THE FAKE GHOST

NUZO ONOH

DEAD SKY PUBLISHING

Published by Dead Sky Publishing, LLC

Miami Beach, Florida

www.deadskypublishing.com

Cover by Shane Pierce

Design & Formatting by Apparatus Revolution, LLC

Edited by Anna Kubik

Copyedited by Nico Vasquez

PRAISE FOR THE FAKE GHOST

Satirical wit meshed with clever societal commentary, a healthy dose of humor, and a highly original storyline, Nuzo Onoh's latest release is literary perfection.

— CANDACE NOLA, *DESPERATE WISHES*

In The Fake Ghost, Nuzo Onoh has created a surreal, intriguing, and hard-hitting tale shining a light on the scourge of corruption in high places. Sometimes shocking, fantastical and hilarious, but also tinged with hope, this ghost will haunt you long after the final page.

— TIM LEBBON, *THE LAST STORM*

Nuzo Onoh's story starts in a near future with a powerful leader, without scruples, willing to do anything to live. After this familiar character's opening I was taken on an unexpected African magical realism adventure that wouldn't let me go. It's a wonder to be in the hands of a master storyteller who values every word/name they use, creating a mesmerizing journey I didn't want to end. Onoh creates a compelling movie in the reader's mind that is unforgettable!

— LINDA D. ADDISON, AWARD-WINNING AUTHOR, HWA LIFETIME ACHIEVEMENT AWARD RECIPIENT AND SFPA GRAND MASTER

This story is dedicated to my beautiful, glamorous, feisty, inquisitive and generous daughter, Candice (Baby) Onyeama, whose eternal quest for social justice and the meaning of life never ceases to leave me in awe of her super-intelligence and compassion. Baby, thank you for choosing me out of all the hopeful mommies that turned up in Baby-Land seeking their forever child. I am truly blessed. I love you to eternity, my child xxxxxxxx

IN THE BEGINNING...

Once upon a time, there was a man, a very rich and powerful man who lived in a very big and opulent house. He had many powerful and important friends—*And enemies.*

One day, the rich man put on his Rolex watch, his Yeezy Crush 950 V25 sneakers, and a bright, red cap. He checked out his reflection in the mirror—tall, taut, no greys in his sleek brown hair, green eyes still piercing, a near-perfect specimen of prime manhood. *Looking good!* He pointed a proud finger at the immaculate image his mirror reflected before grabbing his golden golf clubs. A couple minutes later, he sprawled inside his big black car as his chauffeur drove off, flanked by his security entourage, en-route to a very famous and exclusive golf course.

Later, he planned to enjoy a sumptuous Haute Cuisine dinner before returning to his beautiful wife and even more beautiful tailor-made suits and designer leather shoes. He also planned to meet the most powerful people in the world for a very important conference to determine the fate of mankind.

He never did.

Something bad happened to him and he died—

Or so he thought...

I

THE REBIRTH

He heard somewhere that rats know when people are about to die. They will leave a house enmasse just before the house owner dies, or abandon a ship before it sinks, dragging all to a cold, watery grave.

The man shudders, fighting the dark thoughts torturing his mind as a new tunnel rushes towards him with dizzying speed. At the sight, his head reels, panic quickening his heartbeats. A zillion thoughts buzz in his head like angry wasps—*Holy fuck! When's this nightmare gonna end?* With renewed despair, he wonders if he will be devoured by this silent, spiralling darkness that oozes pure malignancy and bone-freezing terror. If only he had the instincts of the rat, he thinks; the foreknowledge of his own demise. Then he would've fought death with every drop of blood in his body. Instead, he's been caught totally unprepared, and now he's trapped in these dark tunnels, headed for... *Jesus Christ!*

A new tunnel rises out of the dark and sucks him into its chilling darkness. He groans, and his body quakes violently like storm-battered leaves, weakened by cold and fear. He continues to free fall, diving through dark tunnels and icy realms that seem never ending. Every bit of his body is iced up by the freezing air blistering the unknown worlds he's been navigating since he started his escape several hours ago; Or maybe it's been several days? Got no friggin' idea. Not even sure it matters anyway. He could be stuck here for the rest of his bloody life.

A flush of self-pity engulfs him—*I'm nothing now, zippo, zilch!* Just a friggin' bodiless soul on this shitty flight from death. He shudders again, fighting to rein in the panic threatening to steal his sanity. He senses its dark presence behind him, the fearsome hooded one, giving relentless chase. Its killing scythe swishes terrifyingly in the empty air, seeking its target—his soul. He makes the swift choice to veer towards the new tunnel to his right, the only tunnel not spewing hissing, black smoke. It is narrower than the rest, and a pale, blue light emits from its tubular entrance. His eyes are getting tired of seeing nothing but icy blackness. Damn things are now starting to hurt like hell on top of everything else. *Shit!*

Just then, a baby's frail wail pierces the still air. It seems to come from somewhere to his left, another tunnel different from the countless ones he's already plummeted through. His eyes open wide in disbelief, and he almost weeps with relief.

He takes a deep breath, says a silent prayer, and dives. His frosty and translucent form veers towards the baby's cries, seeking it out as a moth to a flame. He has no idea what he'll find at the end of this new tunnel, if the infant's cries will be the harbinger of his own tears when he finally confronts his hooded nemesis. All he knows is that anything is better than *this*.

He squeezes his lids tightly as he spirals, fast and deep, till he hits something soft, something small, yet something so powerful that it knocks him out before he has the chance to open his eyes and confront his cruel destiny.

It is nighttime when he next regains consciousness. The air is warm and rancid like a pigsty in a run-down rural farm. He is lying inside a room as black as a biker's jacket. At first, all he can see is the dim flickering of a solitary candle burnt to half wax. The candle is atop a rickety, three-legged, midget table cluttering up an ugly room that is barely big enough to hold his gold-plated golf clubs, much less a grown man.

His eyes scan the gloomy surroundings with laser-like speed. The first thing he sees is a small, wooden window next to a dwarf door. The ridged window frame is supported by what appears to be red-mud walls—*Huh? What the fuck?*

His mind reels—Is he really seeing red-mud walls or are his eyes kidding him or what? He shuts his eyes and opens them again. This time, it's not only the red-mud walls assaulting his vision, but also a low, thatched roof woven into an uneven mess that resembles a giant bird nest—*Holy righteous shit! Something's not right here! Scratch that; I ain't thinking jack shit. I know something's horribly wrong here; very bad indeed.* It's a nasty and revolting kind of wrong that makes his skin crawl.

His body shudders with revulsion as he feels his face flush with rage. He reaches for his concealed pistol—*Someone's stupid head's gonna roll!* No; several dumb heads are gonna get the full force of his wrath for this mega screw-up. How on earth did he end up in this lousy, fly-dump place? Pansy-Pete had better have some damned good answers to give him or else…

His pistol is gone. No matter how frantically his hands seek its familiar smooth grip, the secret weapon is nowhere to be found. His heart starts to race.

"Pete! Where the fuck are you?" he screams in rage. "Get your bitchass over here at once, do you hear me? And while you're at it, where the hell's this gawd awful place? And why are we in friggin' darkness? Hell! I'm surrounded by a bunch of morons, paying you clowns decent taxpayer's money to sit on your lazy butts and take advantage of my kindness while—"

He stops abruptly, like a rapper cut off in mid-rant—*What the hell?* The plaintive wails of a newborn baby that has dogged his angry cussing ceases as well, plunging the room into a strange kind of silence. It is the silence of a tennis court, the hushed breaths of riveted spectators as the players slug out a tense point, the only sounds being the hard thuds of the balls and the adrenaline grunts of the antagonists.

A deep frown furrows his forehead as he cocks his ears, his body tense—Nothing. Almost total silence. Pete is equally silent and invisible, just like the mysterious crying baby in the gloomy room. All he hears are the thuds of his racing heart and some heavy breathing close by. A weird noise to his right catches his attention. It sounds like soft moans, female sighs—*Heaven help me! That's all I need now; some cheap broad getting herself banged right next to me in this stinky shithole. Fuck!* He is ready to explode, and his body is quivering with ill-suppressed rage—*This insult is beyond pardon. Am I POTUS or AM I FRIGGIN' POTUS!?*

POTUS? His brain scrambles for several dizzy seconds as he tries to recall a distant memory that flits in and out of his fuzzy mind like the dim flickering of the half-candle fighting a losing battle against the all-devouring night.

POTUS! That's his name alright. *POTUS!* He's not sure if it's his first name or his last name, but he knows God-sure it's his name. Something flashes in his mind—a coin-shaped, gold-lettered seal with some weird bird surrounded by blue stars. Before he can make sense of the image, it vanishes in a wink, replaced by a rush of images in dazzling colours that leave him disoriented—a great white building with loads of opulent rooms and long, wide halls teaming with important people all desperate to see him; lush, green golf courses and expensive golf carts weighted with equally expensive clubs and bags; an impressive motorcade with flashing lights, fluttering flags, blaring sirens, and a super-plane called… *Air Force One? Or is it Air Force Two? Fuck!*

His head is suddenly pounding, and he is starting to suspect he's coming down with something pretty nasty—Surprise, surprise, considering the filthy state of the hovel he's trapped in. Even his mind seems incapable of stringing any rational thoughts together. But one thing he knows for sure is that he has no business being in this vile dump—*Goddammit! I'm done with this farce. Pansy-Pete seems to have mysteriously disappeared, just like the rest of my security detail. Well, if Mount Rushmore won't come to POTUS, then I'll damn well race to the friggin' place!*

He lunges towards the shut dwarf-door across him like a quarterback at full charge, and instantly, he collapses back onto the floor

—*Huh?* His brows clash tightly. He attempts another forward thrust and again, the hard floor holds him immobile with a Jacob Marley chain, a prisoner of an unseen jailor that wields a frightening power over him. He feels the blood drain from his face. His heart starts a maniacal race.

"Pete! You no-good mouse, where the fuck are you?" he roars. The invisible baby wails again, right on cue, its cries angry and frustrated. An icy chill coats his skin with goosebumps.

"Pete…?" This time his voice is weak, almost a whisper. The baby whimpers softly as well. The sound is so close he can even feel its soft breath near his lips. He tries to turn his head and find the pesky infant, but his neck has become an iron rod, rigid and uncooperative. Try as he may, he can't seem to see beyond what lies directly in front of his gaze.

And now, he is seeing something else standing in front of him, something big and black that hulks directly over him. The figure leans dangerously low, blocking out his vision with its mammoth bosom—*Sweet Mary and the apostles! A bla…black giantess!* Before he can blink, the giantess pushes something into his mouth, something that looks suspiciously like a pinkie, a smelly, grubby finger that tastes of 1000 MGO pure Manuka honey! *Holy shit!*

His lips clamp on the finger with the frenzy of a blind bat, suckling greedily, shamelessly—*Wow!* He can't remember being this hungry, ever. He could suck this damn pinkie for the rest of his life! The black giantess roars, her laughter like the boom of some native Tom-Tom. It quakes her mammoth body like a sea of roiling, soft flesh, almost dislodging the sweet finger from his suckling mouth. She looks at him with rheumy black eyes and babbles something unintelligible into the gloomy room. He hears a weak voice moan softly once more in the familiar sound he'd initially mistaken for an orgasm. Now, he realises it's a moan of pain. Nobody can mistake the agony searing every hushed groan emitting from the invisible woman's lips now.

The giantess pulls her pinkie from his mouth, and he reaches out to grasp it—*Come on! I ain't done yet, not by a long mile!* Again, she chuckles that booming laughter, mumbles something under her breath and lifts him up whole from the floor in her sturdy arms—*Holy righteous shit!*

His heart sinks right to his feet, and lands smack on the warm, soft body of the giantess. His head is swimming and his eyes are so goggled he thinks they'll drop right out of their sockets—*No friggin' way! The mammoth freak has lifted me as easily as if I'm made of flimsy chicken feathers. Me, POTUS, six feet tall and some three hundred pounds of good American flesh to boot!* His heart is pounding so hard, he thinks he's going to dishonour the American flag and faint. Yes, that's what he'll do; faint before the monster gobbles him up. Good thing there's no one around to witness POTUS' humiliation, nobody to spill the beans about his ignominious death—*Oh, please, Jesus! I don't wanna die, don't wanna die…*

Head reeling, he shuts his eyes and prepares for the excruciating bite of sharp fangs on his soft, pink flesh, every nerve pulled to its breaking point.

He waits… and waits…

Nothing; no pain or giant teeth in his flesh. Instead, the randy bitch starts to touch his naked body—his mighty POTUS body—with hard, callused hands that have never experienced *La Mer* moisturising crème. A weird word flashes in his head as soon as he thinks of *La Mer* moisturiser—*FLOTUS.* He has no idea what it means, apart from the fact it rhymes nicely with POTUS—*Maybe that's my last name? POTUS FLOTUS?* There's a righteous rightness to the name—*Swell!* His memory is starting to return. Now he remembers his name, the rest will surely follow. Just a matter of time.

The giantess starts washing him in warm water. The sensation of the warm fluid on his naked body fills him with indescribable bliss. Instant calm descends over him, coupled with a great sense of relief. His limbs go soft like mushy peas, and his eyes droop languidly. He feels his body melt into the rough hands of his giant masseuse, who is now rubbing some vile smelling, greasy stuff into his skin as she hums some savage lullaby in a strangely soothing voice. What he is feeling isn't a sexual response in any manner or form, just a blissful yielding of a body that has been through unbelievable trauma.

POTUS FLOTUS! He smiles contentedly—*I sure like my name.* It's a solid name for a solid guy like him, and truth be told, it's good to have a complete name again, especially with him not knowing his ass from his elbow, and no one around to have his back. He feels his anger re-awaken, brewing a dark storm in his heart—*The yellow clown, Pansy-Pete! The cowardly pissant in his fancy haircut and cologne! Running away like the shameless Judas he is and leaving me at the mercy of the friggin' ch*nks and filthy n*gger giantess. Just wait till I get my hands on the sono-fabitch!*

The giantess swaddles him in what feels weirdly like a soft nappy. POTUS FLOTUS sighs softly again, yielding to the slumber that pulls at him like a black, syrupy magnet—Who gives a shit what the dumb-fuck does, as long as she doesn't have him for her dinner. He doesn't think the giantess plans to gobble him up after all, not with the way she's cooing all over him as if he were some stupid, precious baby. Speaking of babies, he wonders where the wailing infant is, the one that keeps interrupting him whenever he calls for Pete, his useless Chief of Staff—Whatever the stupid title means, anyways.

Once again, he tries to search for the baby, but he still can't turn his neck. He's starting to suspect he must have sustained a neck injury when he landed in this realm of giants. He has no doubt whatsoever that he's been kidnapped by the crooked Albanians and sold to the greedy Chinese—*Shit! I can bet my clean ass that the friggin' ch*nks have dumped me in this weird planet inhabited by n*gger giants!* Even their women are so mammoth, they can easily lift a full-grown man like him as if he's a day-old infant. As if on cue, the giantess lifts him up again and carries him over to another female giant lying on a thin mattress on the floor—*Aah! This must be the moaning broad, likely the mother of the whining, shitass brat. Now what?*

His stunned eyes catch a glimpse of the woman on the mattress. First thing he sees is that she's half-naked, her exposed breasts full and rounded. Her skin is very pale, and save for her distinctly African features, one could easily mistake her for being Latina. He thinks she's likely bi-racial—Way too many brown people these days with all the globalization shit and randy white and black fools refusing to stick to their own kind, even in this weird world of giants. *Fuck!* He dips his brows and cusses softly as he gazes at the young giantess on the mattress—She sure looks as if she's overdosed on some very bad drugs imported from Albania! *I just hate Albanians! Friggin' dickheads! I'll never forgive that fucker, Besnik, for conning me out of my first million. Corrupt motherfuckers, the lot!*

He takes another close look at the pale woman on the floor—Yep, definitely a goner. Fuckshit Albania strikes again! In fact, he's almost sure the woman is overdue for the morgue when she suddenly opens a pair of pale, brown eyes and looks straight at him. The next thing he knows, the black giantess plonks him onto the drugged woman, right against her exposed breasts, almost suffocating him. Before he can scream his rage, she prises open his lips with her filthy fingers and pushes his face against one swollen breast, forcing a hard, pink nipple into his mouth. His head almost explodes. He's not sure which is stronger, his fury or his shame—*Sweet Mary and the apostles! No! No! This can't be happening to me!*

POTUS FLOTUS shudders violently. He thinks he'll vomit; that all the steak he consumed before his ordeal started will disgorge from his lips in a stinky heap of gooey sick. Instead, to his eternal shame, his lips grab the nipple greedily, suckling so hard he almost chokes on the sweet, warm milk squirting into his mouth—*No! No! Come on man, stop this disgusting behaviour at once! POTUS FLOTUS, have some dignity! Oh, please God, help... help?* His head is screaming at him to reject the nipple but his mouth seems to have a mind of its own, and his lips keep smacking noisily. He guzzles the breast milk with gusto—Damn! This is the sweetest thing I've ever tasted in my entire friggin' life! A warm arm cuddles him closer as he hears the soft sigh of the drugged-out woman on the mattress. The satisfied chortle of the black giantess hulking above them booms in his ears.

"Folake, see how greedily your new baby boy is suckling at your breast, eh?" The black giantess crows in a language that's not English and yet, one he suddenly finds himself understanding as if he's spoken that weird tongue for his entire fifty-four years on Utah's sanctified earth—*Huh? New baby boy? Whose friggin' baby is the mammoth moron talking about?* Surely, the stupid cow doesn't think he's some shitass baby? He'll soon tell her.

He pulls his mouth away from the nipple and yells his rage at the black giantess.

"I am POTUS! POTUS FLOTUS, you dumbfuck!" There! That'll teach them, alright.

The baby's angry cries fill his ears instead—*Friggin' hell!* Again, he cusses loudly at the huge woman and on cue, the invisible baby wails right back at him. The icy chill is back in his spine, and this time, his head is starting to spin crazily like some malfunctioned Disney ride—*I ain't a baby…oh, please Jesus, tell me I ain't some shitass baby!* He tries again to speak and once again, the sound coming from his mouth is the plaintive wail of a pathetic infant. A mighty shudder quakes his body. His heart is racing so fast he thinks it'll crash through the walls of his chest like a F1 car on failed brakes—There's no doubt about it, he thinks in stunned disbelief. None whatsoever. He's been shrunk by some psycho Chinese scientist at one of their secret labs in this fly-dump African country!

His body is trembling. Thoughts run wild like frantic ants inside his head—*Holy fuck! I'm royally screwed!* Everyone knows the Chinese have bought up half of Africa, and who knows what whacky experiments they've been carrying out in the place? Now, he's become part of that evil experiment, shrunk into a baby, and given to the natives to raise in squalor and horrible poverty. *Fuck! This can't be happening to POTUS FLOTUS!* If there's one thing he loathes more than ugly women, it's poverty. Poverty is just so…*so dirty…*

"Pete! Pete!" he shrieks, his voice a desperate baby's wail that reverberates in the little room.

"Ha! Folake, look how gustily your son cries, so? He has a big voice just like his Papa," the black giantess chortles, leaning low to poke his left cheek affectionately with a rough forefinger.

"Fuck his Papa!" The exhausted, light-skinned woman breast-feeding him curses, her voice a bitter rasp. "Just tell me, who does he look like, Mama? Lift him up so I can see him properly."

"He looks like his Papa, alright," the black giantess laughs indulgently. "See how black his skin is, just like his Papa's skin, so? I tell you, even his nose is as broad as his Papa's nose. Now, Tunde can't continue with his shameless lies and deny he's the father of your child.

This little devil is the spitting image of the man. Just you wait till he sees his son."

"No, Mama; Tunde Adeniran will not see this baby," the one called Folake says in a hard voice. "Tunde Adeniran will never see his son if it's the last thing I do."

"Daughter, what do you mean, so? What are you talking about? Jesus forbid evil! Of course, Tunde must see his son and provide for him even if he refuses to marry you. I don't think—"

"Mama, I said no," Folake cuts off the black giantess, her voice like iron despite her apparent weakness. "Nobody will see this child except the rich man from Lagos who'll be visiting us as soon as I let him know I've delivered the baby. I told you my plans, but you didn't listen to a word I said." The woman sighs impatiently as she adjusts the baby's neck under her arm. "I want to go to America, Mama. The rich man in Lagos will give me money to buy my black-market US visa if I give him this baby. So, first thing tomorrow, I'll top up my mobile phone credit and tell him the baby has arrived. Then I can start making plans for America and change our lives for the better," she pauses, inhales deeply before extruding a gust of air in a loud whoosh that ends in a sustained cough.

"Rest, daughter. Don't stress yourself, okay?" The giantess soothes her as she stoops to lift him away from the breast, even as his traitorous lips cling desperately to the milk-squirting nipple. She sits on the floor facing her daughter as she gently rocks him in her arms, assaulting his nostrils with the stench of stale sweat and smoke. He sneezes angrily and delicately burps up gooey breastmilk.

"Bless you, child," the black giantess says in a distracted manner, wiping his mouth with her filthy cotton wrapper. "As I was saying, daughter. Rest yourself, okay? Tomorrow, we'll talk things through and see what happens, so?"

"No, I'll not change my mind, Mama. I promise you, things will be different for us once I get to America and train as a nurse. They say nurses make big money there, and I want to get you out of this horrible village so you can live in a nice house in town. You know yourself that since Papa died and his brothers took everything because they say I'm not Papa's child, our lives have been truly worse than a chicken's life. I trusted Tunde Adeniran and thought he would do right by us. But he turned out to be nothing more than a useless and heartless bastard, just like all men," Bitterness drips from Folake's voice like poisoned molasses and her pale, brown eyes are vicious when they rest on POTUS FLOTUS.

Instinctively, he recoils from her hate, before cussing her out in that familiar baby's wail that is now becoming the most sinister sound to him—*You too, lady. Trust me, you ain't the only one hating here. If I could grow wings right now, I'd be gone from you and this pigsty in a blink.* For good measure, he gives her the rude middle finger, his little hand flailing pathetically in the air as she resumes talking, her eyes blanking him out with complete disinterest.

"So, don't waste your breath on the matter, Mama. Tunde Adeniran will not see this baby boy who is my ticket to America, and that's final," Folake turns her face away and pulls a flowered wrapper over her body. "I'm tired now. Take him away so I can sleep, and promise me you won't tell anyone the baby has come. Later, we'll tell them it died in the womb and we buried it in the bush, okay?"

POTUS FLOTUS' head is reeling. He thinks he's going to die right there in the black giantess' sturdy arms—*My grandmother if I'm to believe the bullshit I've just heard from these whacky natives. There's no way, no friggin' way I'm black! Uh-uh! It's all bull. I refuse to believe a word I've just heard. POTUS FLOTUS ain't black, period! The woman and her mother are deluded, demented. Look at me, for fuck's sake! I'm as white as a lily! And even worse, they're planning to traffic me like a friggin' slave. ME! Goddammit! Good thing I'm now a baby or the filthy bitches would even have me in chains and...*

He pauses, his heart racing. Clarity returns to his mind in a flash, images and sounds flooding his head in relentless waves—*Yes! Holy cow! I'm remembering stuff!* He's practically quivering in excitement. Everything starts coming together in chained perfection. He remembers arriving at the golf course that morning and getting into his cart with one of his security men—which sure proves he's a real big shot even if he can't quite yet remember who he is. Next thing he recalls is the whack of a golf ball on his head, followed by a blinding and excruciating mother of all pains, after which... Nothing, zero, zilch! Just a friggin' black nothingness. Likely when the bent Albanians kidnapped him, before the ch*nks shrunk him into midget size and dumped him with these two ignorant natives. The Chinese must've also messed up the women's minds with some hallucinatory drugs, making them believe he's their little n*gger baby—*The stupid cows!* In fact, for all he knows, Pansy-Pete was in on the whole nasty affair and likely sold him out to the ch*nks for an island paradise in Beijing—*The stinky rainbow!*

Hot blood rushes to his head, almost frying what's left of his brain cells—*Just wait till POTUS returns to full size and back at my house in D.C.… D.C.? Where the fuck's D.C.? Whatever. I'm gonna find all those involved in my betrayal and wreak a mighty vengeance such as the world's never seen. I'm not called POTUS FLOTUS for nothing! Hell yeah! POTUS FLOTUS will get his revenge alright!* But right now, all he wants to do is sleep. *I'm just totally pooped… shit! Have I just shat in my clean new nappy?? Shit! SHIIIT…*

The little room reverberates with the angry wails of a newborn baby while the anxious grandmother desperately tries to hush it to sleep. The neighbours must never know that her unwed daughter has given birth to a new son, a baby whose destiny it is to change theirs for the better if Folake's plans work out. Briefly, she thinks about naming this poor grandson of hers who'll never know its heritage. But with a slight shake of her head, she decides against it. The baby will soon be out of their lives anyway. No need wasting a good name on it. She would have called him Adisa, meaning "he who makes himself clear." With his loud, demanding voice, she has no doubt this tiny grandson of hers will grow up making sure the whole world hears his voice alright —*Hah! Just see how loudly the little devil screeches already, and him just a few minutes old, so?* She wrinkles her nose—*Phew! This pikin's shit smells something horrible.*

BOOK
ONE

2

LITTLE POTUS

The Federal Enquirer
(Breaking News!)
President Jerry King admitted to hospital
PMD Media, 8 July
(Mike Vine and the news desk)

Golf Balls, Jealous Lovers & Family Curses

President Jerry King has been admitted to hospital following a ghastly accident at his favourite golf club in Utah while on the campaign trail. The White House press secretary, Sandra Macpherson, confirmed that the accident happened sometime around mid-morning today.

According to sources familiar with the incident, President King was hit on the head by a golf ball swung by the playboy billionaire, Tad Hunter, rumoured to be the current lover of Miss Madison Hudson, who was once the president's mistress and the mother of his only child, Lisa Hudson. Latest reports from The Walter Reed National Military Medical Center state that President King is presently in a medically-induced coma due to serious head trauma. Doctors are working around the clock to save his life while the nation grapples with this latest tragedy in the King family.

Readers will recall that the president's father, the late Newspaper magnate, Dan King, died tragically at the same Utah Golf club almost ten years ago, after he suffered a similar golf ball accident. A second cousin, Mike King, also suffered a fatal golf-related death, albeit at a different club, leading people to wonder about this strange coincidence. Some are already starting to dub it "The King-Golf Curse," just like "The Kennedy Curse."

As messages of support and well-wishes continue to pour in from world leaders, business leaders, and religious leaders around the globe, the stock market has seen a sharp drop as markets react to the president's accident. Meanwhile, we can confirm that the FBI are now carrying out investigations to ascertain what exactly happened at the golf course, and why Tad Hunter was able to get so close to the president's golf cart that his golf ball hit the president with such deadly impact.

We have reached out to Mr Hunter, but have been unable to get his side of the story. All efforts to reach Madison Hudson have also been unsuccessful. As we pray for President King's speedy recovery, we will keep you informed with further developments. This is a developing story.

"I am POTUS," the little boy in the pristine school uniform glared at his class teacher, Miss Yemisi, his light brown eyes flashing fearlessly underneath his dipped brows, eyes so pale they would have sat better on albino skin than the smooth, dark colour of his face. "My name is POTUS Olupitan."

"POTOOS?" Miss Yemisi's voice sounded as amused as the smirk on her face. "I thought your name was Lanre Olupitan. At least, that's what it says here on your admission form," she turned to the rest of the fifteen, bright-eyed pupils in the cool, air-conditioned classroom, her mocking voice tacitly inviting their derision.

"My name is POTUS," the boy insisted, his voice rising, little fists clenching and unclenching furiously at his side. "It's P.O.T—" He paused, confusion furrowing his brows. Spelling and writing had never been his forté in his seven years of existence, not even when spelling his own name.

"Pot! Pot! Pot!" The rest of the class took up their teacher's unspoken invitation. They broke out in wild laughter, with Miss Yemisi doing little to rein in their rowdy glee. It wasn't her fault after all if Nigerian parents insisted on giving their kids the most outlandish names in creation, just like the little girl in her class stupidly named 'Scandal,' or the other boy in Mrs. Olu's class with the ridiculous name of 'Take-Good-Position.' *Jehovah, have mercy!*

POTUS glared at his jeering classmates, his eyes zeroing in on two children who weren't joining in on the horrible chants. The first was a little Filipino boy, a rather rotund and bookish sort of kid with thick, round-rimmed glasses, dressed as fastidiously as himself. The boy's uniform stood out from the rest of the class, even POTUS' own; such was the dazzling cleanliness of the starched and pressed pair of grey cotton pants, grey bow tie, and starched white shirt. POTUS felt an instant kinship with the clean boy, who smiled shyly at him before quickly averting his eyes. The second child was a petite English girl with the iciest blue eyes on a non-doll entity he had ever seen. Like the pudgy Filipino boy, she wasn't laughing at him either. As their eyes met, the little girl flashed him the widest and brightest smile, as if he were the dearest person in her life.

POTUS' heart skipped, soaring right to the skies. His entire body was suffused with warmth as his face broke into a giddy smile. His lips opened to say the cheeriest "hello" to the little angel, but before he could speak, the girl's face instantly hardened, her thin lips tightening with knife sharpness. In a blink, her eyes went glacier as she totally froze him out, leaving him feeling small and rejected.

His eyes pooled as he glanced away. His fists clenched into tight balls, fury raging in his heart—*Horrible, nasty, bad Abiku girl!* He wanted to go over to the icy little miss and sock her one on those mean, pink lips; teach her the meaning of respect. Then he would punch each of his jeering classmates on their horrible faces, too, before dishing out the same pain to his nasty class teacher. He glared at the class before returning his furious gaze to Miss Yemisi, holding her eyes with a fierce intensity that caused the teacher to swear silently in resentment—*Spoiled little brat!*

Miss Yemisi smiled desperately at POTUS through gritted teeth— God! She just hates the vile, little, rich bastards she's forced to teach! Good thing Mrs. Olu from class 2B had already given her the drill, otherwise she would teach this little brat a lesson he won't forget in a hurry. It was Miss Yemisi's second week at the posh international primary school, located in the exclusive area of Ikoyi in Lagos, Nigeria. The area groaned under the entitled weight of a myriad of diplomatic missions, opulent houses, and affluent residents of every nationality and race. After the terrorist group, Boko Haram, kidnapped the president and overran the capital city, Abuja, there had been a steady exodus of foreign embassies and businesses to Lagos city, now once again the new Capital of Nigeria. They had brought along their horde of entitled kids, who made up the bulk of the pupils in the school. It was Miss Yemisi's first assignment as a graduate teacher at the exclusive school, and she was determined to make a good impression on the rather intimidating headteacher.

Now, as she looked at POTUS' glaring eyes, she gave silent thanks for the crucial advice she'd received from Mrs. Olu of class 2B, who had been in the school for almost a decade. All Miss Yemisi needed to do was be extra nice to the kids of the rich parents, practically her entire class, save the few spawns of the European diplomats, who were notorious tight wads.

"Just be generous with your marks, be blind to their misdeeds, drown the little sods in peanuts and make sure they have enough reasons to sing *your* praises to their rich parents," Mrs. Olu had advised with a grim expression on her plump face. "In return, come Christmas, Easter, or the end of Summer term, you can ask their grateful parents for the moon, and you'll receive both the sun and stars as extra bonuses. Trust me, you won't regret teaching in this school. You'll make more from the parents than you'll ever make from your salary."

Miss Yemisi already had POTUS' mum marked for a Gucci-Hyun handbag, seeing as it seemed to be the woman's favourite accessory. It was the very least she deserved for being stuck with her wretched brat for the whole academic year. It was therefore, with the titillating image of the designer handbag in her mind, that she forced herself to return the little boy's scowl with another manic smile.

"POTUS! Of course, that's your name, my dear. POTUS it is then," she shrilled, rapping her ruler on the table to bring some belated order to the class. "His name is POTUS, and that's what everyone must call him. Are we clear, children?"

The children giggled in response, and POTUS fixed them with a malevolent glare—*Just wait till I get them later. POTUS will teach them a good lesson…well, maybe not the clean boy in glasses who didn't laugh at me!* Looking at his mutinous expression, Miss Yemisi's heart sank. Mrs. Olu was right. Privileged brats like this wretched child justified every form of compensation and bribery teachers received from their equally rubbish, rich parents. It was a good thing Nigeria didn't have stupid laws like America, where parents were chucked into prison for bribing teachers to improve their children's prospects—which, after all, was the whole purpose of having children in the first place—to give them a good start in life by every means, fair or foul. In any case, she reckoned it would be a farce if any such anti-bribery law existed for schools in Nigeria, seeing as everyone, from the senators and state governors, all collected graft and were the very people to lead the Nigerian teacher-bribery schemes for their spoilt and brainless spawns. It was 2031, seventy-one useless years since independence, and she was still earning wages designed for 1960—*Jehovah! I hate this country and its privileged thieves!* She just hopes the new Igbo president lives up to his reputation of being clean and wipes corruption from the country.

Now, looking at POTUS with a maniacal glint in her eyes, something told Miss Yemisi that this newest addition to her classroom was going to prove a right pain in her generous backside.

She was right.

By the time three children had fled from the playground with bleeding faces and wailing voices, she knew that her premonitions were spot on. And later, when she discovered her new handbag savagely massacred with a pair of scissors after sending POTUS to the naughty chair for the assault on the three kids, she was almost ready to tender her resignation on the spot. Thankfully, the saintly Mrs. Olu of class 2B had come to her rescue again and reminded her that she would definitely receive a new replacement handbag of superior quality from the little thug's mother as compensation for his vandalism. Grinding her teeth, Miss Yemisi resigned herself to what she now knew would become a never-ending war of attrition with the little bully that evil fate had so undeservedly dropped into her formerly orderly classroom.

POTUS stood by the set of blue and pink swings in the playground with his arms akimbo, a menacing scowl on his face, daring the rest of the kids to come near the swings. By his side, his newest friend, the Filipino boy, Frankie Potot, weirdly pronounced Fotot, followed his lead, spreading his arms and endeavouring to look as menacing as his new playground mob boss.

"You in the glasses. Yes, you ugly four-eyes. Come over here and say, 'I'm sorry, POTUS, for being horrible to you in the classroom yesterday' and maybe I'll let you get on the swing," POTUS ordered, pointing to the nearest child amongst a group of cowering children, a mixed-race little boy eyeing the empty swings with desperate yearning through his eyeglasses.

POTUS clenched and unclenched his fists as he spoke, silently reminding them of his ferocious attacks on their classmates the previous day. When some of the kids had tried to make fun of his name in the playground again, calling him POT and POO and POTATO, he'd soon made quick work of them with his fists, punching them till they dropped like flies at his feet.

Even at just seven years of age, POTUS was already bigger than his peers in both height and girth. Moreover, he had spent countless hours watching reruns of his favourite HBO World Championship Boxing shows on Hologram-Cable TV to know how to use his fists effectively in combat. His favourite boxer was Wladmir Klitscho—a very good and very nice man and a very big and very good fighter. He hates Anthony Joshua for winning against Klitscho... *not fair.* Maybe he'll be a boxer too, when he grows up. Then, he'll find Joshua and punch his face for what he did to nice Klitscho.

"Olè!" Frankie's pitched voice startled POTUS out of his brooding. "You there. Didn't you hear what POTUS just said? Say, 'I'm sorry, POTUS, for being horrible to you in class yesterday' or you won't get to go on the swings," Frankie tried to bunch his own fists, too, but gave up when his little fingers began to ache. He omitted adding the 'ugly four-eyes' insult since he also wore eyeglasses.

"I'm sorry, POTUS, for being horrible to you in class yesterday. Can I go on the swing now?" The mixed-race boy capitulated. He could see that Miss Yemisi was too busy gossiping with some of the other teachers to notice what was going on at the swings, and he didn't fancy becoming another bloody-nosed victim of POTUS' notorious fists.

"Good. Now you can get on the swing," POTUS ordered magnanimously, a hard smile on his face. As the child scampered atop the blue swing, POTUS caught sight of a little white girl giving him a nervous smile, just like a burglar who discovered that his new friend was the Police Chief. His brows instantly dipped—*Huh! Horrid Emily! The little Oyinbo girl with the nasty smile. I'll soon show her!*

Before he could speak, she did it again. Emily flashed that killer smile at him and murdered it within seconds, as he almost—*almost*—but thankfully not quite, fell for her trick all over again—*Oh, the horrible Abiku girl! I hate her! I'll never let her get on the pink swing, never!*

"That girl is horrible," POTUS muttered to Frankie, scowling viciously at Emily, who turned away and walked off by herself, as alone as ever. She had no best friends as far as he knew.

"You mean, Miss Flash and Die?" Frankie gave one of his cheerful giggles.

"Miss Flash and Die?" POTUS repeated, a baffled look in his pale, brown eyes.

"Yes, that's what Miss Yemisi calls her because of the way she smiles. First, she opens her teeth wide to smile at you, and then when you start to smile back at her, she kills the smile immediately. Miss Yemisi said it's not nice to give people a flash-and-die smile, but Emily can't stop doing it," Frankie shrugged. "We think maybe she's an idiot, you know, like she's not quite alright in her head. Olè! Do you know she's the only kid in our school that doesn't speak Yoruba fluently like the rest of us? Even the American and Chinese kids all speak good Yoruba like me," Frankie's eyes widened in wonder underneath his thick glasses.

Hearing his best friend's words, POTUS felt his heart quicken. He was ready to jump with joy. He hasn't been disrespected after all! Emily is just a poor idiot who can't even speak Yoruba. The insight killed his desire for vengeance and Emily was quickly consigned to his mental box of irrelevancy, especially as he noticed several kids who equally blanked her into disdainful invisibility. Not that the horrid girl seemed to care. Emily continued flashing her evil smile manically at everyone like a malfunctioned doll, her pale blue eyes just as icy as a doll's.

"You! Yes, you elephant ears! Are you going to say 'I'm sorry' to me, or do you want me to force you to say it?" POTUS glared at a boy that was almost his height—*Uh-uh, not quite.* He reckoned he topped the boy by a little bit—Maybe by ten hundred feet or even twenty hundred.

"No. I won't say I'm sorry, and you can't make me say it," the boy returned his glare, folding his arms as aggressively as POTUS.

"Okay, now you've gone and done it! Get ready to fight me," POTUS started to advance menacingly towards the boy who stood his ground fearlessly.

As he got closer, POTUS suddenly paused. His heart started thudding hard. An unpleasant feeling washed over him, revulsion jellying his legs. His eyes were glued on the boy's food-stained shirt and dusty trousers—*Dirt! No! Not dirt; uh-uh! Dirt is poor and horrible. POTUS likes clean. Clean is rich and nice, just like me and my new friend, Frankie.*

"Will you remove your shirt and wash your hands first before we fight?" He asked the boy in a low growl, trying to maintain the threatening scowl.

"Huh?" The boy looked as baffled as Frankie.

"You have to wash your hands before we fight because your trousers are dirty, and you have a stain on your shirt. I don't want you to give me germs with your dirty hands and—"

"My hands are not dirty," the boy cut him off, his eyes flashing with injured pride.

"Yes, they're dirty. You're a dirty pig. Your daddy is poor! You're a poor, dirty pig! Poor, dirty pig! Poor, dirty pig!" POTUS started to chant with glee, and Frankie and several of the kids joined in. In no time, the little boy abandoned the fight and ran off, fighting tears.

POTUS turned around and smiled triumphantly at his admiring minions. A warm feeling coursed through his body—*Wow!* He never realised he could defeat an enemy without using his fists, just like the HBO championship boxers who curse out their opponents real good before a fight.

"Yes, he's a poor, dirty pig," POTUS repeated, savouring the words, the power in their crushing negativity, and the devastation they wreaked.

"Olè! He's a poor, dirty pig," Frankie repeated obediently.

"Why do you say 'Olè' all the time?" POTUS asked with irritation. "Don't you know it means 'thief' in Yoruba? I thought you spoke good Yoruba?" Frankie shrugged, giving a sheepish smile. "Well, if you ask me, I think it's stupid …ouch!" POTUS gasped, clasping his head with both hands. His eyes were squeezed tight and little dots of sweat dappled his forehead as he groaned softly.

"What's the matter? POTUS, are you okay? Why are you holding your head? Is it hurting you?" Frankie looked frightened, and the other kids quickly gathered close, curiosity and anxiety jostling for dominance on their faces.

"Sshh… don't speak…everybody silent…I need to listen…ouch!" POTUS' eyes rolled, crossed and re-crossed, before fixating somewhere towards the high fence with myopic vacancy. Tears rolled down his cheeks as he stood erect like a soldier at attention, seemingly oblivious to his surroundings and the children's frantic questions.

Except he wasn't totally deaf.

Inside his head, he could hear *them,* the strange people that lived inside his body and spoke to each other as if they were right inside their own homes. Even now, they were at it again, multiple male and female voices clamouring inside his head with reckless raucousness. POTUS knew them all as well as he knew his own voice.

Except, there weren't many people speaking, just one person that spoke with many different voices; one terrifying demonic entity that could mimic the voices of every living thing on earth.

And that demon lives inside his body.

POTUS' groaned again. His head throbbed with the familiar pain that always heralded the voices. But this time, it wasn't just the demon's multiple voices inside his head bringing him agony, but rather, the sudden raucous chanting by the horrible children surrounding him.

"Sshh! POTUS is listening, listening, listening.

POTUS is listening for his Mama's car.

Cry-cry baby, cry-cry baby.

Where's your naughty Mama? Cry-cry baby, Mama's little POO!"

The booing voices snapped POTUS out of his trance. He lashed out blindly at the nearest child, bloodying one nose before dishing out the same punishment to another. In no time, the playground descended into the familiar chaos that seemed to follow POTUS like flies to a stinky fart-arse since he had arrived at the school just the previous day. Miss Yemisi abandoned her gossiping cronies—with whom she had ironically been discussing POTUS—as she tried to bring some semblance of order in the midst of bawling kids with bruised faces.

"Lanre Olupitan, what did you—"

"POTUS, my name is POTUS,"

"Shut up, you little devil. Your name is what I say your name is, and it's Lanre, and I don't want to hear another—"

"It's POTUS. My name is POTUS, PO—"

"Shut your stupid mouth or—"

"POOOTTUUUSSSS!" He shrieked at the raging teacher, his features contorted into the batshit crazy mien of a pocket dictator. Eyes psycho-wide, POTUS readied his body to hurl himself on the ground in his trademark fit. But just in time, he remembered that it wasn't as clean as the glossy marbled flooring of his daddy's house. Instead, he flung his arms up in the air wildly and started the terrifying tantrum routine familiar to his parents, but one Miss Yemisi or his classmates had yet to witness. His screams drowned out every other sound in the playground as everyone froze, children and teachers alike, all stunned by the screeching, kicking, hopping, air-punching little demon with the unsettling pale, brown eyes.

POTUS was in his element, watching their panicked confusion with glee, wide eyes totally devoid of tears—*Good! That'll teach them all for being horrid to POTUS. After all, I'm not daddy's Ekùn mi (daddy's little fearless Leopard), for nothing. POTUS isn't afraid of anybody or anything.*

Miss Yemisi watched the shrieking child helplessly, itching desperately to slap his face, but terrified of the consequences, not just from the headteacher, but from the little demon-child who wasn't one to let any slight go unavenged. She was still smarting about her ruined handbag, The wretched child had the gall to tell her his mama would buy her a new handbag if she was good—*Huh! If I'm good indeed, the little Satan spawn!*

Now, watching POTUS, Miss Yemisi was ready to scream, pull his ears, and drag him out of the school gates for good. In the end, money-sense and economic necessity prevailed. She sent him to Mrs. Olu's class 2B to sit out the rest of the day under the supervision of the more experienced teacher while she tried to contain her rage and control her unruly class—*The little wretch is right. His stupid mama will indeed replace her handbag with a new handbag, alright. Except, her bribe price has just gone up from one Gucci-Hyun handbag to two, and maybe a Pharrell-Vuitton as well. It's the least they owe her for raising such a demon thug. Huh! POTUS indeed! Little pretentious hooligan!*

3

THE WATER DEMON

POTUS' name had always been shrouded in mystery. The fact that he talked when he was just six-months old and the first word he had said in the clear distinct voice of a full-grown man was 'POTUS' had become a kind of urban legend around him. According to his parents, Ronke and Kunle Olupitan, the phenomenon had almost driven them into naked madness; such was their horror.

After recovering from their shock at hearing the creepy, raspy voice extruding from their baby's lips, they decided to seek the services of a Babalawo medicine man for more clarity, seeing as no one could figure out why the baby kept repeating 'POTUS' with manic persistence. Moreover, unlike most Yoruba families, his parents didn't do "church" and therefore had no access to Pastors or Prayer Warriors to pray away their troubles.

The story went that, on hearing the child repeatedly chant the strange word, POTUS, the Babalawo had almost passed out in shock, his eyes rolling back deep inside his sockets. When he sufficiently recovered his composure several minutes later, he had stared at the child with horror before turning his attention back to the quaking parents.

"Your son is possessed by a powerful water spirit that goes by the terrible name of POTUS," he stated in a stentorian voice, showering himself with charmed ashes to ward off the evil. "This demon, POTUS, is a terrible one indeed. He's known in the underworld as the greedy fiend, a polluter of men's morals and a stealer of souls."

His parents gasped. His mother clutched POTUS closer, tighter, against her chest. The Babalawo grunted ominously, blowing his bone flute loudly to chase away the demons and spirits.

"Listen carefully," he said. "You will need to offer some sacrifices urgently at the *Bar Beach*. We must appease the fearsome spirit so that the child can live a long, righteous, and healthy life. If not, the great water spirit might make your son sickly, turn him into a fish, a criminal, an idiot, or steal his life in his prime."

His horrified parents had escaped from the shrine on jellied limbs. Within days, they organised the visit to Bar Beach along the shores of the Atlantic Ocean, to free their only child from the terrifying curse. POTUS had no recollection of the famed visit to that popular beach on Victoria Island, Lagos. But his Mama, Ronke, had told him the story over and over till he knew just about every minute detail of that fateful trip by heart.

Apparently, on a warm and muggy midnight, just before the dry Harmattan season, his parents had travelled to the famous beach with live chickens, kola nuts, black crystals, and other ingredients demanded by the Babalawo for the ritual of appeasement. Little eight-month-old POTUS made the trip with them and had been rather subdued on that particular night, quite unlike his usual rambunctious self. The Babalawo explained that the child was aware he was in the presence of his spirit master, hence his quiet trepidation. POTUS had been dressed in a flowing white gown, a bit like a child having a Mormon baptism. He was later dunked into the salty sea several times during the course of that historic night as part of the mystic ritual to rid him of his curse.

His Mama said he'd howled so loudly that even the sharks and crocodiles were scared away from the ocean—*Ha! You always had a powerful set of lungs, my boy, even as a baby*, Ronke always added at that point in the story with a hearty chortle. She would tickle POTUS under his armpits till he eventually joined in her hoarse laughter.

Ronke explained that the Babalawo had sacrificed the live chickens to the water spirit to replace POTUS' life before placing a trio of charmed Black Tourmaline amulets around his left wrist for protection from the dreadful demon. According to the medicine man, Black Tourmaline crystals were native stones to Nigerian soils, ensuring that their natural link to the ancestors would provide double protection for a blood Nigerian child such as POTUS. When the ritual was over, his parents were told to return home with their healed son, who would never again repeat the terrible POTUS-word.

It took just three minutes inside the car on the ride home for little POTUS to start reciting the banished word to his horrified parents with the familiar, gleeful monotony– POTUS! POTUS! POTUS! A quick swerve of the SUV and a hurried return to the Babalawo confirmed that the appeasement ritual had indeed worked, but only partially.

"We are fighting a powerful spirit indeed," the Babalawo said, his brows creased in a deep frown. "The great water spirit, POTUS, has been bound with my supernatural chains and can no longer claim the child's soul. However, he still clings to the child's body and is fighting my charms. But he fights a losing battle, trust me. My powers can stun demons of all colours, realms, shapes and sizes. However, as added protection, your son must be allowed to call on the name, POTUS, as frequently as he wishes, since this name is now a talisman and has become the child's weapon against the demon. Also, you must baptise him with the name, 'POTUS.' Taking on the demon's name neutralises its hold on your son, and becomes a powerful supernatural shield that will wrap the boy in an invincible bubble of safety, protecting him from evil for as long as he lives."

Before they left the Babalawo's shrine, the medicine man left his parents with one final warning, a caution so dire it brought a gasp to their lips.

"Listen well," he warned, fixing them with a steely gaze. "Your son must never be allowed to swim or go near any river, lake, or big body of water for as long as he lives. Moreover, his face must also be covered whenever you cross a bridge, to prevent the water spirit from recognising him and claiming his life in a drowning accident. That is all."

His terrified parents had made their escape from the Babalawo's shrine for the second time. From that fateful day, they adhered to the medicine man's prophecy and instructions with fanatical zeal. POTUS was allowed to mime his favourite word without censor, and everyone that knew the child soon grew used to hearing the chanted word, *POTUS, POTUS, POTUS.* A second baptism was held to add the name "POTUS" to the child's other name, Lanre, meaning, "wealth is increasing, riches are growing." The only person that still called him by the name, Lanre, was his paternal grandmother, Grandma Funke. POTUS figured he could live with that minor aggravation, seeing as Grandma Funke was the only grandparent in his life. All the others were long dead. Moreover, his grandma spoiled him with loads of presents, so he didn't mind humouring her by answering to the detested name, Lanre.

In time, their community of affluent friends grew accustomed to calling the rowdy little boy, POTUS, without the initial smirk or wry amusement the name used to generate. Save for the identical twin sons of their security man, Taiwo and Kehinde, who teased him mercilessly and made fun of his name at every opportunity, little POTUS had little to worry about in his secluded and pampered life of extreme privilege. The twins were an irritation he would deal with when he was older—Anyway, they were too poor for him to be bothered by their meanness.

POTUS knew that poverty was a bad disease which made people mean and nasty. He was glad that his parents were rich. He loved his home as much as he loved his toys. The eight-bedroom opulent house he shared with his parents was sparkling clean, just like his best friend Frankie's house. Incredibly, Frankie's father worked with POTUS' dad at the big oil company, and the boys' friendship had birthed an equally strong bond between the two families. Best of all, Frankie turned out to be very gifted academically, a complicated feat POTUS could never quite master. With Frankie's help, difficult homework was easily completed, despite Miss Yemisi's scepticism. The class teacher, now the happy recipient of his mother's frequent bribes, from Gucci-Hyun bags to Princess Megan's *Lilscent* perfumes, had long tired of trying to get POTUS to write in lowercase instead of the screaming all upper case he seemed to favour. Even the home-lesson tutor hired by his parents soon informed them that, with the exception of a natural flair for drawing crayon artwork of spectacular boxing gloves and gigantic golf clubs, the child had little or no academic prowess whatsoever. He suggested that POTUS should instead be encouraged to develop his drawing skills at an arts school. "Who knows, he may yet grow up to become an architect if given the right tools," the tutor had advised unconvincingly, before quitting in despair.

Little POTUS wasn't fazed by the home tutor's disappearing act. If anything, it gave him more free time to enjoy his online monopoly games. He also took the opportunity to order more prank items like stink farts and faux period blood stains with his mama's credit cards. The prank arsenal did its wicked job on the teachers populating his hit list, blighting their days and raising his street cred amongst the rest of the admiring pupils. His mama didn't mind his abuse of her credit cards. Mama loved him more than planet Krypton and would let him do anything he liked.

Of everybody in the world, POTUS loved his Mama the best, at least as much as his selfish, egoistical, and me-me heart could ever love another human being.

4
THE SECRET

The first time POTUS realised his mama wasn't like other mothers was on the day he turned nine, a bright summer afternoon in the teeming city of Lagos, the commercial capital of Nigeria. That day had started out just like any other day, with his mother, Ronke, dropping him off that morning at his primary school in her black Mercedes SUV with the personalised number plates – RONKE 1. Their house was a mere five-minute drive from the school, but walking was out of the question. It was something only the unfortunate poor endured.

As he endured the torture of reading and writing, POTUS could hardly wait to enjoy the lavish party his parents were throwing for him at their plush Ikoyi mansion after school. He'd already made sure to mention the toys he liked to his friends and minions and expected to receive the proof of their fealty at his party. It was therefore with great anticipation that he dressed up in the new red and pink three-piece suit his parents had bought for his birthday, together with his new gold wristwatch, a present from his parents, lovingly inscribed with their joint initials, R & K—Ronke and Kunle.

Now, standing in front of the wide mirror on his double wardrobe doors, POTUS once again tried to accustom himself to the image of the little black boy with the expensive barber-designed haircut and piercing light brown eyes underneath scowling bushy brows, reflected back at him. Try as he may, he could never understand why his face, his skin, his size, and even his hair—most especially his hair—just seemed all wrong to him, as if they should belong to someone else with a different name and a different home.

It had always been that way for as long as he could remember, this strange feeling of being someone else other than the little black boy he saw every day in the mirror. In his mind, the real him was hiding somewhere behind the mirror, a strange land that existed in an invisible realm unknown to everyone, himself included. When he was nursery school little, he used to open the wardrobe door over and over, searching for himself behind the mirror. His Mama thought it was a funny game of Hide & Seek and always joined him with indulgent laughter. Ronke would open and shut the wardrobe door as she called out, 'POTUS, where are you?', her deep voice trilling in amusement. Her reactions inevitably brought on one of his famous tantrums, until he was distracted with a new toy or taken for a meal at the Burgers N Shakes restaurant for a well-stacked plate of fries and beef burgers.

As he grew older, most of the memories that used to alternately torment and thrill him from birth—the images of lavish homes, extravagant parties, obsequious friends, icy, white snow, and mind-blowing cuisine—had all but vanished. All that remained were the voices clamouring inside his head, the strange whispers, giggles, weeping, conversations, and screeches he heard at the most unexpected times, day and night.

Initially, he used to ask his parents what so-and-so words meant, strange phrases he'd heard inside his head when the demon voices came. They would hurriedly shush him up, terror clouding their eyes, convinced the dreaded water spirit was still haunting him. Gradually, POTUS learned to keep the voices to himself. He was resigned to the fact that his class teachers and home tutors would forever label him as lacking concentration due to his tendency to switch off when the voices came thundering inside his head, accompanied by the blistering headaches that heralded their onset. Save for Frankie, he never mentioned his affliction to any of his friends, for fear of their reaction, something he'd experienced a lot in his nursery school days when he lacked filter and awareness of nuances. Only his trusty fists had bought him reprieve and respect—*Huh! I'll kill anybody that laughs at me. I will, too. POTUS is nobody's fool!* He even used to punch and bite his mama whenever she made fun of his so-called Hide & Seek game, until his daddy spanked him good and proper and put some discipline back into his body.

But today was his ninth birthday, and POTUS was prepared to put aside his habitual unease and accept the smart looking boy in the mirror as himself. If nothing else, he'd receive the myriad of presents intended for this little, black stranger staring back at him in the mirror with wide pale, brown eyes. He shut those eyes tightly and made a desperate wish for the voices to be still today and allow him to enjoy his birthday party. He prayed Frankie wouldn't be late to his party either. His best friend always knew when the voices came and would either lead him away to a private place or create a diversion to distract the class.

He headed downstairs, exiting through their plush inner parlour that housed the grand piano which nobody played. His mama thought it was a classy thing to have. Plus, it displayed POTUS' golf trophies and photos to perfection. His favourite sport was golf, a clean game that left no marks on his pristine, white trousers. He excelled at it with such uncanny brilliance that he was already considered a protégé, even earning himself a glowing piece in one of the local dailies. His proud parents made sure the press article was preserved in a huge, gilded photo frame and displayed atop the grand piano for both their guests and POTUS to admire.

As he walked through the open front door, he could see the balloon-festooned marquees set up in the huge compound, together with tables laden with assorted foods and an impressive six-tiered birthday cake. A couple of bouncy castles and an ice cream van decorated the children's area, while a live band practised some *Afro-Juju* music to entertain the adults expected later in the evening. The weather was kind, too. No hint of clouds or rain in the sky as far as his eyes could see. A cool breeze lazily stirred the leaves of the banana, orange, and Paw-Paw trees dotted around the large compound, disturbing the languid butterflies and greedy birds feasting on the ripe fruits. A few randy red-crested boy-lizards gave chase to the smaller grey girl-lizards, before giving up with their habitual silly nods and scurrying away into the vibrant hibiscus bushes. POTUS smirked at them before inhaling deeply as the tantalising smell of Jollof rice, fried plantain, Egusi soup, and goat-pepper soup wafted up his nostrils. Listening to the strands of music floating in the air, he felt a warm thrill course through his body, bringing on a delicious shiver. He just knew his ninth birthday party was going to be a very special one— maybe even better than his eighth birthday party at the Ikoyi golf club last year.

The gentle purr of a car engine interrupted his musings. He turned and spied the bonnet of a silver-blue Mercedes Benz nosing past the open metal gate. POTUS smiled. His first guest had finally arrived, and his party was now about to enter full swing. He pumped his fists and dashed out—*Yes, yes, yes!*

POTUS was desperate to pee. He'd drunk so many bottles of Fanta at his party that his groin was now crying out for desperate relief. With a tortured groan, he dashed over to the nearest guest toilets downstairs, but some other kids were already inside. It was the same with the third toilet across the lounge, with several kids lined up waiting their turn. He made a dash up the wide flight of stairs leading towards his private quarters, which were also comprised of his ensuite bedroom and adjoining playroom. But the corridor door leading to his quarters was locked, an action his parents had taken to protect his precious collection of Yeezy sneakers and expensive electronic gadgets from wandering children and their "light-fingered nannies," as Ronke called them.

Sweat was now pouring down his face, and he was ready to bawl with frustration. He ran towards his parent's bedroom, clutching his groin and moaning softly under his breath. The door opened, bringing a whoosh of relief to his lips. Dashing across the wide bedroom with its dramatic red walls and massive bronze four-poster bed, POTUS flung open the ensuite bathroom with frantic force and came face to face with his mama, Ronke, in her full naked glory.

POTUS stopped, his mouth dropping in a wide O-shape. His goggled eyes fixated on his mother's body, her small, flat-chested, and wiry, muscular body that had a ding dong between her thighs just like his own and Daddy's own only bigger, longer and… *Oh my God! Oh my God! Mama has a giant ding dong!* For several stunned seconds, POTUS stared in silent horror at the terrifying rod between his mother's thighs, unaware he was peeing all over his nice, new red trousers till the puddle formed at his feet. The sudden, pungent smell of ammonia stank up the bright, tiled bathroom.

"PO… POTUS!"

"M… Mama…?"

They both spoke at the same time, their voices identical whispers that sounded like thunder inside his head. Ronke dashed over and pulled a pink towel robe over her body, tying the belt tightly with hands that trembled so badly POTUS thought she was going to faint, just like Lois Lane in his Hologram Superman films.

Thoughts were running like crazy inside his mind and from nowhere, a strange word popped into his head—*Chinese.* He didn't know where the thought came from, but it was so strong it refused to budge from his mind—*The Chinese have turned my Mama into a man!* His classmate's face flashed in his mind. Hu Lin was Chinese, and his dad was a diplomat. The little Chinese boy was clever, even smarter than Frankie. But POTUS just couldn't see Hu Lin hexing his mama and turning her into this terrible thing before him—*Isn't Hu one of the boys he protects at school? Why would Hu jeopardise his play-ground safety by hurting his mama?* POTUS shook his head, over and over till it ached— *No, it isn't the Chinese responsible for changing my Mama, at least not Hu Lin. Maybe, it's the Albanians… huh?* His brows dipped in confusion—*Who's the Albanians?*

Another strange phrase popped into his head—*Oh, s-sweet Mary and the apostles!* He didn't bother figuring out what it meant or how he'd picked it up. His mind was in free-spin, tripping on its own poisoned candy—*S-sweet Mary and the apostles! Sweet Mary and the apostles!* The phrase played over and over inside his head like a faulty toy in a manic repetitive motion. There was no space for any other thought in his mind. *S-sweet Mary and the apostles! Oh, sweet...*

"POTUS... Baby Boy, please listen, okay?" Ronke's voice was an urgent whisper. "There's something that Mama must tell you, something very important." Tears pooled and tottered at her spiked lids before cascading down her cheeks in a mascara-stained flood. She came close to where he was rooted in his piddle-pool by the open bathroom door and stooped low till their faces almost touched. Her Colgate-scented breath wafted up his nostrils. "Baby Boy, what you just saw... I mean, daddy and I... we always wanted to tell you, but we didn't think the time was right," she swiped away her tears impatiently with the back of her hand before clasping POTUS' arms with desperate intensity. "Oh, Baby Boy, I'm so sorry you had to find out this way. You know the last thing Mama would ever do is to hurt you or do anything that'll make you sad. You're everything to me... to daddy and me. You know Mama loves you more than the whole wide world and planet Krypton." Ronke's face creased in a pathetic little smile as she repeated their favourite bedtime mantra, the one she whispered into his ear every night.

Looking into her tear-soaked, pleading eyes, POTUS could only see the beautiful and glamorous mother he'd always known for as long as he could remember. Even without the familiar flamboyant golden curls on her now bald head, her lovely thick faux-lashes still looked as beautiful as ever despite her tears. Even her full lips shimmered with the familiar dazzling red colour, while her long nail-extensions glimmered on her bejewelled hands.

An avalanche of emotions hit him like a ten-tonne truck, overwhelming him with fear and confusion. Thick brows furrowed—*It's my Mama... I think it's Mama... and yet, it isn't really my Mama, not anymore.* His mind told him something bad had happened to his real mama, something that stole her body and left her head stuck on a strange man's body, just like the Centaur in his *Hercules* films. He wasn't even sure it was his Mama's head for real, seeing as this alien's head was bald, lacking the flowing, golden tresses that were his mama's hallmark.

"Baby Boy, let's get you out of these wet clothes first, okay?" Ronke began to undo his zipper and he allowed her, too stunned to resist or protest. "Afterwards, we'll go to your room and I'll explain everything. But you must promise never to tell anyone about what you just saw, okay? It's really important, POTUS. You must never tell anyone, not even Frankie, about this. But most importantly, you must never, ever, mention this to Grandma Funke, d'you hear? D'you promise?"

POTUS nodded.

"Say 'I promise, Mama' and cross your heart and hope to cry."

"I p-promise, Mama, and cross my heart and h-hope to cry," he parroted in a broken whisper, crossing his heart with a frantic hand and staring into her eyes with wide eyes filled with terror. His heart was pounding so hard it hurt his chest, and his body quivered and burnt with an all-consuming heat. His eyes pooled, and his bottom lip trembled till he bit it hard with his teeth. He hung his head. Crossing his heart had not saved him from crying after all.

A terrible thought snuck unbidden into his head— *I'm afraid of my Mama!* For the first time in his nine years, POTUS was frightened— soul-terrified—of the woman he had known as 'Mama' for as long as he could recall. Terror washed over him in icy waves. Every fibre in his body told him to run, to escape from an alien threat so great it superseded his terror of the water spirit—*I want my daddy.* Daddy will save him from this alien monster that had taken over Mama's body. His eyes searched frantically in vain for his mother's full-breasted body in the new muscled, flat-chested one lurking underneath the pink towelling robe.

"Good boy," Ronke hugged him tightly, briefly, before lifting him into the wide, walk-in shower. He realised he'd never appreciated the comforting softness of her breasts against his face till they were no longer there. Now, it just felt like being hugged by his daddy, a hard and flat hug, devoid of fragranced comfort and soft security. "We'll soon have you back to normal again, and don't worry about your stained trousers. Mama will buy you a better pair tomorrow, okay?" Her gaze held his own with an intensity that had never been there in the past, the way Wladmir Klitscho would look at an opponent he didn't trust before knocking them out flat.

POTUS nodded again, his mouth dry, stealing his voice. Unshed tears stung his eyes, and a hard knot hurt the back of his throat—I mustn't cry. I mustn't do anything to upset it until Daddy comes up to the bedroom. I must say yes to everything it says until I can make my escape. He shut his eyes tight and held his body stiffly as she handed him the soft sponge and waited in the bathroom as he washed himself. Save for the sound of spurting water from the shower head, and the ruckus outside from the squealing kids and booming music, all was silent in the bathroom.

It was a silence that filled POTUS with tummy-cramping terror. The tepid water from the shower spray did little to wash away the revulsion he felt at the bald, male alien wearing his mother's face. And when the alien handed him the soap with a hand that still had his mama's red-polished nails—*But it isn't really Mama's hand anymore*—he flinched instinctively at the alien's touch. He wanted to remind her that he was now nine years old and hadn't needed her help to wash himself for months. But he was too frightened to speak—Best not to trigger the rage of this scary monster. He quickly averted his gaze, trying hard not to meet her eyes.

When he was done in the bathroom, a torturous ritual that seemed to have lasted a million years, Ronke gave him one of the numerous large towels folded on the bathroom shelf to dry up. When he was done, she led him back into the red-painted bedroom she shared with his daddy and guided him to the plush, leather sofa. Then she picked up the red remote control from the sofa and instantly, the heavy door he'd left open when he crashed into their bedroom earlier began to shut with a slow motion that filled him with terror. He heard the security lock seal them in with a loud click, instantly trapping him inside with her—*Oh no! No... no... no!*

His desperate whispers reverberated inside his head, feeding his terror anew—*Now, I'm truly doomed!* The alien will surely kill him now for discovering its secret. He glanced around the room fearfully, seeking an escape route. But all the windows, even the high French window leading out to the bedroom balcony, were sealed with iron bars to keep away the menace of armed robbery that afflicted both the rich and the poor in the city of Lagos. Now those bars had become his cursed prison, trapping him inside the bedroom with a terrifying alien lurking inside his Mama's body.

Ronke switched on the 100-inch Xiaomi telly that almost covered the entire wall.

"Baby Boy, why don't you watch telly while I change into something suitable for your party, okay?" She smiled at him as she offered him the black remote control. Her yearning smile begged him to smile back and make things normal between them again. POTUS averted his gaze as he perched at the edge of the massive sofa. He could feel the slight tremors of his body, and his hands slipped by themselves between his knees, as if also seeking escape. He squeezed them tightly with his thighs, rocking himself forward and backward in a frantic, robotic motion. He wished he had Superman's strength to break through barred windows and fly away.

After several taut seconds, Ronke heaved a deep sigh and looked up to the ceiling. Fighting her tears, she gently placed the remote control by his side before heading to the brightly lit dressing room adjoining the bedroom. POTUS also released a silent sigh that had lodged beneath his chest in a tight knot. Heart thudding, he jumped off the sofa and began to tip-toe around the room, edging closer to the window. He hoped to catch a glimpse of his father amongst the throng of guests outside and holler for help.

Just then, he heard the familiar heavy footsteps on the marble flooring outside the bedroom corridor, and his heart soared—*Daddy!* He ran towards the door, just as the doorknob turned impatiently a couple of times. Several loud raps on the door soon had Ronke dashing out of the dressing room half-dressed.

Except she no longer wore the terrible alien's body.

POTUS stared at her, his mouth hung open like a goldfish gasping desperately for water—*Huh? B-but how?* In the few minutes it had taken for his daddy to arrive, the alien had morphed back into his mama, with full breasts hidden behind a black lace bra peeping through her dressing-gown, and the familiar long and golden tresses flowing past her shoulders.

"Is that you, Sweetie?" Ronke called out in her familiar husky voice, a deep pitch which now had a sinister ring in POTUS' ears, sending chills down his spine. He'd now seen the real alien hiding inside his mother's body and finally knew why her voice always sounded deeper than his friends' mums' own.

"Of course, it's me," his daddy chuckled behind the door. "Who else do you think it is or are you expecting someone else, you naughty girl?"

Ronke made a pained noise that sounded half cackle and half moan. She quickly unlocked the door, and before his daddy could step into the room, POTUS flung himself at Kunle, pulling his arm, trying to drag him away from Ronke and push him back out of the bedroom.

"Hey! Hey! What's this, eh?" Kunle's voice was a combination of humour and surprise. "Ekùn mi, my little leopard, what's wrong, son? Has Mama been naughty to you on your birthday? We can't have that, can we, eh?" Kunle laughed again, pulling POTUS into his arms, even as he struggled frantically to wiggle free.

"Kunle, he knows," Ronke whispered, tears pooling once again in her eyes. "The child knows everything now. I didn't tell him, I swear. He came into our bathroom and saw me… you know… without my wig or clothes…" Ronke's voice trailed away, choked by soft sobs.

POTUS felt his father go suddenly still. He looked up and saw a look on his daddy's face, a terrible ashen look that said more than a million internet search results on his shiny blue laptop. Instantly, he ceased his struggles, his glazed eyes going from his father to his mother. His heart was thudding louder than the drums of the live band playing outside—*Daddy knows! Daddy knows all about Mama's shapeshifting! B-but, if Daddy knows, what does it mean? Is daddy also a shapeshifting alien like Mama and the ones in my* Women in Green *movie? Does it mean I'm also an alien? Oh, please… no, no…*

"POTUS… Ekùn mi, come with me. It's alright, my son. You don't need to be afraid. Come. Let's get back into the room and we'll explain everything to you. Come now; be a good boy," his daddy gripped his arm firmly and pulled him back into the bedroom as he watched Ronke click the lock once again.

POTUS opened his mouth to let out one of his famed shrieks, but something told him this would be the worst time to throw his usual tantrum—*Uh-uh!* It would be a terrible mistake that could well cost him his life. Hot tears finally trailed unchecked down his cheeks. He made his body go slack and heavy as his father dragged him over to the plush, red sofa. Kunle sat him down next to himself and released a deep sigh. POTUS pressed his fists hard against his lips, stopping the terrified howls that threatened to escape his mouth. He could feel his hands trembling, just like his body. Ronke came over to join them on the sofa, and POTUS flinched away from her, pressing hard against his daddy, his actions instinctive. He saw the hurt look in her eyes before she resumed her gentle sobbing, her face covered with her ring-littered hands.

"Sweetheart, it's okay; come, stop crying. Stop it now," Kunle reached over to pat Ronke gently on her left shoulder. "It's not your fault, alright? You haven't done anything wrong. It was bound to happen sooner or later. After all, the boy is growing older by the day and would've soon put two and two together and come up with the truth. Now's as good a time as any to tell him the truth, don't you think?"

Ronke nodded. "Ju-just a second while I dry my face, alright?" She got off the sofa and hurried back into the bathroom, her movement fluid and graceful as ever. An overpowering combination of Yves Saint Laurent's *Opium* and Princess Megan's *Lilscent* trailed her in the familiar waft of heavenly intoxication. Both POTUS and his father followed her retreat in silence, a brooding silence of conflicted emotions and tortured thoughts. POTUS leaned away from his daddy, edging himself to the far side of the sofa. Kunle gave him a tight smile, but said nothing. The wall clock ticked away relentlessly, pounding insanity into POTUS' head till he thought he would scream after all.

Ronke returned with a box of tissues and perched herself at the edge of the bed facing them. She gave POTUS a tremulous smile, which he returned with a scowl—*Uh-uh! She isn't my Mama! She might try to trick me with her disguise, but I'm not stupid. POTUS is nobody's fool! I'll never smile at her again – never!*

Kunle cleared his throat noisily. "Son, I know what you saw must've been a great shock for you, and I can understand how you must be feeling now and the thoughts going through your head," his daddy took hold of both his hands in a tight clasp, covering them completely in his large, warm hands. "I'm sure you're wondering how we can be your parents if we're both men and of course, you're right."

POTUS wasn't wondering about that at all but now his daddy mentioned it, it suddenly became the most important question to him in the world—*Who are my parents then if Daddy is saying that both him and Mama are men, real human men, not aliens from a super kryptonite planet and...?*

"We're not your parents, Ekùn mi," his daddy's voice interrupted his thoughts. "That is... I mean, we're your Mama and Daddy, of course. Nothing can change that. It's just that Mama didn't actually give birth to you. I brought you back to Mama as a very special present when you were less than a day old and ever since, you've been the most precious thing in our lives, and we wouldn't have it any other way. Remember that you're Daddy's little Ekùn mi and Mama's Baby Boy. You're a very, very special child. It doesn't matter that we're not your real blood parents. To us, you'll always be our son, and we hope you'll always accept us as your Mama and Daddy. Nothing has changed. We're still the same parents you've always known, despite everythin—"

"NO! YOU'RE NOT!" POTUS screamed, stunning them all into boggle-eyed, wide-mouthed silence. In a blink, he snatched his hands from Kunle's own, leapt from the sofa and dashed towards the locked door, twisting the knob, and banging on the thick mahogany door with his fists. "LET ME OUT! LET ME OUT! SOMEBODY HELP ME!" POTUS was screeching hysterically. His eyes were wild, terror turning their pale brown colour to a deep brown that was almost black. The towel slipped from his waist and he stooped to pick it up just as his daddy lifted him full-body into his arms, still kicking and screaming.

"POTUS! Stop this now! Stop right now, or I won't be responsible for my actions," his daddy's voice was the harshest he'd ever heard it, and POTUS instantly ceased his histrionics. Kunle retied his towel briskly around his waist and returned him to the sofa. He hulked over him, arms akimbo, a deep frown of displeasure on his face. "That's better. Now listen up, young man. There's no need for you to behave in this manner, causing your Mama unnecessary pain. I know it's hard

for you to understand why your Mama is a man and why your real
parents aren't around. It's a very long story which will take the entire
day to explain, and we just don't have the time for that right now." His
daddy glanced at his gold Rolex watch, his tall, muscular body oozing
impatience. "Listen, your birthday party's already in full swing and I
only came to get both you and Mama for the cake cutting and photo-
shoots," he turned to Ronke who was perched at the foot of the four-
poster bed, still sobbing softly. "Ronke, try and get a hold of yourself,
alright? Look, I'll take POTUS to his bedroom so he can dress up
while you get yourself ready. Try and be quick, Sweetie. We'll be back
in a bit."

Kunle led him out of the room and shut the door behind them.
Once again, POTUS seized his opportunity and started shrieking at
the top of his voice, calling on his grandmother, his aunties, Frankie's
parents, and every adult he could remember, to come and rescue him.
Kunle quickly placed a hard hand over his mouth, glaring at him with
eyes that were icy, cold pebbles.

"Enough of this abominable behaviour, young man. Do you hear
me?" Kunle's voice was harsh, as though he were speaking to their
security man. "Now, listen carefully to me. No one—repeat, no one—
must ever know about your Mama, do you understand? Nobody. Not
even Grandma Funke or your teachers or your friends. Are we clear?"
Heavy sweat coated Kunle's face, dampening the collar and armpits of
his white shirt. He wiped his face with the habitual white handkerchief
he always carried, and fixed POTUS with an angry glare.

POTUS' legs melted into soft corn pap as he nodded, his heart
pounding hard and fast. Kunle grunted as he removed his hand
covering POTUS' mouth. His eyes were still flinty and his fists
clenched and relaxed, flexing with the familiar menacing repetitiveness
that POTUS had always admired and imitated. Now, he found himself
fearing those flexing fists like a raging river.

"Good. You must keep your mouth shut about what you just saw.
After the party, I'll explain everything about Mama and I. But you
must never, ever, tell anyone, are we clear?"

POTUS frowned, his face a black cloud of mutiny. He hated being
ordered around. His fists clenched so tight his fingers hurt as he

instinctively began flexing them in the familiar motion that mirrored his daddy's own—Maybe this is the right time after all to throw another tantrum, perhaps even refuse to attend my party? Yes, that'll teach them a lesson, and they'll be sorry for being mean to me. Even before the thought left his mind, POTUS flung himself on the floor and began to scream, kicking his legs and flailing his arms wildly in his familiar M.O.

"Grandma Funke! Grandma Funke! Help! Aaaah! Grandmaaa!" *Oh, please, please! Let Grandma Funke hear my shrieks and come to my rescue!*

"POTUS! Stop this foolishness at once and behave yourself," Kunle's voice was now like thunder as he grabbed POTUS by the left arm and yanked him to his feet. His fingers were so tight, POTUS winced and howled even louder in pain. Everything was turning into scary darkness, his whole reality collapsing around his bare feet. "I'm tired of your bratty behaviour. Now, listen up, you; I need you to shut up and behave, are we clear? ARE WE CLEAR?" He waited for POTUS' reluctant nod. "Good! Now, you must promise me you'll keep our little secret, because if you don't, you'll soon find that things won't be very nice for you around the house anymore. Believe me, you won't be happy with what I'll do to you if I ever find out you've talked about this to anyone. In fact, I want you to think about your curse by the scary water spirit and consider what it'll feel like to take a swim with that fearsome demon in the Atlantic Ocean tonight."

Kunle paused as POTUS started to hiccup, gasping for breath. A pained look clouded his eyes as he looked into POTUS' terrified face. He dropped to his knees and enfolded POTUS in a tight embrace, stroking his back gently.

POTUS pushed him away violently.

"I hate you! I hate you and Mama! I'm going to find my real Mama and Daddy and live with them forever and ever and ever!" POTUS screamed, his eyes mutinous, blazing with fury as he glared at his father. A hard look coated Kunle's swarthy features, replacing his earlier warmth as he got to his feet.

"I see you're still not ready to see sense, and that's fine. But just remember what I said about the water-demon and what will happen to you if you ever tell about your Mama and me. So, just behave yourself and don't give me or your Mama any trouble for the rest of the day. I've gone to great expense to throw you a wonderful party as usual, and it'll be good if you showed a bit of gratitude for once. You've been so spoiled that you don't appreciate just how fortunate you are to have us as your parents."

Listening to his father's words, POTUS thought he might pee on himself again. Kunle's harsh behaviour was a second shock coming fast on the heels of his mama's terrible transformation. His eyes filled with tears again, real water-tears this time, not the dry ones he faked for his tantrums. His tummy hurt so much, he almost doubled over in pain. He didn't think he'd ever throw tantrums again, not to these new parents he now had, two frightening aliens he struggled to accept as strangers despite everything—*But if they aren't my real parents, what am I to call them now? How will I find my real Mama and Daddy and escape from these two horrible people?*

POTUS meekly allowed himself to be led into his bedroom. An unfamiliar rage was slowly brewing inside him, replacing his terror. Something hard lodged in his heart as he recalled Kunle's speech in the corridor. Now, his mouth tasted like bile to him—*I hate my Daddy and my Mama more than anything in the world and planet Krypton! I hate my party too! I don't want to take the stupid photos either. I'll run away to Frankie's house, and later, I'll find my real Mama and real Daddy and I'll never come back to this horrible house again – never! I'll show them, alright. I'll show them that POTUS IS NOBODY'S FOOL!*

He wiped his face with a vicious swipe of his hand, sniffing hard and fast. His eyes scanned his room rapidly, even as Kunle rummaged through his wardrobe for a fitting attire to replace his soiled, red, birthday suit—*Yes, I'll take all my toys and my games and my consoles and my laptop and my mobile phone and my golf clubs and my Superman costume and my boxing gloves and my Yeezy Crush 350 sneakers and my bicycle and my electric scooter and my...*was he forgetting anything else that belonged to him? He shook his head viciously—*I don't want their stupid gold wristwatch present with their horrible initials. I'll chuck it into the bin when I escape. Yes, I mustn't forget to take all the new presents my friends brought, and the new OppO phone from Grandma Funke. They're* *mine, after all, and POTUS always keeps what belongs to POTUS. And when I find my real Mama and my real Daddy, I'll keep them with me forever and ever and ever...*

A treacherous tear trickled down his cheek, and was quickly swiped away with a raging fist.

5

BLACKMAIL

The Federal Enquirer
Coma Countdown!
Day 3 of President Jerry King's Coma
(PMD Media, 11 July)
Mike Vine and the news desk

President King's Family at War!
(First Lady and First-Sister Battle Over Life Support Machine!)

The countdown to President Jerry King's coma continues as we enter into the 3rd day, and things are starting to heat up in the president's domestic arena. As the entire country and the world come together in prayers for the president's recovery, sources close to the family have reported that the First Lady, Portia King, was involved in the mother of all fights with the president's sister, Dr. Delores King, over her decision to terminate the president's life support machine. It has been reported that the president's medical team believe that the life support should be switched off eventually, as it is unlikely the president will ever regain consciousness from the coma.

. . .

According to our sources, Dr, Delores King accused the First Lady of being "a gold-digging whore," determined to finish off her brother for his considerable wealth. Eyewitnesses to the altercation between the two women at the hospital claim that it took the intervention of the Secret Service and the Vice President, Franklin Flint, to defuse the situation. The vice president is yet to make his thoughts public, seeing as he stands to automatically become the next President of the United States.

In the meantime, we can confirm that the playboy Billionaire, Tad Hunter, has been questioned and released without charge as the investigation continues. In what has become known as "Cough-Gate," Tad Hunter has been accused of failing to shout out "FORE" when he saw his golf ball, which was travelling at an estimated speed of 150 miles per hour, heading towards the president's golf cart. Mr. Hunter is said to have suffered a bout of coughing spasms at the very moment he shouted, or attempted to shout, "FORE" and warn about his bad ball. Needless to say, conspiracy theories now abound about the so-called "Cough-Gate," and we will update our readers as more information is received.

As readers may recall, Mr. Hunter is currently in a relationship with Miss Madison Hudson, who was once President King's mistress and the mother of his only child, Lisa Hudson. It is no secret that the relationship between the two men has not been the best over the years, and Mr. Hunter has been quite vocal in his criticisms of the president, whom he once referred to as, "the dumbest fool in the White House." Meanwhile, it remains to be seen if Mr. Hunter's golf ball incident was a genuine accident or a weapon of love-rival-destruction as some people are insinuating; not forgetting the fact that Mr. Hunter is amongst the biggest donors to the Democratic Party. With the presidential elections looming, certain quarters are already hinting at dark Machiavellian plots behind that notorious tee and "Cough-Gate."

· · ·

President King's approval ratings since the accident have skyrocketed in the latest opinion polls, and if the intention was to derail his re-election bid, then that strategy has failed spectacularly. Not that this report is implying that the golf ball was anything but a genuine accident, of course; but try convincing the president's supporters otherwise. Meanwhile, efforts to reach both Mr. Hunter and Miss Hudson have so far been unsuccessful.

As we continue our coma countdown, doctors are still working around the clock to save President King's life despite the dire prognosis. Our sources tell us that a team of the world's top neurologists might be flown in from Germany to assist the medical team caring for the president. Several other countries have offered their assistance, including the Chinese government. But as is well known, President King has very strong opinions about the Chinese, as well as the Albanians, and certainly won't be happy to learn that he owes them his life should he recover. As we all pray for President King's speedy recovery, we will keep you informed with further developments. This is a developing story.

He's in a brightly lit living room that gleams with the kind of opulence he's never witnessed in his seventeen years of life in Nigeria. Everything about the room screams of stupendous wealth, an affluence that is even greater than his parent's impressive riches. The heavy brocade curtains covering the tall windows shut out the night and its stars, sealing the room and its secrets from the outside world. He can feel the sweat drenching his body underneath his silk shirt and the hard pounding of his heart. His eyes are glued on the shut door just beyond the heavy bookshelf against the wood-panelled wall, and every limb in his body trembles with feverish panic.

Once again, just as always, his legs start leading him towards the shut door. He doesn't want to go to that door, doesn't want to turn the knob and open its wooden shield. But his legs have a will of their own, and he's helpless to halt their strides. In seconds, he stands before the shut white door,

feeling the terror rush up with renewed force, threatening to steal his sanity
—No... no... oh, please God, no! *He won't open that door; he'll shut his eyes and refuse to look. That's what he'll do; refuse to look.*

His hand starts turning the knob, slowly opening the door as his breathing quickens, coming out in harsh gasps. He stands by the open door, fighting the urge to flee, to put thousands of miles of distance between him and the cursed room that lies beyond the white door. For several seconds, he lurks outside the door, fighting the pounding in his chest, his eyes tightly shut. But eventually, a familiar gritty hardness forces his lids to flicker. Then they open, and a low moan escapes from his lips as he stares at the prone figure stretched out on a white slab in the centre of the room. An overhead bulb shines directly above it, and in its cruel glare, he sees the horror he's dreaded and avoided.

It is the body of a young girl, maybe eighteen or nineteen years old. She is dressed in a bright yellow dress that has a white lace collar with mother-of-pearl threaded through it. Her blonde hair flows below her shoulders in a soft wave that shields one side of her face. Her skin is pale, a ghastly white colour that betrays the absence of life in the still body. For a brief second, his gaze lingers on her face and a hard knot in his chest brings a low groan to his lips—Oh, Jesus... fuck... fuck...

Of its own will, his gaze travels down the prone corpse of the young woman till it comes to a point just below her stomach. This time he is unable to stop the choked sobbing that causes him to double over in pain—blood... blood... oh, sweet Jesus, blood; so much blood...

From her hips to her toes, a thick sludge of blood coats the dead woman like a blanket drenched in red paint. The blood spreads across her stained yellow dress, dripping down the metal edges of the slab to the marbled floor, till the entire area gleams with the death-hue of her life fluids. There is so much blood on the floor that he wonders how one human could have carried that much blood without collapsing from the sheer burden—Poor Mary-Beth. I'm sorry... I'm really sorry... I didn't plan for this to happen... you know that I... Jesus Christ!

The woman's corpse starts to rise from the slab. Her eyes are shut, like someone in deep meditation. As he opens his mouth to scream, her eyes fly open, her icy gaze fixated on his face. She glares at him with loathing and rage, and he feels the menace oozing from every closed pore on her pallid skin. Her eyes are no longer the baby blue hue he recalls, but are now as blood drenched as her lower body. Her arms stretch, reaching out to him, and a terrible gurgle issues from her lips. A sludge of black blood disgorges from her gaping mouth, trailing a bloated worm down her chest.

He stumbles backwards, whimpering softly as he backs away from the room. He bumps into something and trips, falling and crashing against the glass-topped side table. The shattering noise of the broken glass fills his ears, together with the heavy shambling footfalls from the room—Oh, J-Jesus… oh, God… fuck!

He tries to get up, but he's not fast enough. In a blink, she slumps over him, trapping his body beneath her icy weight. Her cold, cold hands reach for his neck, squeezing, pressing, pushing with a strength beyond the realm of man. He feels the breath dying in him, his life force draining. In seconds, his soul starts to fly from his body. He is thrashing his legs, clawing with desperation at the icy fingers digging into his windpipe. His breathing is harsh and raspy, and his body jerks manically in tortured spasms. With superhuman strength, he pushes her off and hauls himself into…

POTUS wakes from his nightmare, gasping and coughing, his eyes wide with terror. His body is drenched in sweat despite the air conditioner humming in his bedroom, and the thudding in his heart was like hard rocks crushing out his life—*Jesus! When will this nightmare stop?* It was the same dream he'd been having from his childhood. The nightmare was like the voices he heard inside his head, except that unlike the voices, this ghastly dream came to him once every year instead of every day.

On exactly the twelfth day of December, POTUS had the recurrent nightmare that left him shaking with terror on awakening. It was always the dead young woman in her blood-drenched yellow dress and blonde hair, and just like always, he had fought himself into wakefulness from the attack of the terrifying corpse. In his younger days, he used to run to his mother, screeching with terror. Listening to him recount his nightmare, Ronke would cover his mouth with her trembling hand, her eyes wide with a terror that mimicked his own.

"Shh… Baby Boy, don't talk about it anymore, you hear?" She would hug him close, so tight he struggled to breathe. "It's just a wicked dream from enemies jealous of our good fortune. Maybe it's even the water demon trying to frighten you. We'll visit the Babalawo tomorrow and ask him for another charm to protect you from the evil white witch in your dream, okay?"

But with each passing year, POTUS realised the futility of the Babalawo's potions. They only chained the dead white witch for one year until she returned once again the following December 12th to torment his dream. These days, he no longer bothered telling Ronke about the nightmares seeing as they terrified her more than they did him. Anyway, he's now seventeen and old enough to handle a stupid yearly nightmare without freaking out like some scaredy girl. He's lived with this long enough to be used to it by now—*Stuff the bloody white witch and the water demon!*

POTUS pulled his blanket over his body and shut his eyes, willing sleep back with grim determination. But this time, just as he had done on previous December 12th nights, he left the lights on and his music playlist on a reassuring loop.

Ever since that fateful day POTUS witnessed Ronke's male body on his ninth birthday, nobody had spoken about it to him. Sometimes he wondered if what he'd seen that day was real or something he'd imagined. Save for Kunle's brutality from then onwards, he would've likely forgotten all about it. Instead, their heavy burden of secrecy was borne in uncomfortable silence within the thick walls of their luxurious home. Even now, eight years later, the thought of the lies and secrets they kept as a family hung over his shoulders like a sack of sharp blades, poised to slash him to pieces should he stumble. He couldn't remember the last time his father had addressed him with the old endearment, "Ekùn mi"—*Not that I give a Kobo. Who wants to be his stupid leopard, anyway?*

POTUS scowled, resisting the urge to rev up his motorbike. Last thing he wanted was for Ronke to wake up from her usual Sunday lie-in before he escaped from the compound. He also didn't fancy yet another fight with his legal father. These days, they fought about everything and anything, just like the previous night which had ended with more shouts, accusations, and threats—*Stupid man! Useless hypocrite!*

POTUS didn't doubt that he would best Kunle in a fist fight, what with the way the man had let himself go over the years. While he wasn't quite as tall as Kunle, he rocked the solid, muscled body of an athlete at his peak, unlike Kunle's over-blown girth padded with soft fat. In his younger days, POTUS remembered a different Kunle. Then, his daddy used to be tall and taut, his stomach as flat and hard as his chest, a doppelgänger of Terry Crews in *White Chicks*. POTUS smirked—*Huh!* Dude was just a flabby, sweaty, pile of dog mess now.

With a muttered curse, he rolled out his motorbike from the garage before fitting his helmet over his head. As he hopped on his motorbike, his thoughts took a rapid descent down the years of relentless family friction, to the last time Kunle had taken the belt to him. It happened just before his fifteenth birthday, brought on by a minor misdemeanour POTUS now struggled to recall. Kunle had gone crazy with rage, flaying POTUS with his belt till Ronke pulled a kitchen knife on him, enabling POTUS to escape. He'd spent the night at Frankie's house, nursing the agonising belt welts on his back and legs. By the time he returned home the next morning, he had come up with the plan that would bring an end to his abuse at Kunle's hands for good—*Give me my freedom and money, otherwise Frankie's parents and my teachers will know about your disgusting secret!*

He recalled the stunned look on both their faces when he shouted the threat, Ronke's tears, and the rage that turned Kunle's eyes into ticking twin blood moons. Tight muscles had bulged beneath Kunle's neck, his fists flexing manically.

"Who the hell do you think you are, you little bastard?" Kunle had bellowed in a deafening roar as he approached POTUS with bristling menace. "What right do you have to judge us or threaten us? What are you without us, eh? Answer me, you bastard retard. What are you without us?"

POTUS had tensed as Kunle pushed his face into his own, his breathing harsh and hot. He expected Kunle to charge at him again with his belt, and his heart pounded as he geared himself up for more violence. But as their eyes clashed, he saw the terror lurking behind his father's dark gaze. In that split second, POTUS felt a heady rush of triumph—*Kunle fears exposure more than anything! Crazy man fears me!*

That illumination had wiped away POTUS' fear and had stayed with him. In time, he added Grandma Funke, the church pastors, and the police to the threat list, as well as *Naggle, Chiggle, AssBook,* and Instagram. He didn't need to remind his parents that Africa wasn't as tolerant of gay rights as the West, and when he demanded a motorbike as his seventeenth birthday present, Kunle had paid up, even as he cursed and stomped around the house for weeks afterwards with rage-reddened eyes and flexing fists. A few months later, when POTUS demanded to be sponsored for his university degree in America the next year, Kunle's weary silence confirmed his forced acquiescence. His mother had already paid for the person to take his exams for him, and he knew his high grades were guaranteed.

Still, despite his blackmail victories, POTUS constantly watched Kunle with the wariness of a cat lurking near a Rottweiler—*If the dude ever finds out how terrified I am of their secret getting exposed, he'll never hand over the bribe money again.* He knew that Kunle believed his weekly bribe money bought his silence. But truth was, he would rather die a hundred water deaths than reveal their family's shameful secret, bribe or no bribe—*God!* He would never live down the shame if his mates discovered his conventional Yoruba parents were really two gay guys. POTUS shuddered, overwhelmed by the hidden terror that stalked him with relentless grit.

Despite everything he knew about his adoptive mother, he could never get himself to hate Ronke the way he wanted to, with the same passionate loathing he harboured for Kunle. To him, Ronke was just Mama—*She, her.* He could never think about her in masculine terms, not with her tender-hearted femininity and easy tears. It hurt him that she had to masquerade as a female underneath her flamboyant wigs, faux-breasts, heavy makeup, and heavier jewellery. After all, Ronke couldn't help the way she was, which was more than he could say for his adoptive father—*Huh! Kinky-Kootch Kunle! Dude struts around like Superman, all macho and Mr. Perfection himself, all the while skulking inside the most cowardly closet ever.* Even on the rare occasions when some glimmer of the old affection resurfaced in Kunle's heart, like when POTUS was hospitalised from a near-fatal burst appendix and Kunle spent a night with him in hospital, smiling and talking to him with the long-forgotten warmth, POTUS still sensed Kunle's unease in his caged behaviour. And when they returned to their usual brawls after his recovery, he had welcomed Kunle's vitriol with the relief of an old friend.

In public, Kunle styled himself as a traditionalist, with a healthy contempt for the West. His clothes, speech, mannerisms, and even his diet (save for his expensive Whiskey), were epitomes of Yoruba culture. One would never see him wearing anything save the Agbada, Danshiki, and Aso-oke native clothes. He always wore his Fila caps to the right side of his head to show people he was in a heterosexual marriage. Unless Kunle opened his mouth and spoke in his impeccable English accent, nobody seeing him decimating a full bowl of Eba with his hands amidst bawdry jokes would ever believe he'd seen the four walls of a classroom, much less hold a Master's degree in Engineering from a top British college in Oxford.

POTUS' brows dipped viciously as he lifted his fingers briefly from the handlebars of his motorbike and lit a cigarette, savouring the thick smoke swirling around his face. Smoking was one of his few joys, a habit he'd formed solely to frustrate Kunle's fastidious sensibilities. As he took another puff, he eyed the trio of black Tourmaline amulets on his wrists with a scowl—*Stupid things!* The Babalawo insisted that he continue wearing the charmed amulets to protect him against the dreaded water spirit. His last visit to the famed seer had been on his thirteenth birthday, when Ronke had literally dragged him to the Babalawo's shrine for fresh amulets, before he rebelled and refused to afflict himself with that superstitious foolishness. In fact, he would have chucked the stupid amulets into the bin, save for the fact that Ronke begged him with desperate panic to desist— "Just for my sake, Baby Boy, please. Give your poor Mama peace of mind by wearing your amulets, you hear? Just do this one favour for your Mama, and I'll never ask you for anything else."

POTUS knew when he was beaten; not that Ronke needed to

emotionally blackmail him into wearing the charms. He had found out not too long after that final visit to the Babalawo's shrine that he was a prisoner to the sinister trio of Tourmaline bracelets. He had tried to pull them off after some minor argument with his mum, only to find that he couldn't yank them from his wrist no matter how hard he tried. The more he pulled, the more they bit into his skin till his wrist was raw and sore. Not even the scissors or knives he applied could cut the thin thread holding the beads together. Ronke had stared goggle-eyed, just like POTUS. Even Kunle gaped slack-jawed in stunned disbelief, before bursting into wild laughter. The humiliation had been too much to bear, and POTUS had run out of the room after cursing Ronke and threatening to tell everyone about her real gender, unless she got the Babalawo to remove the charms—ASAP!

In the end, it had all been just talk. Even though he still nursed a desperate need to go to America and find his birth mother, a woman that went by the common name of Folake, of no known village, his love for his Mama was unwavering. Gradually, he learned to accept the triad of black amulets as permanent body-guests, despite knowing there were no benefits in wearing them. The voices inside his head and his annual nightmares continued to ruin his peace, and the charms weren't doing much to destroy them. Still, they gave Ronke some peace of mind, which was the least he could do for her.

With a deep sigh and another deeper inhalation of his cigarette, POTUS manoeuvred his bike out to the streets of Lagos with Kamikaze glee.

6

THE DEMON VOICES

POTUS weaved his red Honda VFR800F motorbike through the busy morning traffic. Cars and buses blared their horns in annoyance, while street hawkers hurled colourful curses at him for almost knocking them down with his expensive ride. POTUS howled gleefully and gave them the middle finger. Revving the throttle with maniacal zeal, he embarked on an impromptu road race with a white van in front. Beads of hot sweat dotted his forehead underneath his black and red *Iron Cool-man* helmet as he quickly overtook the van before slowing for maximum vexation-effect. The van driver remained glued to his horn in a furious and prolonged blare as POTUS continued with his manic disruption of traffic. Knowing how angry his parents would be when they awoke from their Sunday lie-in and found him gone—again—filled him with vicious satisfaction. Who cares? POTUS can do whatever POTUS likes.

His brows dipped in a scowl as he recalled the first time he informed his mum he was visiting the Hill of Fire Church at Bariga several months ago.

"Bariga!" Ronke had exclaimed in horror. "Baby Boy, you can't go there. The place is full of kidnappers and robbers. What will—"

"I've told you not to call me Baby Boy," POTUS snarled. "I'm not a kid anymore. I'm seventeen years old now and can go anywhere I like."

"At least let me give you a ride in my car, okay? You're still learning how to ride your bike, and heaven forbid you get knocked down by some crazy bus driver," Ronke insisted.

"For God's sake, Ronke, stop babying the boy!" Kunle snapped, giving POTUS a vicious look. "Just let the fool find his own way to his stupid church on his stupid motorbike."

For once, POTUS was grateful for his father's hostility, and he had used the opportunity to escape Ronke's smothering attention. Not that it had done him much good. Ronke's response had been to trail his motorbike in her Mercedes SUV every Sunday, till he arrived safely at the church premises. She would then hang around the street till service was over before once again trailing his bike to wherever he was taking his latest conquest to, be it the cinema or the restaurant. No matter how long he dallied or how many angry holo-messages he sent to her mobile, she would remain sentinel inside her car till he was ready to go home. Then she would trail him back to their safe neighbourhood and safer compound, ignoring his rants as she glided into her bedroom in a cloud of Saint Laurent and Princess Megan.

POTUS glanced back to make sure the white van wasn't gaining on him. It wasn't—*Yah, babes!* It was a good way to start the day. He hoped his luck would hold till he got to the church. It was a known fact that the hottest girls in town generally hung out at the churches in this bustling part of the city on Sundays in search of eligible bachelors to snare into holy matrimony. Thanks to Kunle's bribe money, POTUS' purse was always well-greased, and he rarely failed to score with the girls. With his five-eleven height, well-toned physique, unusual piercing pale, brown eyes, hoarse booming voice, and designer trimmed hair, POTUS knew he was a class above the rank-and-file losers hoping to snag the birds outside the church grounds. He'd had lots of people come up to him to ask if he was John Boyega's brother, a fact that flattered him no end, albeit he felt he was better looking than the famous actor. If nothing else, he was definitely more blinged up than Boyega any day.

Being a golf celebrity equally tanked up his sexiness barometer, something he never failed to mention in every company, male, female, and child. His motto was, 'If you have it, brag it.' Frankie sometimes called him a Philodox, whatever that meant—Fool liked to use big words that only made sense to himself. According to Frankie, POTUS had a special skill for one-way conversation, all going down his own lane. Frankie's dissing was fine with him. Frankie was his soul brother and spoke from a place of love, unlike some other demons he could think of—Kinky-Kootch Kunle, for one!

POTUS thoughts were interrupted by a rush of wind that almost toppled him from his motorbike. He frowned as he realised the white van had finally overtaken his motorbike, horns still blaring furiously.

"Idiot goat! Yeye man! Vamoose your motorcycle before I squash you like voodoo chicken!" The van driver screamed at him through the open window, his eyes dark with rage. POTUS returned the compliment with a middle finger. Sudden mania glazed his eyes. Adrenaline pumped up his heartbeats—*Idiot peasant! I'll show you who's a Yeye man!* He weaved across the road in a dangerous overtake, almost causing the van to swerve onto an oncoming lorry. The blasting horns and angry shouts of numerous irate motorists followed his fast disappearing back. POTUS cruised ahead serenely. He'd already lost interest.

Just then, a motorcyclist in a black hoodie zoomed furiously past him. Lost in thought, POTUS almost ignored the cyclist till he noticed the guy was on a dirty, cheap machine—*Huh!* The bike was likely rescued from some second-hand junkyard. A new surge of excitement hit him—Fool needed to be taught a Honda VFR800F lesson in superior speed and respect.

POTUS gave chase, weaving past cars, buses, pedestrians, and everything in his path with reckless grit and laser determination. The offending motorcyclist, blissfully unaware of the impromptu race, continued on his route, leading POTUS down a lane that ended at a bridge.

POTUS braked suddenly—*Sweet Mary and the apostles! I almost crossed a bridge!* He did a rapid sign of the cross, stalling his motorbike several feet from the bridge, breathing hard—*POTUS! Man, you're one stupid, yeye fool!* He wanted to punch his own face as he watched the motorcyclist ride across the bridge. He rested at the side of the road, engine lolling, helmet now in hand, heaving and panting as he wiped hot sweat from his face. The Babalawo's voice rang loud inside his head —*Never go near a river or cross a bridge, otherwise the water demon, POTUS, will steal your soul!*

POTUS laughed nervously. He didn't really believe the Babalawo anymore, but it was better to be safe than sorry. He lowered his head and sniffed his armpits—*Phew!* Now he would arrive at the church smelling like a pedestrian. He'd be lucky if he scored with any of the girls today. *Stupid!* He restarted his machine.

Just then, he spotted a familiar black Mercedes SUV with the personalised number plate, idling by the roadside across from him. He already knew who sat behind the wheel—*Mama! Not again!* His lips tightened, and he swore softly through clenched teeth. Anger flared briefly in his heart before morphing into resigned irritation—*I should've known better.* He'd thought he had successfully escaped her. Seemed he was wrong—*Yet again.*

Ronke wound down her tinted window and waved frantically at POTUS, her face wreathed in the sheepish smile he'd come to recognise as her attempt at a meaningless apology. They both knew she had no plans to quit re-offending, and he was tempted to ignore her presence. Her large designer sunglasses hid her eyes while simultaneously drawing attention to her. POTUS scowled as he noticed several pairs of curious eyes watching their interaction in the busy street. A barrow boy in a filthy Adidas cap and an obese woman in a flowered headscarf stared at them with avid interest.

POTUS' body wilted with familiar mortification, his mind screeching the words he couldn't scream aloud without incurring the disapproval of the nosey onlookers—*Just get lost, Mama! Leave me alone, alright?* He didn't need telling he'd be lynched in seconds by the self-righteous crowd for showing such disrespect to his mother. 'Honour thy mother and thy father' was a big one in their Jesus-obsessed culture, despite all the other evils they committed with unholy blasé in the Lord's name. POTUS kept his lips tightly shut and instead raised an impatient arm to wave Ronke away.

With no warning, the voices roared inside his head. The familiar blistering headache hit him like a tonne of bricks. He groaned softly, biting his lips. This time, the conversation wasn't calm, but a shrieking, manic ruckus. POTUS wobbled on his motorbike—*Oh, God, no, no, no! Not now!* He tried to maintain his balance on his ride. He was gulping air through his open mouth, all his attention focused on the deafening voices clamouring inside his head. He recognised each of the voices shrieking their rage. They were the multiple tongues of the water demon, POTUS—

Or as he used to believe.

These days, he knew better than to accept it was solely the water-spirit speaking inside his head with different voices. POTUS was convinced the people inside his head were as real as his parents—except he had no idea who they were. From their accents, he knew they were not Africans. Americans or Canadians, perhaps. With painful meticulousness, POTUS picked out each torturous voice, from the deep, authoritative male voice that always used the phrase, 'National Intelligence,' to the petulant female voice that peppered every sentence with the words, 'POTUS, honey.' And finally, the cultured female voice that constantly called out desperately in a half-sobbing voice, "Jerry… Come on, little brother, speak to me. Wake up now, please." There were other voices that also called out the demon's name, POTUS, on several occasions. POTUS knew them all as if they were his own family, and just like his dysfunctional family, they were now warring inside his head, cursing each other, threatening each other, till the voice he recognised as "Doctor" told them all to leave the room because their presence was agitating the patient.

A few years ago, POTUS had started to record the voices with his *Mind Zoome* device, the memory-chip recorder that transported thoughts and sounds from the mind straight into the small recording disk attached to the forehead. Mind Zoome was the flagship invention by Africa's biggest tech company, *54gene*, a Nigerian firm that were the world leaders in innovative and game-changing technology. POTUS hoped the mind-files stored away in his Mind Zoome keys might one day help him crack the mystery of his demonic possession. He desperately wished he could record now. Live-recordings minimised the intensity of his headaches, but he was caught in morning traffic and his Mind Zoome device was at home. There was little he could do but download the voices later.

POTUS was distracted from his throbbing head by the petulant lady and an oily-voiced male conferring in harsh whispers together with the authoritarian man. Their words filled him with sudden horror. What he was hearing seemed vital, terrifying. If his hearing was right, the people inside his head were planning to murder the patient called Jerry—*Oluwa! God in heaven!*

An icy chill gripped his heart. His hands started trembling—*This is real! God! What to do?* A murder plot was happening inside his head, and he couldn't do anything about it because he didn't even know who the victim or the plotters were! POTUS pushed his right hand up his helmet and against his ear, hoping to shut out the voices and make the evil disappear. His motorbike wobbled again, violently. He heard Ronke scream, just as a car blasted its horn so close it even out screamed the voices.

Something hard hit him like a million-tonne boulder, sending him flying from his motorbike and right across the bridge. He saw the water below, the deep flowing lake rising, rushing towards him—*Oluwa! I'm finished! The Babalawo's prophecy has finally come true!* He heard the terrified screams of the onlookers, Ronke's shrieks, and the roaring sound of the water just as he plunged into its cold depths. The last thing he felt was the salt water filling his mouth, his nostrils, his ears, and his eyes.

In a wink, the world and all its sounds, ceased to exist.

BOOK
TWO

7

THE OYINBO GHOST

He is surrounded by a horde. He can see the moving lips, the gesticulating arms, and the animation of vocal communication on the faces of the crowd. Yet, he hears nothing. Not a whisper or a sigh. He is lying on soft, sandy soil, though he can't quite figure out where or how he's ended up in this undignified position. His body is writhing in revulsion at its close contact with dirt, and he's starting to hyperventilate.

    Suddenly, he remembers the water, the iciness of death—Oluwa! I drowned! The water demon got my soul in the end! Oh, God! Oh, Sweet Mary and the apostles! *He trembles, terror jellying every limb in his body. Something strange infiltrates his hysterical mind, bringing a modicum of calm. He notices that the air, usually redolent with the scents of fruits, exhaust fumes, fried foods, and the sweat of honest and dishonest labour, is strangely odourless. It feels as if he's been transported into a foggy bubble of nothingness.*

    People gather around him and he holds his breath. The last thing he needs is the halitosis of the pedestrians leaning over him. He has no doubt their breaths will smell sour, and bad breath is one thing he simply can't stomach. In his experience, poverty and bad breath go hand in hand, just like the congenital foul onion-breath of their security man. When his chest is close to bursting and the people are ignoring his feeble attempts to push them away, he finally inhales a desperate gulp of air that smells of...

Nothing. *No onions, garlic, tobacco, palm wine, fermented food, or sweaty body odour. He sniffs, inhales deeply again, even when another sweaty pedestrian leans low into his face as he speaks. Still, he smells nothing, no smell of life. A fat woman with a flowered headscarf and a boy in a dirty Adidas cap are both leaning over him, their faces wreathed in panic. They're talking frantically to the others gathered nearby and gesticulating to several people hulking above him, but he hears nothing. The silence is deafening in its sheer solidity.*

Just then, he sees his mother. Ronke is standing a few feet away from him, her body drenched in water that pours from her like a gushing waterfall. Her eyes regard him with intense pity and love.

"Mama!" he shouts, relief overwhelming him. He never knew the day would come when he'd be ready to weep from joy at the sight of his mother. "Mama, bring your car, quick. Let's get away from this filthy place, God!"

Ronke remains at her spot, tears mixing with water down her face. With the same sad smile, she turns and walks... no... glides away from him—Huh? How can Mama walk like that? And why is she ignoring me? *An icy chill slithers across his body, cold terror weaving its spindly claws behind his neck*—Something is wrong, an evil kind of wrong. *His mind is telling him to get up and run, to get out without delay. He starts to rise when a movement to his right catches his attention. He turns to look.*

His mind explodes with bone crushing terror.

He shrieks. His skin sprouts goosebumps fertilized with putrid corpses. There is a man standing a few feet from him. A tall, bulky man with straight hair the colour of the silver moon, except he doesn't look like any living human he's ever seen. A dull light surrounds the stranger, a sick yellow hallow that shrouds him like a dying lamp on a stormy night, obscuring the details of his face. All he can see is a blank mask devoid of those double appendages that form a human face. The stranger wears shrivelled skin the hue of milk splashed into blood. He is dressed in a pair of white trousers and a white polo shirt that bears an insignia he can't quite decipher. A bright red cap rests over the stranger's straight white hair, and his sneakers are a distinctive brand he instantly recognises—Yeezy Crush

950 V25. In the midst of a bustling crowd adorned in the familiar colourful garbs of the vibrant Lagos metropolis, the strange man stands out like a grey duck amidst a muster of preening peacocks.

Then the faceless man coughs, a hacking kind of cough, like somebody trying to spew out poisonous pellets lodged tight inside their gut. The rasping sound of the cough is like thunder in the silent space of heaving humanity. Relief washes over him in waves—I can finally hear again!

Just then, he sees a tall man carrying a bulging plastic bag rushing towards him, a tomato-red mobile phone pressed close to his ear. The man doesn't look as if he's watching his steps, and before he can shout out a warning, he collides with the faceless man and smashes into him …

And simply walks right through him.

His jaw drops and his eyes goggle. He rubs them furiously, so hard they burn inside their sockets—There's no way I just saw what I think I saw. Uh-uh! No way! *But the silver-haired apparition remains porous. More people continue to walk through the faceless apparition in blissful oblivion as he stares on in quivering horror.*

Clarity hits him like a bolt of lightning, sending hot piss to his groin— Oluwa! I'm seeing a ghost! I'm seeing an Oyinbo ghost, a white man's ghost! I'm really seeing a proper, haunting ghost like the ones in *The Shining 3* film! Oh, God! Oh, God!

He shudders violently. His head swells up, expanding and contracting painfully. More goosebumps layer his skin as his dazed mind scrambles to find a rational explanation. All he knows is that a white man's ghost is haunting the streets of Lagos, a faceless ghost who could be benign or malignant, lost and confused, or something worse. He can't tell. For some strange reason, he's the only one that can see the ghost, and he's ready to piss on himself—Oh my God! What will the ghost do to me now it knows I've seen it?

He looks around desperately, seeking help, an escape, anything but the sight of the pale and strangely incorporeal figure hovering nearby. He tries to speak to the fat woman gently wiping his face and stroking his arm. He opens his mouth to ask for her help, but terror reduces his words to whim-pers, a low groaning that inexplicably goes unheard by the people around him. His fingers fold in, tight fists pressed hard against his thighs. Once again, he tries to get up from his prone position, but his body is trapped by an invisible weight. He sees the Oyinbo ghost shudder like a wind-buffeted tree as it glides closer to him. Its movement is sluggish, wobbly, as if it's drunk on Ogogoro *local gin and suffering from the drink's notorious grogginess.*

With a small whimper, he recoils, shutting his eyes as he used to do when he was a frightened child crouching under his blanket, hiding from the terrifying flashes of lightning during an African thunderstorm. He can sense the ghost drawing insidiously nearer—No…no… please Jesus! *Before he can stop himself, he opens his eyes…*

… And finds himself staring up at the glowing horror hulking right above him.

He screams. The reverberating echoes of his shrieks startle him so much he's stunned into hyperventilating gasps. No one seems to hear his screams, and everyone carries on as usual. He stares at the ghost in wide-eyed terror—Oh my God! Its feet aren't touching the ground! *What he took for a stumbling gait is actually an unsteady levitating glide*—What is this? Why is everybody gliding in this place? Please… somebody… anybody… save POTUS!

He mumbles prayers in an incoherent babble. Time is like a thousand agonising, crawling hours, and still, the faceless ghost is there, right before him, in the midst of the bustling crowd that is blissfully blind to its presence. Now he knows for sure that the Oyinbo ghost is there for him and nobody else. He's the only one that can see it. He forces himself to look again at the ghost's face, a face that is now unshrouding its white veil, revealing ears, eyes, nostrils, cheeks, and lips in startling detail.

This time, his gasp is one of wonder—and shock. For even though it is a face he's never seen in his entire life, a face that is terrifyingly alien, he instantly recognises it as easily as a mother would know her own child. From the heavy scrotal bags under pale green eyes, to the thick, bushy brows scowling over the hawkish features, it is a face that is so familiar it tugs at his heartstrings—I finally remember! I know his face! I know him!

He stares transfixed at the ghost, like a snake-hypnotised mouse. He thinks he now knows who the Oyinbo ghost is, why its face is so familiar. It is little POTUS' lost face, the face he's searched for behind the wardrobe mirrors and desperately yearned to find. What he's now seeing, staring down at him, is the exact face he expects to see each and every time he looks into the mirror, but has never seen—till now! Oh my God! I'm looking at my own ghost, my true image! This is what I really look like, a decrepit, old, white man instead of this black face I see in the mirror every day. This can only mean one thing; I'm d-dead! I'm a rotten corpse! I'm looking at my own ghost!

He starts to shake uncontrollably. Horror drenches him in icy sweat—I can't be dead… oh, please God! POTUS isn't dead! No! No! *Just then, a small voice whispers sanity into his petrified mind—* "Don't be stupid," it sneers in a tone laden with contempt. "Just remember, POTUS is nobody's fool. Come on, look at it. This is an Oyinbo ghost, just an old white man's ghost. You're not dead. It's just a stupid coincidence, that's all. You'll soon wake up from this nightmare. It's just a stupid dream."

He feels something tight inside him slowly loosen. A sense of calmness descends over him, and he even feels sorry for this lost ghost stumbling around the streets of Lagos when it should be back in its own country haunting its fellow white people. He wonders which country the Oyinbo ghost came from—It looks too Caucasian to be Chinese or Bharatian. Poor ghost will soon roast under the Lagos heat. If it were possible, I'd put it inside a taxi and send it straight to *Murtala Mohammed International Airport* so it can hitch a flight back to its country.

"*Wh-who are you?*" *He finally stutters, his voice a hushed whisper.*

The spectre stares down at him for a few seconds. It coughs and clears its throat noisily.

"*I am POTUS,*" *the Oyinbo ghost says in a disquieting voice. Its eyes burn a sickly green colour, and an aura of death clings to it. Its words fill him with horror, and he starts trembling in involuntary spasms.*

"*I am POTUS,*" *the ghost repeats. This time, its voice is triumphant and booms like hollow drums in the unnatural silence—*No, no, no! It's not possible. Please, God, don't let it be true! *He's shaking his head, a head now swimming in a churning sea of dizziness—*Did it just call itself, POTUS, the great water demon the Babalawo freed me from?

He struggles to rein in his terror. All his life, he's had to retain the water spirit's name to protect himself from the evil eye of the deadly spirit, the terrifying green eyes now staring down at him from its hovering height.

Despite all Ronke's precautions, his destiny has finally caught up with him. His drowning has released the demon and damned his soul to eternity. Now, that terrifying deity has finally come to reclaim his soul—but I'm not ready to die! Oh, please God, not yet! POTUS doesn't want to die and be dragged down into the Atlantic Ocean!

Instinctively, with blind desperation, he reaches for his charmed amulets around his left wrist, designed just for an event such as this— Surely, they'll subdue the great spirit's powers and preserve my life as Mama has always assured me… Mama, where on earth are you? Just come here now, you hear? Please…

To his shock, his arms obey his will, breaking free from their paralytic hold even as his body remains trapped on the ground. He starts rubbing the charms with manic frenzy, feverishly willing the hovering ghost to vanish. But his efforts are wasted, and the spirit continues to stare at him from its great height like a manic scientist scrutinising an insect under a microscope. Then, it straightens its shoulders and flings back its head in an arrogant angle befitting a king. Pumping its right fist into the air, the ghost roars a deafening "Yes!"

Before he can calm his panic, the ghost winks at him, a slow, wicked wink that seems to hold a bucketful of choking laughter. It's as if it's enjoying his terror. Instant resentment flares inside him, flooding his body in unexpected heat. Demon or ghost, nobody has the right to look down at him with such condescension—NOBODY! God! I wish I could get up.

"No, I am POTUS," he finally challenges the ghost, despite the terror pounding his heart. "My name is POTUS. Tell me who you really are. Who are you?" His voice is hoarse, and he's struggling to add bravado to it. Disjointed words run wild inside his mind, bits and pieces he's picked up from the various churches he frequented in the past—The Lord is my shepherd… though I walk through the shadow of death… no… the valley of death… I shall fear no evil… Hear, oh Israel, the Lord your God, the Lord is one… Our father, who art in heaven…

"I AM POTUS," repeats the ghost emphatically, gliding closer till they are mere inches apart. Anger creeps into its voice, sending great hailstones of terror into his head. He opens his mouth to speak but quickly swallows his words—Uh-uh… I'd be a fool to challenge the great water spirit. Only a fool fails to recognise and bow to a greater spirit. And POTUS is

nobody's fool. He's thinking he should shut up and agree to everything the demon says. There is an aura of immense power still radiating from the tall, hulking figure, and he knows with chilling clarity that killing him will be as easy as swimming for the water spirit—What's in a name after all? What's the sense in dying for a stupid name like POTUS anyway, a name that was never mine in the first place?

Yet, something within his deepest core refuses to yield without a fight. The familiar small voice of sanity whispers frantically inside his head about a sermon he'd heard at one of the Pentecostal churches he frequented. It was a sermon about Jesus' temptation by Satan, where Lucifer offered the Lord the whole world if Jesus bowed down and worshipped him. The pastor giving the sermon, a small man decked out in a flowing Agbada kaftan of glittering green sequins and matching sequined shoes, had thundered from the pulpit to the riveted congregation—"A man's true name is all he has," *the pastor had proclaimed, shaking his green-sequined Bible furiously in the air.* "To sacrifice it is to sacrifice his very existence and eternal life in our Lord's bosom."

Now, he realises he is faced with the greatest temptation of his life, just like the Lord Jesus. He can either fearlessly challenge Satan and save his soul, or he can give up his name to this water demon and be damned—Uh-uh! I've been called everything by Kinky-Kootch Kunle, but never a stupid coward.

"I AM POTUS!" He shrieks in his loudest voice. "I AM POTUS!" He repeats, his voice a great thunder as he glares at the spirit, daring it to do its worst—I'm not a pathetic coward. Oh, please amulets, do your work. Come on, do your stupid magic! *He rubs the trio of black crystal bracelets on his wrist with manic desperation as the ghost hovers above him. Its pale skin burns a brighter hue as it leans low, dousing him with its icy breath. It reaches out a hand towards him, and he screams, recoiling instinctively from the ghostly touch.*

That's when the magic happens.

There's a searing heat on his left arm, and he turns to look. The three black talismans around his wrist begin to glow, burning so bright he's dazzled by the light. In seconds, his entire body is shrouded in a bubble of rainbow fire, a kaleidoscope of brilliant effervescent lights that brings a soft gasp to his lips— Sweet Mary and the apostles! No way! The charms are actually working! Wicked! Woah! Thank you, Babalawo! *He reaches out a hand to feel the bright shield surrounding him, and his hand connects with an icy, solid wall.*

The Oyinbo ghost reaches out to touch him. It is flung away with such force that it crashes right through the bodies of several of the oblivious crowd, before landing flat on its back on the sandy soil several yards away.

He stares in open-mouthed shock, seeing the equally stunned and confused look on the ghost's hawkish features. The spectre picks itself up from the floor in a fluid, floating motion and begins to glide once again towards him, its movements now cautious. It hovers several feet away from him, watching him with an intensity that fuses its thick brows atop its high bridge in a deep frown.

A sudden burst of elation engulfs him. He wants to jump up and shout —I'm safe from the water spirit! I've been saved! Mama was right after all, and my curse is real! God bless the Babalawo forever and ever! I'm invincible now! POTUS is indestructible! Nothing can touch me now!

His euphoria is brought to an abrupt end as his skin begins to itch. It's as if he's been bitten by a hundred mosquitoes. He starts to scratch his arms, his legs, his face, even his fingers. He's like a man possessed as he writhes frantically inside his dazzling cocoon. His eyes search wildly for the sudden bug infestation but see neither mosquitoes nor ants. He tries to resist the itch, but his body is an inferno. The fire bubble shielding him begins to wane, growing dimmer with each manic scratch, till its glow is nothing more than a dying torch running on run-down batteries—Oh, God, please no… no…

The water demon glides closer again, emboldened by the dying light shield. POTUS doesn't know which is worse, his terror of the malevolent spirit or the agonising pins of the itch. Just when he thinks he'll go naked-crazy, he feels himself yanked away by invisible hands. The next thing he hears is the roar of the lake, a cacophony of raging voices and total madness, as he returns to excruciating consciousness and reality.

~

POTUS slowly opened his eyes. The first thing he saw was his mum, Ronke, dying right before him on the sandy beach, torn to bloodied bits by a screaming mob. With zealous brutality, they tore her expensive clothes, her faux breast-pads, and her dignity from her body. Their eyes burnt with bloodlust and their voices roared with righteous, unforgiving judgement.

"Mama! Please Jesus! Mama!" POTUS was shrieking, cursing, begging, but no one paid him any attention. He struggled to rise from the soft soil and annihilate Ronke's attackers, but he was trapped by his broken limbs and the hard hands pressing him to the ground, forcing him to witness the daylight murder of his mother. Ronke was screeching, running towards him, her tear-soaked face, bald head, and slight, naked body covered in bloodied cuts and bruises. The terror in her swollen eyes mirror the helpless fright raging in his heart.

"POTUS! POTUS!" Ronke's desperate shrieks were like hammer blows inside his head.

"Mama! Mama!" He screamed, fighting the hands restraining him —*Oh, God! Please... no... I'll kill them all... kill all the filthy demons myself...*

The mob crowed with gleeful malice, mimicking his words. "Mama! Mama! Chei! See how the idiot boy is calling a man his Mama!" they mocked. Even the fat woman in the colourful scarf and the young boy in the dirty Adidas cap were amongst the jeering, murderous crowd. They were calling Ronke a sick pervert, an abomination, a degenerate, and a corrupter of public morals. In a blink, they hung a dusty tyre around her neck and set it ablaze with a whoosh of petrol and a lighter. In an instant, the tyre exploded. The mob cackled in wild triumph.

POTUS watched in helpless horror as his mother was sent to a screeching and agonising hell. Ronke's killers were still laughing as they watched her burn, her melting body writhing on the sandy beach that had now become her noonday grave. A solitary policeman stood aloof from the murderous crowd, feigning ignorance.

POTUS was screaming, howling, cursing. His voice went hoarse, his hands bruised from scratching the soil. He heard the piercing siren of the approaching ambulance the crowd had called when they rescued him from the lake—*What's the use? What's the use of saving a worthless life I no longer wish to own?*

The Oyinbo ghost, the evil water-spirit he now knew was behind everything, was nowhere to be seen. His charmed amulets had no doubt banished it into an unknown realm. The Juju beads had miraculously saved his life but had failed to save the life of his innocent mother. With his mammoth stupidity, he had killed his mother. Now he knew why her spectre had turned its back on him in his dream. Was it a dream? A vision? A visitation? He wasn't sure, and nothing mattered anymore.

POTUS started howling again. By the time the ambulance attendants arrived by his side, he had given in to the blissful darkness of unconsciousness.

8

REVELATIONS

The Federal Enquirer
Coma Countdown!
Day seven of President Jerry King's Coma
PMD Media, 15 July
(Mike Vine and the news desk)

**President King's Life Support to Be Switched Off in Days!
A Nation in Mourning!**

The countdown to President Jerry King's coma continues as we enter into the 7th day. Today, the United States of America officially went into red alert. The president's physician, the WHMU Director, Dr. David Frankel, earlier advised the cabinet that President King is no longer fit to discharge the powers and duties of the Office of The President of the United States. Consequently, the Senate President confirmed in the daily press conference that the cabinet, the First Lady, and the medical team have reached the harrowing decision to switch off President King's life support machine within the following days.

There's no date set yet, but we can report that if all goes according to plan, President Jerry King, our great and powerful leader, will no longer be with us by the end of this week. We can also confirm that the House will begin holding talks on temporarily removing power from the comatose president and transferring it to the Vice President, Mr. Franklin Flint, in accordance with Section 1 of The Twenty-Fifth Amendment. When that happens, Mr. Flint will become the next President of the United States.

The news has plunged the entire nation into mourning as friends and supporters of the dying president continue to gather outside his hospital to stand vigil and protest the planned medical procedure. Many in the crowd carry banners with the message, "The President of the United States will not be Murdered by the Jews!" Dr. Frankel is Jewish-American. Another group of counter-protesters are also demanding that the constitution be followed and the VP sworn in without delay. Their banners scream, "USA V POTUS! Set Him Free, Set Us Free!" We gather that several arrests were made by the police during clashes between the two factions, and no lives were lost. We can also confirm that President King's sister, Dr. Delores King, has today filed a stay of execution on the planned switching off of the life support machine. She believes that the First Lady, Portia King, is rushing the event, despite the expert opinions of some of the physicians treating the president.

Reports coming in from the White House states that there are over two million cards from children across the United States wishing the president a speedy recovery. Readers will recall that President King had waged a vendetta against paedophiles and single-handedly spearheaded an overhaul of the American judiciary, culminating in the new federal law imposing a life sentence on paedophiles and an automatic death sentence where victims are under the age of seven years. This has seen a drastic reduction in sexual crimes against minors and has made the president a hero to children and parents across the nation and beyond.

. . .

We can also confirm that the American Association of Pastors have today released a joint communiqué, stating that a 3-day joint prayer vigil for the ailing president will commence tonight. Billed "The Nights of Miracles and Deliverance," it is expected that over fifty million people both in and outside the United States will participate in the three-night marathon prayer vigil. President King has always been a great supporter of the evangelical Christian groups, and now, it would appear that his support is yielding dividends as they unite in the singular goal of resurrecting our president from the jaws of death.

We all join hands with them in prayer for President King's speedy and miraculous recovery. Meanwhile, we will keep our readers informed with further developments.

∼

When next POTUS opened his eyes, it was nighttime. A fluorescent light lit up his room with dazzling brightness. The first thing he saw was the shut white door of a private hospital room. Pasted on the back of the door with black sticky tape, was a large sign in bold red and white lettering bearing the profound message— **Jesus is your Saviour. The Doctor is His divine Tool**. A huge wooden cross was nailed to the white wall by the door, dominating almost the entire space. The effigy splayed on the cross was a black Jesus, complete with leopard skin loincloth, braided cornrow hair, and heavy ivory bands clasped around his arms and ankles. Oil paint faux blood poured from invisible holes in his hands, feet, and chest. His sad, black eyes seemed to bore right through POTUS' heart.

My mama is dead. My mama... kind, loving, sweet, Mama... she's dead, and I killed her. Oh, God! Oluwa! Just kill me now! Chei! Thoughts swirled inside POTUS' mind like turbulent waters. Tidal waves of pain smashed against his skull. Total recall flooded his mind with graphic 5-D images of the most vivid horror movie ever—Ronke's battered and bloodied body, her terror-widened eyes, her skin melting under the furious flames of the burning tyre, the bloodthirsty mob, the awful sound of her screams and the roaring of the waves... *Oh, God, have mercy! Will I ever forget the sound of Mama's dying shrieks and that horrible, horrible stench of burning flesh?*

A hard knot bunched behind his throat so tight his ears ached. POTUS shut his eyes, shutting out Black Jesus and His judgemental eyes that seemed to damn his soul to eternal hard service in Satan's hell. Every limb, muscle, and vein in his body throbbed in addition to his head. He welcomed the pain, the raw intensity of his anguish, even as he groaned into his pillow, praying for death.

The door opened and a fat-arsed nurse entered, followed by the last person he wished to see—*Kinky-Kootch Kunle! Oh, God!* His adoptive father was dressed in an unfamiliar flowing kaftan with a hood that shielded most of his face. It would have been hard for anyone to recognise him, but POTUS' weary eyes zeroed in on the distinctive puffed-out walk and the heavy signet rings on the incessantly flexing fingers that were the unique hallmark of his adoptive father. Kunle's unfamiliar dejected mien brought instant anxiety thuds to POTUS' heart—*God! Dude looks like someone that's played poker with Death and lost.* His father's face had aged at least ten years since the last time POTUS saw him... today? Yesterday? He could only tell it was night-time by the dark skies behind his glass windowpane and the bright lights dazzling his room. But apart from that, everything else had a surreal quality that left him feeling like a drugged-out cat jiving at a Rottweiler rave.

Kunle was clutching what appeared to be several bundles of news-papers and magazines, and the sight brought a deeper frown to POTUS' face—*The man had better not try to taunt me today of all days. Come on! When have I ever read a newspaper in my entire life apart from the articles about my golf wins?*

"PORTOOS! I see you have finally wake up, eh?" Fat-arse nurse laughed as she blissfully massacred his name, waddling towards his bedside with the silver tray containing the blood pressure monitor and temperature gauge. Her garish makeup, wide gap teeth, and curly blonde wig did little to enhance her already challenged looks, and when she drew closer, POTUS had to hold his breath from the assault of her cheap perfume.

"You have been sleeping since yesterday morning. Look, your Papa has come to visity you. Chei! Let us thank God for His greaty mercy, eh?" Fat-arsed Nurse chittered on, oblivious to POTUS' distress. "You're a very lucky boy, I telly you. If Doctor Okoye was not here when they broughty you in, I don't think your Papa will see you alive now," she turned her small, bright eyes to Kunle. "Oga Olupitan, you must give testimony in the church later, because this your son is God's miracle. He died many times before Doctor Okoye broughty him back to life. You must be a good man for God to do you this greaty favour. Dr. Okoye is the besty doctor here. Any other doctor, and this poor boy will be a corpse now. That kind of motor accidenty and the drowning, kill people very easy, just like this," she snapped her fingers to demonstrate.

POTUS' eyes widened—*Aahh!* So that's what it was. A stupid car accident that knocked him over the bridge and into one of the Lagos lakes. Figures. At least, now he knew why he was sprawled uselessly on that filthy beach as they massacred his poor Mama. At the recollection, POTUS' heart plunged deeper into an even thicker molasses of pain, tears pooling again in his eyes.

Kunle smiled at the nurse, a ghastly stretch of his lips that mimicked the look of a man nursing a jagged rock up his arse. POTUS didn't know if he should howl in laughter or rage at the nurse's ironic words. If ever a person deserved zero favour from God, that person was Kinky-Kootch Kunle—*And myself.* The thought snuck into his mind, unwanted and dreaded, numbing every vein in his body —I'm no better than Kunle. Neither of us is worthy of poor Mama. Her useless husband had better not cry any crocodile tears, or I swear to God, I'll do him in. Broken limbs and all, I'll kill the useless man!

"POTUS, how are you?" Kunle fake smiled, all teeth and icy eyes, before quickly averting his gaze. He turned to admire Black Jesus— *Huh! Bet you're thinking He's the sexiest butt at a gay club, you devil man!* POTUS glowered at him.

"Your son is fine, sir," Fat-arse nurse answered for him before he could respond. POTUS felt a wave of affection for her. The last person he wanted to talk to was Kunle. "He's a strong young man, I telly you. They heal very quick when they're young like this. Don't worry, Ọga Olupitan. Your son will be discharged very soon, you hear?" She smiled reassuringly at Kunle before stooping to take POTUS' vital stats.

POTUS kept his eyes shut, shutting out Kunle's face. He wished the nurse would stay in the room forever. Last thing he needed was a confrontation with his legal father.

"See? I told you he's okay," Fat-arse nurse smiled again at Kunle as she finished injecting POTUS with whatever, before waddling away with her silver nurse's tray.

"Thank you, nurse. You've been very helpful. Please take this little "thank you" for your shopping. I insist," Kunle handed a wad of Naira notes to the smiling nurse, who bowed so low in obsequious gratitude that she was almost prostrating on the floor. POTUS turned his face away in distaste—Yeah, yeah. There goes Mr. Big Stuff again at his fakery best. Let's see what the nurse will think about you when she finds out you're a lying, useless queer!

Something knocked hard inside his head, a concrete ball of shame that rolled through his body and settled heavy in his heart—Why did I say 'queer' with such vitriol? What do I have against queer when my poor Mama has just been brutally murdered just for being queer? An indefinable emotion surged through his body. It was as if a black shadow had been chased away from his heart and replaced with the light of compassion. He was drained of a bitter poison that had dogged him for as long as he could remember. Suddenly, he no longer wanted to hate. He may loathe Kunle, but Ronke's death had killed everything in him, including his long disgust with their sexuality— God… I'm just so, so, tired...

He sighed and shut his eyes. He needed solitude to digest this new reality, but Kunle's presence was a solid wall blocking him from the peace of aloneness. He heard the door shut behind Fat-arse nurse, and silence descended in the room. He kept his face turned away, every pore in his skin on pinpoint alert as he waited for Kunle to speak.

He didn't have long to wait.

"Your mother is dead," Kunle's voice was flat. POTUS' heart fluttered. Guilt stole his speech—What should I say? What can I say? Does Kunle expect me to say something? For the first time in his life, POTUS found himself speechless.

"They killed your mother because you lured her to her death, you disgusting bastard," Kunle still spoke in that low tone of icy calm, despite the viciousness of his words.

POTUS winced inside at hearing the detested curse, 'bastard.' Of all the insults that Kunle heaped on him, the one that hurt the most was "bastard." He sensed the rage seething underneath Kunle's calm demeanour, and for the first time in a long time, he was afraid of his legal father. He was used to Kunle's schizo, split personality; his explosive fits of rage, his shouting threats, and stomping feet, interspersed with booming laughter and bawdy jokes; the occasional gentleness before the return to explosive rage. This new man, this tightly restrained stranger, filled him with unease—*What if Kunle decides to kill me right here in my hospital bed?*

"But for the fact Ronke panicked when you were knocked off your bloody bike into the lake and her wig fell off as she dived in to save you, nobody would've discovered her secret. So, yes, your mother died to save your worthless life. Not that you give a shit. Ha!" Kunle barked an arsenic-laced laugh, a hard vein throbbing violently in his neck. His blood-shot eyes kept blinking as if he had sand grains lodged inside them, and his forehead glistened with hot sweat. "I bet you must be dancing with joy now the whole of Lagos is aware of our secret. It's what you've always wanted, isn't it? To expose your mother and I to ridicule and abuse. Ha!" Kunle shook his head over and over, flexing and cracking his knuckles till POTUS' ears rang. "Well, you've now got your wish, and I hope you rot in hell for the rest of your wretched life. I curse the day I brought you into our lives," Kunle bit out between clenched teeth, coming close to POTUS' bedside and glaring down at him with black eyes ablaze with hate.

POTUS flinched, shrinking away from him, biting his lips to stop himself from groaning in pain—Oluwa! I'm right! Kunle is going to murder me right in my hospital bed... *Huh?*

POTUS froze—Murder... hospital bed... hushed voices in my

head… Oyinbo ghost… God! How could I have forgotten about the great water spirit?

"You don't have to look so frightened, you little piece of turd," Kunle barked a short, humourless laugh, his dark eyes glittering icy malice. He leaned so close to POTUS their faces almost touched. "I'd be a fool to kill you here, not after your stupid nurse has assured everyone you're as fit as an ox," he straightened, stepping away from the bed. "It's not necessary. I think we both know that your days of blackmail and threats are over. My secret is now out in the open. The whole of Lagos is now talking about us. And how about this; you've single-handedly created a new craze in this vile city. People are now going about yanking off wigs and groping women's breasts, just to be sure they're not like your mother. Here, check out some of the head-lines in these papers. I think you'll find them happy readings."

Kunle tossed him the bundle of tabloids, watching his pathetic attempt to catch them with a grim smile. "You'll discover that your mother and I have now become national caricatures, all thanks to you. I've had to switch off my phone to avoid the deluge of sick calls I've been receiving since she died yesterday. You should hear what some of our so-called friends are saying to me. Not to mention my superiors at the Oil-refinery headquarters in Port-Harcourt. You'll be thrilled to know I am now finished. My job is on the line, and my family has disowned me, just like Ronke's family did. I'm not even sure if anyone —apart from you and I, that is—will attend her burial, what with the scandal and all. Your Grandma Funke has refused to take my calls and left it to my stupid sister to inform me I'm no longer welcome in the family home. Ha! The family home indeed! The same family home I built for them, the ungrateful bastards!"

Kunle barked another of his bitter laughs. Tears pooled in his eyes before he quickly turned away from POTUS and strode towards the window. For several silent minutes, Kunle stared into the night skies, his shoulders as stiff as an iron rod. The sight touched something raw in POTUS' heart, a compassion that caught him unawares—*Huh?* He quickly pushed away the unwanted emotion, his thoughts zeroing in on one crucial word Kunle had mentioned—Phone! My mobile… where's my *OppO* mobile? I'm dead without it! Oh, please God, don't let it be that those sickos at the beach have stolen my mobile while I was unconscious. Bloody demons! Filthy peasants…

"Anyway, that's not your business," Kunle's dull voice broke into his raging thoughts. "All you need to know is that you and I are now finished. Our relationship is over. You'll not get a single Kobo from me, starting from today. I hope you managed to save some of the blood money you extorted from me all these years. You'll be needing it, otherwise, you might have to start auctioning some of that Yeezy and Adidas junk, plus the stupid golf clubs you've been collecting. You'll need the money to maintain yourself and pay for your needs. No need to mention that your USA university programme is now off the table too."

Kunle's eyes gleamed with malignant triumph. "Don't worry, I'll cover your hospital bills, of course. But that will be it. As soon as we bury your mother, you'll pack your things and leave my house for good. After all, that's what you've always wanted, isn't it? Your independence. Well, now, you'll get your wish, except you won't be getting it with my money. As the hymn goes, 'He that is down needs fear no fall.' There's nothing you can do to me now that everyone knows what I am. You've opened wide that closet you've been yapping about all these years, and there's nowhere left for me to hide. Ha!"

Kunle paused, lost in thought, his eyes staring at the ceiling, at the walls, before returning again to Black Jesus. Sweat poured down his face. He didn't seem to notice or care, and POTUS wondered what had happened to his ubiquitous white handkerchiefs, even as Kunle's words gripped his heart in an icy fist—Oluwa! What's to become of me? Where will POTUS go? How can I survive without my weekly allowance and our house? Now, I can't even study in America anymore or find my birth mother, and I'm without Mama who'd always come through for me, no matter what…

The migraine was so painful he thought his head would split. The seconds ticked away in ominous silence as they both grappled with their thoughts and demons. Beyond the door, somebody cried out in pain and another cursed loudly in vulgar Yoruba. The sounds startled Kunle, who shook his head in a disoriented manner before returning his attention to POTUS.

"Well, I'll leave you to your conscience if you have any left inside that selfish, useless body of yours. Just remember that, but for you, your mother would be alive today. I won't visit you again. Make your way back to the house with a taxi whenever you're discharged. In the meantime, you might start thinking about your future and where you'll go next. Trust me, you'll soon discover that not all friends are friends, and what you viewed as your safety net has numerous hidden and dangerous holes in it. Welcome to the big world, my boy. You think you know a rooster until the wind blows up its feathers and you discover it's got a stinky arse, ha!" Kunle walked out of the room without a backward glance, shutting the door gently behind him. The soft click of the door rang with the same ominous clack POTUS recalled from all those years ago inside his parent's red bedroom, on that fateful afternoon of his ninth birthday party that destroyed all their lives.

Tears pooled in his eyes. He let them fall unchecked—What do I care? My life is now ruined anyway. Kunle is right. I'm a useless bastard! Soon his shoulders were shaking, his body convulsing violently, wracked by hard sobs. He felt like the little nine-year-old he'd been on the morning of that terrible birthday—*I want my Mama… Oh, God, help me! I want Mama so, so bad. Mama, I'm sorry… I'm so sorry. Please forgive me. Forgive your Baby Boy, Mama…*

~

POTUS was still sobbing when he picked up the first of the newspapers scattered on his bed several minutes later. Through his tears, he managed to read the gleeful headline in the front page of the tabloid:

Lagos Socialite, Wife, and Mother murdered in Broad Daylight for Being a Man!

A large photograph of Ronke in her glamorous best was splattered across the page, below a prime example of Nigerian putrid reporting, mired in a sludge of toxicity. It was a picture POTUS had never seen, and the sight broke down the last of his reserves. He began to howl, heaving hard, choking sobs that hurt every pore in his body. His wails alerted Fat-arse nurse, who dashed into his room with excessive zeal. Her mien was overly solicitous, courtesy of her Naira-greased palms. She was accompanied by a second obese nurse whose buttocks almost rivalled Fat-arse nurse's own. She patted his convulsing shoulder with the zealous tenderness of a fake mother.

"*Chei!* Enough, you hear?" Fat-arsed Nurse urged him in a hushed voice. "You musty have faith in Jesus and Jehovah's goodness."

"Enough, you hear? You must have faith in Jesus and Jehovah's goodness," the second nurse parroted with a cheery smile as she, too, stroked his arm gently.

POTUS cringed in repulsion at the feel of the nurses' hands on his body. He was certain they hadn't washed their hands and were now dowsing his body with hospital germs, which everyone knew were the worst kind of germs in the universe—*Oluwa! God! I can't take this anymore!*

"I want a cigarette," he gasped, eyes wide with desperation. "Get me a cigarette, now. Any kind, I don't care."

"You cannot smoke in the hospital," Fat-arsed Nurse gave him a disapproving look. "What is a young boy like you doing with cigarette? Don't you know it is a sin to smoke?"

POTUS let out a mighty shriek that stunned the two women into wide-eyed silence— "Can't you see I'm dying? Can't you Jesus nutters see that POTUS is suffering more than any living soul in the world? That my mother has just been brutally murdered? That I'll never study in America now? That my limbs are so damaged I'll never play golf again? I'll be lucky if I ever score with a bird again in my current disabled and penniless state. What do I care about Jehovah's goodness when He didn't care about my poor mother's life? Stuff Jehovah! Do you hear me? I said, stuff Jesus! Stuff everyone!"

POTUS was screeching, ready to punch both their shocked faces when Fat-arse nurse jabbed a needle into his arm and stunned him into silence. It was now his turn to gape wide-eyed at them, like a naughty child who realises his parents can actually take away his toys. Without waiting for him to recover from his shrieking, the nurses switched off the main light, leaving just his side lamp on as they exited his room.

Stupid cows! POTUS started to wipe his face and paused—*Huh?* His bling-rings were gone. A quick check on his neck and left ear confirmed his bling-medallion and diamond stud were equally missing —*Thieving demons who killed Mama have stolen my bling! Useless peasants! God! I really hope Mama haunts all those animals that killed her and stole my bling, and my mobile, and…*

POTUS hiccupped. Then he yawned, long and loud. Within minutes, he collapsed into a drug induced slumber, courtesy of Fatarse nurse's Diazepam injection. In his dreams, he was fighting with three-headed ghosts and machete wielding mobs, all determined to behead him and steal his charmed amulets. And at one corner of the open marketplace where the battle raged, the terrible Oyinbo ghost watched, winked, and cackled maliciously, his voice hollow, spooky, ghastly.

9

THE FAKE GHOST

"Finally! Sleeping beauty awakes! Let's ring the New Year's bells and throw an Alleluia Party! Holy righteous shit! I was starting to wonder if you've crossed over too," the Oyinbo ghost was clapping his hands sarcastically as he glided towards POTUS' bedside, his eyes squinting at him in the familiar wicked wink. In the midday brightness of the room, the ghost appeared even more insubstantial, like a bulky shadow made of talcum powder, only lighter, creepier.

The air in the room dropped to an unnatural chill, just like his skin. He could swear the ghost was draining every source of heat like an evil alien invader from a dying planet. The heavy pounding of his heart and the jellying of his limbs were stark reminders of the terror his first encounter with the spectre had bred.

POTUS whined softly like a day-old puppy. His breath came in hard, fast gasps, and his head felt as swollen as a rotten mango, ready to pop and spill the bloody pulp of what remained of his brain matter.

"So, kiddo, tell me, what's your name again?" The Oyinbo ghost asked, staring down at POTUS with those terrible green eyes. Once again, it squinted in the familiar conspiratorial wink, as if it knew something terrible about POTUS that it wasn't sharing. "And while we're at it, where the hell's this fly-dump? Sweet Mary and the apostles!

I've been waiting for what? Five? Six? Seven days, probably, to escape from you, and when I'm finally free, what happens? Get a load of this. You go and get your ass busted by a fucking car and almost drown in the lake, that's what. Whatever. Well, let's start getting some answers. Who are you and what's your name?" the ghost's voice dripped with irritated impatience.

"P-POTUS. M-my name is POTUS." *Sweet Mary and the apostles! The great water spirit is before me!* Had he nurtured any doubts before about its identity, the spectre's use of the expression unique to him alone, just confirmed everything. Only the water demon would know the phrase, 'Sweet Mary and the apostles!'

"Shit! I thought I heard you right that first time," the demon snapped its fingers before tapping the side of its head. "I see your brain is still scrambled. Listen kiddo, I wasn't asking you my name. I know I'm POTUS, and you know I'm POTUS. Hell! The whole world knows I'm POTUS, so all hunky-dory. Now let's see if we can get your brain cells working. Listen carefully and read my lips, samba-sambo? What. Is. Your. Name?" The water demon pointed a pale forefinger at POTUS as it spoke. 'Your name? Me, POTUS. You…?"

Something about the water demon's condescending tone jarred a hypersensitive nerve in POTUS. He glared at the spirit.

"POTUS. My name is POTUS," he said. This time his voice was stronger, not the whispered stammer he'd managed to gasp out the first time—What's this samba-sambo anyway? "Yes, mighty spirit. I know your name is POTUS, the great water spirit. But my name is also POTUS, named after you for protection. We share the same name since the appeasement ritual the Babalawo performed that night at the *Bar Beach*." Even as he spoke, POTUS was surreptitiously rubbing his trio of amulets under his bed clothes with the usual frenzy—*God!* Surely, there must be a faster way to activate these amulets. He saw the spirit's eyes widen, first in shock, then in wild glee.

"Great water spirit? Is that what they call me here? Jeez! And you say you clowns performed some wacky mumbo jumbo ritual for me? Holy righteous shit! Now I've heard it all. Who fed you that kooky bull?" The spectre roared in backbreaking laughter before coughing itself into normalcy. When next it spoke, it had to fight the hiccups occasioned by its mirth.

"Listen, kiddo, take it from me; there ain't no water spirit or land demon that goes by the name of POTUS, right? I am POTUS, get it? President of the United States, and this fly-dump sure ain't God's Own Country the last time I checked," the ghost broke into more giggles. "Listen, I don't know who's been messing with you, but there's only one POTUS and that's me. Friggin' hell! I'm gonna kill Pete once I get my hands on that pansy rainbow. Shit!" The water demon ran a frustrated hand through its unruly silver mane and glided away from POTUS towards the huge crucifix of Black Jesus. For several seconds, it stared at the black figurine, seeming as fascinated as Kunle had been with it.

POTUS' mind was in a whirl—If it isn't the water demon, who then is it? He didn't believe its story about being the President of the United States, not one bit. Huh! It must think he's really dumb! Everybody knows that the American president, whatever his name is, is a young man. Well, defo not as old as this demon with its silver hair and wrinkled skin. Nah, he's not letting himself get fooled like some pathetic illiterate. POTUS is nobody's fool. Still, the demon's amusement and derision had touched a raw nerve, returning his embarrassment and disdain about the whole Babalawo superstitious junk. He didn't want to appear like some ignorant villager as the demon was trying to make him out to be—*Nonsense! I'm POTUS after all, the coolest dude in the city of Lagos, a junior golf celebrity and nobody's fool.*

"Wow! Take a look at this!" The water spirit shook its head, turning to look at POTUS before returning its amused gaze at Black Jesus. "Ain't this something! Gotta hand it to you nigg…I mean, you coloured folks. You sure have some mighty imagination. Fancy having a witch doctor Jesus. All he's missing are some chicken feathers and war paint, and he'll be just perfect for a right voodoo crucifixion, right? Ha!" It turned and glided back to POTUS' bedside again. "Now, where were we? Right, we were trying to get a name for you, but I guess we're wasting our time and time's one thing I ain't got enough of, in case you haven't noticed," the smile vanished, and its voice now had a menacing quality.

"Stay away from me, d'you hear? Don't come near me, or I'll kill you with my amulets, see?" POTUS raised his left hand and for a second, he couldn't tell who was more stunned, the demon or him.

They both stared goggle-eyed at the glowing amulets around POTUS' wrists, a light that grew stronger and brighter even as they looked. The familiar warmth was starting to flow through his body once again—*Yeees! I didn't dream it all!* It was the water spirit alright, not some white man's ghost as he'd wrongly believed. There was no other reason for the charms to activate, save to protect him from this water demon.

"Holy Guns! Not again!" The demon dived swiftly away from him, smashing into the wall, and vanishing in a wink, only to reappear again before POTUS' stunned eyes in seconds. Its face looked even whiter than before. POTUS felt the return of his natural confidence and bravado—Yes! I'm invincible again! His face creased in a grim and triumphant smile—Who's the man now, eh? Who's the man now?

"What's that stuff you've got around your wrist, kiddo? That's one heck of a gadget, right?" the demon's brows were dipped. Its mien was no longer combative. It was as if it was suddenly injected with Buddhism, oozing easy calm and warm Zen.

"I told you the Babalawo did a ritual of appeasement to you when I was a child; but you didn't believe me even though you know I'm speaking the truth," POTUS felt a rush of anger engulf him. "You are POTUS, the water spirit. I recognise you despite your attempts to trick me. You finally caught me when I fell into your lake, after the Babalawo warned me to avoid all bodies of water. I know you've come to take my soul and return me to your water realm. But you can't, see?" he raised his left arm again. "You can't kill me! I'm protected against you. The Babalawo gave me these charms and told my parents to name me POTUS, just like you. So, stay away from me! Stay away!" He was screaming as he glared at the ghost. "Don't come near me or my charms will annihilate you, d'you hear?"

The spirit paused, a frown furrowing its brows. For several tense seconds, the two antagonists observed each other in silence. Then the demon smiled, a charming smile that lit up its pale, wrinkled features a million watts.

"Hey! Take it easy, kiddo; Just relax, alright?" It raised its hands in a placating gesture. "Listen, believe it or not, we're friends. You and I are closer than you actually realise. I need you to trust me in this, right? I've something really important to tell you, and if you keep activating that military gadget on your wrist, then I'll never get the chance to fill you in and time ain't on my side, trust me."

"It's not a military gadget," POTUS snarled, his eyes once again ablaze with rage—*Why won't this stupid spirit listen to me?* "I told you the Babalawo gave me these charms to protect me from you. How can we be friends if I need to be protected from you, eh? Answer me. Why should I trust anything you say when you keep lying?"

"Because I ain't no dumb water spirit, that's why," the demon raised its voice. "I told you I'm Jerry King, the President of the United States and—"

"No, you're not," POTUS cut in savagely. "You're a liar, and if you look in the mirror, you'll see that you don't look anything like the American president. You're a horrible old ghost-demon. I've seen photos and videos of the American president—whatever his name is— and he's still a young man with brown hair and no wrinkles, like you. So, stop saying we're friends when you're still lying to me about who you really are."

POTUS saw the stunned look on the spirit's face, and his heart swelled with grim satisfaction—*Ha! Got you! POTUS is nobody's fool!* The demon touched its hair, then glided to the ensuite bathroom. Next thing, POTUS heard a shout, then a ghastly groan as the water spirit glide-staggered back into the room, banging itself clumsily against the door, the wall, and the visitors' chairs. It looked as old as all the old people in the world combined, and POTUS recoiled instinctively from it.

"What happened to me? Sweet Mary and the apostles! What in hell's name happened to me?" It turned a pair of dazed, green eyes to POTUS as if seeking answers from him. "No wonder you don't believe me. Seeing that face in the mirror, holy Christ! I wouldn't believe myself, either. Damn motherfuckers! This is bad, even worse than I ever imagined. We got no time to waste, boy. You gotta quit this bull-shit about water demons and—"

"No, it's you that has to quit your lies and own up to who you really are," POTUS shouted, his eyes flashing. "After all, it was you that put the name POTUS into my head, you and all those other people that have been talking inside my head all my life. I'm sick of you all, d'you hear? I'm sick of all of you messing with my head. I wouldn't have had the accident if it weren't for them fighting inside my head and plotting murder right inside Jerry's hospital room and…"

POTUS stopped, his mouth hanging open as the significance of his own words hit him—*Jerry! OMG! It's not possible! No way!* The demon said its name was Jerry King. That meant the patient who lived inside his head all his life was really Jerry King, the President of the United States! *But how?*

His skin went cold. The shield dimmed and winked out even before the itching hit him. The demon—*no; ghost… half-ghost… what the devil is it, anyway?*—glided closer, just as his hospital room door opened. Another obese nurse dashed in with her silver tray, all flustered and sweaty. POTUS almost died from relief.

It didn't last long.

"PORTOOS, why are you shouting? What is the matter with you?" She mimicked Fat-arsed Nurse's massacre of his name.

POTUS winced—No, what's the matter with you idiots? Why can't you fat fools pronounce my name right? And is obesity a job description for nurses in this stupid hospital? *God!* His angry glare spoke volumes, and the rotund nurse quickly exited the room. He noticed the ghost—yeah, it'll have to be a ghost till he can figure out what it really is—gliding towards him again, its face wary, yet ominous.

"That's right, kiddo. See? You're starting to remember who I am, right?" The ghost's voice was urgent, excited. "Those voices you heard were coming from my hospital room. I've been in a coma for a while and I don't know how many more times I gotta tell you that I ain't no stupid water demon, right? I'm Jerry King, the President of the United States of America, and if you don't believe me, then you gotta be the dumbest guy on earth. And while we're here wasting precious time, I'm dying right in front of you. The clock's ticking away my life, and I've got even less time than I thought, if that mirror's anything to go by."

The demon groaned in frustration, fixing POTUS with desperate green eyes. "Listen, kiddo. I need your help badly, right? You're the only one that can stop me getting murdered by that gold-digging whore and slimeball, motherfucking vice president—vice being the operative word here, believe me," the ghost punched the wall furiously and its fist promptly disappeared into it. "Goddammit! I can't believe this is happening to me. Fuckshit! The rotten, no-good, sonofabitch dickheads! Friggin' bitchass jerkoffs! Just wait till I get my hands on the shitass cocksuckers! I'll wipe the fucking floor with the lot, you wait and see," the ghost was apoplectic, marinating in a thick sauce of lalochezia. POTUS felt something stir in his heart as he observed the spectre. Its every action bore the stamp of authenticity—Is it possible? Could it be telling the truth? He has to be sure, really sure. He can't afford to make a deadly mistake that could cost him his soul. After all, POTUS is nobody's fool.

"Look, if you're really President King, then tell me how come I've been hearing your voice inside my head all my seventeen years if you say you've only recently been in a coma? And how is it that you ended up here in Nigeria if you're still in a coma in America?" He said, his voice loaded with suspicion.

"Nigeria? Did you say Nigeria? As in scam boondocks Nigeria? Damn! So that's where this is. I did wonder," the ghost whistled.

"Hey! Don't insult my country," POTUS snapped, pale brown eyes flashing fire.

"Sorry, kiddo. But all this has rather thrown me somewhat. Hell! That's what you get from trying to cheat death. You should—"

"What do you mean 'trying to cheat death'?" POTUS interjected.

"Just that," the ghost said unpleasantly, gliding closer to him. Again, POTUS shrank away from it, sinking deeper into his uncomfortably soft mattress. The temperature around POTUS dropped so low his teeth rattled. He quickly pulled the bed cover tighter around his body with his good arm.

"I used you to escape death, right?" The spectre nodded grimly. "I'm not known as 'Jerry the wheeler-dealer' for nothing. You can call me the great escape artist. When that golf ball hit me at the back of my head, I felt the dark presence of the almighty soul collector hovering around me. Just for a brief second, mind. But it was enough to scare the bejeebers outta me. Hell! I wasn't about to let death get the better of me, not while I still have an election to win. Hell no!" Its green eyes glinted malevolently for a second. "And by the way, I heard you asking the nurse for a cigarette. Bad habit, kiddo. Dirty, too. Bad breath and bad romance. It'll kill you faster than a car crash, trust me." The ghost gave him the same reproving look as Fat-Arsed Nurse, only more contemptuous, as if POTUS was tainted with filth. He felt himself wilt under the look, checking his breath surreptitiously—*God! No more stupid smoking for POTUS!*

"Anyways, as I was saying, I wasn't going to be caught by the hooded one," the ghost resumed. "So, I did the next best thing and jumped. That's it. I wasn't even thinking. I just jumped into the first emerging infant I could find to hide from that scary scythe wielder. Next thing I know, I wake up as some little shitass black baby in some fly-dump mud shack and—"

"Hey! I told you not to insult us!" POTUS yelled again, anger surging, even as his mind reeled—*OMG! This is weirder than any Frant Gwo SF film I've ever watched!*

"Sorry, kiddo, but—"

"And stop calling me kiddo. My name is POTUS!"

"Come on, not that bull again! I thought we're done with all that hubbub. I'm POTUS, right? I've been living inside your body for days... well, I guess it must be years in your real time, though it's only been days in my spirit time. I mean, all this shit is new to me, right?" The president ran his fingers through his hair with a distracted air. "Listen, I don't claim to understand anything or how things work, or why the time difference is so vast, or why I've aged beyond my years. All I know is that I've been stuck in your body like some damn, bug-eyed zombie, aware of everything going on in my hospital room, but unable to do anything or speak to anyone about it. I'm guessing I was kinda feeding you everything I heard, hence your ability to hear everything going on in my hospital room, too. I'd almost despaired of ever escaping till you had the accident which brought you close enough to death, allowing me to finally escape your body. Huh! Some escape."

The president looked around wild-eyed, shaking his head over and over. "Well, here we are. I'm outta ya body, which is a good thing, I guess. Hell! I'm a fucking fake ghost, but at least, I can finally speak to you and you can see and hear me. On the other hand, I'm in a bit of a fix. Now there's no human body to sustain my spirit, I'm slowly fading away; basically dying. I don't have much time and need to stop those vipers from killing me off under the guise of turning off my life support machine. Believe me, kiddo… sorry, POTUS," the president bowed mockingly in POTUS' direction. "Believe me when I tell you there ain't nothing the matter with me. I don't need the friggin' life support machine. Maybe initially, but not anymore. I simply suffered a nasty concussion and panicked, and the assholes grabbed their chance to fuck me up. Bet you'd like to know the dirty details, right?"

POTUS nodded, his eyes saucer-wide. His body shivered deliciously in excitement—*Whoa! Whoa!* This is really The President of the United States for real! Who'd believe this? Him, POTUS Olupitan, is talking with The President of the United States himself! No way! This is sick! Even better than being on *The Serena Williams Show* any day!

Listening to the ghost, all doubts he previously harboured about its identity vanished. Everything now made a weird kind of sense, inexplicable things finally falling into place. He could even see the resemblance to President King now in the ghost's pale features—not that he knew much about the American president. It would be a different matter if he were dealing with the Chinese president—after all, the whole world knows what the Chinese president looks like, what with China now the master of the universe and outer space. Still, with the little he knew, there was definitely something about the ghost's facial expressions that was similar to the American president's own in real time, right down to the piercing green eyes and hulking gait that looked a lot like Tom Hardy in one of his favourite James Bond films, *To Kill Again.*

The door to his room swung open and a jostling group of rotund nurses shoved their way into his room, led by Fat-arse nurse with her ubiquitous silver nurse's tray. POTUS glared at them, his brows dipped in a frown. They didn't seem bothered by his scowl. In fact, if anything, they looked more pissed off than he was.

"I hear you have been shouting," Fat-arse nurse's voice was cold, all previous friendliness gone. One would swear her palms had never been greased by Kunle's Naira notes. "This is a busy hospital, in case you haven't noticed. If you wanty anything, just ring your bell instead of shouting like a little spoilty boy," she turned to the other five nurses crowded behind her. "I telly you, these children of rich people are mannerless somethings. All of them, even when their mother is a man, Jesus forbidy bad thing!" She crossed herself. The other nurses quickly imitated her, making the sign of the cross with their lips twisted in pious disdain.

POTUS' eyes widened as the penny dropped—*Oh, you stupid fat Cow!* He should have known it was just a matter of time before they discovered his identity, the useless religious nutters. He opened his mouth to tell them exactly what he thought about them, before quickly swallowing his words—Stupid beach whales have his life in their dirty hands and ugly chipped fingernails. He wouldn't put it past them to inject him with poison, using the biggest needles out of spite. He could see the avid curiosity in their eyes, the way they all shuffled closer to get a proper look at him, the son of two abominations. He could read the pious judgement in their disapproving eyes, see their self-righteousness in their sneering lips, the same petty prejudices he himself used to harbour until only recently—*Bet the ugly melons can't wait to get back to their dirty little shacks to gossip about me and my degenerate family. God!*

"Sorry," he mumbled, keeping his eyes down so they wouldn't see his fury.

"Psss!" Fat-arse nurse hissed, twisting her lipstick smeared lips in disapproval as she quickly turned him over and pushed the needle into his arse, dosing his body with agony. Then, she turned away without a by-your-leave and waddled out of his room, followed by her gang of rotund minions. POTUS gave their righteous backs the middle finger before letting out a big sigh and a muttered "Fat cow!"

"Sorry, kiddo. That was rough. A right Albanian bitch she is, right?" The president glided back to his bedside, his voice sympathetic, his eyes gleeful. There was something familiar about 'Albanian,' but POTUS couldn't grasp it. "You gotta admit it was kinda funny, right? Shucks! It looked like a Miss Fat-ass beauty pageant for a minute there," he chuckled, his face creased in mischievous delight. It was the happiest POTUS had ever seen him.

"Yeah, you're right," he gave a wry smile. "Funny you said Miss Fat-arse pageant. That's exactly what I call the cow in my mind—'Fat-arse Nurse.' She really gets on my nerves."

"Don't let her bother you. She's small fry. We've got bigger things to cook. So, where were we before we got interrupted by the fat-squad?"

"You were about to tell me about the assassination plot against you,"

"Yeah, that's correct. I mean, don't get me wrong, I ain't afraid to die, right? But I got family; my sister, Doctor Delores, and my daughter, Lisa, in particular. Hell! They need me, and I need them. Take it from a guy who's seen everything, there ain't nothing like blood family, trust me. And when I say blood family, I don't mean wives and broads, right? They'll stab you in the back and sell your soul to the highest bidder. By the time they're done with you, even your own mother ain't gonna recognise you," the president twisted his lips in distaste.

"I have no blood family," POTUS muttered sourly, his voice sullen as he rubbed his sore arm.

"That's right? How come?"

"I'm adopted,"

"That's tough, kiddo," the president's voice oozed sympathy. "Anyways, I reckon you'll do just fine as you are. I can sniff success a mile off, and you've got it stamped on your forehead with a capital S, with or without your blood family," the president smiled at him and POTUS felt tears pool in his eyes. A warm flush washed over him, and he felt like throwing his arms around the president and hugging him —Now I know why this dude is the second most powerful president in the world. He's totally ace! The coolest dude ever! I'll happily shoot the traitors trying to assassinate him!

"Thanks," he smiled shyly at the president, who returned his smile with another one of his wicked winks, which POTUS was starting to think were the coolest thing ever. "But Your Excellency, who are these people plotting to kill you, the ones I keep hearing inside my head?"

"Your Excellency… I like that," the president flashed POTUS a wide smile. "Yeah, right. Well, let's start with FLOTUS, the mean bitch," the president's voice was as bitter as lime, his former good cheer vanished in a blink.

"FLOTUS?" The name rang another bell, a distant memory that flitted in POTUS' mind like a dandelion and disappeared just as quickly.

"Yeah, FLOTUS is the other bit of POTUS, the girly bit if you like. Ask those bloody rainbows and they'll tell you a gay president, heavens forbid, can call his bitchass boyfriend FLOTUS, even though both of them are gay men. More like GLOTUS if you ask me, you know, Gay Lady Of The United States. But I digress. That's another thing," he grimaced. "Anyways, the current FLOTUS, my dear wife, Portia, or should I say, Poison—she ain't Attila the Hen for sure—no balls whatsoever. Bitch just plays dirty. She's a sour-crotch dime-broad with an axe to grind. She wants me outta the way, ASAP. If you heard everything going on in that shitty coma room, then you'll recognize her as the stupid cunt constantly telling the viper VP she loves him, while calling me "POTUS, honey." Fake bitch! How's that for fidelity and marital vows, right?"

The president shook his head again, a baffled look on his face. "I mean, look at the man for fuckssakes and tell me how anyone in their right mind can possibly fancy that righteous tightass prig, apart from his poor wife who ain't clued-up right anyways," he tapped the side of his head. "Thing is, the First Lady's never forgiven me for my affair with Madison and the daughter we share, my only child, Lisa. Now, there's a beautiful and wonderful gal who's got her daddy wrapped around her pretty littl' finger, ha!" The president's face glowed with pride as he stared into a far distance. "Anyways, where was I? Yeah, Poison Portia. I offered her a divorce, but she ain't having none of it. Bitch signed a prenup and isn't about to lose out on my billions. Now the dumb broad's gone and found herself another sucker to leech on. She's convinced herself she's in love with Flake-Frank, can you believe it? Broads! Take it from me, kiddo, never trust a woman, not even your own mother."

POTUS didn't bother reminding him to use his name—What's in

a name anyway, especially since, in all fairness, he got his name in the first place from the president?

"Flake-Frank is your Vice President?" POTUS asked.

"Yeah, slimeball extraordinaire and as greasy as they come," the president gave him an approving smile for parroting the derogatory name. "He's desperate to become POTUS, but I've got the shit on the little prick. You know, recordings of the sanctimonious faker frolicking at some secret brothel with high class hookers, whips, chains, and baby feeding bottles filled with brandy-milk. That's right, no kidding. That's the way to ride the world. Hit the clowns where it hurts. Nicey-nicey is pussy-whipped and loser-stamped. You gotta whack them with everything you got, right?" The president nodded in emphasis, his eyes glittering with malicious glee. "Flake-Frank knows I got the dirt on him, so the dickhead will do anything I tell him to do unless I'm outta the picture, savvy?"

POTUS nodded, gripped in the thrall of the dastardly conspiracy.

"The other viper is Rawlings, the CIA Director, a right snake. Both the VP and FLOTUS are in cahoots with him, though he's got no idea they want me dead. He just thinks they'll help him get me outta the White House by hook or crook. The CIA sees me as a security threat, coupled with the fact that I sacked a lot of their power grabbing, blackmailing, and corrupt asses. They like China, you see, and I like Bharat. So, I get rid of the ones that hate Bharat, and they're running to Mummy *CNL Anderson Corp*, crying about how mean I've been to them, fucking deadbeats," the president's voice dripped with disdain, his head cocked in that arrogant angle that screamed privilege and power. POTUS felt his admiration for the ghost increasing with every word he spoke.

"As for *CNL Anderson Corp*, well, let's just say they don't like me because I got no time for the gays and pedophiles, and they're tighter than a nun's crotch with the queers and trans, right? Pity I can't sort them out the way I dealt with the sick paedos; chuck them all into prison with a life sentence and roll that fake news channel straight into bankruptcy, that's what," President King's voice was hard and ugly, but POTUS was no longer paying attention. His mind was now in a whirlwind journey to a heated argument he had witnessed between his parents a few years earlier.

Ronke had been unusually voluble, challenging Kunle fiercely in a manner that had surprised POTUS.

"Yes, the man might be a bigot and homophobe as you say," Ronke had said, frowning at Kunle. "But he's the only world leader that's had the courage and conscience to give the sick paedophiles the death sentence and a whole life sentence too. That's what we need in this useless country; good leaders who will protect our children by hunting real criminals instead of wasting taxpayer's money attacking people like us who haven't committed any crime apart from choosing to live our lives as we wish. So, don't tell me any bad thing about the American president. He's my hero and the hero of every parent that cares for their kids," Ronke had glared at Kunle in a manner that said he wasn't a good father that cared for his son.

Now, POTUS was staring at the ghost with new eyes filled with awe—*Oluwa! This is the man that Mama liked, the one she called her hero, the only world leader with the courage and conscience to give sick paedophiles the death sentence! Mama won't believe this—that I'm actually talking to her hero!* In that instant, POTUS felt a strong bond with the ghost, as if they were brothers—If Mama trusted him, then he'll trust him too. How strange that the Babalawo had seen him all those years and saw evil, not good!

"Anyways, everyone knows I'm a shoot straight kinda guy. No messing about. I say things as they are, and people don't like my kinda truth, right?" The president was still talking… and talking. "All the clowns now have a massive axe to grind with me. You can see why they're plotting to assassinate me, and what better opportunity than to install their own corrupt medical team and fake all this life support circus to enable them bump me off without suspicion. Rotten jerks! Dumbass pussies!"

"Who's the other lady that's always begging you to wake up?" POTUS asked. "She's the only one that always cries whenever she visits you, although I've also heard another guy that calls you 'POTUS-Sir' crying."

The president gave him a queer look. "You really heard a lotta stuff, didn't you?" There was something in his voice that flushed POTUS with guilt, as if he'd been caught eavesdropping even though he'd had no choice in the matter. "Yeah, that's my big sister, Dr. Dolores King, a real swell dame. She's the one person I trust completely in the entire world. Dels always has my back and will protect me with her life. The other guy is Pansy-Pete, my Chief of Staff. He's the only one that calls me POTUS-Sir, the little robot," the president chuckled softly. POTUS could see the affection in his eyes when he spoke about his Chief of Staff, even though he called him by the offensive name. "Yeah, I think I can count on Pansy-Pete's loyalty. He's got his heart in the right place though he can be a bit of a wuss at times. Too polite and too nice. And you and I know niceness never got anyone anywhere, right?"

"Right," POTUS nodded enthusiastically. He liked the president's use of 'You and I.'

"Is there anything we can do to stop them killing you, Your Excellency? I mean, I can send someone a message for you if you want me to. It's just that I don't have my phone here with me right now. I think they stole it when I had my accident. But I have other spare phones at home and can use them to send a text or holo-message to your sister or your daughter if you like."

"That'll be great," the president smiled down at him. "We've gotta hurry, though. I don't have much time. As you've probably noticed, you haven't been hearing the voices inside your head since your accident, right?"

POTUS' eyes widened. The president was right. He hadn't heard a thing, not even a whisper since the last attack just before his accident. If he needed any further proof of the authenticity of everything he'd heard, this was it.

"Since I'm no longer in your body, I've lost my ability to hear anything happening in my hospital room anymore. Even as we speak, the snakes could be bumping me off and there's nothing to stop them. Worse, the longer I'm outta your body, the more my life force is drained. So, I may well die in that induced coma without any help from them assholes. Either way, I'm royally screwed, right?" The president swore again, albeit not as violently as before. "If I'm inside you,

you can't hear or see me, and if I'm outside you, I can't survive for long either. Not good, right? So, first thing is, we figure out how I can get back into your body to—if you like—recharge my batteries so to speak, and see what else I can pick up from my hospital room."

POTUS' heart missed a bit—Uh-uh! No way! I'm ready to help the president, but I'm not sure I want a ghost, or fake ghost—whatever —living inside me again. Even if he's a rich American ghost, I can't make an exception for him. Now that I'm finally free of the voices and the excruciating headaches, I'm not ready to go back to that nightmare again. And speaking of nightmares, maybe I might even be free of that horrible 12ᵗʰ December nightmare now...

"No, no... sorry, Your Excellency, but I don't think I want you inside me again," POTUS shook his head, shrinking away from the president as one would a deadly viper. "D'you have any idea how horrible it's been for me living with those voices inside my head all my life? Everyone thinks I'm stupid, well, a bit crazy, because of how I react to the voices. If it weren't for the fact that I'm a golf champion and my parents are rich, nobody would treat me with respect. So now—"

"Did you say you're a golf champion?" The president cut in, his eyes alight with unbridled joy.

"Yeah," POTUS flushed. "I'm actually a kind of local celebrity. In fact, I was a golf protégé from childhood and have won practically all the local junior championships so far. My dream is to go to America and train professionally and maybe meet Tiger Woods one day. He's my all-time icon even though he's retired and Guan Tianlang has been winning all the majors for years now. But my dad won't send me to America. He's just told me to pack out of his house now my mum's dead," POTUS felt the darkness of recurrent grief threaten to over-whelm him once again.

"Damn! That ain't right," the president sounded outraged. "You can't treat a kid like that. Might as well adopt an orphan from Ukraine and abandon it in the street when you're tired of playing mummy and daddy. I think I'll be paying your dad a visit soon, to whip sense into his stupid head, damn it!"

POTUS felt tears pool in his eyes. It was the first time someone, apart from Frankie, had felt outrage on his behalf over his father's abuse, and he allowed the tears to fall unchecked.

"Sorry, kiddo," the president's voice held genuine compassion. "Life's a bitch, right? I saw everything that happened out there when you had your accident. It was terrible, the poor man. I mean, I don't like queers, and they don't like me either, so we're even. But hell! You gotta feel for that poor guy. Imagine having to masquerade as a woman and then being lynched publicly. Heck! I even saw a coupla cops amongst the crowd, but they did jack. Just watched as that poor rainbow got roasted. No arrests, nothing, zilch. I'm guessing you've got no laws in your country protecting the gays and trans like we have in The States, right?"

POTUS shrugged, struggling to suppress the renewed rage the president's words wrought.

"I'm not sure. I think I heard my dad once say that the law in Nigeria is twenty-five years imprisonment for being gay. It used to be fourteen years, but they increased it."

The president's eyes widened gleefully. "Twenty-five years imprisonment? Holy Mackerel! That should do it alright, keep the rainbows as straight as an arrow. Much better than any conversion therapy we have in some states back home. Just as I did with the sick paedos. Brought back the life and death sentences for the disgusting bastards and clipped their perverted wings for good. Mind you, not that your gay laws seem to have worked with your parents, right? They still found a way around it. I'm guessing there are lots of queers in your country who masquerade as straight couples. Damn, crazy! At least, you ain't got the whacko trans problem we have in The States. So, were you close to your mother even though you knew he was a man? I mean, you knew, didn't you?"

POTUS nodded. It felt strange hearing his Mama referred to as a man. Anyone else and he would have been furious. But he could see the president was really curious about his unusual family dynamics rather than coming from a place of malice.

"Mama was the kindest, most generous and caring person in the world," his voice broke despite his best effort. He cleared his throat noisily, feigning a cough. "I'd hoped to save up enough money from my tournament prize money to get her away from my dad's abuse someday, but now it's too late. I'm not even sure I'll ever be able to play again, what with this accident and the damage to my leg and arm," POTUS' voice was as glum as his face.

"Don't you worry about that, kiddo," the president consoled, his voice kindly and wise. "Trust me, you'll be able to play golf very soon and play even better. That's my game, you know. As I told you, that's what I was doing on the day of my accident. I'll soon teach you some clever tricks to get you where you need to be at, winning more tournaments and trophies. Best trick is to repeat the mantra, 'I'm the best of the best of the best.' Love Will Smith. Anyways, you gotta repeat that mantra when you shave, piss, or eat. Hell, even while you're dreaming! Just keep saying, 'I'm the best of the best of the bestest.' I jazzed it up a bit with the last bestest. You gotta look at photos of the top golfers and shout that mantra as loud as the Pentecostal alleluia-amen nutters. Look at the holes and the balls fearlessly, and speak the mantra loud and clear. You may not believe it, but trust me, by the time you've said it a hundred times daily over 365 days, you'll become Mohammed Ali, the greatest. That's my special tip, kiddo. You won't hear this anywhere else. That's how I became a billionaire and the President of the United States. Now, let's see how we can get you to be my host again if you like, ha!" The president's laughter held a nervous ring to it.

POTUS' head was ringing with the president's words—*I'm the best of the best of the bestest... I'm the best of the best of the bestest...POTUS Olupitan, you're the best of the best of the bestest... I'm the best of...*

"Hey kiddo, are you listening?" President King's voice cut into his bliss. "Are you ready to host me again inside your body?"

POTUS felt the return of his terror. "Your Excellency, I told you I don't want to do it. You have no idea how horrible my life has been while you were inside me. Anyway, my amulets won't let you enter me now that you've been expelled from my body," POTUS pointed at his trio of black bracelets. Nobody looking at them now would believe the incredible power they possessed.

The president frowned. "Yeah, what are those damn things anyways? They almost knocked me to smithereens when I touched the pod-shield thing they created around you. Where did you get them from?"

"I told you the Babalawo gave them to me to protect me against you, well, against the great water demon. I mean, I guess I now know you're not a water spirit, but the charms were created to fight a supernatural entity, which is what you are, really. Sorry," he shrugged in embarrassment. "I've tried to ditch them multiple times, but they're stuck to my wrist. I think the Babalawo is the only person that can remove them, and I don't even know where he lives. I'll have to ask my Grandma Funke, that is, if she'll speak to me after all this news about my mum. I mean, she now knows I'm not really her blood grandson as she always believed."

"That's sad," the president sounded suddenly bored. "Listen, we gotta get moving fast, right? If you don't want me inside you, then you gotta get calling, holo, texting, whatever. Just do anything you gotta do to get my sister and my Chief of Staff over here ASAP. In fact, I want them all here, the FBI chief included."

"D'you have their address… I mean, their telephone numbers?" POTUS garbled, again caught off guard by the president's mercurial change of subject.

"Well, I once had a mobile with the phone numbers of all my contacts. But I'm guessing it's now in the grabby hands of Poison-Portia. Bet the bitch is scrolling through it to catch me out with some bird, the dumb broad. As if I'll be stupid enough to store info on any woman in my official phone when I know the snakes from The CIA are monitoring it. Anyways, I don't keep numbers in my head unless it's dollars."

"So how am I going to call them for you if you don't have their numbers?"

"Don't know, kiddo," the president sounded irritated, running his hand through his silver mop. "You're in the driver's seat here. You gotta use your imagination, get those creative juices pumping. My mind's starting to tire, and I'm not sure how much longer I can hang around."

"Well, I could call the American Embassy and see if they'll give me some contact details. But I'm not sure I'll even get through to them, unless you have someone on the inside I can speak to?" Surely, as the

President of the United States, President King would know some top guys at one of his own embassies. Plus, it would be nice to make personal connections with such important guys. One never knew.

"Naahh. Don't know anyone there personally. Don't even know who the ambassador is. Too lowly for me to bother with. Can't help you there, I'm afraid," President King looked as unconcerned as if the problem were all POTUS' own and had nothing to do with him.

"Okay, just in case I'm able to get through to them, how will I convince them that you sent me? I mean, as far as everyone's concerned, you're still in a coma in America, while I'm here in Nigeria. They'll think I'm a fraud-freak unless I can convince them with some secret code only you and they know about," POTUS couldn't quite suppress the irritation in his voice.

"Ha! I see what you're trying to do," the president was animated once again. He gave POTUS a piercing look, suspicion smeared across his features. "You're trying to steal state secrets from me and trade it in with an enemy state for money. No siree Bob! I'm not disclosing any codes to you. Next thing you'll be asking me the secret codes to activate the nuclear bomb," he wagged a playful finger at POTUS, his green eyes as steely as iron.

"I don't give a shit about your codes. I'm just trying to help you, in case you've forgotten," POTUS snapped.

"Sure, sure. My bad," President King gave another of his charming grins. "Anyways, I reckon I could share the code with you if it'll help."

"You actually have the secret code to nuke the entire world just like that?" POTUS snapped his fingers, his eyes as sceptical as his voice— Dude may be the president of America, but surely, he can't carry such a dangerous code all by himself. It's not even as if he's the Chinese leader. POTUS is nobody's fool.

The president preened. "Yeah, I got it. I carry the Gold Code card with the random launch codes generated daily, you know, just to screw the hacking Chinese and Albanian clowns. Obviously, that's useless now because it changes every day, right? Anyways, listen up. I've come up with a great idea. It's mighty stuff and if I should say so myself, really genius. Are you ready for it?"

POTUS nodded, slowly—Got to watch it with him. Maybe he

thinks I'm an ignorant native he can fool with tall stories. But I'll show him POTUS is nobody's fool.

"What's it, Your Excellency?"

"*The Great America News Inc.*!" President King roared triumphantly.

"Huh?"

"Yeah, *The Great America News Inc.* Now, listen real good," the president glided closer. "Everyone listens to *The Great America News Inc.*, right? Well, everyone except the communist Dems. They get their fairy tales from the big liar, *CNL Anderson Corp*," he screwed his face in disgust. "Anyways, I know all my guys tune into *The Great America News Inc.*, including my sister and Pansy-Pete. So, what better way than to call in live or text the cable station—whatever—and tell them you got a message from me, right?" The president's eyes glittered malevolently. "In fact, guess what? Let's get those jerkoffs at the White House shitting in their slimy butts. I'll give you the last 6-digit code for the Big-N, the same one generated on the day of my accident. It's not as if you can do anything with it anyways, since it's already obsolete. Moreover, no one'll believe you except those in the know, and there are only four people in the know and you're looking at one of them," the president puffed out his chest, poking it with a proud finger. "Now, you're gonna receive the code too, kiddo. Ain't that something special, right? Bet you're feeling mighty proud."

POTUS's mouth was so wide he could have swallowed an elephant.

"No way!" his voice was hushed—*The president was actually telling the truth? He's one of the four people that holds the secret nuclear code? Mega sick!*

"Yes friggin' way! Now, you ready?"

POTUS nodded, eyes wide in awe.

"Great. Memorize these numbers," the president whispered six numbers into his ears, his breath so chilly POTUS thought his ears would freeze up and drop off his head. "Got it?"

"Y-yeah," POTUS repeated the six digits through chattering teeth.

"Great. Now get that mind of yours working. You didn't have my great mind feeding you pure genius all this while for nothing. Mind you, I'm not sure how far you'll get with *The Great America News Inc.* when they hear you're calling from Nigeria. No disrespect meant here, little buddy, but you gotta admit that despite being a member of G7, Nigeria has patented the copyright to the trade name 'Scam,' right? I mean, right or wrong, you guys have got your eyeballs deep in real scam shit, and it's gonna make things a bit trickier for you with this covert mission. So, maybe we gotta try a different approach, right?"

"We're not the only scammers in the world," POTUS retorted, the scowl back on his face. He wished the president would stop saying bad things about Nigeria. It wasn't as if America wasn't just as bad—well, maybe not as openly bad as Nigeria since they're richer. But still, Nigeria is his country, and he'd rather be the one dissing it than an outsider, especially an Oyinbo fake-ghost.

"Sorry, kiddo, my bad. But before I forget, when you call *The Great America News Inc.,* tell my sister, Dr. Delores, that I said, "Remember Belly-Bury." You got that? Belly-Bury. Dels will know it's me for real once she hears that. We're the only two who know what that means."

"Berry as in the fruit, yeah? Remember Belly-Berry?" POTUS confirmed.

The president looked startled, then his eyes glowed with a malignant glint before he gave another of his wicked, slow winks.

"Berry... sure! That's it, kiddo. You got it pat. Remember Belly-Berry, swell. And don't go asking me to tell you what it means. This one stays with me. You've got enough State secrets as it is to sink the entire U.S. of A," the president stretched and yawned. "Okay, I'm beat. Gotta get me some rest. Don't call me. I'll call you, as the lady says," he winked again and started to fade.

"Hold it just a minute, Your Excellency," POTUS rushed his words. "Before you go, I need us to clear up a couple things," POTUS tried to sit up on his bed, but the effort proved too much. He collapsed back against his pillow, panting and wincing in pain.

"Take it easy now," the president solidified again and leaned low, his face concerned. "You gotta remember you're still a very sick guy and learn to take things easy. What's on your mind?"

POTUS groaned and cleared his voice. "Well, Your Excellency, my thoughts are that I'm the one doing all the giving here, and I'm not getting any receiving, you know…" POTUS managed to gasp out.

The president's eyes widened in surprise. Then he whistled, a long toot that bounced off the walls and pierced his eardrums. POTUS clenched his fists, steeling himself for a fight—POTUS is nobody's fool. The dude's the President of the United States after all. When am I going to get a chance like this again in my lifetime? I'll be an idiot goat if I don't make use of this incredible opportunity.

The president observed POTUS silently for several intense seconds. POTUS held his gaze, his eyes two golden orbs of hard steel. Then the president gave a short, loud bark.

"Ok, I see I'm dealing with a mind that's as ruthless as mine. I like it. I like it. Alright, shoot! What do you want from me in exchange for your help? That's assuming we're successful and I return to full flesh and memory."

"I want an American passport and a scholarship for myself and Frankie,"

"Who the hell's Frankie?"

"He's my best friend. I'm sure he'll be visiting me very soon once he hears about my accident,"

"And all you want is an American passport and a college scholarship for both of you, right?"

"Yeah, and a house too, plus some cash, you know,"

"A house for both of you…hey! You're not queer like your parents?" The president looked alarmed.

"No! God! No way!" POTUS' face creased in distaste, an image of his father flashing in his mind.

"Great! That's good. You had me worried there for a second. I'm guessing you're like me and don't take to the gays, right? Can't blame you after having to endure them as parents all your life."

"It's not that," POTUS said, his eyes flashing. He hated it when anyone spoke bad of his mother. "I don't have anything against them, well, my mum anyway. Mama was wonderful. Just my adoptive dad, who's a hypocritical bully. I just think people should be open and stand up for whatever they believe in, good or bad, rather than pretending. You know, saying one thing, and doing the opposite. I guess you politicians are like that, aren't you?" POTUS' eyes squinted, suspicion coating his face. "Hey! You mentioned something about your memory just now. Is that your way of wriggling out of the deal by claiming you don't remember afterwards? Because if that's the case, then—"

"Hold it, kiddo!" the president raised his hands up in a placating motion. "Listen, I know you've been through a lot, and I don't blame you for feeling the way you do and looking out for number one. I feel exactly the same. I told you I like you, and I'm not lying. Hell! We've shared a body together for so long that you're practically my mini-me, right?" He laughed.

POTUS' face remained stony—*Uh-uh! POTUS is nobody's fool.* He won't let this Oyinbo half-ghost sweet-talk him. "So how are we going to ensure you keep to your end of the bargain, Your Excellency?"

"You just gotta take my word for it, I'm afraid," the president raised an arrogant brow. "You and I gotta trust each other and work together to get me back to my body, otherwise nobody wins except those vipers at the White House."

POTUS knew he was beaten. He felt very tired, as if all his blood-batteries had been drained from his body. He didn't think he wanted to get into another marathon chat with the president. The guy could talk for the whole of Africa and Asia, and he just wanted to sleep and never wake up.

"I guess you're right," POTUS muttered.

"I know I'm right. Now, I really gotta go. Don't forget to tell Dr. Delores to remember Belly-Berry, alright?" The president did another one of his slow winks before winking out like a sozzled star.

POTUS sighed again, extruding air from his mouth in a loud whoosh. His head was reeling with everything he'd heard. He wanted to analyse every word exchanged with the president, savour the incredible experience of chatting with the American president almost like an equal, but Fat-arse nurse's needle had done its work with brilliant efficiency. Soon, he felt his eyes drooping, lethargy seeping into every limb in his body—*God! This dude can talk! And Frankie thinks I'm a Motormouth. Ha! He needs to meet the president. Belly-Berry… what does it mean anyway?*

10

ALIENS AMONGST US

POTUS was having a nightmare, a horror-scape filled with corpses, ghosts, and snakes of every size, colour, and threat level. A fat hag that looked suspiciously like Fat-arse Nurse cackled as she chased him with a blood-dripping giant needle, while a black cobra raised its head in readiness to strike his exposed ankle as he fled from the fat witch. A multitude of wispy ghosts floated out from the putrid corpses littering his path, wailing and flailing as they crowded around him. POTUS saw Ronke amongst them.

"Baby Boy! Baby Boy!" She shrieked his pet name, her voice so shrill it sent his heartbeat into overdrive. Then, she swooped down on him so quickly that he started choking and gasping, desperate for air.

He woke up, his arms flailing wildly, still struggling to breathe and... *Oluwa! God have mercy!*

POTUS stared with horror into the pale, glowing face of President King, hulking so close their noses almost touched. The president was blowing icy air over his face, freezing his lungs.

POTUS screamed. It came out a choked whimper. He caught a gloating glint in the president's eyes in the split second before his amulet blazed into blinding brilliance. The shining pod shrouded him within its protective shield, hurling the ghost with such force that it crashed through the wall and vanished.

POTUS was panting, inhaling deep gulps of air as his skin broke out in tiny rashes of icy terror—*President King has tried to kill me in my sleep! Oh my God!* The president had tried to freeze him to death and would've succeeded but for his Mama's voice calling him into wakefulness from his nightmare! No wonder he'd dreamt of snakes, the ultimate sign of treachery. He shuddered again—Why? Why would President King want me dead after we'd chatted and parted like good friends? Is it because I'd asked him for the scholarship and house and money? Is he angry because I disrespected him by saying I didn't trust him to honour the deal or because I refused to let him back into my body?

The room went icy again, and he knew without looking that the ghost was back. He saw the president's pale spectre hovering by his bathroom door.

"Heck! What the fuck's wrong with your gadget? So friggin' schizo!" The president's voice was breathless like someone that had run a marathon. He pushed a shaky hand through his silver mop, eyeing the glowing bubble warily.

"Why did you try to kill me?" POTUS wasn't beating about the bush. Anger was starting to replace his initial terror—*God!* He would happily kill the president if the dude wasn't already a ghost! In his book, people shouldn't smile and then stab you in the back. That was the worst kind of treachery, something the president ought to know considering his own betrayals.

"Try to kill you? Is that what you think?" President King laughed, his face breaking out in that charismatic smile that was impossible to resist. "Now, why on earth would I go do such a kooky thing? If I kill you, who's gonna help me return to my body or get a message through to my sister?"

It made sense, and POTUS started to feel a bit stupid for speaking out. *Still...* he shook his head—*Uh-uh! I know what I saw and what I felt when I woke up.* His protective amulets wouldn't have kicked in if there'd been no danger to him from the president.

"You were trying to freeze me to death," he insisted. "I saw you blowing icy air on my face. Why would my protective shield come up if you weren't trying to harm me?"

"No idea," the president shrugged indifferently. "You tell me. I don't know what you think you saw, kiddo. All I was doing was trying to make sure you were okay. You were moaning as if you were having a nightmare or something. You're my little buddy now, so I gotta look out for you, right? Maybe your little gadget is faulty, or it just doesn't like me. I don't know. You gotta figure that one out yourself," the president shrugged again.

"Sorry," POTUS mumbled. The horrible itching returned to his body with a vengeance. The bubble began to dim, getting hazier as he scratched, till it completely winked out.

"If you ask me, I think that stupid gadget doesn't like either of us," the president glided closer to his bedside again with the disappearance of the threat. "It sure makes you pay for the protection it gives you, right?"

POTUS said nothing, massaging his skin to ease the burning sensation.

"So, since I'm guessing you won't be catching some Z's tonight, why don't we get to know each other better, right?" President King suggested. "You seem to know everything about me, and I know jack about you, apart from the fact your dad's some big shot queer fella. So, tell me how it was growing up in such a kooky home. I mean, it must've been one hell of a job trying to keep such a big secret, right?"

POTUS nodded, touched that the president realised just how difficult it had been for him carrying the terrible burden of secrecy. Before he knew it, he was telling him all about their family dynamics, his parents' struggles within their larger family circle, the stigma of homosexuality in the country and the way it had impacted his relationship with his parents and his life.

"That's really tough, kiddo." The president seemed genuinely sorry for him and his compassion touched a core in POTUS' heart once again. He had to swallow back the tight knot behind his throat several times—*Life isn't fair. Why don't I have a real dad like President King?* He couldn't ever imagine the president raising a fist or a belt to his daughter. "Anyways, if things work out swell, you'll soon be visiting the Big Apple or any one of our marvellous states. We've got fifty-four states since we split Texas and California into two. America is now the greatest, and you, lucky boy, are now speaking with the ruler of the entire damn world—"

"China is the new ruler since—"

"Fuck China!" The president snarled. "I'm the most important guy in Terra Firma. Hell! Even aliens from Mars speak with me, and I ain't kidding you."

POTUS' eyes widened into saucers. "No way! Your Excellency, you've actually seen real aliens, like in the films, *Liberation Night* and *Independence Day* and *Women in Green* and *Men in Black*. Real mothership aliens?"

President King preened, chest all puffed out, a grim smile on his face. "Yep. This is top secret, right? I'm not supposed to tell that we got aliens running wild amongst us, but take it from me, there are loads of them and—"

"Are there any aliens that are famous?" POTUS cut in, his heart thudding with excitement—*Oh my God! Just wait till I tell Frankie. Mega wicked!*

"Sure. Listen, promise you won't tell, right? Swear on your life, and I'll give you a coupla names."

"I swear on my life," POTUS crossed his heart feverishly. His love affair with sci-fi was only second to his boxing reruns on archive hologram channel.

"Okay. You know the actor guy, Tom Cruise? Yep! He's one of the Martians."

"No way! Tom Cruise?" POTUS' ears were literally burning—*Tom Cruise is an alien! Oh my God!*

"Yep! Ever ask yourself how come he does all his own stunts despite his age? I mean, the guy's older than me in human years, right? Last time I checked, he was almost seventy years old, and he's still scaling walls and jumping parachutes and driving cars over cliffs. Hell! It's even rumoured the guy never bleeds, never sleeps, and never been sick either. Now, who wouldn't want that kinda power, right? A real charmer and superman, literally," the president shook his head, his eyes glittering with admiration. POTUS could tell he liked alien Tom Cruise a lot.

"Are there women aliens too, Your Excellency?"

"Sure thing. The singer broad, Taylor Swift. Yep. Little green girl, I'm afraid. Psycho-bitch is a cloner and can split herself into thirteen alien Taylors, ensuring she has enough of herself to wreak chaos on humanity whenever she wants. Why do you think she always wears those creepy number 13 earrings? The alien bitch claims she was born on the 13th of the month and turned 13 years on a Friday the 13th, but we know who her real parents are and trust me, they ain't humans; alien mummy and daddy, just like their spawn. As I said, that psycho bird is the mistress of chaos. She can sow anarchy, cause riots, and destruction just by showing her friggin' face and opening her big mouth to spout garbage. And boom! Instantly, humanity turns into crazy zombies; wild, rabid squad dogs who just want to cancel out everyone without having a friggin' idea why they're doing it. And she has thirteen clones to help her sew unrest around the world. Most times you see her having a concert in different countries, it's actually one of her thirteen alien clones performing. But as I said, this is top secret, got it? Just between the two of us, right?"

"Right," POTUS nodded. He was so relieved Rihanna wasn't amongst the named aliens. It would've killed him if his all-time celebrity crush was one of the little green people from Mars. She might be older now, but he still had endless hologram recordings of her in her hay days to feed his besotted eyes.

Something niggled him.

"Your Excellency, are all the aliens white people, or do we have any black aliens too?"

President King barked a grim laugh. "Sure thing. We got loads of black aliens, even yellow ones. They hold annual Alien Zoom meetings to catch up with their alien stuff. I hear Will Smith's been begging them to let him into the meetings but they keep voting him out. I reckon the alien motherfuckers think he has too many lethal *Men in Black* anti-alien arsenals. So, they don't trust him and who can blame them? Mind you, Will's no alien, but the fashion designer guy that used to be a singer, Pharrell Williams, and the F1 champion, Sir Lewis

Hamilton…" he paused and nodded grimly as POTUS' eyes goggled. "Yep! Sorry to disappoint you, kiddo, but they're both little green men too. Not forgetting the Korean megastar singer, Taemin. That guy doesn't even need to hide the fact that he's an alien. He looks like one and moves like one. Little wonder they call him the reincarnated Michael Jackson, who was another alien freak, by the way. Yeah, these alien fuckers have got their people practically in every country, although we have the most in America. I'm guessing Martians know a quality country when they see one. Fuck China!" The president glided closer till he was practically whispering. "You see, they send them down with special powers. The aliens we gotta fear are the singers and the drivers."

President King caught the stunned look on POTUS' face and nodded again with that hard smile that POTUS was starting to admire. It was a smile of power, of strength, of knowledge and ruthlessness. It was the kind of smile that said the president had the aliens well sourced and could handle them with ruthless ease.

"Take the racing guy, Sir Lewis, for instance," the president's eyes glittered with malice. "Did you ever stop to ask yourself how come a little black kid from a dirt-poor family living in some shitty place in England got to make it so big in a sport previously reserved for the kids of white billionaires? I mean, twelve championship wins at the last count, right? Right?" The president insisted, and POTUS nodded obediently. "Damn right. He only let the Dutch kid win so people wouldn't get suspicious and start wondering why he never loses."

POTUS frowned, thoughts buzzing inside his head like bees on crack. The president observed the confusion on his face with smug satisfaction.

"Now you get it!" President King nodded vigorously. "Sir Lewis is the alien with the powers of movement and manipulation of machinery. He controls the engines of everything that moves, from scooters to rockets. If he decides to cripple humanity, all he gotta do is think it and just like that," the president snapped his fingers. "Planes will tumble from the skies, submarines will float, cars will stall, and rockets will explode, boom! Gone! China and Albania destroyed in a blink! Everything! I told you we gotta fear the drivers, right?" The president nodded grimly, his gleaming eyes boring into POTUS' wide eyes. He was pleased by the reaction his words were causing.

"But, you ain't heard nothing yet, kiddo. I mentioned Pharrell, didn't I?" POTUS gave a dazed nod. "Arsehole alien is now trying to get all humans dressing like aliens at his Pharrell-Vuitton fashion house that dominates the whole industry. Well, get this; he and that Christmas cocaine broad they call Mariah are the other two dangerous black aliens. Ever wondered why Mariah's voice cracks glass and mirrors? I've been told by the FBI that she can explode bombs too, just by singing. So, they're making sure she doesn't get anywhere near our military bases. She and Pharrell control the emotions of mankind and if they want us to be happy—simple! They'll just release a happy song and next thing you know, everybody's hopping around in Santa's costume or clapping their hands like some fucking morons on heroin, just as Mariah did with her Christmas song after the OJ Simpson drama. Then the mind-fucker, Pharrell, decided mankind needed some serious cheering up with his friggin' *Happy* song after the Boston bombing, right? Chew on that."

POTUS did.

He chewed on his lower lip till it was tender and sore. His head was spinning as if he'd just gotten off a malfunctioning Ferris Wheel. He had no idea what the Boston bombing was all about, or who OJ Simpson was, but it didn't matter. What mattered was the fact that he suddenly remembered just how happy he too had been as a child, watching the crazy, yellow minions and clapping along to the joyful happy song without realising he was being manipulated by the aliens —*Oluwa! Still… uh-uh! POTUS is nobody's fool.*

"Your Excellency, everyone knows Mariah Carey's family, and she and Pharrell have kids. I've seen their kids and they look human. So, how can they be aliens and still have kids with humans? I just don't know and…"

"You think the president of the USA is feeding you bullshit?" President King bristled, his eyes flashing. "You think I share this kinda classified information with just anyone? You also doubted me when I told you about the nuclear code, and I'm starting to think you don't like me."

"Sorry, Your Excellency!" POTUS tried to clear the air. He didn't want to offend the president. As the guy said, there was no reason for the President of the United States to feed him fake news about aliens or anything else for that matter. "I didn't mean to imply anything. It's just my usual scepticism, you know. If you lived in our country and heard some of the wild stories our people tell, you'd understand why I'm struggling with this," he shrugged, giving the president a wry smile.

President King beamed, rewarding POTUS with another one of his winks.

"I got ya, kiddo. But trust me, Mariah and Pharrell are definitely from the green planet. I got secret information on every single alien on the planet, so take everything I say as straight from God's lips," the president puffed his shoulders, a maniacal glint in his eyes. "Imagine if those mood aliens wanna destroy all mankind, right? All they gotta do is sing a suicide song and boom! Everyone's jumping the friggin' bridge or blowing out their brains, right? Or in the case of the Japs, trouping to the Suicide Forest. Yep! They can wipe us out with the power of a song because they hold the secret to mankind's mind. As I said, drivers and singers, real bad news. These alien fuckers are dangerous, but I'm keeping my eyes on them. Don't get me wrong, some of them are okay, like Tom Cruise, for instance."

"I like Tom Cruise," POTUS smiled, happy the president didn't have anything bad to say about one of his favourite actors so far.

"Yeah, you and the whole friggin' world," President King gave a soft chuckle. "Mind you, the other celebrity aliens aren't on the Cruise bandwagon. They resent his popularity and the fact that he's the only one allowed to return to the mother planet frequently. I'm sure they'd love to touch base and shed their human skins for their reptilian alien ones, but they ain't lucky like Tom. He's the ultimate alien spy, and each time he goes back to Mars, he rejuvenates and returns to earth looking even younger. That's another thing you'll find with these aliens," President King's voice now rang with an authoritative boom. "They never age, forever young, just like vampires, right? As I said, Tom's okay. The mothership just sent him on the charm offensive, you know, show us their good side and disarm us. Guy even gets to shoot all his mega successful movies these days on his alien planet." The president glided over to the Black Jesus effigy, glaring intently at it for several seconds before turning back towards POTUS. His eyes glittered with rage, and POTUS wasn't sure if his outrage was directed towards the offending crucifix or the super alien, Tom Cruise.

"Anyways, I've already spoken to Tom about sharing the secret to eternal youth, and I expect to receive the age antidote any time soon. Tom's my good pal, and he'll play ball unless he wants to be kicked outta earth. I got the FBI watching them carefully. Trust me, I got your back, kiddo. Yours and every damn human in the world. I one-thousand-fucking-percent-guarantee you that. So, don't you go worrying your little head about a thing."

POTUS nodded again and again, as if nodding would wipe out what he'd just heard. He was worried, a clammy hands kind of panic—*Oluwa! The world is doomed! Everyone is doomed! Who will believe this stuff? Armageddon is here. An alien invasion can happen anytime!* He didn't doubt a single thing the president said about the aliens anymore. If anyone would know the truth, it would be the President of the United States. The fact that the almighty FBI were investigating the aliens proved that the threat was real. Thoughts went round and around inside his head like psychedelic ants at Glastonbury—*God! Who'll believe it! Tom Cruise, Pharrell Williams, Taemin, and Sir Lewis Hamilton, all green men! Who can be trusted now?*

"Are the aliens only in America, or do we have them here in Nigeria too?" He needed to know so he wouldn't stumble in ignorant blindness and end up in their green claws.

"Relax, kiddo," President King smiled indulgently. "I told you I got your back, right? Sure, you had one of them in Nigeria, but he's long been deleted. A musician guy called Fela Kuti. Know him?"

POTUS nodded vigorously, his eyes like saucers—*Oluwa! Fela was an alien! No way!*

"Yup! Guy was also a mood alien with the same powers as Pharrell & Co. I heard he could sing madness into the minds of the people too. That's why as soon as he left, the mothership quickly replaced him with the other big guns, Mariah, Pharrell and Psycho-Swift. Anyways, no sweat. We have all the Martian fuckers on our radar, trust me. As I said, just chill, alright? Everything's under control."

POTUS chilled.

His teeth rattled, and his body froze under his thin blanket. He'd been so wrapped up in the president's incredible words that he didn't realise how much the ghost had iced his room. By the time they finally called it a night and the president vanished, POTUS had ceased wondering about President King's strange nocturnal visit. Too many thoughts were churning inside his head, and as for his charmed amulets, the president was probably right about them—Stupid things could've been faulty and just got triggered when they detected the supernatural presence, even if the president meant him no harm.

This time, when POTUS finally fell asleep again, his slumber was deep and peaceful, devoid of nightmares and celebrity green aliens from Mars.

II

SAVING THE PRESIDENT

Frankie came to visit him that evening, right after the famed Dr. Okoye had done his rounds and informed POTUS he would be discharged in a couple of days.

"Motormouth!" Frankie high-fived him on his good left hand, his eyes glinting delight behind his thick-rimmed glasses, the ubiquitous lollipop stuck in his mouth. His long silky hair was held back with a green band, giving him the look of an overweight, nerdy hippy. He pulled a chair close to the bedside and plonked his chunky frame on it.

"Einstein!" POTUS laughed in a rush of joy he hadn't felt in what seemed like forever. Frankie always had that effect on him. "Wondered where you were, you goat."

"Olè! I kept calling your mobile phone and getting some idiot woman telling me you weren't around. Then it just stopped ringing after a while. I had to call your dad to find out where you were,"

"Dogs! I knew it! They stole my mobile when I had the accident. That's why I couldn't call you or anyone."

"That's some bad luck you've been having recently," Frankie's voice was low, his pitying gaze speaking volumes. POTUS knew he'd heard about the scandal. "Listen, I'm sorry about your... mum," Frankie hesitated slightly before saying the word, 'mum.' He was literally squirming on his chair.

"It's alright; you can say it to my face. Mama was a man; big deal."

"I'm sorry, Motormouth. Didn't mean it that way," Frankie blushed, averting his eyes.

"It's okay. She was still my mum and nothing can change that," POTUS paused, forcing back the brewing tears—*Not now, POTUS; you won't cry before anyone.* He weighed his next words carefully. "So, how did your parents take it?"

Frankie shrugged, mortification contorting his gentle features in a painful blush. "You know them and their Catholic beliefs. Dad says their oil firm has put your dad on indefinite leave, and we're not to have anything to do with him anymore. But he feels sorry for you and says he now understands why you were always fighting with your parents and spending so many nights at our house. Now, whenever he and mum mention your name, they always add, 'the poor thing' to it, no jiving you," Frankie laughed as he mimicked his parent's solemn tones. POTUS forced his own laughter, breaking the unfamiliar awkwardness between them. Soon, they were chatting with their usual ease, and Frankie filled him in on how their friends had reacted to the news of his parent's sexuality. Apparently, a few people were already questioning POTUS' sexuality as well, as if homosexuality were a disease that one caught or inherited from their parents—*Idiots*!

"Listen, is it okay to stay at your house when I'm discharged from the hospital?" POTUS mumbled the request, fighting his humiliation. "Just that Kunle has disowned me and kicked me out of the house."

"Olé! That guy is a monster," Frankie cursed in unfamiliar rage. "Of course, you can stay in our house for as long as you want."

Frankie's anger towards Kunle was like a balm to POTUS' bruised heart, just like the president's earlier outrage. Before he knew it, he was sharing his surreal ghostly experience with Frankie, revealing every-thing that had happened since the accident, albeit he avoided mentioning the aliens. He had given the president his word and he meant to keep it, despite his desperation to reveal all to his best-friend —Maybe later, when they were both safely settled in America.

"Get ready, Einstein; you and I will soon be going to The States on a college scholarship, with our own house and loads of cash to rock the town," he was almost beside himself with glee.

Frankie was quiet. His face had a look that doused POTUS' enthusiasm with ice.

"What?" POTUS barked, his voice as aggressive as his frown. Frankie winced, fidgeting on his chair.

"Motormouth, I don't want you to get upset, okay? I mean, I know how you've always heard voices inside your head from when we were kids. But I'm just thinking that maybe the accident kind of made things worse. You know, a kind of hallucinatory effect which might be responsible for what you think you've seen," Frankie looked at him apologetically. "Do you think you might mention it to your doctor, just in case they need to do a proper head scan to make sure, you know, that you're okay?" Frankie shrugged, averting his gaze.

"I don't believe I'm hearing this!" POTUS roared. Frankie was the one person he'd always thought would understand. It never occurred to him that his best friend might doubt him. All his earlier elation deflated, leaving in its place an empty void filled with despair.

"I'm not imagining stuff, Einstein," POTUS' voice was dull. "Believe me, I wish I were. President Jerry King has actually been living inside me all my life, and if you hang around long enough, he might come back and you'll see him for yourself... my mistake, I'm the only one that can see him," POTUS hissed again, his pale brown eyes glaring his frustration. Then, they brightened as he reached out and gripped Frankie's arm. "Einstein, give me your phone let's Naggle him and see if he's really in a coma," POTUS snatched Frankie's phone. He quickly typed in President King's name into Naggle, Nigeria's biggest search engine.

"OMG! Dude, this is awesome!" POTUS's voice was hushed in awe. "I told you. See for yourself. President King is really in a coma. He was telling the truth. And look at his picture. I tell you, it's the same guy I saw. He's just younger in these photos. Here, read for yourself. This is mega sick! The Oyinbo ghost is really legit, I tell you." POTUS was almost bouncing on his bed in excitement—*I'm not crazy after all! The president's half-ghost is real! Everything I heard inside my head was not some moon-madness!* "Listen, Einstein. Maybe the president might do something to show you he exists. Honest dude, I'm not making this up. POTUS is…"

"Yeah! Yeah! POTUS is nobody's fool," Frankie finished for him, his eyes oozing that special brand of kindness reserved for the hopelessly insane by the rigidly sane. "You always say that, yet you and I know just how many times you've been taken in by people after I've warned you. Then later, you tell me that you should've listened to me," Frankie shook his head wearily. "Trust me, this is one of those times you should listen to me, okay? I know you're the last person that'll make anything up, but you've got to admit that this ghost stuff is a bit far out. And you claim your bracelets glow and shroud you in a fire bubble. Come on, Motormouth. I've known you all my life and seen these three strings round your wrist from when we were kids. In all that time, not once have they ever displayed any signs of magic. If there was any magic in them, why didn't they protect you from your dad's beatings?"

"Because they're designed as protection against supernatural entities, not humans!" POTUS bellowed. "The president is a kind of ghost-thing, even though he isn't properly dead-dead," POTUS sighed, reaching for the TV remote control. "Anyway, let's see if they have *The Great America News Inc.* channel on, so I can check out their newscasters and figure out who's best to call with my message."

Frankie looked aghast. "Olé! No way! POTUS, please tell me you're not going ahead with that crazy plan?" His eyes were pleading, like a child that doesn't want his mummy to disgrace him before his classmates with a kiss on his cheeks, or worse, an inappropriate pet name.

"Of course, I am. Haven't you been listening to me? I made a deal with the president, and I'm going to honour it if…"

POTUS froze as the president materialised in front of him, glaring at Frankie with enough venom to annihilate a battalion. The temperature immediately dropped, and both Frankie and POTUS shivered involuntarily.

"He's here," POTUS whispered to Frankie. "The president has just appeared, and he's standing right next to you. Don't move, okay? Just sit still."

Frankie's eyes widened. He looked as if he were about to faint. Even though he doubted the story, Frankie was affected by the strange chill in the room. His lollipop hung uselessly in his mouth, and his eyes darted around as he tried to maintain a brave, sickly smile.

"President King, I'm glad you're back," POTUS called out with unrestrained joy, looking at a point just above Frankie's head. Frankie glanced behind, looking as if his blood had curdled in his veins. "This is my best—"

"I should've known you weren't to be trusted, you little punk," the president snarled, glaring at POTUS. "You couldn't wait to make a quick buck with the Chinese, is that it? Minute my back turns and you're hooking up with the ch*nks to sell confidential info, you dirty weasel. And after I paid your fairy daddy a visit too as a favour to my supposedly little friend. Well thanks for nothing, you little shit."

"Hey! Hold it!" POTUS yelled, causing Frankie to jump from his seat. "Frankie's not Chinese. He's Filipino, and he's trying to help us, okay? Just chill, alright? I'm trying to make him believe that you actually exist, but he thinks I'm crazy," POTUS returned his gaze to Frankie, who was looking almost as white as the president. "Is there anything you can do to show him you're really here so he knows I'm not making it up?"

The president's scowl vanished, and his face broke into a sheepish smile. "Sorry, kiddo. Shoulda known you wouldn't stab me in the back. That's not your style. You and me are the same, right up front and fuck the motherfuckers, right?" He gave his slow, wicked wink. "That's why I visited your daddy last night and scared the holy jeebers outta him. You shoulda seen his face when I made the pen write on his book—THIS IS GREAT WATER SPIRIT, POTUS! BRING HOME MY BOY, POTUS, AND BE GOOD TO HIM OTHERWISE…! That's what I wrote while raising hell inside his bedroom. Ha! You shoulda seen the guy's face when he saw the message and the crashing ornaments and flying stuff. Trust me, he'll be coming for you ASAP to take you back home, and damn right too. It's wrong for parents to abandon their kids. Very bad stuff." The president shook his head with a deep frown.

POTUS teared up. He wanted to hug the president tight, give him a hundred fist bumps. "Anyways, you say your friend here thinks I'm a figment of your imagination, right? I guess we'll have to show him he's wrong," the president laughed, leaning close to Frankie and blowing so hard on his head that his green band snapped. Frankie's hair spiked up in a vertical bush, as if swept by a whirlwind.

"Olé!" Frankie screamed, bolting from his bedside and dashing to the foot of POTUS' bed, his eyes like saucers. The president swooped down on him and blew harder. This time, he blew so hard that Frankie's T-shirt rode high up his back and bunched just beneath his fleshy ribcage.

"Olé! Olé! Stop! Stop! Please…" Frankie dashed for the door. Just then, the remote control sailed in the air in slow motion towards him, and he froze, staring with horror at the flying device. He looked ready to pass out.

"Einstein, come back!" POTUS called out. "Listen, it's alright, okay? Trust me, he's not harmful at all. He's just trying to show you he's real. Please dude, just come back, okay? I can't do this without you." POTUS leaned forward, forcing himself not to groan with pain as he fixed a cajoling smile on his face. He turned to the president who was smiling smugly, ready to blow again. "Your Excellency, enough now, please? I think he believes us now. Don't frighten him away, or we'll have no one to help us."

The president snapped his fingers with a muttered, "Damn!" and glided away from Frankie, who remained rooted by the door.

"Einstein, come on, dude. Don't leave, alright? Come on," POTUS cajoled. After several tense seconds, Frankie released a deep sigh and slowly made his way back to the bedside with tentative steps, like a mouse trying to avoid waking a tomcat.

"Olé! Diyos ko po!" Frankie whispered repeatedly, merging the Yoruba and Filipino languages as he stared at POTUS with stunned disbelief. His owl eyes behind his thick lenses kept searching the room with suspicion and fear.

"I told you," POTUS couldn't resist the smug dig. "He's just by the bathroom door and he's laughing. And don't go screaming 'Olé' again you little goat," POTUS laughed, knowing he was wasting his time. Frankie's attachment to the Yoruba word for "thief" had stayed with him from their nursery school days and into adulthood. It was now an inappropriate and natural part of his general vocabulary, together with the ubiquitous lollipop.

"But seriously dude, I need you to help me make these calls without delay. Every second that passes brings the president closer to death. We can crush this together, and then, the USA is ours. Just think about that."

Frankie was thinking, alright. "I got an aunt in the States and that girl, Gloria, you know, the one I've been chatting with on *AssBook*. She lives in Miami. It'll be nice to hook up with them, I guess," his voice was shaky but POTUS knew he was now a believer.

"Don't guess, Einstein," POTUS laughed. "It's in the bag if we pull this off. The president says he'll set us up with a house... hey, why not two houses?" POTUS called out to the president. "Your Excellency, could you give us a house each? Please, please?" He wheedled, flashing his most dazzling John Boyega smile.

"You little punk!" The president glided closer, his eyes glinting dangerously. "Do I look like your daddy? The deal was one house, two scholarships and some cash for—"

"Loads of cash, not some cash," POTUS cut in, unfazed by the ghost's mien now that he had his best friend by his side. "I'm thinking two million dollars, maybe three. Come on, Your Excellency. Just make it two houses and a million each and it's a deal. I mean, it's not as if you can't afford it, and what are two miserly houses compared to your life anyway?"

The president stared at him intently for several seconds, his green eyes calculating and hard. Then finally, he nodded.

"Okay, done. But that's it. Kaput! You don't ask for anything else and you get right down to work without delay. No half-ass work, right?"

"You're the man!" POTUS grinned at Frankie. "He's agreed; a house for each of us, a college scholarship and a million dollars each. Whoopeee!"

"Yeees!" Frankie high-fived POTUS before jabbing his fist into the air. "Yeees! So, what do we do now?"

"Now we call the American embassy first and then start calling everyone at *The Great America News Inc.* or *CNL Anderson Corp.* Basically, any TV station in America that'll carry our story if the Embassy doesn't help. Come on, let's start earning our money, dude!"

"No *CNL Anderson Corp*, remember? Just *The Great America News Inc.*," the president quickly interjected.

"Sorry. Okay, just *The Great America News Inc.* I hear you."

"And don't forget Belly-Berry."

"Belly-Berry confirmed," POTUS laughed.

"Belly-Berry?" Frankie looked confused.

"Belly-Berry," POTUS giggled. He and the president exchanged simultaneous winks. "It's a special wine, dude. I promise you'll really dig it."

POTUS was laughing, Frankie was laughing too, and the president was laughing even louder than all of them.

≈

KSB12 NEWS RADIO –
Salt Lake County's favourite Station
105.9FM

Good morning folks, and welcome to Salt Lake County's favourite radio station, bringing the latest and hottest news from around the globe right into your bedrooms. This is your Sunday morning host, Ron Doyle, wishing y'all a wonderful and righteous day.

So, my fellow Utahns, to kick things off, here's a little bit of light relief for your enjoyment! Folks, get ready for this. We got an exclusive for you right from our sources at *The Great America News Inc.*, and no, we ain't telling you the who or the how. Just take it from us, it's real. And remember, you heard it first from KSB12 NEWS RADIO, your Salt Lake County's favourite station!

. . .

So, what's the story? Well, get ready for this. It would appear that our dear president, Jerry King, has a double in Africa, and by a double, I mean a doppelgänger that goes by the identical name of POTUS. Yeah, you heard right, folks! We have an African POTUS, and believe it or not, this guy actually goes by the first name of POTUS. How crazy is that I ask you? Imagine being called POTUS Jackson or POTUS Smith or in this young fella's case, POTUS Mugabe or POTUS Mandela or whatever. Real crazy shit, right?

The story doesn't end there, though. The African POTUS who was recently in touch with *The Great America News Inc.* station, claims to be hanging out with our president in his little African village. This is the same president who is currently in a coma here in the USA. Even more incredible, this fella says he has a message from the president for the Chief of Staff, Pete Daniels, as well as the president's sister, Dr. Delores King, who was given the secret message, "Remember Belly-Berry".

Now, that's a puzzle for y'all to crack. Anyone heard of Belly-Berry? Perhaps a special kind of berries grown in some secret vineyard in Utah? Maybe it's even somebody's name? Come on, people! Someone out there must know what, who, or where Belly-Berry is. All our attempts to contact Dr. Delores King have so far proved unsuccessful, but trust me, we'll keep trying. So, phone in if you got the answer to the riddle. Our lines are open all day eagerly awaiting your call.

But still on this incredible story, we gather that our guy from Africa also gave six numbers supposed to be the president's secret code to activate the nuclear button. Yes, you heard right. The nuclear button activation code! Now, we ain't sure yet if it's the real deal, mind you. But we gotta remember that many parts of Africa, take Nigeria for instance, have a reputation for scams and hacking, a bit like the

Russians and the Chinese. So, anything's possible, and this guy may have just cracked the most secret of secret codes in the universe.

Did I hear you ask if this means President King is out of his coma? I mean, is he running around in some remote African village giving messages and selling national security codes to our enemies? If that's the case, then surely, he's gotta be awake, fit and healthy and doing brisk business with Air Force One, right? The answer is an emphatic no! As far as we know, the president is still on day 9 of his coma and has neither recovered consciousness nor left his hospital room for the White House or Africa. And it's still expected that his life support machine could be switched off any day now according to our sources. So, your guess is as good as mine on how the African POTUS managed to communicate with President King.

But get this, folks; it would appear that the phenomenon of the African POTUS is catching on like wildfire. Now, a well-known USA psychic known as Madam Lula is claiming to have received messages from the president from beyond as well. Madam Lula gave an interview with KTX-TV in Texas claiming to have been in astral communication with President King who she claims is trapped in a cold, dark realm inhabited by a horde of pinching goblins. The psychic Madam says the president's been pinched black and blue by these vengeful goblins who are angry with him for refusing to release his gold to them. Madam Lula claims President King has asked her to help him escape his torture by getting the First Lady, Portia King, to declare his gold reserves to the IRS so the goblins can receive their ransom in gold, which it would appear is their preferred currency. How's that, eh? I'm sure we could all do with a bit of gold too, ha!

The psychic claims that the president will be released by the goblins and wake up from his supernatural coma once FLOTUS complies with the instructions. So now y'all know what's really keeping our president holed up in the hospital. Needless to say, the Republicans are calling this another orchestrated and sick political stunt by the Dems, while the Democrats accuse them of desperation and disseminating false information to manipulate the elections, especially now that President King is seemingly out of the picture. No one's sure yet which party Madam Lula will be voting for. What a racket, eh? Well, your guess is as good as mine whether the president has a cache of buried gold or not or whether the First Lady will reveal the whereabouts of the said treasure, which I'm sure the IRS will be very interested in acquiring.

Nobody knows whether the African POTUS is really in communication with our president or not. But, hey! That's not for us to figure out, right? We'll leave all that craziness to the clever folks at the FBI while we continue to send our well-wishes for a speedy recovery to President King and his family.

As I await your calls about the secret message, "Remember Belly-Berry," what better way to show our solidarity with our ailing president than with a bit of great country music from our very own beautiful Dolly. So, come on folks, let's stand by our man, the great President of the United States, the real and only POTUS, President Jerry King!

∿

POTUS reached for the remote control first thing after waking up in case something had been reported about his long call with the guy from *The Great America News Inc.* last night. It hadn't been easy getting through on the international call with Frankie's mobile until the president instructed him to ask for someone called Don and to tell Don, "The Donkeys are ready to fly." POTUS was starting to discover that President King liked cryptic riddles, as if he were working on some WW2 Morse code.

The riddles obviously worked for the president because within minutes the guy, Don, was on the phone, and POTUS immediately set the mobile on speakerphone as instructed by President King. Soon, he was telling Don his story in its minutest detail, with the president hulked impatiently over him. But it wasn't long before POTUS was asking the president to give him room, his teeth chattering and his fingers frozen by the iciness that permanently trailed the spectre. It was at times like this that he remembered he was dealing with a supernatural entity and experienced a return of unease.

The Great America News Inc. anchor, Don, kept asking him how he knew about the code, "The Donkeys are ready to fly." Over and over, POTUS repeated that the president was by his side and had given him the information.

"If what you say is true, then ask the president where we were when we came up with that phrase… oh, and who else was with us at the time," Don said, his voice hard. POTUS could imagine him viciously breaking several pencils in half as he spoke, half-smoked cigarette dangling by the side of his lips.

"Chubby-Chuck was with us at the back game room of Old Martha's, you moron. And hey, just so you know, I plan on collecting my gold pen from you once I'm back, in case you think I've forgotten," President King shouted into the mobile phone, even though nobody could hear him except POTUS.

By the time POTUS repeated the president's words verbatim, Don was repeating, "Oh my God! Oh my God!" over and over till POTUS cut in and asked him if he was now ready to air the news.

Don was more than ready.

Just as the clock struck midnight on the ninth day of the president's coma, *The Great America News Inc.* broke the highly redacted bulletin of the African POTUS under their "weird and funny" news section. The coverage also included a different story about a Native-American shaman in the Amazon jungles doing some secret rituals to figure out the ailing president's chances of recovery, as well as Madam Lula's goblin messages. The female presenter ended the segment by repeating the phrase, "Remember Belly-Berry" with a voice that was one-part humour, two-part snigger, and three-part unease.

Just as POTUS switched on the telly to check the news, his door opened, and Fat-arse Nurse waddled in with her sadistic silver tray, ready to deliver more early morning torture. POTUS slapped away her hand as she made to wash his groin in the detested bed wash routine.

"I can do it myself," he snarled, holding her furious gaze—*Stupid fat witch! What else can you do except stick another needle in me?*

Which was exactly what she did, jabbing his arse so hard he actually screamed.

"Ha! Cry-cry baby," she mocked, waddling out of his room with a smirk. Hearing the reviled teasing rhyme from his school days galled him like nothing else did.

"Fuck you!" He shouted at her retreating back—*Yes!* It felt really good to use President King's cool cuss words. That should show her and her idiot Christian righteousness...

"Fucky you!" She shrieked right back at him before slamming the door with a loud hiss—*Oh, the balloon witch! I'd happily explode her fat arse with a dynamite stick!* He reached down to rub the tender spot on his backside.

When he was done cursing, he rolled over to face the Xiaomi flatscreen mounted on the wall and scrolled to *The Great America News Inc*. But there was nothing in the news, just some documentary about trans babies and the rise of parents seeking transitioning for their female babies in communities that value male children over females. *CNL Anderson Corp* didn't yield any results either when he switched to their channel—*Surely, all the international news outlets syndicate their coverage, so something as big as his story must be on every news channel.*

Twenty boring minutes later, POTUS realised with brooding irritation that he wasn't going to get anything from the news stations or get famous either—*Useless idiots!* What if all his efforts were in vain and the president never returned to his physical body again? Worse, what if he couldn't recall his promises or feigned convenient amnesia if he miraculously returned to his body? The thoughts didn't sit well with POTUS, and he hurriedly pushed them away—*Come on, POTUS! Focus on the outcome as a done deal. The president will never let you down. He's too kind and honest for that. Remember that Mama* trusted him. Just see how he fought your battle with Kunle... he even called you his mini-me and shared his golf-success tips with you, not forgetting trusting you with the secret about the aliens…

A wide smile spread across POTUS' face. He decided he liked President King—*A lot lot.* The man was funny and chill, no stupid airs or pomp. Just a regular top dude. Moreover, any man that could love his family the way the president did, or do what he did with Kunle, must be a good man at heart. Not forgetting how he dealt ruthlessly with the paedophiles in America—*Nay! President King is a top, top guy. In fact, the best of the best of the bestest!*

12

UNEXPECTED VISITORS

The door to POTUS' hospital room opened, and five people barged inside. And barged was the word—literally; just the way men in power strode into rooms, taking up every space as if they were working hand-in-hand with God when He created the universe. One of the men was dressed in military uniform and looked uncannily like the American actor, Ben Stiller. The only difference was he was draped in more medals than even a Russian general, and just like Ben Stiller, he was white.

POTUS stared goggle-eyed at his unexpected visitors—Who on earth are these people? His eyes zeroed in on the singular female member of the group. Like the military guy, she was also white and slightly older. She was immaculately dressed in an expensive grey trouser suit that matched her glossy grey coiffure. She had a dignified yet authoritative air that reminded POTUS a bit of Doctor Okoye, albeit in a white female body. The lady stared intently at POTUS, her steely green eyes niggling a memory in his mind that refused to linger or be caught. POTUS held her gaze till the woman looked away.

A warm glow of satisfaction spread across his body—*Yes! POTUS has never backed away from a gaze fight!* He's ready any day to stare down the next man, woman, or even Jesus Himself. Staring down people was power, and POTUS had mastered that art.

The third member of the group was also a white guy. He was blond and slender, with a neat, clean cut appearance. His tie was a bright pink colour that matched his glowing skin. POTUS reckoned he was the youngest of the group, what with his colourful fashion and wrinkle-free face. Of the five visitors crowded inside his hospital room, he liked the young guy the most. There was something about him that reminded POTUS of Frankie, a harmless and good energy that radiated from his bright blue eyes. He smiled nervously at POTUS when their eyes briefly met, and POTUS returned his smile.

The remaining two guys were both black, although POTUS was sure only one of them was Nigerian. There was something about one of the black men that told POTUS he was a foreigner, an African-American most likely—Moreover, who's ever seen a black guy with such striking green eyes unless they're foreigners? The second black guy was dressed in a dark uniform which had "Nigerian Police" emblazoned atop the jacket pocket. He was a huge man with a scarified face and bloodshot eyes. POTUS quickly averted his gaze from the policeman's brutal face. The four foreigners were now gathered in front of the huge sculpture of Black Jesus on the wall, as if drawn to it by an invisible magnet. They stared at the crucifix, pulling their ears, tapping their lips, and scratching their chins in bafflement. With weird synchronicity, they cocked their heads to the right and then to the left —What is it with everyone and this Black Jesus crucifix?

"Are you POTUS Olupitan?" the Nigerian policeman asked, his voice loud and raspy.

POTUS nodded, slowly, reluctantly—*God! What have I done now?* What trouble has he got himself into now? Has Kunle accused him of killing Mama? But why should the white people be here with the Nigerian police when it wasn't their business anyway?

"My name is Inspector Kayode, the Inspector General of Police," the big man announced, turning his scarified face to his companions. "These men are from the American embassy, and they want to have a private chat with you—"

"And lady, if you please," the posh white woman inserted in a quiet, cultured voice that was surprisingly deep. The policeman gave her a stunned look. It was clear he was unused to being challenged or interrupted, especially by a woman. He opened his mouth to speak but thought better of it. With a scowl, he nodded curtly at the woman and returned his attention to POTUS.

"As I said, these men and woman are from the American embassy. It's my duty to ensure that you're not being coerced into doing anything you don't want to do. I will call your father over since you are a minor, or if you wish, I'll be happy to stay here with you instead," the man's eager eyes told POTUS that he was desperate to stay. "Are you willing to talk with them?"

POTUS' eyes widened with excitement—*OMG! No way!* His heart soared. He now knew why the lady with the steely green eyes and expensive trouser suit seemed familiar—He'll bet his Yeezy Crush that she's none other than Dr. Delores King, President King's sister! *Wow!* Which meant the young dude with the pink tie must be Pansy-Pete. He was ready to bet a Yeezy on that too. Goosebumps layered his skin —*This is real! I've really done it! Me, POTUS Olupitan, has brought the most powerful people in the United States right into my hospital room!* He wanted to pinch himself, and before he could stop them, his fingers obliged him.

"Ouch!" He moaned softly, rubbing his thigh and hoping nobody heard. He looked up and caught Pansy-Pete observing him with amused eyes. POTUS gave a wry smile and an invisible shrug. Looking at the guy, he now knew why President King dubbed him with that nickname. On first glance, one could easily mistake Pansy-Pete for a gay man, but there was something about his carriage, something in his quiet gaze that told POTUS the guy was as straight as a ruler. After all, he had lived with two gay parents all his life. He should be able to recognise a gay man with his eyes shut. He reckoned Pansy-Pete was just a guy that loved his unconventional fashion and impeccable grooming. Moreover, knowing the president's aversion to homosexuals, POTUS thought it was unlikely he would have hired one as his Chief of Staff.

"My boy, did you hear me?" The policeman's impatient voice interrupted his thoughts. "Do you want to talk to these people or not?"

"Y-yes, thank you, sir. I'm fine," POTUS stammered. "I'll talk with them alone,"

"Are you sure?" The police chief wasn't ready to give up his chance to ferret out more information.

"Yes, thanks," POTUS nodded again. He saw a flicker of approval in the eyes of Ben Stiller's clone—He still didn't know who the guy was. After lingering for several seconds, the police chief shrugged in resignation, nodded brusquely at the men, shaded the lady, and walked out of the room with mega attitude.

Suddenly, POTUS found himself alone with the four foreigners.

POTUS' heart was racing with rocket speed. Hot sweat turned his palms clammy. His eyes searched out the sole black man in the group, the green-eyed Terrence Howard look-alike, the only one amongst the strangers that shared his skin colour, if not his nationality. The man's face remained remote, his eyes cold and hard—*Thanks for nothing, bruv.*

"Do you know who we are?" Ben Stiller's clone asked. His piercing blue eyes glinted with manic zeal, as if he were rearing to do a thousand push-ups before tackling an obstacle course in the Amazon forest. On his starched uniform, multiple military medals gleamed wickedly under the fluorescent bulb, and his teeth sparkled with cosmetic perfection.

"I think so," POTUS nodded towards the sole lady in the room. "She's Dr. Delores King and…"

He stopped. The president had just materialised. His face glowed ecstatically as he glided towards his sister, shouting her name in unrestrained joy.

"Dels! Dels babes! You made it here! Holy righteous shit! I can't believe my eyes!" He flung his arms excitedly around Dr. Delores, babbling words nobody apart from POTUS heard. Everyone, especially Dr. Delores, shivered involuntarily before looking at each other with baffled frowns. Terrence Howard's look-alike's cold, green eyes zeroed in on POTUS, suspicion written all over his chiselled, bronze face.

POTUS ignored him and instead pointed to the young guy in the pink tie. "I think he's Pansy-Pete and—"

"What? What did you just call me?" Pansy-Pete was almost apoplectic, yet POTUS saw the incredulity in Dr. Delores's eyes.

"It's not me. It's him, President King," POTUS pointed somewhere towards the window, where the president now hovered. Four pairs of startled eyes followed his finger. "That's what he calls you... what?" he cocked his ears. "Oh, he says that was only at the beginning when he wrongly thought you were gay. He only told me your nickname out of anger when he thought you'd betrayed him and joined forces with little poo-face and had him shrunk at some Chinese lab before transporting him to this fly-dump... hey! Your Excellency, I've told you to stop the insults or you're on your own. I mean it!"

He saw the blood drain from Pansy-Pete's face as he turned his stunned eyes to the medal-laden Ben Stiller clone.

"Oh my God! It's true! It's really the president! No one knows that he calls the Chinese president 'little poo-face' except me. No one else, I tell you!" Pansy-Pete was almost whispering.

"I know," Dr. Delores' voice was hoarse, her face ashen. "I know. He uses the same name when we talk. I also know he calls you Pansy-Pete when he's mad at you for whatever reason," she spoke with an unexpected English accent at odds with her very American Michelle Pfeiffer features. When she turned to POTUS, her eyes were wet with tears, her face haggard. "Tell me quick. Is my brother here in the room with us right now? Are you telling me you can actually see Jerry and speak with him?"

POTUS nodded. "He says you gotta put away your stethoscope and listen to his lips, not his heart."

"Oh, sweet Jesus! It's Jerry! It's truly Jerry! He's here!" Dr. Delores looked ready to faint. "Jerry, can you hear me? Speak to me, little brother. Oh, dear God! I can't believe this." She slumped into one of the chairs, quickly followed by Pansy-Pete, who POTUS noticed managed to cross his legs elegantly despite his shock. Only the Ben Stiller and Terrence Howard doubles remained standing. The president glided over to his sister, whispering soft words of comfort into her deaf ears as she shivered incessantly, icy smoke fogging her breath.

"Everyone, calm down," Terrence Howard's clone finally spoke, his voice gravelly, hard as steel. Raw power oozed from his voice, the calm authority of the very powerful. He walked over to POTUS and leaned over him, radiating icy menace. POTUS recoiled instinctively—*Uh-uh. I'm not scared of this big bully, not one bit.* Just wait till he got out of this bed and see who's tougher. His eyes flashed hostility back at the African-American.

"My name is Chief Daniel Jackson, and I'm the Director of the FBI. You've already correctly identified both Dr. King and Mr. Pete Daniels. The gentleman in uniform is the Secretary of Defence, General Mike O'Neill. So now you know everyone. Are we whom you were expecting when you pulled your little stunt and sent your silly message to *The Great America News Inc.*?" His voice was hard, his eyes icy jade.

POTUS' blood curdled in his veins—*Sweet Mary and the apostles! The FBI! I've got the head of the FBI in my hospital room! God! I'm finished unless the president can pull something!* He turned desperate eyes at the president, who was busy whispering frantically into his sister's ear. Dr. Delores kept shivering and wringing her hands, her teeth chattering softly.

"She can't hear you, Your Excellency!" POTUS screamed at the president, angry at him for abandoning him to the human wolves. All eyes returned to him, ashy faces staring at him as if he held the miracle of creation in his hands. "They're all here as you wanted, see? What do you want me to tell them?"

"Ask him if he knows Portia is planning to switch off his life support machine next week," Dr. Delores said.

"Ask him if he knows that Richard Patterson is withholding the donation he pledged, and that the vice president has yet to return the gold case to the White House," Pansy-Pete cut in.

"You'll ask him nothing because there's nobody here to ask anything," the FBI chief's voice thundered, bringing instant silence into the room. "From here on, no one says anything to this punk. First, we're gonna scan this room for bugs to ensure he ain't hiding any secret gadgets. Then, we're gonna figure out how he managed to hack into the president's private files to steal his code. Now—"

"But Chief Jackson, how can you doubt that Jerry is here?" Dr. Delores asked, her voice reproachful. "We all heard what the kid said. I'm telling you, even without coming here, I already knew it was my brother because no one else knows about Belly-Berry, just Jerry and I and—"

"Yeah! I meant to ask. What the hell's Belly-Berry?" General O'Neill cut in, his piercing, blue eyes still glinting maniacally. "All the country's going crazy trying to solve the puzzle. Hell! Even the gambling shops are taking bets on it. Any chance you might clue me in on the secret?"

Dr. Delores maintained a dignified silence, her eyes icy. General O'Neill shrugged and turned his attention to POTUS. "Chief Jackson's correct. I want you to tell me how you got the president's secret code. Who are you working with, and what do you hope to achieve by bringing us all here? Speak up, kid."

"I'm trying to save President King's life, that's what," POTUS yelled, anger darkening his eyes into a deep brown colour. "I'm sick of you guys accusing me when all I'm doing is trying to stop him from getting killed by the CIA snake and Flake-Frank and Poison-Portia… his words, not mine,"

"What?" everybody chorused. Dr. Delores jumped from her chair while the FBI Chief and General O'Neill crowded close to his bed, their eyes goggled. Only Pansy-Pete remained seated, manically crossing and uncrossing his legs over and over.

"Repeat what you just said, young man," Chief Jackson ordered, his face thunderous, green eyes flashing danger. POTUS turned desperately to the president.

"President King! Your Excellency!" he yelled. The president looked dazed, and his face wore an uncharacteristic vulnerable look. "Listen, you've got to do something now. Like, right now? Just do the stuff you did with Frankie, otherwise they won't believe me."

The president seemed like he was on some kind of sedative, his movements slow, his face haunted. It was as if seeing his sister and all his people in the flesh brought home to him the direness of his situation. The man looked ready to vanish and POTUS felt panic building —He mustn't vanish before they see him! *Oh, please God, keep him solid for as long as it takes to fix this mess, or I might as well kiss my American dream goodbye, not to mention the possible jail time for me!* "Come on, Your Excellency. You can do this. Just do something now or everything is finished for us."

"Do I look like your friggin' performing monkey, you little punk?" The president snarled, recovering himself.

"Who gives a Kobo about your performing monkey?" POTUS yelled back, startling everyone in the room, including Chief Jackson, who followed the direction of his gaze with a suspicious squint. "Listen, Your Excellency, if you don't do something quick to convince these guys that I'm not faking it, then don't blame me if they leave without saving you," he hissed and scowled at the president—Imagine shouting at me like that! President or no president, nobody disrespects POTUS, especially not an Oyinbo ghost in my own motherland, even if he's an important American ghost and not some petty ghost from a poor country!

He heard the loud gasp in the room and saw everyone staring at him in disbelief. Chief Jackson muttered a low oath and began circling the room, holding out some shiny black gadget. The device beeped loudly with metronomic regularity till it came near the bedside and released several frantic beeps. Chief Jackson's eyes glowed triumphantly as he glared at POTUS as if to say, "Gotcha, punk!" As the beeper hovered over the TV remote control, it intensified its beeps. The FBI chief quickly proceeded to dismantle the device with vicious zeal till he was satisfied it was clean. POTUS read the disappointment in his eyes as he reluctantly returned the scanning gadget to his open briefcase.

As Chief Jackson straightened up, the remote control began to lift by itself from the bedside table in a silent and slow motion that nearly creeped the piss out of POTUS. As everyone stared in stunned horror, it made a short journey in the air and smashed hard into the back of the FBI chief's head.

"WTF?" The Director turned a pair of raging eyes at POTUS, his hand rubbing his tender skull.

"He didn't do it, Jackson," General O'Neill rushed in, blue eyes stunned. He stared at POTUS as if he were the real water demon himself.

"The thing lifted by itself. We all saw it," Pansy-Pete added, his face drained of all colour.

"It's Jerry. I told you, Jerry's here," Dr. Delores trilled, her voice happier than POTUS had heard since they arrived. She was the only one that seemed pleased.

"I don't give a damn what anyone thinks," Chief Jackson lost his cool, striding towards POTUS' bed with the familiar menace, his hand still pressed against the growing bump in his head. "Let me cut to the chase. We're done with your stupid games. You're going to tell me who you're working for, or I'm having you arrested and extradited to the United States for international espionage and more federal charges than you can dig yourself out of in your stupid lifetime. Are we clear?"

POTUS was shaking. President King was shaking too, a quake of unbridled rage. This time, the black briefcase belonging to Chief Jackson lifted by itself and smashed down on the floor with such force that its locks broke, spilling the contents all over the worn carpet. Even as everyone gasped in stunned disbelief, Chief Jackson's mobile phone lifted out of his pocket by itself and landed next to his feet in a silent thump, quickly followed by General O'Neill's mobile. The window curtains started to flap crazily, whirling furiously as if caught in the eye of a hurricane. Everyone scrambled away in panic from POTUS' bedside.

All, except the FBI chief.

"It's a trick!" he shouted. "Calm down. The kid's telekinetic. That's how he's been able to do everything—"

Chief Jackson shut up abruptly, his eyes widening in shock. POTUS watched in glee as president King blew so hard in the guy's face that his breath froze in his nostrils. His necktie was yanked so hard the man started choking. His hands clawed and pulled frantically at his necktie as he staggered helplessly around the room. He tried to punch his attacker, but his fists went through the president's porous body. Everyone rushed to his aid, shouting and stumbling around as helplessly as the asphyxiating FBI chief.

"Your Excellency, stop! You'll kill him," POTUS finally yelled at the furious president. "If anything happens to him, then who's going to trap Flake-Frank and the rest? You'll die even before they get back to the States to save you."

President King let go of the necktie with a cuss, and the chief slumped into the chair vacated by Dr. Delores, wheezing loudly. His eyes were stunned, and his face wore an ashen colour. POTUS never knew a black guy could turn grey.

"Get him some water, quick," Dr. Delores said to Pansy-Pete, who dashed over to POTUS' bedside table and grabbed a bottle of still water. In seconds, the director was taking small sips, his eyes bloodshot, his tall body trembling like violin strings. When next their eyes met, POTUS knew all doubt had vanished from his mind.

POTUS heaved a deep sigh of relief. With the hardest resistance now gone, it was easy to pitch the president's wishes.

13

TREACHERY EXPOSED

For almost two hours, POTUS narrated his life story to his rapt audience, now crowded around his bedside. Speaking in a low, hoarse voice, he started from when he first began hearing the voices inside his head in his childhood years, to his recent accident. The president stayed close to his sister, as if afraid she might vanish if he strayed from her side.

"Oh, sweet Jesus!" Dr. Delores looked ready to faint when POTUS fell silent. All colour drained from her face. Rage twisted her features, turning her green eyes almost obsidian. "I can't believe this! This is just too horrible to stomach. I'll kill that Portia bitch! Just wait till we get home."

"Atta girl!" President King cheered, leaning low to hug his sister. Dr. Delores shivered violently and wrapped her arms around herself. "Tell her to make sure the dumb broad gets zilch, absolutely nothing from my estate if I don't make it back."

POTUS complied. "I can also get you my Mind Zoome keys so you have the recording of everything I heard if you like," he added, feeling rewarded by the warm gratitude in Dr. Delores's eyes. Mind Zoome recordings had long been accepted as legitimate evidence in legal proceedings.

Just then, the president glided close and began whispering into POTUS' ear, even though they both knew no one could hear them. POTUS itched to push him away. His ear was frozen enough to drop off.

"Dr. King, the president says you should go to his attorney, James Michigan, and ask for a copy of his latest will. He says to tell James he sent you and that 'The Eagle has Landed' … Come on, Your Excellency! Not another one of your riddle codes again," he glared at the ghost before turning back to the astounded group. "He says his will gives you sole power of attorney and with it, you should go to his bank, the one at Main Street and ask for his vault. The number… what? Oh, okay. He says to whisper the security number to you alone."

Dr. Delores rushed up close and pressed her ear close to POTUS' lips as he whispered the number. When she straightened, her eyes were wet, filled with awe.

"You wonderful, beautiful boy!" She whispered hoarsely, shaking her head and staring at POTUS as if he were Satan and Jesus morphed into one human wonder. She took his hand and shook it warmly, patting him on his shoulder over and over. "Jerry, you son of a gun! I should've guessed you would use that number! Belly-Berry to you too, you rogue," her voice trembled with laughter despite the tears welling in her eyes.

Everyone stared at the doctor as she returned to her chair once again. The physician now looked pensive and somewhat glum, and POTUS wondered if he'd done something wrong or had somehow upset her—*Oh, well. I'm only a mouthpiece. Don't shoot the messenger, Ma'am.* He shrugged inwardly. He was starting to get tired anyway and needed this whole business over and done with—like ASAP. The president continued to whisper instructions to him, which he diligently repeated.

"Dr. King, the president says you'll find all the evidence you need against both the Vice President and FLOTUS inside the vault. And Chief Jackson, the president says you should be able to get a confession from the snakes once Dr. King hands everything over to you. He says that with the power of attorney, Dr. King can halt the pulling of the life support machine until he figures a way to return to his body,"

POTUS returned his gaze to Dr. King. "He says you're not to worry and to remember that he's the original wheeler-dealer and great escape artist and will be back before you know it."

POTUS stopped. Tears were trailing down Dr. King and Pansy-Pete's faces. Even the manic-looking Defence Secretary was fighting back his emotions, while Chief Jackson pretended to be busy sorting out his damaged briefcase. But POTUS could see his eyes glistening with tears like the rest—*Wow! This president is truly loved by his people!* His admiration for the American president skyrocketed.

"Tell Jerry we'll do everything he's asked and more. Damn it, much more," Dr. Delores's voice was as icy as her eyes. "Tell him we'll ensure nothing, no harm whatsoever, comes to a single hair on his body. Tell him all those involved in this dastardly plot will be indicted and punished," a hard nerve ticked in her throat as she strove to suppress her rage. POTUS was glad he wasn't on the receiving end of it.

"I'd like to have those Mind Zoome recordings you mentioned, if you don't mind," Chief Jackson said. And for the first time ever, he smiled at POTUS, his piercing green eyes glinting with warmth. His approval made POTUS feel as if he'd won a ticket to St. Peter's pearly gate.

"It's at my dad's house, but I can get my friend, Frankie, to bring it over," he offered. A light bulb flashed in his mind. "Your Excellency, what about our deal? Will you tell them to start getting it ready?"

"What deal?" General O'Neill asked, his eyes squinting in suspicion. "And by the way, it's Mr. President, not Your Excellency. We call him Mr. President."

POTUS wasn't paying him any attention anymore. His head was cocked as he listened to the president speak before turning back to Pansy-Pete. "The president says you should take care of it. He wants you to contact Callahan at Jefferson College about two scholarships for my friend and I and to find two houses near the college for us. He says you should also sort out our Green Cards while you're at it. He says Dr. King should be able to write us a check of a million dollars each and help us open a bank account," POTUS turned to the doctor. "Ma'am, he says to tell you he'll square with you when he comes back, though he says you never repaid him for the loan to invest in the A-shares that went burst."

Dr. Delores gasped. She stared at POTUS in wide-eyed disbelief, shaking her head over and over. Pansy-Pete kept straightening his already straight pink tie, nodding his head again and again like a stunned grey lizard that's stumbled from a tree while trying to mount a bigger, red female lizard. POTUS felt a twinge of righteous smugness as he continued to relay the president's instructions—That'll teach them all for doubting me in the first place!

"General O'Neill, sir. The president says to tell you he's sorry he had to give me the secret code, but that was the only way to bring you guys down here," POTUS had no idea why he added the 'sir' to the general's name. It wasn't even something he'd done with the president himself. But with the general, it just seemed right, a well-earned and well-deserved title. The respect wasn't lost on the general who gave him a warm smile.

"The president says he's sure you've scraped the code already and says to thank you all for your faithful service to him. He says that you guys are the only people he trusts in the White House… What? Oh, Chief Jackson, he says to tell you he knows you play things by the book and your word is your bond. So, he's grateful to you for making this trip and says he's looking forward to strengthening his relationship with you. Oh, he says to also tell you he apologises for the little trick earlier on, just that you were acting like a dickhead robot and he needed to knock some sense into y'all—his words, not mine."

The FBI chief straightened even more, if it were possible. He turned and saluted at the empty space by the door.

"Mr. President, sir! It's my honour to serve you, sir. I promise I'll do everything in my power to protect your life and bring those responsible to justice."

POTUS didn't want to tell the guy that the president was now standing near his sister again and was no longer by the door.

"Dr. Delores, the president says he has a message for you. He says, 'Tell Dels I love her dearly, and no, I ain't turning into a sissy. I just wanna say it before it's too late, just in case.' What? Oh, okay. He says to also tell you to tell Lisa that he loves her too and will see you all soon, if all goes well."

Dr. Delores was sobbing softly, tears trailing down her cheeks unchecked. POTUS looked away, embarrassed.

"Mr. Daniels, the president says he hopes you're not mad because he called you Pansy-Pete and to tell you he can't wait to hear you call him 'POTUS-Sir' once again, and he's glad you didn't call me POTUS, because he's sick of me appropriating his name and… Hey! I didn't appropriate anything, and if that's the thanks I get for helping you, then you can take your name and everything else and just stuff it, dude. I'm totally done."

"Calm down, kid," Dr. Delores laughed, getting up and patting his shoulder kindly. "I'm sure he didn't mean it that way. Jerry always did have a nasty sense of humour. Hey, Jerry, if you can hear me, then behave yourself, alright? This kid has done you more service than the entire Republican Party put together," she turned to the others. "Are we done here now? I'm eager to get back before anything else goes wrong."

"Yes, we're done. Do you mind giving me your friend, Frankie? Frankie, right. Let's have his number and we'll drive over and pick him up so he can collect your Mind Zoome key," Chief Jackson walked over to POTUS and extended his hand in a handshake. "Thank you, young man. You've just single-handedly saved not just the President of the United States, but the fate of the entire world. I personally look forward to welcoming you and your friend when you eventually land on American soil."

"Ditto," General O'Neill said, his manic blue eyes smiling warmly at POTUS. "You're a credit to your parents, young man. You should be proud of yourself. We need more young people like you in the military, and should you ever think of enlisting once you settle in the States, just let me know and we'll set you up nice and sweet."

"Thank you, sir," POTUS said, resisting the urge to do a hand salute. "Thanks a lot," his voice cracked.

"No, *thank you*," Dr. Delores stressed, pumping his hand over and over. "I want you to know you have a new family in the King clan for life, alright?"

Again, POTUS nodded and cleared his throat noisily—*Got to play it cool, dude. Be cool now, alright? Can't let them know you're fazed.*

Pansy-Pete gave him a gentle smile. "I'll get on right away with the president's instructions and make sure everything is ready and waiting for you and your friend when you arrive."

"Needless to say, nothing that happened here today leaves this room." Chief Jackson was all business again. "I know the Inspector General of Police will be back to interview you, and I want you to just tell him that we came to ensure you didn't hack into the defence computers. We'll ensure we mention that we found nothing on you," Chief Jackson winked at him. His wink reminded him of the president's wink, just not as wickedly cool. POTUS decided he really liked the FBI guy after all. He was cool in his own way with that special Obama-swagger in his walk that only black men could slay with authenticity. In fact, he planned on watching all reruns of Terrence Howard's films once he left the hospital.

"Do you have any idea when we might expect Jerry back?" Dr. Delores looked apologetically at POTUS as if she might be offending with the question. POTUS gave a little smile and turned towards the president, but he had gone, vanished as if he'd never been there.

"I'm sorry, but he's gone," he said to Dr. Delores, seeing her face fall. "But don't worry, he does that all the time. You know, appears and then vanishes. I know he'll be back again, and I'll ask him and get back to you with any other messages he has for you if you let me know where to call you,"

"Sure, here's my number—"

"Don't worry, POTUS. We know where to find you, and we'll be in touch very soon," Chief Jackson cut in before Dr. Delores could give him the number. He exchanged a significant look with the elegant doctor, causing her to flush.

POTUS was impressed. He was thinking, perhaps when he gets to America, he might train as an FBI agent instead of the military. The quiet power the FBI Chief exuded was totally intoxicating to him. By the time his visitors left, he was so hungry that he was ready to devour the entire menu at *The Oprah Hotel* and *The Radisson Blu* combined—*OMG! I can't believe what's just happened! America is real! Everything's been sorted. My life is about to change in an incredible, mega wicked, cool and crazy way!*

From nowhere, the devil snuck a horrible thought into his head, as ever determined to throw sands of misery in his Jollof rice—If only Mama were alive to see all this! If only she had waited just a couple more days and everything would've been alright when we start our new life in America. God! If only I hadn't gotten on that stupid, stupid motorbike…

The tears returned again, this time with a vengeance. He cried till the headache came, till his eyes went dry and gritty, till his throat hurt, and the darkness returned to drag him down into welcome oblivion.

14

RATTLESNAKE

A couple of days following the visit by the American delegation, the esteemed Doctor Okoye confirmed that POTUS was fit enough to face the outside world and hobble around safely on his double crutches. Even without the doctor giving him the green light, POTUS had already made up his mind not to spend another minute under the same roof with his nemesis, Fat-arse Nurse, and her crew of obese minions. He had refused her injection last night, resulting in a battle of wills he'd won hands down, followed by a battle of insults, which she'd won without contest. By the time she bristled out of his room with her giggling goons, he'd learnt that he was a "scandalous scally-wag, a bombastic amoeba, a jingoistic nincompoop, a rascally-some-thing, and a pompositacious ignoramus."

Frankie walked into POTUS' room later that morning nursing his habitual lollipop at the corner of his lips. His plump face wore an anxious frown, as if he expected to be attacked by the president's half-ghost any second. He looked around nervously, loitering by the door.

"Einstein, hey!" POTUS called out, waving him closer and high-fiving him with his good hand.

"Motormouth, how you doing?"

"Cool. All ready to leave this stupid joint."

"Mum's got a room all prettied in pink for you. She's hung these girly pink curtains with matching beddings and table lamps. Olè! It looks just like Cinderella and Barbie's bedrooms combined, no jiving," Frankie crossed his heart, his eyes glinting mischievously behind his glasses. "I think you'll love it. She says to tell you to make yourself at home for as long as you want."

"Idiot," POTUS paused. "Listen, thanks, okay? I really appreciate it. And hopefully, it won't be for long. By the way, did you tell her about our scholarship?"

"No, not yet," Frankie shrugged. "I thought it's best to wait, you know, and see how things go."

"Basically, you don't believe it'll work out despite everything you saw?" POTUS shook his head. "I really give up on you sometimes, Einstein. By the way, I forgot to ask you about your visit to my house with the Americans. Did you have any problems with my dad when you got to our house that day?"

Frankie looked uncomfortable, looking away and fiddling with his mobile phone.

"Einstein, what?" POTUS' heart started racing. Kunle always created that tension in him even when he wasn't present.

"I guess you'll find out eventually," Frankie shrugged, playing with his lollipop with that peculiar squeamish motion that told POTUS he was uncomfortable. "Your dad was attacked by your security man's sons and—"

"What? Taiwo and Kehinde? They attacked my dad?" POTUS felt rage that took him by surprise by its very existence and intensity—*The useless pedestrians! I'm going to kill those two stinking maggots!*

"How's my dad? Did he tell you what happened?" He couldn't believe how angry he was with the attack on Kunle. Sure, he couldn't stand the dude, but that didn't give anyone else, especially those twin idiot sons of their security man, the right to attack him. Kunle was his own devil and nobody else's.

"It seems they jumped your old man outside the compound because of all the stuff about your mum," Frankie executed his familiar shrug, averting POTUS' gaze. "One of them had a knife, but apparently, they didn't know your dad was a karate black belt and he—"

"What? Did you say my dad's a karate black belt?"

"Yeah, didn't you know?"

"Of course not, he never said," POTUS shook his head in wonder —*Holy righteous shit, as the president would say!* It was a good thing he never egged Kunle into a fight as he'd been wanting all these years. Dude would've killed him, easy as pie. Imagine him being a black belt and never letting on! "Is he alright? Do you know what's happened to the stupid twins? I could never stand those two yeye goats."

"He was stabbed in the arm before he managed to knock them both out. I hear they're still in the police cell awaiting bail. Motor-mouth, your dad doesn't look too good if you ask me. He actually asked me to tell you he's been trying to call your phone but not getting through. I told him it was stolen, and he said to tell you to come home once you're discharged and that I should drive you back to your house in my car. Motormouth, I think he really regrets everything. It'll be a pity if you two can't work things out, especially now."

"Don't blame me. He caused everything," POTUS scowled. "And anyway, he's the one that told me to pack my stuff and get out of his house when my mum died." Kunle's words still rankled—*I bet he's only inviting me back home because he's scared of the president's ghost. I'm not sure I trust him.* Still, he felt better hearing about his father's troubles. It had bothered him that Kunle hadn't come seeking him out immediately as President King had promised. Now, he felt hope flower in his heart—*Not that he'll make it easy for Kunle when he comes apologising and begging him to come home; just because the president's ghost had scared him into doing it. Huh!* He'll go home with Frankie today and then go back to their house tomorrow or maybe the next day… *We'll see…*

Frankie's mother fussed over POTUS in her typical boisterous manner till he was ready to weep in frustration. He couldn't count the number of times he had to say "No, thanks auntie" with desperate politeness to yet another bottle of Coke and fried snacks offered with insistent kind-ness. After he finally escaped her smothering attention, POTUS settled tensely inside his new bedroom, looking around with dazed numbness. Just as Frankie said, the room turned out to be a vile, pink nightmare. The smell of fresh paint was still strong, and he knew that his best friend's mother had gone to great lengths to accommodate him.

POTUS stretched out flat on his pink sheeted bed, creasing his face in distaste. Briefly, he wondered if there was a hidden message in the pink furnishing Frankie's mum had used for his guest bedroom; if perhaps she believed, like some of the ignorant nurses and now ex-friends, that his parents' homosexuality had rubbed off on him like an infectious virus, leaving him with a preference for girly pink colours. He'd always thought Frankie's mum was a bit dumb anyway and could never figure out how she could've given birth to a genius like Frankie —*Unless the poor sod wakes up one day, just as I did, to discover he's been adopted as well.*

With a deep sigh, he rearranged his plastered leg gingerly on the mattress. The effort brought a dizzy spin to his head. He shut his eyes and exhaled loudly. He hadn't realised how much he'd been dreading the meeting with Frankie's parents. He was glad he was going back to his own bedroom the next day, thanks to President King.

As he looked up at the bare magnolia ceiling of the room, the only thing not painted the garish pink, he found himself weirdly missing the Black Jesus crucifix on his hospital bedroom wall—At least, the crazy thing wasn't pink. There was just something powerfully weird about it that gripped his fascination despite himself. It was as if the sculptor had decided to offend the indoctrinated sensibilities of the traditionalist Christians and their unwavering belief in a white Jesus for the sheer bloody-mindedness of it. He was surprised Fat-arse Nurse hadn't set that blasphemous artwork on fire with her Pentecostal fanaticism.

Recalling the fat nurse and her prejudiced minions brought back the familiar depression. Searching for ulterior motives and meanings behind people's words, actions, and expressions had now become a new and unsettling habit for him. Paranoid suspicion had snuck insidiously into his DNA since his mother's death and the subsequent exposure of his parent's homosexuality. Even in the days when they all lived in the closet so to speak, he'd never bothered about the nuances in humanity that had now become his daily reality. The unspoken words, the eye-flicker, the snide smiles, the hisses, or worse, the subtle and unsubtle shifting away from him to avoid contact with his sinful and gay-contaminated body, were now daily challenges he navigated. He'd never even imagined such discrimination for the simple reason that the primary responsibility to remain closeted had rested with his parents, not him. He wasn't gay, so he had no business thinking about something that wasn't his burden, apart from keeping himself and his friends far away from its tainted vicinity.

Until now.

Once again, his mind returned to the ghastly image of his mother's gruesome death—*Oluwa!* Will he ever be free of that nightmare? And this soul-crushing guilt! When will he ever wash away this feeling of treachery in his heart?

POTUS shivered, hot tears seeping through his shut eyes to trickle down the side of his face. He let them drip—*Why did it take Mama's death for me to finally understand the terrifying shadow under which she'd lived all these years? Or the magnitude of the burden she—and even Kunle—had carried, mostly for my sake, to protect me from the kind of judgement and spite I'm now experiencing?* The new awareness brought an unfamiliar feeling of shame. It was sharp and overpowering, hitting him with an intense headache. It was a bad feeling POTUS neither wanted to confront nor dissect.

With a slight shake of his head, he pushed the thoughts away, willing sleep into his eyes with desperate grit

The temperature in the guest room plummeted. POTUS shivered violently. He didn't need to open his eyes to know a familiar visitor had arrived, one he'd been expecting since he left the hospital that morning.

President King hovered at the foot of his bed, swaying like a paper kite. He looked ghastly in fact, so grey and porous, POTUS feared he might evaporate with a tiniest puff. The familiar glow that used to surround him was now murky, like the pale glimmer of a dying candle.

"Your Excellency! God! What happened to you?" POTUS whispered, his eyes agog. He started to sit up on his bed, lifting down his plastered leg once again to the floor—*Shoot!* He must try and keep his voice low so Frankie's parents don't hear him. Good thing the guest room is downstairs.

"I'm dying, kiddo," the president's voice came from a distance, as if he were speaking across vast realms. "I think I used up all my energy for the hocus-pocus stuff I did the other day for our American friends, not to mention your daddy too. Now, I got nothing left in the tank. Unless you can host me again, I'm afraid that's it for me. They'll be burying the President of the United States sooner than you and I can share a peace pipe."

POTUS' heart dropped. He'd been afraid of something like this cropping up—Just not so soon. The last thing he wanted was the president inside him again, bringing back those terrible voices and blinding headaches. Now he'd had the chance to enjoy the bliss of total silence inside his head, he couldn't dare mess things up again—*Uh-uh! Please, God, no!*

"Your Excellency, I'm really sorry. Honestly, I feel for you," he placed his hand on his chest. "But, man!" he shook his head over and over. "Your Excellency, I like you; you know I really admire and respect you. I mean, you're even like an idol to me and I worship everything about you. I really want to do everything I can to help you, and you know I've been doing everything in my power to get you back to your body. But I'll be honest with you; I don't want your half-ghost inside me again, like, you know…" POTUS shrugged, his eyes pleading with the president for help. "I mean, no offence meant, Your Excellency; but surely, there must be another way we can save you?"

"If there was, d'you think I'll be here asking an ungrateful little punk like you for help?" the president snarled, his eyes flashing uglily.

"Hey! Who you calling ungrateful?" POTUS yelled, before quickly muting his voice. Rage darkened his pale brown eyes. "I've been doing everything for you and you know it. If not for me, you'd be a dead ghost now. I kept you alive all these years… weeks… whatever. Not forgetting bringing your friends and sister from America over here. Without me, they would've murdered your body by now. So, don't go forgetting and calling me ungrateful. It's not fair. You're the one that should be grateful, not me."

"I ain't forgetting a damn thing, buddy. But it goes both ways, right?" The president retorted. "You just remember that without me, no friggin' green card or sweet American dream for you and your little ch*nk friend in God's own country. Chew on that," the president glided so close their faces almost touched. His breath was icy on POTUS' face. "You help me, I help you. That's how the cookie crumbles. Anything happens to me and you can bet your little black ass the deal's off. The plan's only as good as my word, and if I ain't there to speak it, then you can kiss all the American goodies goodbye too." President King brushed back his hair with an irritated hand. "Damn it! What's it with you n*ggers anyways, huh? You people just can't be trusted to seal a simple deal. Y'all too damn lazy to work for anything you want. You just expect it to be handed to you on a silver plate without doing the hard work. You think the whole world owes you a friggin' living just because of the slavery bullshit. That's why your continent has stayed a fly-dump despite all the aid poured into it by us white folks."

The president glared at POTUS. Rage burnt in his green eyes. "Well, here's news for you, buddy. America owes you jackshit! You only get what you've earned. Shit! I don't even know why I bother. I thought perhaps you were different, that I've made you different, better. But I see you're just like your kind; gimme, gimme, gimme. Well, I'll give you when you give me, right? You want a piece of the American pie, then you gotta quit ringing the alleluia tinkerbell and put that gym body of yours to work, and I mean, literally. Now, let's cut to the chase; are you in or out?" President King's voice dripped all the arrogance, contempt, and disrespect that power and extreme wealth had always rained on their less privileged victims. The smirk on his face rubbed salt into the raw bruise of POTUS' pride.

POTUS bristled—*Oh, the wicked devil man! God! I can't believe this!* He wanted to howl; to punch his fist through the vile pink wall of the bedroom. The smug smile on the president's face told him the man knew he had won. POTUS was his pawn once again to do with as he pleased, just as he'd done when POTUS was a defenceless infant, too weak to fight for his body when he possessed it.

POTUS ground his teeth and glared at the grey spectre with enough loathing to annihilate a million cockroaches—*The lying demon!* He wanted to kick himself, slap his face and scream abuses at himself —*POTUS is nobody's fool indeed! Ha! You pathetic idiot fool! Frankie was right. You're just a Motormouth idiot! God!* The president's words hurt, and his cocky smirk made his blood boil, but he knew he was boxed, with no exit hole in sight.

He had been out-foxed by the conniving politician who now had him by the short and curlies. He desperately needed America at all costs—*I must find my birth mother if it's the last thing I ever do!* Even if Kunle capitulated as Frankie indicated, he doubted Kunle would still send him to America to study. There was nothing for it but to yield to the president's wishes. And for the first time, POTUS understood the blind desperation that drove the migrants to the killing boats.

"I said, are you in or out? I got no time to waste, buddy," the president's voice dripped with icy arrogance. Once again, the man's attitude brought a hot flash of anger in POTUS' eyes.

"Yeah, I'm in. So, what next?" POTUS' voice was coated in resentment. He struggled not to show just how frightened he felt—If only Frankie was here in the room with him! He was sorely tempted to call out to his friend, but he knew he dared not alert Frankie's parents to his plight. He had zero doubt they would chuck him out of their home and accuse him of demon possession on top of his other dubious afflictions and affiliations.

"What d'you mean, what's next?" The president snapped. "You're the one with the fucking voodoo gadget to keep me away. Last time I tried to get back into your body in the hospital while you slept, the damned thing almost killed me."

"Oluwa! Oh my God! So that's what you were doing that night at the hospital! I knew it! I knew you were up to no good! You lied to me. You lied!" The president came tumbling down from the invisible high pedestal POTUS had built for him.

"So what? Everyone lies. Big deal," President King sneered. "Just take the damn stuff off your wrist and let's see what happens."

"I told you I can't," POTUS snarled, raising his arm for the president to see while tugging viciously at his black bracelets. "Didn't you hear me last time? I can't remove them. Only the Babalawo can and—"

"Then let's go find this Barber fella now and get him to remove it."

"Now? Have you any idea what the time is? In case you haven't noticed, it's almost midnight, and I'm squatting at my friend's house. I don't plan on asking Frankie for a lift at this time of the night, and I don't even have any idea where the Babalawo lives. I told you my parents took me there when I was too young to remember."

"Then ask your fairy daddy for the address and call a yellow cab. Come on, speed it up. Let's hit the road," the president ordered, his spectre oozing impatience and annoyance.

"You're not listening to me, dude. I'm not going anywhere at this time of the night, not to some strange place I don't even know in Lagos. I've just left the hospital today, and I'm bloody tired. Do you hear me? I'm tired, tired, tired," POTUS shouted, frustration bringing tears to his eyes. "Just come back tomorrow, and we'll talk, okay? I'm just going to crash out now and that's all I'm going to say. If you don't like it, you can go stuff yourself and your stupid scholarship. I don't care anymore." He lifted his plastered leg back onto the bed and stretched down again, glaring at the president mutinously, daring him to do his worst—*Selfish man doesn't even care! I've just got out of the hospital today. I lost my mum and my grandma Funke too, lost the use of my limbs, and practically lost my entire future, and yet, he expects me to up and wipe his buttocks because of his rubbish scholarship and visa! Well, fuck you, dude. Fuck you, fuck you, fuck you!* He wiped his tears with an impatient hand, hating himself for crying and displaying such weakness before the president, but he couldn't help it.

The president seemed to read POTUS' thoughts on his scowling face and immediately reverted to his familiar, disarming friendliness.

"Hey, kiddo, pipe down, alright?" He winked and flashed his dazzling teeth in an expansive smile, as if POTUS were his dearest, long-lost friend. "I can do tomorrow, sure thing. I ain't got much time as you can see, but as long as I know we're on the same page and I can count on you, then what's one more day between friends, right?"

Wrong! POTUS said nothing. He wasn't getting tricked anymore by the man's smiles. In fact, he was starting to think the president must've been little *Miss Flash and Die*'s father in another life, what with that fake smile he was fast discovering couldn't be trusted. He clenched his fists, fighting his rage—*I've been a proper fool to think I could be friends with the President of the United States! After all, the horrible man didn't get to be president by dishing out his friendship to every pedestrian. Well, it suits me just fine. From now onwards, it's every man for himself, or as my pastor would say, 'To your tents, oh Israel!' I plan to look out only for Number One from now on!*

POTUS turned his head away from the president, feigning sleep. The heavy concrete of disappointment weighed him down, the toppling of this great icon from the highest pedestal he'd stupidly erected for him. It felt like losing a parent all over again; such was the painful knot in his chest. He finally knew he was dealing with a slippery individual whose words couldn't be trusted. President King had used him with ruthless contempt. His fault really. After all, the president had told him exactly the kind of man he was from the word go— What was it he called himself? Wheeler-dealer and great escape-artist. Yeah, he should've listened more with his head rather than his heart. *Ha! So much for POTUS being nobody's fool!*

What shocked him the most was the sudden unexpectedness of everything, the vicious one-eighty degrees U-turn by the president, the rattlesnake savagery of his attack and the ugliness of his voice. It felt like seeing a complete stranger from the kindly, fatherly, and powerful figure he had naively believed President King to be—*What did I do wrong? What terrible crime did I commit to deserve these horrible insults? What is it with older men that makes them so mean and unreliable, even when they're Oyinbo ghosts? Well, no more Mr. Idiot for me, uh-uh.* The president was right; nobody can be trusted. From now on, he was going to trust and depend only on himself. He'll do whatever it takes to be independent, even if it meant sacrificing his body to this Oyinbo demon. At least, in America, he'll have a birth mother, plus a better chance than he has now in Nigeria where everything was who you knew and who your connections were. Kunle was definitely no longer a connection anyone would want to claim, and his grandma had wiped him out of the family register for good. Just wait! He'll show every-body that he's the best of the best of the bestest…

POTUS sniffed and swiped the tears trailing his cheeks with an angry hand. He slammed a pillow over his head, shutting out every-thing and every ghost. He hated himself for his tears, the shame they placed in his heart, and the sense of helplessness they wrought in him. But there was little he could do to destroy this new person he had become since his mother's death, a pathetic weakling that now cried with the ease of a girl.

He heaved a deep sigh of weariness, wishing he could sink into a warm bath. He felt tainted from his latest interaction with the half-ghost. The only consolation was that Frankie's house was as clean as his own, and the guest bedroom, even with its appalling pinkness, sparkled with enough fragranced cleanness to lull even the crappiest of babies to sleep.

POTUS slept.

15
RECONCILIATION

Kunle let POTUS and Frankie in through the high security gates when they arrived the next day just before noon. The sight of Kunle fiddling clumsily with the security locks on the gate cut POTUS' heart with a sharp, unexpected blade. It was a menial job his father had never had to do, an act that brought home to him the full, harrowing impact of Kunle's downfall from grace.

POTUS stared at Kunle with disbelief. The man was a ghost of his old self, haggard and unkept, his beard an overgrown bush that covered his face. His left arm was strapped in a thick, white bandage, and his eyes were bloodshot, as if he hadn't slept in weeks. A strong, sweaty odour told POTUS his adoptive dad hadn't visited the shower room in a while either. He never realised it was possible for someone to drop so much weight in just a space of a week, but Kunle looked as if he had dropped several kilos at the very least. The angles of his face were sharper and the Terry Crews look appeared more striking than before, in spite of the overgrown beard.

"POTUS, I see you're walking again," Kunle said, leading them through the smaller front living room and into the massive, plush parlour usually reserved for their important guests. POTUS figured there would be no more VIP guests gracing that lounge anymore, not after the whole terrible business with his mum—*Stuff them all! Who needs the two-faced idiots anyway?*

"Yeah, I'm managing okay thanks to these geriatric crutches," he tried to make light of things, using humour to hide the unexpected tightness in his throat—*WTF? Dude, what's wrong with you? Why are you even feeling sorry for the guy?*

"Motormouth, I'll pop up to your room and wait for you," Frankie, ever the diplomat, dashed out of the parlour and headed up the flight of stairs before POTUS could reply. He'd spent so many years in the house that it was like a second home to him.

"Sit down, POTUS," Kunle waved him over to one of the intricately carved chairs with excessive politeness, as if he were a stranger. He reeked of alcohol, and POTUS struggled to hold his breath. "You don't have to keep standing like a stranger in your own house, you know." There was a wry weariness in Kunle's voice that dispelled the resentment the words would have roused in the past.

POTUS sat down. Right across his chair, occupying almost an entire section of the wall, was the life-size photo of his mother in one of her most flamboyant Ashoke attires, resplendent in her familiar, bejewelled glamour. Ronke's smile was winsome and wistful, as if pleading with the camera lenses to love her and accept her. That photo had always been one of POTUS' favourite pictures of his mother, and the sight sent him into hyperventilating grief.

His head dropped to his chest as he started sobbing softly, shoulders convulsing.

"Ma-Mama... I'm so sorry. Forgive me, Mama... I'm so sorry," the harsh wail burst from his lips. It was as if his grief had been capped in an airtight bottle, buried in a deep hole, trapped in a metal jail, awaiting release at the right place and time. Now, he was a child all over again, devoid of pride, of strength, and of hate. All he wanted was his mother, a return to the past, even the dysfunctional past they'd shared as a family. At least his mother was in that past alive, vibrant, loving, and constant.

He felt a gentle hand on his left arm, quickly followed by an arm wrapped tightly around his shoulders.

"It's okay, you hear? Don't cry, alright? It is fine," Kunle's voice was hoarse with ill-suppressed tears as he perched on the arm of POTUS' chair, his body also shaking. "It is well. Wipe your tears, POTUS. Come now, hold your grief."

"I'm sorry... I'm sorry... I'm sorry..." The hiccups were stealing POTUS' words and his breath.

"Shh... jowo... please, don't cry. Your mother is at peace now, nobody can hurt her again. They've done their worst. There's nothing more anyone can do now," Kunle's voice was a soft croak that increased, rather than decreased, POTUS' tears. His body heaved as he continued to bawl like a child.

Lost in his grief, he had no idea how he ended up with Kunle's arms folding him in, his face sniffling against Kunle's broad chest. He only realised where he was when the strong pong of sweaty skin hit his nostrils. Even then, he wanted to remain where he was in the warm safety of a father's arms, held once again as he used to be held a long time ago when he was still a beloved son and Kunle a proud and loving dad who called him 'Ekùn mi'.

For several minutes, father and son stayed together, bound by their shared grief.

"Come, dry your tears. Rest here, and I'll get you something to drink, okay?" Kunle released him gently and shuffled his way towards the large bar at the far end of the parlour, his shoulders hunched, his gait that of an old man, unsteady and slow. POTUS' head remained bowed, his shoulders hunched low, looking at the shiny, marbled flooring, the white hardness of his plastered foot, and the rich leather of his Yeezy Crush 950 V25 on his good foot. His mind was numb and his head empty. He felt like a bottle of rich wine emptied of its sweet contents and washed clean of everything, right down to its fruity scent. Even if Rihanna materialised in front of him and offered him her lips, he doubted he would have the strength or desire to kiss her.

"Here, drink this. It'll make you feel better," Kunle gave him a glass of cold Pimm's sans fruits, his favourite drink. He was surprised Kunle knew about his illegal imbibing of the stuff from when he was fourteen.

"Thanks," he mumbled, taking a long sip of the drink, savouring its sweet freshness. "I'm sorry."

"You don't need to keep saying sorry, you hear?" Kunle's voice was gruff, as he returned to his vacated chair. "I'm the one that should be saying sorry to you. What I said to you at the hospital was unforgivable and cruel. I was hurting, and I wanted you to feel the same pain I felt. I didn't mean it. None of it, I promise you. If anyone is to be blamed for your mother's death, then that person is me. I know I failed both of you in so many ways through the years, and I have no excuse for how I behaved except my own ignorance, or rather, my stupid pride and fear." Kunle's voice was low, his fingers gripping his can of beer like pincers

POTUS gave him a sharp look, his brows dipped in a frown as he kept wiping his tears.

"Yes, fear," Kunle said with a slight shrug. "You have to understand, I was my father's first son. They invested everything in me, as per our custom, in the expectation that I would succeed in life and take care of them and the family. When my father died, that burden became mine. I was expected to provide for my mother and siblings; to marry and provide sons to carry on the family name. You know how it is with our people."

Kunle shrugged again. POTUS kept still, afraid of making even the slightest movement. He didn't want anything to break the spell. He never knew he craved a backstory; this backstory—*Finally! I'm getting the history behind my adoption from Kunle's mouth and not the little scraps Mama had fed me!* A shiver of anticipation slivered across his body.

"I knew I was different from other men from a very young age, even younger than you are now," Kunle gave him a sidelong, weary glance before looking away again, staring at Ronke's photo with intense concentration. "It was while studying in England that I finally gave in to that truth about myself. When I returned home after my studies, there was no way I could come out to anyone, most especially my family, who already had several women lined up for me to marry. By the time I met your mum while I was at a conference in Abuja, I knew that no power on earth would force me to enter into a marriage contract with any of the women your grandma Funke had in mind. That was when we devised the plan for Jimmy to alter himself and become the woman everyone knew as Ronke. With his family having disowned him a long time before we met, there was no fear of discovery, especially since we came from different ethnicities. The rest is history."

Kunle shrugged again and took a long drink from his can. He was silent for several minutes, his eyes staring into space. POTUS began to worry he might not continue.

"What about me?" He finally asked, his voice soft, almost a whisper. Kunle looked up startled, like someone woken from a bad dream.

"What about you?"

POTUS nodded. "Yes, how did you find me? Why did you choose me, you know…?" He shrugged like Frankie, his voice trailing off.

Kunle grunted. "Hmm… Well, my mother was starting to fuss about Ronke's delay in giving her a grandson. As you know, your Grandma Funke never liked your mother, especially as she was from a different tribe. Worse, we also had a registry marriage instead of a big traditional and church wedding as is the norm, denying my mother the chance to participate in it. Ha! Some marriage!" Kunle twisted his lips in a bitter sneer. "Needless to say, that wedding is now nothing more than a piece of toilet paper, seeing as we lied about Ronke's gender. This country doesn't recognise gay marriages, and I expect I'll be arrested for several crimes under the *Same Sex Marriage Prohibition Act* after your mother's burial. The only thing still keeping me here is the hefty bribe I'm paying the police DPO to help the corrupt bastard become blind to my existence and develop amnesia about my crime," Kunle barked a harsh laugh and took another gulp from his beer can.

"Anyway, as I was saying, when the pressure from my family became too much, we decided that our only hope was to adopt a child. So, when a good friend found your birth mother for me, it was time for Ronke to start wearing the pregnancy prosthetics. As you know, your birth mother was an unmarried woman called Folake from some village I can't even recall now. I'm truly sorry, but that's all I know about her. She desperately needed money for a black-market American visa, which I gave her in exchange for you. She brought you down to Benin City where we made the exchange, and I've never heard from her since then.I have no idea if she's still in the country or succeeded in making her way to the States. You were less than a day old when I collected you, and from the day I brought you back, you were the greatest joy and blessing we ever had. I want you to believe me when I tell you that despite everything, despite the evil I spoke at the hospital out of my grief, you were the best thing that ever happened to your mother and I."

Kunle paused again. He leaned back his head against his chair and shut his eyes. POTUS wasn't sure if he was shutting out a bad memory or holding in a good one. He desperately prayed it was the latter. His heart thudded so hard against his chest, he thought it might burst. It yearned for a healing, a bonding, a return to the good past. He desperately craved the happy days of his childhood, a time that was seen as a blessing because of his very existence—*Oluwa!* Right now, He would give everything to turn the clock back and skip one year of his life so that that accursed ninth year is forever obliterated from his history. He never realised how much he missed being called Baby Boy and Ekùn mi till he'd lost both.

"From the day I brought you home, we wanted to wrap you in innocence, shield you from the hate and attacks we knew would follow should the truth be discovered. I didn't want you to carry the burden of secrecy we endured since I knew there was no way we could openly live as man and man in our society," Kunle was talking again, his voice as dull as the brief glance he cast in POTUS' direction. "Unfortunately, it was all in vain. The rest you know." Kunle hung his head before leaning forward to fix intense, bloodshot eyes at POTUS.

"I didn't handle things well that day, son. I'm ashamed to say I let my fear get the better of me and resorted to stupid and cruel threats instead of understanding the confusion and fear you were experiencing," he shook his head violently, as if raging at himself. "Believe me, I've spent endless days and nights regretting that terrible afternoon of your ninth birthday and wishing I could take back the things I said and did. I know that was the day I lost you, your love and your respect, and for that I am sorry, truly sorry from the bottom of my heart." Kunle's voice broke as he hung his head again, clutching his beer can like a lifeline.

A heavy burden lifted from POTUS' shoulders. It was as if the sodden soil covering him in a deep, dark grave had been dug up, and he could finally raise his head to inhale fresh, life giving air. This was what he'd been yearning for all his adult life, what his bruised soul had been craving; an acknowledgement that he did nothing wrong on that fateful day. That he was not to blame. The imposter syndrome that had been the secret shame he carried from the day he discovered his adoption status melted into a bright pond. He was no longer a fake son. He hung his head just like his dad, fighting to swallow away the dryness in his mouth and the tight knot behind his throat.

"I thought you hated me," his voice was hoarse when he finally forced himself to speak, as if he nursed a cold. "You just kept beating me and cursing me. I hated you as well for forcing me to keep the secret and for hiding who you were, you know…"

"I know I did wrong, son, and you're right to be disappointed in me," Kunle said, shame layering his voice. "Your mother and I thought we were doing the best for us as a family by asking you not to talk. We were wrong… I was wrong. I was a bad father to you. It was cruel and heartless to take out my frustration on you, even if you were acting up due to your own fears and confusion. I failed to realise what a great burden I was putting on you, and in hindsight, I should've done things differently." Kunle lifted his head to hold POTUS' gaze with imploring eyes. "POTUS, I want you to know that your mother's death has made me confront my past and my actions. I realise just how much I've failed you as a father, and I am truly, truly sorry for everything. It is too much to ask for your forgiveness now, but I hope that one day, you'll be able to see me once again as your father. Nothing would make me happier than for you to continue to live in our house. I promise you'll see a change in me. I'll become the father you once knew and loved if you will give me the chance again. I'm begging you, Ekùn mi," Kunle paused, fighting his tears.

POTUS looked up sharply, stunned by Kunle's use of the endearment Ekùn mi, *daddy's little fearless leopard*. The last time he heard that word on Kunle's lips was just after his ninth birthday, just before things deteriorated beyond repair between them. Now, POTUS was fighting his own tears—*Even if he's saying this because of the president's*

ghost, I think he really means what he said. I don't think he's faking it…
he's really sorry for what he's done to me and wants to make up…

"POTUS, I must ask you a question, and I need you to tell me the truth, okay?" Kunle's voice pierced through his thoughts. He looked up to see Kunle's blood-rimmed eyes fixed on him with piercing intensity. There was something in Kunle's gaze that told him he wouldn't like the question coming his way.

POTUS nodded, his heart pounding.

"I need you to answer me from the deepest part of your heart without fear or shame, you hear?" Kunle said. "It's important for me to know the truth, and believe me, it won't change a thing no matter what you say. One thing I've always admired in you is your uncompromising honesty, and that's what I need from you now," Kunle paused, before sighing deeply. When next he spoke, his voice was low, almost hesitant. "Tell me, son, do you hate gay people? Is that why you've loathed me all these years?"

"No!" POTUS shouted the denial. "No…" this time his voice was hushed, almost a whisper. Shame gripped his heart, his mind doing a laser scan of words he'd used in the past, thoughts he'd had, emotions he'd felt—*What to say?* Should he lie, make himself look good in Kunle's eyes, especially in view of their recent conversation? It would be good for Kunle if he lied and denied everything. If nothing else, it would make him feel he wasn't despised for being gay.

POTUS sighed deeply, his head bowed. Several silent seconds ticked away on the mounted square clock as Kunle waited tensely for his answer. Finally, he raised his head and leaned forward on his chair so he could look Kunle squarely in the eyes. He, POTUS, who had prided himself on being able to stare down the devil himself, was finding this particular eye-to-eye contact the hardest of all. He steeled himself—*Truth demands the respect of a full eye-hold.* He cleared his throat.

"The honest truth is that I hated you and Mama. I really did," he finally said, his voice neutral, even hard. "I resented you guys for being different, for not being like other parents, and worse, for making me keep secrets. Knowing what you were created a sense of fear and anxiety that's still with me even as I speak. There was no day that my heart didn't jump in panic at even the most innocent of questions, like, 'How's your mother? Is she well?' Oluwa! Have they heard something? Have I inadvertently said something to reveal our secret? Will I get into trouble with you guys? These were the kind of thoughts that continued to stress me right up to the day they killed Mama. So, yes, I hated you, especially for threatening me with the water spirit and scaring the hell out of me, not to mention constantly being beaten for the slightest offence," POTUS shrugged, looking briefly away before returning his gaze once more to Kunle's stricken face.

"Yeah, so, if that makes me homophobic, then I guess I was, though God knows I had no idea what homophobic meant or what being gay was all about in my younger years. By the time I was older and understood things, it did affect how I viewed you. I'm sorry, but you asked for the truth. The pastors at the churches I attended condemned homosexuality as Satan's evil. I heard people making derogatory remarks about gays. So, yes, that did affect how I viewed you. I just thought you were a hypocrite and a coward for pretending to be straight. I didn't fully understand things then, the risks involved. But where Mama was concerned, it made no difference to me whatsoever because she was living the way she saw herself, as a woman, and I loved her for her steadfast love, her kindness and …"

"Yet, you returned from your friend's house and threatened to expose us unless I started giving you money," Kunle cut in, holding his gaze, watching him with quiet intensity. "I read the hate and loathing in your eyes that day, and it was something that killed our hearts. I know I behaved terribly, disgracefully, and believe me, it still shames me when I remember that your mother had to pull a knife on me that day. Even so, I always believed that somehow you would understand our complicated situation and hopefully, have more compassion in your heart. I truly believed that in time, we would return to our previous bond as a family. So, for you to blackmail your mother who worshipped the very ground you walked on was too much for me to stomach and…"

"I didn't mean it," POTUS rushed in, desperate to explain himself, fighting back the tears that had once again gathered in his eyes. "I would never, ever do anything to hurt Mama. I love… loved Mama.

She was everything to me, the one thing that was real and rooted in my life. I just thought you hated me since I wasn't your blood child, and if you ever knew how much I loved Mama and how I would never expose her secret no matter what, you would revert to hitting me again."

POTUS paused, wiping his face angrily with the back of his hand —*Why can't I stop crying for God's sake? Why can't I just stop crying?* "I didn't care about the money, I swear. At least, not at the beginning. It was just something to hurt you, you know, have some power over you the way you had power over me. It was stupid, but I was angry and just wanted to make you pay for everything. And later, when I got used to having money, I continued blackmailing you so you wouldn't cut it off. So, yes, I admit at a point, I was homophobic, against just you, though. Your actions told me it was something to be ashamed of and something that was wrong. Otherwise, why go to such extremes to hide it? As I said, the pastors also preached against it in church and my friends mocked that celebrity, Bronky, who's practically in Mama's situation, being a man who dresses like a woman. So, it just seemed normal to dislike gays, apart from Mama. I didn't know then what I know now, so I blamed you for everything."

POTUS paused and shrugged again, nerves tightening his stomach in painful knots. Shame saturated every pore in his body, and he didn't try to stop it this time as he'd been prone to do when his conscience occasionally woke up from its deep slumber. He wanted to suffer— Maybe his pain will atone for his crimes, even if he didn't think he was completely to blame.

"I was also angry with you for the way you treated Mama. I mean, you used to hit her the same as me. I could understand why you beat me, but why Mama? Why?" His voice was almost a wail as he sought for answers that had eluded him for a long time, "Mama never did anything to you, yet you kept attacking her till that last time I challenged you when I was fifteen, and you said you'd kill both of us. Remember?"

Kunle broke eye contact fast, but not fast enough. POTUS saw the shame and guilt clouding his eyes. Kunle sighed deeply, opened his mouth to speak, but instead, his shoulders began shaking as fresh tears flooded his face. POTUS watched him sobbing, embarrassed. Yet, a cynical part of his brain told him it was maybe a ploy, a play for sympathy by someone guilty as charged—*Uh-uh, I won't let myself be gaslighted or manipulated. POTUS is nobody's fool anymore!* He knew what he had witnessed, how nasty Kunle became towards his mum.

"You're right, Ekùn mi," Kunle's voice was hoarse, his eyes even more bloodshot than before. "I was the worst husband to your mother, and I am ashamed to even speak her name. My only reason is that I was angry with her. I was consumed with rage and acted with petty vindictiveness. I wanted to punish her, make her suffer for the way she'd made me suffer. You're old enough now, so you might as well know," he paused, pulled out one of his ubiquitous white handkerchiefs, and blew his nose noisily. "Your mother had HIV. I didn't give it to her, she gave it to me."

POTUS gasped, his eyes wide with shock.

"Oh my God! Oh my God!" POTUS stared at his father with stunned eyes.

"Yes, I know it's hard for you to hear, but your mother wasn't perfect. None of us are, but one thing I can swear to you is that I was faithful to her—always. I never went with anyone else. She said it was just the once, an accident, someone she met when she visited a club at Abuja. I don't know, and it doesn't really matter anymore. But it killed something in our marriage. It made me feel I'd sacrificed everything in vain. I... well, she was nothing when I first found her, just a cheap rent-boy squatting between sofas and hotel rooms. But there was something special about her, a vibrancy and glamour that had me enslaved from the first minute," Kunle paused, staring at Ronke's imposing portrait as if spellbound. POTUS' heart was ready to burst —This is what he'd been wanting to know, but now he wasn't sure he wanted to hear anymore. *Uh-uh... too much info!* He'd rather keep Mama's memory as sacred and pure as it'd always been. God! If only he'd known all this stuff earlier. How different things could've been.

"Are you okay? I mean, are they treating you for it? Are you going to...?" POTUS paused, unable to speak the terrifying words aloud—*Oluwa! Please, don't let my dad die, not now that I've rediscovered him!* He glanced around nervously—Thank God Frankie didn't hear this latest news. He didn't think he could deal with any further stigma. People already thought his parent's homosexuality was contagious. He didn't want to imagine what would happen if they ever discovered his dad was HIV positive—*God! Another horrible secret to hide!* And just when he thought he was done with secrets! He shuddered inwardly, grateful that Kunle couldn't read his thoughts.

"I'm doing just fine, son," Kunle said, his smile gentle. "Don't worry yourself, alright? If I'm going to die, I promise you it won't be from AIDS. Gone are the days that AIDS killed, not with the new antiretroviral drugs that cure it completely within five years. So, I'm doing just fine," Kunle paused, standing up from his chair and stretching with exaggerated exertion, as if to prove he was perfectly healthy. "Do you want another drink?"

POTUS shook his head. "I haven't finished the one you gave me," he smiled, feeling shy as his eyes connected with his dad's. Kunle nodded and sat down again. It was as if ten years had dropped from him since POTUS saw him at the gate.

"I've not yet decided on a date for your mother's cremation. I wanted you to be home from hospital first since I know she'd like you there," the lightness vanished from Kunle's face.

POTUS nodded, a tight knot in his stomach. It felt wrong, somehow unnatural, talking about his vibrant mum and cremation in the same breath. He would give anything not to be there on the day, but he owed Ronke that final filial duty, at the very least.

"I'm okay with any date you chose. Who else will be coming?" His voice was muted.

"Nobody else as far as I know," Kunle shrugged. "You know how things stand. I'm even surprised Frankie's parents still allow him to come here. Everyone we know has turned their backs on us, but that's to be expected, I suppose. People will be people. After all, my own mother and siblings, whom I did everything for, no longer want to hear my name or see my face. That's life," Kunle shrugged again.

"Stuff them all!" POTUS swore, rage flaring in his heart. He didn't think he would ever speak to Grandma Funke and his aunties and uncles again. In fact, he doubted if he would even spend another night ever under Frankie's parent's roof—Certainly not if they aren't loyal enough to stand up for friends they've known for many years.

"It's okay, son. Don't let it bother you. After all, who else would your mother need but you and I, eh?" Kunle waited till POTUS finally nodded, albeit with frowning reluctance. "Good. Now, should we give Frankie something to drink? Poor lad's been upstairs in your room getting bored all this while," Kunle started to rise again just as POTUS also struggled up from his chair, reaching for his crutches. Kunle dashed over to assist him.

"Thanks..." He wanted to add 'Dad' but it had been such a long time since he last used the word that it stuck behind his throat. He guessed it was too soon. It was fine with him, though. Eventually, everything would flow normally, naturally—*I hope?* He looked again at his mother's picture again—Was it his imagination, or was Mama's face smiling differently, a happier smile that showed her silent approval? He fervently prayed so. It might be wishful thinking, but it didn't hurt to think his mother had been present with them in the parlour to witness everything. He knew it would make her happy to know the family she left behind were united once again and healing.

"Son, you know you don't have to leave your home, don't you?" Kunle's eyes were pleading. "This is your home and will always be."

"Thanks. Thanks a lot. I'll be home later today." He saw the startled look in Kunle's eyes before his face broke out in the widest and happiest smile POTUS had seen in forever. He rubbed POTUS' head roughly with his hand, trailing the hand to his shoulder.

"Good boy. Good, good!" Kunle nodded again and again, his eyes brimming. "Do you boys want to eat something? I'm not sure if there's any food in the house, but we can order something from the restaurant for home delivery. Otherwise, if you wait, I'll dash up and have a quick wash, and we can all go somewhere for a bite," Kunle's eyes were eager, and it hurt POTUS to turn him down.

"Thanks, but not now. Maybe later after I come back. Frankie and I need to go somewhere. Actually, just wondered, do you still have the Babalawo's address?" He looked up anxiously into Kunle's startled face.

"Sure, I have it. But why?"

"I need to visit him so he can take these stupid bracelets off my wrists."

"No! Don't!" Kunle shouted, grabbing his wrist, his fingers hard, eyes wide with terror. "You mustn't remove the amulets. Trust me, the water demon exists and it's still seeking your soul. So, please son, keep the amulets on, you hear? I have my reasons for asking, and it's not a trifling matter."

POTUS smiled—*President King actually visited my dad for real!* Once again, he felt his heart constrict as his recent dislike of the flawed ghost warred with his previous affection and admiration. "It's okay, trust me," he said, holding Kunle's gaze. "I've met the water demon, and it no longer seeks my soul and..."

"You've met the water demon? How? Where?" Kunle's eyes widened in horror.

"It's a long story, but all is okay now, honest," POTUS smiled. Kunle searched his face intently for several seconds before nodding, slowly, reluctantly.

"Okay, if you say so. Do you want me to drive you there? It won't take me a minute to get dressed."

POTUS shook his head. "It's okay, thanks. Frankie's taking me there, and anyway, you need to rest your arm. Which reminds me, what happened with those idiot twins? Frankie told me some of it but not everything."

"It was nothing," Kunle brushed the question away with an airy wave. "They were just two ignorant fools I should've kicked out of the compound long ago. It was a pity to sack their father as he was a good security man, but there's no way I'm having those two thugs in this compound again. They're still at the police station as far as I know. I'm not bribing the bloody police anymore to keep them behind bars and charge them to court. They can do as they like." Kunle shrugged, a bitter look in his eyes. "Anyway, I've bigger things to think about. Good thing is, I don't have to hide anymore. They've taken your mother away from me and there's nothing more they can do. I'm forever grateful to the ancestors that you don't have to share this burden in your life. Just appreciate the freedom you enjoy as a straight man in this our Nigeria."

POTUS did. Or if he didn't before, he now did with intense savagery. He realised he hated people just as much as he now hated President King. Maybe even more. He finally understood what his dad had meant at the hospital when he'd said, "You think you know a rooster until the wind blows up its feathers and you discover it's got a stinky arse." He was discovering so many stinky arses amongst their family, friends, and extended acquaintances, it was a miracle his nostrils could still function from the stench of betrayals and lies—*And speaking of lies, where is the biggest liar of them all? When will that horrible Oyinbo fake ghost invade my space again?*

BOOK THREE

16

THE BABALAWO

President King appeared in the back seat of Frankie's car just as they drove out of Kunle's compound. One minute they were inside the sweltering car waiting for the air-conditioner to kick in. The next thing they knew, the temperature dropped so suddenly their teeth started chattering.

POTUS and Frankie looked at each other startled. Then with a manic frenzy, they began to wind down their windows to let in the humid air from outside. Frankie hurriedly switched off the AC, blowing on his hands to warm them up. POTUS knew instantly the president was in the backseat.

"Dude, you need to pull over now, okay?" Frankie gave him an incredulous look. "Just do it, alright? The president's in the back seat with us," POTUS' voice was weary, like a wife resigned to her husband's bad jokes.

"Olè!" Frankie swerved to the side of the road, slamming the brakes so hard they lurched forward violently. He froze in his seat, gripping the steering with shaking hands.

"See what you've done now," POTUS turned and snarled at President King. "You're lucky you didn't kill us."

"Count me out of your body bags, kiddo," the president laughed without repentance. "In case you've forgotten, I can't lose my life in any accident, see?" He raised a phosphorous arm.

"Stuff you, dude. Just fuck off, okay? I told you I was going to get the Babalawo to remove the amulets today. So why are you here? Fuck!"

"Watch your filthy mouth, kiddo," President King's eyes flashed angrily, and POTUS returned the glare. "Anyways, I don't have time, savvy? I want to be at your Barber's place with you in case we need his services should anything go wrong during my re-entry into your body."

"Stop calling them stupid gadgets. I've told you they're not—"

"Of course they're stupid gadgets," the president cut in. "I mean, we're talking about the moron that told you I was a great water spirit. Oohh! Aahh!" The president made spooky sounds from the back seat, feigning terror.

POTUS scowled at him. "Whatever, do as you please. Just don't talk to me while we're driving unless you want Frankie to have an accident. Remember, if anything happens to me, then as you said yesterday, no deal, and defo no living body for you to possess. You need me just as much as I need you," his voice was as vicious as the look he gave the president.

POTUS turned and nodded at Frankie, whose face was still pale with fear.

"Is he gone? Olé! It's still chilly inside this car." He shivered before restarting the engine.

Behind them, President King smirked but kept quiet. POTUS glared at him through the rearview mirror and also held his peace. Frankie shrugged, popped a lollipop into his mouth, and obediently hit the pedals with his feet. The car lurched forward, settled, then began rolling.

Soon, they were cruising down the busy traffic of Chiwetel Ejiofor Avenue, burning the rubber with absent-minded recklessness, each lost in their own thoughts. POTUS set his mobile phone to Frankie's Bluetooth and began to scroll through his playlist. He was about to play Drake's latest hit, *Sing Now, Dance Later* when he changed his mind —*Nah!* Let the yeye ghost have some heavy Fela Kuti music drum insanity into his stupid Oyinbo head. After all, he claims Fela is a mood alien. Come on, Fela! Bring the demon some proper mental chaos! That'll teach him, alright!

The pounding beat of Fela's mega-hit *Shakara* began quaking the car from the mean surround speakers. Frankie shook his head in sync to the heavy drumming, his face grinning with approval. The guy had always been a fanatical Fela fan and knew both the Yoruba and pidgin English lyrics of all the Afro Juju king's songs. As they meandered through the congested roads, Frankie screeched along to the song, blaring his horn in metronomic sync to the rhythm. POTUS joined him gleefully, his voice loud and out of tune. He cast a malicious glance in his rearview mirror at the president, whose face was screwed up in distaste.—*Good!* He pressed the volume key, upping the ante.

I go beat you, I go nearly kill you,
Na Shakara.

They arrived at the Babalawo's residence an hour later. Thanks to the constant bombardment of Fela's music, the president had grudgingly, and with a great deal of swearing, decided to make himself scarce. His disappearance meant they could enjoy their drive with the sensible air conditioning rather than the iciness the president's presence wrought. As they turned into the untarred, dusty road that led to the Babalawo's residence, sticky sweat dampened POTUS' armpits and hands despite the air conditioner roiling inside the car. He cast a sidelong glance at Frankie, but his friend was just frowning, his bottom lip chewed mercilessly as he tried to navigate the bumpy dirt road. Waste of every kind littered the street together with noisy kids and even noisier dogs that barked gleefully for the sheer bloody-mindedness of it.

"I think we're here," POTUS said, pointing. "This place looks familiar. Park your car here, just outside that white house."

Frankie complied, manoeuvring the Nissan into a small space in front of a dilapidated whitewashed bungalow. He kept the engine running for the air conditioning as he turned towards POTUS with raised eyebrows. "What now?"

Before POTUS could answer, a small crowd of boisterous kids gathered around their car tapping at the shut windows with excitement. Their smiling faces glowed with that peculiar blend of mischief and joy common amongst Nigerian children when they are congregated in a rowdy group.

"Oyinbo, give us money," they called out to Frankie with savage glee, their eyes twinkling as they made exaggerated gestures of supplication.

POTUS frowned—Little sods don't really care if they receive some coins or not, the tiny devils! It was merely part of their street games to harass foreigners for money since those people were known to be naïve, bleeding-hearts who were easy to fleece. He wound down his window and glared at the rascals nearest to him. They quickly backed away realising they were dealing with one of their own despite the presence of the Oyinbo, Frankie, in the car.

"We're looking for the Babalawo," POTUS said. "Do you know where he lives?" Before he could finish his question, several of the urchins turned around and started shrieking out a name.

"Olu! Snake-head! Come see Oyinbo and his friend who dey look for your Papa," they screeched in the familiar pidgin English of Lagos city.

A little bare-chested boy in red shorts and dusty long dreadlocks ran up to them. He looked around nine or ten, and his bare torso was littered in ritualistic occult symbols tattooed to his skin. His wrists and ankles were draped in amulets, some of which resembled POTUS' own.

POTUS stared at the child, surprised the Babalawo could have such a young son. He recalled from his last visit that the medicine man had been pretty shrivelled, way past his prime. But then, this was Lagos city where geriatric men with one foot in the grave could still marry young brides and somehow impregnate them without Viagra. It was usually left to the family to demand a DNA test of the kids or get the Babalawo to confirm paternity when the guy died and property inheritance became an issue.

"You want to see my Papa?" The little boy asked, his shoulders puffed up all important. He looked around haughtily at his friends as if to say, 'This is important business which you hoi-polloi wouldn't understand,'

"Yes, is he in?" POTUS asked.

"You get money first?" the boy demanded. He stretched out his hand imperiously, holding POTUS' fierce glare with his own.

"Get lost, you little rascal," POTUS hissed. The dirty surroundings were playing havoc on his sanity. He felt like soaking himself inside a bath for the whole day.

"Olé! If you no show us where your Papa dey, I go come swallow you at night, even with all your yeye amulets," Frankie threatened in perfect Yoruba-pidgin, leaning across POTUS and glaring at the Babalawo's kid.

"Oluwa!" All the children shrieked and scampered away from the car, stunned. "This Oyinbo na evil spirit, oh!"

POTUS' face creased in a malevolent smile—Good, that should teach you little devils! *Actually, where's the president?* As if summoned, the icy chill returned, bringing thick smoke to their breaths. This time, Frankie didn't react beyond his eyes being agog and hands tightening on the wheel.

"It's okay, Einstein," POTUS said, glaring malignantly through his mirror at the president behind the car. "We're here now, and we'll be done in no time. Just relax in the car while I see the Babalawo, alright?"

"Are you sure you'll be okay by yourself?" Frankie whispered, looking both terrified and concerned. POTUS waved away his worries.

"Chill, dude. This is between him and I. I can handle him. He's not even a real ghost," he cast another sour look at the president, who arched his brows in hauteur. POTUS wanted to yell curses at him just to rile him and have him experience the same fear he was now feeling.

POTUS fought his terror with an angry frown—*Can't let the dude know I'm scared out of my wits. Uh-uh! No way!* He checked to make sure he had cash in his pocket for the Babalawo's fees before stepping out of the car with the aid of his crutches. President King glided alongside him as he hobbled to the front door. A quick look behind showed him that Frankie was okay. He was now surrounded by the street urchins, who had apparently overcome their initial fear and were now chatting away eagerly with Frankie in Yoruba.

POTUS knocked loudly on the black, wooden front door. Instantly, it opened, as if the Babalawo had been expecting him. But it wasn't the old medicine man who stood at the open doorway, but a tall, young man, perhaps a couple of years older than POTUS. He was dressed in a pair of blue jeans and a Chez Guevara T-shirt.

"Oh… hi," POTUS smiled sheepishly, embarrassed to be seen at such an uncool place by one of his peers despite said peer being a part of the occultic household. "Em… is it possible to see the Babalawo?"

"You have an appointment?"

"No, but it's very urgent. I need to see him ASAP."

"Wait; I'll check and see if he can see you," the young man shut the door and left them cooling their heels outside.

"Huh! Who needs an appointment to come to a shithole shack like this?" The president sneered, floating beside him.

"Fuck you, dude," POTUS said quietly, wondering why he even bothered. The president's prejudices about Lagos city ran deep. But it made him happy to swear at President King. Right now, any revenge was better than nothing.

"Fuck you too, *dude*," the president repeated, stressing the 'dude' to an insult. Before POTUS could respond, the door opened again, and the young man ushered them into the bungalow.

"Follow me to the shrine," he said to POTUS, oblivious to the presence of the president's half-ghost.

The minute they entered the bungalow, the murky glow that always shrouded President's King's body vanished, swallowed in a blink by the invisible magic within the charmed space. It was as if the seer's house had devoured the president. Even the temperature inside the house remained a normal, warm gauge.

POTUS gazed around in awe—*Oluwa! This is the real thing! I'm walking in hallowed space!* He couldn't remember walking through the house the last time his mother brought him. The president looked a bit queasy, as if he expected skeletal hands to reach out from the walls and grab him at any moment. The young man led them through a long, gloomy corridor which ended with another black door. He opened the door, and POTUS found himself in a backyard littered with squawking chickens, bleating goats, and a couple of stone tripods with empty cooking pots over cold ashes—*I remember this place!*

Shivers ran through POTUS' body as he cat-pawed his way across the sandy ground littered with goat and chicken mess, his crutches clumping noisily before him. Sweat dripped down his face and his limbs felt so jellied with revulsion he feared he might faint—Oh, God! Please, don't let anything stick to my expensive trainers. I'll just die if I find animal dung on my Yeezy Crush 950 V25 or my Plaster of Paris and my crutches!

Their guide led them across the familiar dirty backyard till they arrived at a round mud hut, topped with copious thatched roofing. A dwarf-like wooden door led into the hut, but it was shut. Its surface was littered with white bones, blood-splattered feathers, and leering masks. POTUS noticed several bunches of dry leaves tied up with cord strings as well as shells, beads, and other items of ritualistic juju hanging on the shut door. He recalled seeing them in prior visits, and as always, the sight sent icy claws across his back.

"Enter. He's expecting you," their guide said, turning to leave. POTUS watched him return to the bungalow through the open back door. He wished he could follow him and escape right back into the clean freshness of Frankie's car. For several seconds, he remained standing outside the shrine, feeling the hard pounding in his chest. Then, with a deep breath, he knocked and pushed open the rickety door with unnecessary force.

POTUS stooped low and entered the Babalawo's shrine.

The shrine was gloomy despite the afternoon sun streaming through multiple holes in its thatched roofing. More occultic items and ritual-istic inscriptions littered the ground and walls. A musty smell of smoke, herbs, stale palm wine, and fresh blood pervaded the air, and POTUS almost gagged from the pong.

He found the Babalawo seated on the hard mud ground of his shrine in the same wide-legged position POTUS recalled from his last visit. The seer was dressed in a full Agbada Babariga regalia, resplendent with expensive beads and ivory amulets. His grey head was topped with a colourful Abeti-aja cap that was crowned with multiple feathers. There was the familiar Opon Ifá divination bowl with its intricate carvings by his side, together with red kola nuts and a keg of palm wine. The Babalawo's face shadowed the ground, his lips silently counting the black kennel nuts spread out on the floor before him.

POTUS coughed softly. The president chortled loudly. The Babalawo looked up, startled. Then his eyes goggled and he screamed.

"Oluwa!" The Babalawo fell back, shrinking away from the president, his face ghastly. "Ancestors and Ògún keep us safe! What do you want with me, great water spirit?" He shrieked in their Yoruba tongue, turning raging eyes at POTUS. "Why do you bring this curse on my grey head, eh?"

"You can see him?" POTUS' voice was filled with wonder. "You can actually see the president? He's not a water spirit; he's just… "

"Oohh! Aahh! Me, I am Massa, the great water spirit and I will curse—"

"Just shut up, Okay?" POTUS snarled, glaring viciously at the president. "You've no idea what you're dealing with here. So, just quit the fucking insults now."

"And you watch your filthy mouth, buddy, and remember who I am,"

"I don't care who you are. When you get back to your country, that is, *if* you get back, then maybe I'll remember who you are," POTUS stressed the 'if.' "But right here, you're nothing but a freaking half-ghost who needs to respect our culture and our elders while you're floating around on our turf."

"I'll remember what you just said come the time," the president's voice was ugly, an odd look on his face that unsettled POTUS—*Uh-uh! Maybe I've gone too far now and ruined things for myself.* Still, the dude has no business disrespecting the Babalawo.

He returned the president's glare with a hard, uncompromising look. "Whatever, let's just finish this rubbish once and for all," he turned his attention to the Babalawo who was observing his interaction with the president with incredulous eyes. The seer now clutched two long, white bones that looked suspiciously like human humeri in his hands. "Great Seer, you might not remember me, but I—"

"I remember you, POTUS," the medicine-man cut him off, scooping a handful of ashes from the calabash at his side. He blew the ashes at POTUS with a vicious frenzy, covering him in grey dust that caused him to sneeze till his eyes watered. "I have been expecting this moment since the day I first saw the spirit inside your body and bound it with my charms. I should've known that one can never keep a great spirit chained forever. Sooner or later, it will break free from its shackles and wreak its mischief as it pleases. Now, I see the great water spirit, POTUS, has escaped at last, and I beg you, oh great spirit, to forgive me for binding you all these years." The Babalawo bowed low to the president who wore a broad smile despite not understanding a word the seer spoke. POTUS wanted to swipe the smirk from his face.

"He's no water spirit, Baba," he said viciously, speaking in English to rile the president. "Listen please, Baba. He's just the President of the United States, an ordinary human who's sick in a hospital room in his country even as we speak."

"I'll have him know I'm no ordinary human as you so ungraciously introduced me," President King cut in, his voice arsenic. "I'm the leader of the free world and—"

"China is the leader of the world as far as I'm—"

"Fuck China and fuck you too!" The president cut in savagely. "I know I'm the leader, and that's a big, tremendous deal to important people that matter."

"Whatever, dude. I'll—"

"And I'm sick of hearing you parrot, 'whatever dude' like some dumbfuck. If you've got nothing else to say, then shut the fuck up, right?" The president shouted at him, menacing.

"No, you shut the fuck up," POTUS yelled back, fear and frustration roasting his brain cells.

"No, you shut the fuck up," the president thundered, gliding closer. His spectre loomed threateningly over both POTUS and the sitting Babalawo who began waving his two bones furiously, chanting mysterious invocations.

In a blink, the president was sent hurtling across the room by a powerful, invisible force. He crashed against the wall and vanished, only to reappear again dazed, his face as ashen as his hair. POTUS wasn't sure who was more stunned, the president or himself. But there was one feeling he could validate and that was his glee. Before his eyes, President King was slowly morphing into a caricature from a children's cartoon. His skin became a phosphorus green colour and his hands— *Oh, sweet Mary and the apostles*—his hands had stretched into two humongous claws that resembled a giant Slimer from the *Ghostbusters* movie on the archive channels.

"Great spirit, I will protect us from you with everything in my power," the Babalawo said to the dazed president, his voice steely, his rheumy eyes icy. "You may be a great deity, but I am the servant of a greater deity by whose great powers I operate. You will leave us and return to your realm across the vast waters, or I will call on my deity, Ògún, and the ancestors to fight you to the death." POTUS saw the stunned look on the president's face which mirrored his own—*No way!* He would've never believed the old man knew a decent word of English, much less speaking it with such grammatical accuracy and dignity!

For the first time, he saw President King lost for words. Terror coated his eyes, a fear laced with grudging respect. The usual cockiness disappeared from his mien as he realised how badly he had underestimated the Babalawo.

"Dude, look at you!" POTUS squealed. "You've turned into Swamp Thing and Slimer combined! Oh my God! And your hands! Freaking hell! I told you, you don't understand what you're dealing with here, didn't I?" He crowed, seeing the president's eyes flash green fury. "So just do us a favour and let me handle this or you might end up getting yourself killed. Trust me, this guy can kill you in your current spirit state just like this," he snapped his fingers, watching the president's face go even greener.

The president said nothing, but POTUS read the reluctant acquiescence in his eyes, even as he kept staring with incredulity at his gigantic green hands, muttering "Damn!" over and over. POTUS returned his attention to the medicine man who was still busy invoking his powers.

"Ha! This demon is the soul eater, the ultimate consumer," the Babalawo reverted to Yoruba, his face grim. "Look at its hands; it is the sign of its greed; grab, grab, grab. None of the demons can enter my shrine without revealing their true nature. This one will eat a man's strength, his bravery, his loyalty, his honesty, his conscience, his values, his land, his wealth, and his family. It will not stop until it has devoured the man whole and spat him out like a pile of vile sick." The Babalawo looked up at POTUS. "You have no idea how lucky you are that this demon is out of your body. Only yesterday, I exorcised another terrible demon. Ògún have mercy!"

The seer shuddered with revulsion. "That demon was the king fornicator, the debaser of men. It had possessed a young boy just like you, and this boy had gone around ravaging every female in sight until he almost ravished his own sister. When they brought him to me, he was spewing corrupt words until I dragged the demon out of his body!" The Babalawo shuddered again and spat into the red mud floor. "You should have seen that demon. Its penis was so long it jutted almost to the roof of my shrine. But as I said, each demon must show its true colours in my presence. By the time I finished with the young man and his demon, I knew he would run ten miles should he ever come across a woman again," the Babalawo grunted with grim satisfaction.

POTUS' head reeled as his mind grappled with the bizarre image of the demon penis extending to the roof of the shrine—*Gross!* He shook the thought away and forced his attention back to the Babalawo.

"Baba, wise father, your name is known all over the world of men and demons; that's why I've brought this lost spirit here to seek your help. I need you to remove these amulets you put on me so that he can return to my body."

The Babalawo stared at POTUS as if he had sprouted horns, tails, and feathers.

"Did I hear right?" The medicine man was incredulous. "Did you just say you want the demon to re-enter your body after you successfully expelled it? Did you not hear anything I just said?"

POTUS nodded, adjusting his bad leg, which was starting to throb. He leaned as low as he could to speak to the Babalawo.

"Baba, he needs to return to my body so his spirit can find its way back to his own body. But these charms keep repelling him and unless you remove them, he can't re-enter my body and time is against him. If he doesn't return to his human body soon, he'll die for real," POTUS held up his arm so the seer could see the trio of amulets around his wrist.

"Good son, I do not think you understand what you're asking for," the Babalawo leaned close as he whispered into POTUS' ear in Yoruba language, his voice hushed, urgent. "The first time this demon possessed you, you were a powerless infant, unable to resist. Your innocent spirit fought it bravely, but it was too powerful for you. It completely took you over and spoke through your mouth. When your parents brought you to me, it had almost taken over your soul," the seer gripped POTUS' hand tightly, his hands tremulous. "Thankfully, my charms subdued it and bound it. We could not expel it at the time, you see. You were too young then. The exorcism could have killed you. Had I not chained it, it would have taken you over permanently and consumed your soul."

The Babalawo cast an odd look towards the president who remained by the door, his translucent, green body swaying like a drunk alien from Mars. A deep frown creased his face. "Look at it, son. Take a good look at the demon," the Babalawo urged. "It is now released but should you invite it into your body again, then you have given it power over your soul. There's no guarantee that it will leave your body without destroying your soul and turning you into an idiot. Even worse, it could consume you whole and leave behind a young corpse for your parents to bury. My advice is this; let it die. Do not invite it into your body. It is a locust that will devour everything in its path and leave nothing behind but waste and tragedy."

POTUS shivered. His head was pounding, and his body trembled uncontrollably—*Oluwa! What to do? What to do?* He had always known it wouldn't be easy to resolve this horrible business with the president. But he never anticipated the horror the Babalawo just described. He didn't need anyone to tell him the president couldn't be trusted, but he needed the man as fish needed water—I have to think everything through… a house in America and one million dollars, not forgetting a green card… Uh-uh! POTUS is nobody's fool. They weren't cheap bites to spit out just like that, not when there was the possibility that he might find his birth mother as well. Even Kunle would be proud of him.

"I hear everything you've said, Baba, but I need him," POTUS' voice was a desperate moan. "He's the President of the United States of America, and he's promised to give my friend and I houses, green cards, scholarships, and one million dollars each," he saw the Babalawo's eyes widen with incredulity and nodded vigorously. "It's true. I even met his sister and his FB1 people who are all working towards it even as we speak. But if he dies, then everything is over and—"

"But how do you know it will keep to its words even if it survives, good son?" The Babalawo asked softly, tapping POTUS' knee delicately with one of his bones. "You have to remember that demons are devious entities, with tongues filled with falsehood. One must always keep one step ahead and trap them the way you trap a slippery eel, otherwise, you're the one that will end up the loser in every way." The seer's eyes glittered with a cunning light as he turned to the irritated president who was gliding around the room, knocking impatiently on the mud walls and generally making a right nuisance of himself like a spoiled child.

"Are you guys done jabbering away over there? How long am I gonna be stuck in this shitty place?" The president was in a big huff and wanted everyone to know it. POTUS looked askance at the medicine man, and the Babalawo looked at the president's hands.

"I want my son to go to America too," the medicine man spoke again in English, tapping his bones gently on the floor before averting his gaze.

POTUS gasped softly, and the president spluttered, his face apoplectic. Then he burst into an ugly hoot, his eyes glittering with malice.

"I can't believe what I'm hearing. I've sure landed myself in a den of stinking shysters. No wonder you fuckers hold the scam trophy of the world," he turned to POTUS with rage. "First you fleece me, and then, you bring me to this quack so he can shake me down as well? Hell no! You can tell him I say no, no can do. No visa, no America, no nothing for his son and that's the end of it. Nothing, zero, zilch. Goddammit! Now I've heard it all!" He stood arms akimbo, great green hands stretched comically all the way down to his knees, glowering at both POTUS and the Babalawo. POTUS would have laughed had the situation not been so dire—*Stupid Motormouth! Why did I go open my big mouth and blab everything to the Babalawo?* He should've known the man would want his own share. After all, how many times does a man get to have the President of the United States at his mercy? *God! Now what?*

The Babalawo smiled, a gap-toothed grin, unfazed by the president's insults. He put down his bones carefully on the floor and carefully adjusted his flamboyant Agbada Babariga flowing gown. With delicate hands, he patted his hair, adjusted his feathered cap and preened himself like the father of a beautiful daughter about to meet his prospective in-laws for the first time. When he was done, he stood up from the floor and straightened himself to his full miniature height, puffing his arms out like a proud peacock before facing President King. His mien was as haughty as the president's own, and even though President King towered over him by over a foot, they each looked as formidable as the other.

"My name is Chief Obamidele Rufus Ògúndipe," the Babalawo announced in a proud, Stentorian voice, his rheumy eyes focused somewhere just above the president's head. "I am the keeper of the shrine of Orisha Ògún, He who rules the battleground of great warriors and the iron of powerful weapons. Hear this, great spirit! My Orisha can strike you dead before you can call on your own name. I did not come to you; you came to me. My power can return life to you in an instant, and yet, you will deny me a very small favour that will give my son the same chance you would want for your own child should our fortunes be reversed." The seer paused, watching the thunderous frown on the president's face with calm resolve.

"I need you to calm down, great spirit," the Babalawo continued cordially. "After all, you are still a spirit even if you are a president, and we must always accord every spirit their due respect," he bowed low to

President King and turned to POTUS. "Young man, you say you want the spirit to possess your body again, and it will be done as you wish. I will now remove this charm I myself placed on you as protection from this very spirit when you were very young."

The Babalawo reached again for his bones and started to tap them on POTUS' head, his shoulders, his back, his stomach, and his chest. Again and again, he blew ashes over his head, reciting charms of purification and protection. The president watched the ritual with bored contempt, an ugly sneer twisting his thin lips. The seer leaned forward and took hold of POTUS' arm. With a swift and fluid motion, he slipped the three bracelets off with grease-ease and hurriedly dropped them into the calabash of ashes as if they were made of flames.

POTUS stared in stunned disbelief into the mystical bowl. The president's soft gasp mirrored his own.

The amulets came alive.

They scuttled inside the calabash like little black beetles, making a terrifying clacking noise that doused his heart with ice. Then they began to glow, each crystal sparking tiny dots of fire before engulfing the entire bowl in a blazing inferno that lit up the gloomy hut like a fluorescent bulb.

POTUS staggered back. Before he could wrap his head around what was happening, the flames died out and the charred amulets dissolved into the bowl. Now, there was nothing left of them save the familiar grey ashes in the charmed calabash. He was stunned to see that the calabash still retained its cool, orange colour and rounded contours, as if it had never encountered the fiery flames he witnessed.

Something inside POTUS wept silently. It was a cry of loss, sudden and unexpected. The charms were the last link binding him to his mother. Ronke had always begged him never to remove them as a personal favour to her. Now, they were gone and their protection vanished forever. The skin area that wore the amulets his entire life had formed little pale dots around his wrist. He rubbed his flesh, swallowing the hard knot lodged in his throat—*I'm sorry, Mama. Please forgive me.*

There was a sudden shout. The Babalawo was pointing frantically at the president who was swooping down at him with terrifying speed like a great bird of prey. His humongous green hands spread out like giant wings, aiming greedily for his neck. Before POTUS could duck, the president slammed into him in a powerful rugby tackle that should have knocked him off his knees had President King possessed a solid human form.

POTUS fell, but only because he had tripped on his own foot in panic. His head swam, his vision foggy as he tried to rise from the ground. His heart was pounding from a cocktail of adrenaline, terror, and rage—*The fucking, cheating, evil devil! Snuck up on me before I could prepare and stole my body again!* Now it was too late to do anything. He might as well resign himself to having nothing since he didn't think the lying cheat would honour his word now. For all he knew, the devil man was even right now trying to kill his spirit and turn him into a drooling zombie. *Fuck! Fuck! Fuck!*

17

THE POSSESSION

POTUS lay on the floor gasping and cursing. Already, he felt an intense burning inside his body confirming the presence of a malignant entity inside him. He shut his eyes, groaning softly.

The Babalawo's loud cackling drew his attention. The medicine man was doubled over in laughter, pointing a gnarled finger towards the door. His eyes twinkled with tears of hilarity. Before he could turn his face towards the door, POTUS heard a sound that sent his spirits soaring.

"Holy righteous shit! Fucking dumb n*gger freak! You almost killed me, you dumb cocksucker! What the hell was that all about?" The president was apoplectic, his face now so white he resembled Akamu, the mushy corn cereal fed to toddlers. The foiled attack had drained his lifeforce and turned him back to his original, pale transparency instead of the vile green shade.

POTUS stared at him wide-eyed, unable to believe his luck —*OMG! Thank you, God! Thank you, Babalawo! I'm free! The cheating demon hasn't possessed my body after all!* Just then, a hot vibration in his body made him look down. He gasped, his mouth a big O.

His body was surrounded by a radiant, shimmering light. This light was different from the rainbow blaze of his defunct amulet induced shield. It was a fiery shroud of the purest blood hue, and incredibly, it seemed to emanate from every pore in his skin rather than from an external crystal source. He quivered like violin strings as a low humming emitted from the red shield. Before he could take in the miracle, he heard the Babalawo as if from a distance.

"You were too greedy," the medicine man scolded the president gently, his face still wreathed in mirth. "You did not wait for us to complete the ritual before you tried to possess the boy's body and consume his soul. Ha! This fool demon!" The Babalawo shook his head, his gaze fixed at the president's gigantic hands. "Hear this, great spirit! Even though I removed the charms, the boy has to first invite you into himself. I activated his Ori and Emi, his guardian spirits, as soon as he entered my shrine with you. I knew he would need them against you. Furthermore, what you just tried to do is an impossibility. For you to re-enter the boy, there has to be both a bond of blood and a bond of truth between you. Ha! Just see how his guardian spirits protected him and rejected your assault." The seer turned away, shaking his head sadly like a human who had tired of ever training a recalcitrant pet that would insist on defecating inside the house rather than outside.

The Babalawo's words sent rage into POTUS' head.

"I always knew I couldn't trust you," he screeched at the president. "You're just a shameless liar, that's what you are." He noticed the red shield fading rapidly from his body and shivered—*Oluwa! But for the Babalawo's incomplete ritual, I'd likely be dead by now.* He had no doubt that the president intended to get rid of him and wipe the slate clean. After all, if he died, he would never reveal any secrets or demand anything.

"Ditto, you little bitchass shit," the president snarled, his eyes glinting an ugly green. "You fucking lied as well. Listen up, buddy. You and your little shyster witch doctor here had better come up with the goods otherwise our deal's off. You'll get nothing. Zero, zilch, savvy?"

"Our deal's already off since you never planned on sticking to it anyway," POTUS raged, hobbling menacingly towards the spectre. "You might be the president of America, but you're nothing but a liar and a cheat and I don't chill with people like you. Dude, you're just pathetic."

"And you're nothing, do you hear me? A big, fat nothing!" The president screamed, almost foaming at the mouth. "You're a fucking zero. Just a stupid, little jerkoff from this shitty fly-dump. You and I know damn well that you need me to make you a big shot with our great American dollars. I say we finish this joke now. Right now!" The president elevated higher, hulking over POTUS, his eyes shooting fiery daggers.

"Everybody, calm down," the Babalawo interjected. "Let your tempers cool so we can discuss this with sensible heads," he turned to POTUS. "Son, do you still want this demon inside your body?"

"Hell no! He can freaking die for all I care."

"What? And give up the American pie, your American scholarship, green card, house, and oh! Not forgetting one million sweet dollars for you and your ch*nk friend? Give me a fucking break," the president's voice dripped with contempt as he drifted down to the ground.

"I've got news for you, dude," POTUS leaned close to him, his eyes blazing. "You can take your American pie and stuff it up your anus. I wouldn't touch anything you offer even if you serve Jesus Christ Himself on God's golden plate. This fly-dump as you call it may not be as wonderful as America, but guess what? I think we're really blessed not to have you as our president."

"Does that mean you're ready to turn your back on everything just because your little pride's been hurt?" The president's voice dripped icy mockery. "And here I was thinking you were made of stronger stuff. Guess I was mistaken. Shoulda known a dumb fuck like you would punk out of the deal. If I were in your shoes, I sure wouldn't turn my nose up at something so mightily beneficial to you and your friend," the president paused, a sudden gleam in his eyes. When next he spoke, his voice was low, his tone casual. "By the way, I thought you were desperate to find your birth mother, right? I would've easily made that possible for you with the awesome resources of the FBI. Still, I guess you gotta make your own choices. I'm just saying if I were you, I'd do things differently, that's all," he shrugged, pretending indifference.

POTUS could see the desperation in President King's eyes, and he knew he now held the trump card in this dark game of occultic Bridge. Dude was right though. He really wanted to find his birth mother more than anything else. There was a hole, an emptiness inside him that could only be filled by seeing, hearing, touching, and being with the woman that gave life to him. Even with Ronke's love, it was never enough. He needed to find that person whose DNA he shared, find out his roots, his ancestors, his history, and what made him part of his true community. He needed answers to questions that had haunted him since he found out he was adopted, questions such as why his mother hadn't loved him enough to want to keep him, who his birth father was, and if he had siblings, a blood tribe he belonged to. If the president would use the powerful arsenal of his FBI to find his birth mum, then he might just reconsider. But first, he must find a way to tie down the slippery devil-man so that he keeps his word and doesn't try to kill him once he retook possession of his body.

POTUS turned to the Babalawo and spoke in rapid Yoruba.

"Baba, is there any way you can make this demon keep to his promise if I let him back into my body? Will he even remember anything that's happened here when he wakes up in his own body? I desperately need to find my blood mother, and he's the only one that can help me find her. So please Baba, help me. I beg you."

The Babalawo smiled gently and took POTUS' hands in his own withered ones.

"Of course, there is a way. There has always been a way. I told you demons are slippery, but we in the trade have also found ways to counteract their trickery and coat our hands with supernatural glue to catch them," the seer spread his fingers, admiring them as if they were formed of precious metals. "So, have no fear, my son. The demon's memory will be intact when it wakes up, and it will remember everything that happened, right from the moment it entered your body in your infanthood. But even without that, there's a more powerful weapon in my arsenal. Either way, you'll win," the Babalawo gave POTUS a significant look he didn't understand. For some reason, it brought unease in him.

"I will now commence the ritual," the Babalawo continued. "But first, I need you to think carefully about a question you will pose to the water demon. It is a question that will require it to give an honest answer, otherwise it will not be able to enter your body even if you give it permission. Until it answers that question honestly, your Ori and Emi, your two guardian spirits, will keep rejecting it, just as they rejected it now. However, once it has given a true answer, then it is bound by its promises and must comply. The juju I'm performing is a powerful one and will not give it peace until it fulfils its promise to you."

The medicine man paused, leaned closer to POTUS, his rheumy eyes pleading. "Good son, I am an old man, and as you can see, I have small children to feed. Our deities do not let us make money from our trade, otherwise they will withdraw their powers from us. My first son is a fine young man, just like you. If he goes to America, I know he will be able to provide for our family as he's a very intelligent boy and scored very high in his JAMB exam. Just that there's no money to send him to university," the Babalawo grabbed POTUS' hands in desperation. "I am begging you, good son, add my son to your request to the spirit. Tell it to bring my son to America. My son's name is Adeleke. You just met him. Tell the spirit to bring Adeleke to America, and I will bless you for the rest of my life. When you ask it the question for the possession ritual, just ask it if it promises to honour the agreement and take my son to America too, please."

POTUS smiled and squeezed the old man's hands gently. "Baba, it'll be my pleasure to do so," he said. "I think I know the question to ask the demon, don't worry. Let us begin the ritual now. I'm ready," he turned to the president and reverted to English. "I hate to admit it, but you're right, Your Excellency. I shouldn't let my pride get in the way of what I want. I guess I'll have to let you back into my body," the words stuck in his throat, making him feel like puking.

"Atta boy! Of course, I'm right. I'm always right. You forget I'm the world's only true wizard. So, you've told old Katanga here that you're back on the ride, right?"

POTUS nodded, an unpleasant smile on his face. "Not quite. I've decided I want nothing from you except to find my birth mother. As for the scholarship and all the perks, you can give them to the Babalawo's son, the guy that let us in. His name is Adeleke and I reckon he'll appreciate it more than I will. Also, my friend, Frankie, naturally."

POTUS didn't know who was more stunned by his words, the president, the Babalawo or himself. Until he actually said the words, he never believed he would speak them aloud—*Oh, God! Am I really giving up on my American dream? I'm actually kissing this once-in-a-life-time opportunity goodbye! Fuck!*

The president's eyes were like saucers. "Lemme get this straight. You've allowed yourself to be suckered by this old wizard here and decided to gift his son with your loot?"

"Not my loot, as you call it," POTUS gritted his teeth. "I think I've more than earned the payment for all the services I've rendered you. But I don't need a thing from you. My dad's rich enough to take care of my needs here in Nigeria, and thanks to you, we're good now." Maybe it's a good thing he's not taking a thing from this dude. The Babalawo always said that his doom lay in water and that he must avoid large bodies of water. He wouldn't be surprised if the plane taking him to America crashes into the Atlantic Ocean. *Nah! President King can stuff his green card, dollars and all!* "So, are you agreeing to take care of the Babalawo's son and Frankie so we can finish this rubbish now?"

"Sure, kiddo, if that's what you want. Your loss," the president shrugged and gave that wicked wink POTUS was starting to loathe more than anything else in the world. "So, what now?"

POTUS turned to the Babalawo and reverted to their Yoruba tongue. "Baba, we're ready now. As you heard, he's agreed to take care of Adeleke."

The Babalawo's eyes filled with tears as he grabbed POTUS' hands again and shook them over and over in gratitude.

"May our ancestors bless you, my son. Òshún, Ògún and Shango shall protect you and fight your battles for you. Oshe! Ese gan! Thank you, my good son," the Babalawo wiped his eyes and turned to the president, even as he averted his gaze again. "Great spirit, are you ready to return to your realm?" he asked, his voice grave, his face austere.

"Hell yes! I've been ready forever! Let's get the kooky ball rolling," the president glided close to the medicine man who quickly shrank away from him. POTUS could see that the old man was still very wary of President King's half-ghost.

"First we shall commence the blood bond. I will cut your flesh so you can both swear a blood oath,"

"What the fuck are you jabbering about?" the president was outraged. "I sure ain't doing no rat-ass blood oath with anyone, and in case you've forgotten, I'm not flesh and blood, samba-sambo? Savvy? I'm some astral being that can go through doors and walls, so I reckon you'll have to do without my blood," he smirked.

"The ritual cannot be done without the blood bond," the Babalawo said, as if he didn't hear the president's words. He stooped and poured palm wine into the Opon Ifá divination bowl. As both POTUS and President King watched, one with fascination, the other with morbid irritation, the seer stirred some of the ashes into the bowl as he muttered incantations in a hoarse and trembling voice. When he was done, he straightened and passed the bowl to POTUS.

"Drink," he ordered. "Only a little, you hear. Very little."

POTUS took the bowl and stared suspiciously into it. The pungent odour of palm wine and something else he couldn't define was strong in his nostrils, and everything in him rebelled against it— Oh, God! What horrible germs are lurking inside the bowl? He shut his eyes, his face all screwed up as he took the tiniest sip possible. It tasted just as vile as he expected. He shuddered, and he passed the bowl back to the seer, but the old man shook his head and nodded towards the president.

"Give it to the spirit so it can drink as well," the Babalawo instructed. "Tell it, it must finish it, every last drop of it." POTUS wondered why the man was so reluctant to address the president directly, even though he could speak perfect English.

"What's in the bowl?" The president took a sniff and screwed up his nose. "Phew! It smells disgusting. I ain't getting poisoned, thank you very much," he passed it back to POTUS who kept his hands on his crutches, ignoring the bowl. Strangely enough, since having the small sip of the drink, he felt himself growing heavy and lethargic, as if concrete had been poured into his body. He shook his head to clear the fog.

"You can't get poisoned. You're not human, as you keep reminding me. It's nothing. Just drink it so we can get this rubbish started. I've drunk it and I'm still standing."

"Yeah, yeah, yeah. But you n*ggers are used to germs, aren't you?"

"Quit the N-word, alright? Just fucking quit right now, or I won't be responsible for my actions," POTUS snarled, surprised by the ease with which he now used the "F-word" since coming in contact with President King. But he was starting to discover its placebo effect on his rage and now understood why the president seemed addicted to it.

"What? You gonna sucker punch me? Come on, big guy! Give it a try and see where your stupid punches land. Come on! I'm waiting. Show me what you got," the president egged him on with his hands, his eyes glittering malice, his hulking figure gliding closer.

POTUS glared at him helplessly before shaking his head wearily —Devil-man knows he can't be hit; not in that stupid translucent state anyway. "Whatever, dude. Just drink it. Unless you're happy to remain as you are now, an insignificant, fake-ghost loser that nobody respects or gives a fuck about," he knew his insults would hit home. If there was one thing he shared with the president, it was a very healthy ego.

He was right.

"Screw you," the president gave him a sour look and tipped the bowl over, downing the contents in a long swig. POTUS stared in wonder as he followed the slow journey of the fluid travelling through the president's transparent body. The ubiquitous white golf outfit he wore might as well be invisible for all the good it did. The drink quickly congealed into a thick sludge of molasses, spreading in a slow, brown mass across every limb, bone, and vein, till he stood solid, a living black man of flesh and bones.

The president cussed and chucked the bowl away with a disrespectful flick. He wiped his mouth, making a disgusted face.

"Okay, what next?" He glared at both POTUS and the Babalawo.

POTUS stared at him in stunned disbelief.

"What? What?" The president asked aggressively, seeing the incredulous look in POTUS' eyes. The Babalawo just smiled serenely.

"Dude, you're human!" POTUS' voice was an awed whisper.

"You're human, Your Excellency! Look at yourself. You're a brother! Oh my God!"

The president looked.

Then he looked again. His mouth widened, horror glazing his eyes.

"Holy righteous shit! Sweet Mary and the apostles! What have you fuckers done to me?" He glared at the Babalawo before returning his gaze to his arms, his two black, fleshy arms stretched out before him. Even his giant hands had shrunk back to their normal human size.

POTUS was mesmerised. President King looked as if he'd just stepped out of a Nollywood movie on the massive TV screen in Kunle's living room. Gone was the pale, white haired semi-ghost that had haunted him for over a week. In his place stood the familiar middle-aged, dark-haired, and smooth-skinned charismatic leader that had graced every television screen in the world and was instantly recognisable as the bona fide President of the United States.

Except he was now black-skinned—*Holy Righteous Shit, as the president would say!*

POTUS grinned malevolently. Seeing the president in black skin was a balm to his raging heart—*Yes! There's justice, after all! Should I call him n*gger just for the fun of it? If only the bloody guy would remain black for the rest of his yeye life.* Even so, confronting President King in the flesh, so to speak, intimidated POTUS. The prospect of having the president inside him, especially seeing him as he was at the moment, all solid and flesh, sent his heart racing with dread.

"Answer me! What the fuck have you shitheads done to me?" President King roared again, apoplectic.

"Tell it not to worry," the medicine man smiled at POTUS. "It's just the effects of the Àwòrán juice. It is very temporary. We just need it to get its blood for the blood bond. We must not delay before it starts to fade," the Babalawo spoke in English and POTUS saw the president's face morph into a ghastly, ashy mask.

"Holy Mackerel! I can't believe what I'm seeing," President King shook his head. "This is impossible. I'm no fucking ni*gger! No friggin' way! It's a hallucinatory effect of the drugs he just fed me, that's it."

"Dude, this is no illusion, trust me. Otherwise, I wouldn't be seeing you too in the black flesh," POTUS said as the bizarre impact of the situation hit him. He hobbled over and pinched the president hard on his nice, soft, black arm, just to be sure.

"Ouch! Fuck! Why the hell did you do that, you little prick?"

"Just to prove to you you're now human. You're a black brother, bruv." POTUS laughed, a hard, loud chuckle that earned him a sour look from the president—*Wow! The old Babalawo is truly awesome! Respect, dude! Respect with a capital R!* POTUS finally understood the reverence his late mother had for the guy. He too was permanently done with the churches and their pastors for good, even with all the pretty girls on offer—*This is the real deal, the religion of his ancestors! I'm truly born again! Alleluia!*

The Babalawo grunted and withdrew a small blade from his sack before picking up his Opon Ifá divination bowl from where the president had chucked it away. Arms outstretched like a surgeon about to operate, he approached POTUS.

"Raise your right arm," he ordered. "Your palm must be facing up."

POTUS complied, gritting his teeth. With a quick flick of his hand, the Babalawo slashed three straight, vertical lines on his inner arm just below his elbow. POTUS shut his eyes and groaned softly. He felt the flow of warm blood on his arm, and opened his eyes to look.

He instantly regretted it.

His head swum and his body swayed. He staggered back, his horrified gaze fixed on his mutilated arm. His blood literally poured into the wooden bowl like warm stew. The president looked ready to faint as well. POTUS discovered another thing he regrettably shared with the American president—they both didn't handle the sight of blood well. *God!*

"Are you sure that damned blade is sterilised?" President King's voice was hoarse. "Because I sure as hell ain't got no plans of leaving this fly-dump with AIDS or Syphilis or whatever horrible diseases you Africans have."

POTUS ignored him, nursing his throbbing arm. The Babalawo sprinkled some of his sacred ashes on the cuts, and instantly, the bleeding stopped. He could even swear the pain diminished, almost non-existent now. POTUS shook his head with wonder—*Wow! The*

Babalawo washed the blade with the palm wine before cleaning it with ashes and some palm fronds. Then he advanced towards the president with the bowl and blade. The president backed away from him, his eyes goggled.

"It's alright, Your Excellency," POTUS said, an unexpected air of cordiality in his voice. "It doesn't really hurt, and that magic ashy stuff literally kills any little pain you might feel. Look at my arm. It's not even bleeding anymore, and I swear it doesn't hurt either," he raised his arm to show the president who glanced quickly at it before fixing his wary gaze on the steadily advancing seer.

"I ain't worried about now. It's later, after all this voodoo stuff is over. That blade ain't sterilised, and I don't care what you say. I'm not opening myself up to any of your weird, tropical diseases. That's final," President King pursed his lips, folded his arms across his chest, a stubborn frown on his face.

"Your choice, dude," POTUS shrugged. "I've done my bit. You heard the man. The effects of the drink don't last long, and you'll soon revert to your ghostly form and then it'll be too late for you. So, if you really want to ever see your country again, then this is your last chance. Because after today, I promise you, I'm done, and I don't think you can survive much longer."

President King bit his lips, opened them to speak, and pressed them shut again. With a mumbled curse, he stretched out his arm to the Babalawo, turning his head away so he wouldn't see what was happening—*Cry-cry baby!* POTUS almost crowed.

The president gasped at the first cut and continued to groan while the Babalawo drained his blood. POTUS smiled, loving President King's discomfort. He wished he could take a photo with his mobile, but he didn't think it was the right time or place—*Pity.*

"Now we're done," the Babalawo returned to his sitting position on the floor and started stirring the blood inside the bowl. He added some salt, oil, herbs, ashes, and other ingredients to the mixture. The president glowered at the medicine man, nursing his cuts as if he'd lost a whole arm.

POTUS studied him surreptitiously, stunned by how solid he was and how black he looked in his white golf attire and bright red cap.

"I have now finished the blood bond," the Babalawo announced in his familiar Stentorian voice, turning to look directly at the president for the first time. "From now on, you two are bound by blood in the spiritual realm. You cannot harm the other without harming yourself. It is now time for the bond of truth between you, after which you can begin the possession that will lead you back to your rightful realm. You need to stand and face each other now."

"Huh! More hocus-pocus, I see," the president sneered as POTUS shuffled closer to him.

The stuffy shrine drenched him in sweat, and his plastered leg and arm were starting to throb painfully. He wiped his face with the back of his hand. A couple of feet from the president, he stopped and looked back at the Babalawo with an inquiring frown.

"Ask him your question now," the medicine man instructed. "He must give you a true answer to gain passage into your body."

"Shoot," the president said, his green eyes glinting mockingly. "Ask away, boy."

POTUS squared his shoulders as if in readiness for a fist fight and stared him straight in the eyes. He inhaled deeply, exhaled noisily, cleared his throat, and asked.

"What does 'Remember Belly-Berry' mean?"

18

REMEMBER BELLY-BERRY

The Federal Enquirer
Coma Countdown!
Day Twelve of President Jerry King's Coma
PMD Media, 20 July
(Mike Vine and the news desk)

First Lady, Portia King, Exits The White House!
President King Showing Signs of Recovery!

The countdown to President Jerry King's coma continues as we enter into the 12th day. But things are starting to shake up in the White House. We can confirm that the First Lady, Portia King, has vacated the White House for an undisclosed address in a dramatic move that has stunned the nation. According to our sources, the move came out of the blue and took the White House aides by surprise. As the president is still in a coma, the First Lady is expected to be at his side supporting him.

We are also gathering from sources familiar with the situation that both the FBI chief, Daniel Jackson, and the Chief of Staff, Pete Daniels, made an unscheduled and clandestine visit to the African country, Nigeria, in the company of the president's sister, Dr. Delores King and the Secretary of Defence, General Mike O'Neill. Nobody knows the nature of the visit, but it would appear that following their return, there has been a major shake-up in the White House, culminating in the First Lady's abrupt departure. We understand from our sources that more shocking departures are lined up as news of the First Lady's exit continues to send ripples down the entire nation, especially coming so close to the elections. We have reached out to the office of the First Lady for comments but have yet to receive any response.

In other developments, there has been a complete overhaul of the president's medical team. Yesterday, Americans listened to the first briefing by the new team who have confirmed that the president has been showing signs of improvement. As a result, the planned withdrawal of the life support machine has been abandoned.

The positive news saw a spike at the stock exchange as the markets rallied, closing above 10% and bringing a great sigh of relief to investors worldwide. Speaking to reporters, the president of the New York Stock Exchange, Kim Soo-Young, stated that the latest rallying of the Nasdaq can only mean great news going forward. It even raises the possibility that the country might yet head to the polls come November with President King on the ballot after all. As we pray for our president's speedy recovery, we will continue to keep you informed with further developments.

"What does 'Remember Belly-Berry' mean?" POTUS repeated his question as the president continued to stare at him, his mouth opening and closing like a bloated fish trapped on a hot, sandy beach.

"Ask another question, anything, and I'll tell you," the president pleaded, his voice hoarse.

"No. I want to know what 'Remember Belly-Berry' means," POTUS insisted.

For several seconds, President King held his gaze. Then a malignant gleam entered his eyes.

"Okay, if you insist," he shrugged with disdain. "It's not Belly-Berry, you dumbfuck. It's Belly-Bury, get it? As in bury a belly. In other words, an abortion. You have your answer, and I hope you're satisfied. It's not my fault you can't spell shit. Now, can we get on with the business so I can get myself home without further delay?"

"No. You still haven't answered my question," POTUS insisted, glowering at him. "Even if Belly-Bury means an abortion, what does the message mean? Why did you send it to your sister?"

"Shit! I don't feel too well," the president said weakly, stumbling against the wall and collapsing on the floor. POTUS rolled his eyes—Yeye man is up to his usual tricks. Then he looked closely.

"Oluwa! He's really not looking too good," he called out to the Babalawo in alarm. The medicine man glanced briefly at the prone president and promptly returned to his divination with an air of disinterest.

"Don't worry. It's just returning to its spirit form again and losing the mortal flesh the Àwòrán juice gave it. I did tell you its effects are temporary," the Babalawo sounded bored.

He was right.

Even as POTUS stared, the president began to fade right before his eyes. It was like watching a dying sun, the pale shadow replacing the once golden rays of the midday sun till nothing was left except the night skies. He shivered involuntarily. He feared the president would continue fading till there was nothing where his porous body now lay, save an empty, gloomy space.

The president groaned, cussed, and slowly floated up from the

floor, threading air as was his habit. POTUS released a sigh of relief—
Nothing must happen to him till he finds my birth mum!

"Fuck! The clown's turned me back into the Invisible Man again,
just as I was starting to get used to being human," the president grum-
bled, glowering at the Babalawo. "Still, better a white ghost than a
black human, right?"

"He did warn you the effects of the drink were temporary,"
POTUS parroted the witch doctor's words, watching the president
carefully—*Dude sure looks okay and back to his racist shit.* "Anyway, I'm
still waiting for your answer. Trust me, you haven't got much time. If
you looked in a mirror right now, you wouldn't want to waste a second
longer," he shrugged.

The president looked at himself, his fading arms and vanishing
fingers, and cussed again. He gave POTUS a dark look, green eyes
glinting pure malice.

"Damn motherfucker! You're right. Let's be done with this shit
show now."

"So, what does 'remember Belly-Bury' mean?" POTUS repeated
for the third time.

"It means a broad I was dating got knocked up and Delores gave
her an abortion, satisfied? That's it. In case you've forgotten, my sister's
a doctor, and we didn't want any scandal as the girl was from a very
conservative family. So, Dels sorted it out. Are you happy now? Can
we be done with this circus?"

POTUS stared at him saucer-eyed, his heart racing in excitement
—*Finally! I now know the whole sordid meaning behind that weird
phrase!* Why isn't he surprised? It's exactly what he'd expect from the
selfish liar, to have everyone cleaning up his mess after him. His lips
curled down in disdain as he turned and nodded to the Babalawo.

"We're done, Baba. He's told me the truth at last."

"So why are you disturbing me?" The medicine man sounded irritated. "If it has told you the truth, then you have formed the bond of
truth with it. Invite the spirit inside yourself and let us be done with it.
We've wasted too much time here as it is, and my stomach craves
food," he ·hissed. "I swear, I have never seen a more argumentative
spirit in my life than this one. I pity its wife, I tell you," he sent a sour

gaze at the president who returned the favour with a nasty scowl. POTUS would have smiled if his heart wasn't thudding so hard—*This is it! This is really it! It's happening… Fuck! I'm not ready, not one bit…*

"I guess I'll invite you in now," he muttered, fighting his terror. "But just to confirm, you'll help me find my birth mother once you get back to America, and you'll also give the Babalawo's son, Adeleke, and my friend Frankie everything you would've given me before, right?"

The president nodded, his eyes bright with excitement. "Sure, sure. That's the deal, kiddo."

POTUS stared hard at him. He didn't trust a word the man said. He just had to trust the Babalawo's juju to do its magic should the president renege as he fully expected him to do. He expelled a deep sigh and squared his shoulders.

"I guess this is goodbye, then. I won't lie and say it's been great knowing you," he sneered. "I'm sure you feel the same. Anyway, here goes. I, POTUS Lanre Olupitan, invite you, President Jerry King, into my body." He opened his arms wide, shut his eyes and waited. He didn't want to see the president possess him—*Please God, don't let it hurt…*

POTUS waited…

… And he waited. His body was as tense as high-tension wires. Then he heard a shout and the familiar wicked cackle from the witch doctor. He opened his eyes and found the president splayed on the floor, cussing and spluttering. Once again, his own body was surrounded by the mysterious, dazzling, and vibrating red aura.

"This spirit is clearly a congenital liar," the Babalawo gasped in between chuckles, finally staring straight into the president's eyes. "I told you, you cannot enter the boy's body unless you tell the whole truth and form the bond of truth, just as you formed the bond of blood. See how his body has rejected you again. And now, your energy is almost gone," he chortled again, shaking his head. "You don't have much time to waste, so if I were you, I would start speaking before your time is up," he turned to POTUS and smiled. "The good news is that the spirit has depleted its energy completely, so it will not have enough strength to battle your soul when it possesses you. It will be lucky if it has enough left to get it back to its own body."

POTUS' heart soared—*Thank you, thank you, Jesus... I mean, thank you, great Ògún!* He heaved a deep sigh and squared his shoulders once again. He hadn't realised how much he had dreaded the spiritual battle with the malicious half-ghost till he heard the Babalawo's words. He turned back to the president and bore his eyes into his defiant green ones.

"Dude, you're something else, I swear. You just never learn. When will you realise that you're now in the presence of a greater power than yours?" He shook his head wearily. "Anyway, you heard the man. You only have one more chance left. If you mess it up, then you're done," his voice turned hard. "So, you lied the first time about Belly-Bury. Well, guess what? Our old deal is off. Here's my new demand. I now want you to lift all visa restrictions to Nigerians visiting America. That's right," he revelled in the stunned look in the president's eyes. "I mean it. No more visa requirements for Nigerians visiting America. Add that to finding my birth mother and taking care of the Babalawo's son and Frankie and we're even. That's my new deal. You can take it or leave it."

"You gotta be kidding me," the president's voice dripped with mockery. "Why the heck should I lift all visa restrictions for Nigerians? Hell no! We already got half your country in the United States, and you expect me to do the open sesame for the rest of you crooks? You're outta ya little mind, buddy."

"No, I'm not," POTUS snarled, bristling at the president's contemptuous tone. "After all, you're the one that keeps calling us fly-dump and crooks and whatever. I reckon it's poetic justice to have those crooked flies in America so you can turn us into honest butterflies."

"Don't be sarcastic, kiddo. It doesn't suit you," President King tried to sound unbothered, but POTUS could see the president was bothered; very bothered—*Cunning liar.* "Listen, I like you guys, right? And I know you guys like me here, too," President King's voice was all friendly, his mien oozing the irresistible charm that had trapped POTUS in the past like a stupid fly in a spiderweb. "You ain't like the blacks in America who cuss me and call me a racist pig just because I didn't give them the post of VP or Secretary of State. But they didn't vote for me, right? So why should I reward them for hating me? You can understand that, can't you, kiddo?" The president flashed him another winning smile, which POTUS returned with a scowl. Not that the guy paid any notice. "Anyways, you folks here understand me much better than them back home. If you don't believe me, just go out into your streets and ask anyone what they think of President King, and they'll look you square in the eyes and tell you he's a swell guy who says things straight up and holds the same decent, God-fearing values as you folks. Trust me, kiddo, they wouldn't thank you for being this mean to me. So, what d'you say we just drop this free visa nonsense and wrap things up ASAP, right?"

"Wrong," POTUS shook his head violently—*POTUS is nobody's fool! I'm no longer a dumb Eve to be tricked with a stupid apple by an evil snake!* He now knew the real man behind the presidential façade, the badly flawed man dripping poison and lies with dazzling magnetism. "You can quit your divide-and-rule trick because it isn't working with me. I really don't care if everyone in the world loves you. I don't love you, and that's all that matters. The visa deal stays. I won't change my mind. After all, you'll be getting yourself the fattest flies from this fly-dump anyway, seeing as the people that can afford the exorbitant visa and flight fees are the most corrupt Nigerians," POTUS imitated the president's mocking sneer.

"You're a friggin' jerk, d'you know that?" President King glowered at POTUS.

"Ditto, Your Excellency. You brought this on yourself by lying 24/7 and trying to shaft me. Well, this is payday, and I'm here to collect," POTUS gave him a gleeful smirk. "What was it you said? Nicey-nicey is pussy-whipped and loser-stamped? Well, I've taken a page out of your book. I'm just going to listen to your latest story this time, and it's up to you if you lie again or not. My body will reject you again if you do, and then, that'll be it for you—nothing, zero, zilch," he parroted the president's favourite mantra and saw his eyes narrow before he swerved violently away from him and glided towards the door.

POTUS waited. His bad leg throbbed under the hard plaster and his stomach growled with hunger. Worse, the heat inside the shrine was rapidly becoming unbearable, and he was starting to feel light-headed. Just as he was about to tell the president to speed up, the fake-ghost glided back to him, looking so ghastly that POTUS feared another collapse. When he spoke, his voice was almost inaudible.

"Everything I told you before was true, alright?" President King's voice was dull, weary like someone facing the executioner's guillotine. "The girl's name was Mary-Lou Johnson, and she was nineteen, a year younger than I was. It was just before Christmas of '97, and we were hanging out at my college digs. When she told me she was pregnant, I panicked, right? I mean, here I was, about to graduate and this broad was looking to tie me down in unholy matrimony," the president shrugged again. POTUS was starting to recognise that deceptively casual shrug as a sign of stress. "Anyways, I suggested an abortion, but she was having none of it. She was catholic, you see, and they don't do abortions," the president pulled a face. "You gotta realise it was a different era, and I was a different person in those days, too young to know my ass from my dick. As you know, these days I'll have nothing to do with the Roe vs Wade feminist shit." The president paused, his eyes staring into a distance too far for POTUS to see. Whatever he saw there didn't appear to bring him any joy because when next he spoke, he sounded like a man about to face judgement day at St. Peter's gate.

"Anyways, I spoke to my big sister. Dels had just completed her medical school residency in surgery and knew what to do. We agreed to invite Mary-Lou to Dels' house to meet a member of my family, you know, give her the impression I was seriously considering marriage. So, we drove to Dels' place that Sunday evening. We chatted for a while, then Dels went and got her a drink. Well, a spiked drink—whatever. A coupla minutes later, Mary-Lou was knocked out completely and sprawled out on the sofa in la-la land. Dels and I carried her into the spare room so she could perform the abortion on her," the president stopped, just like a toy that had run out of batteries.

POTUS' eyes were ready to pop—*OMG!* This was worse than he'd expected! Something was telling him to prepare himself for much worse—*Oh my God... not my nightmares... don't let it be my nightmares...*

"Everything was going well when, suddenly, there was blood everywhere," the president shut his eyes briefly as if to shut out the image. "The blood just kept gushing from Mary-Lou, and there was nothing we could do to stop it. We daren't call an ambulance or they'd know what Dels had done and then her career would be over. Not to mention possible prison terms for both of us. Soon, Mary-Lou went all white and then she went blue, and by the time she turned cold, it was almost midnight and we were in a daze trying to figure out how to dispose of her body," the president shuddered involuntarily, inhaling deeply.

POTUS' skin broke out in goosebumps, and a sick feeling settled low in his stomach. He had wanted answers, and now he wished he'd never asked. The more President King spoke, the more vividly he recalled his nightmares. Except, they weren't just dreams after all. Somehow, he had tapped into the president's own nightmares during their shared existence, and now, he had even more reasons to be terrified. The more he heard from President King, the more convinced he was that the president wouldn't let him live once he returned to his body. He was now a walking corpse, bullet fodder for the blasted FBI —*Oluwa! Fuck! Fuck!*

After several tense seconds, President King resumed his story, oblivious to POTUS' torment.

"It was Dels that came up with the idea to bury Mary-Lou in her backyard, and that's what we did. Later, Dels turned it into a porch with concrete layering over the grave. Mary-Lou was never found despite a nationwide search, and Dels has never moved from that house. That's why she's never married, either. I told you she's fiercely loyal to her little brother," the president gave a small laugh that was almost a sob. "Anyways, Mary-Lou died on the twelfth of December '97 and that was the number I gave Dels when we met in your hospital room. It's the secret code I use for everything, 121297, and if you know what's good for you, you'll forget you ever heard this number, right? Of course, you know you can never repeat any of this, don't you?" The president's eyes were steely flints, a ruthless glint in their green depths.

"Or you'll get me killed, right?" POTUS turned to the Babalawo, terror widening his eyes into great saucers. "Baba, this bond of truth has placed my life in danger. Now I know his secret, he plans to kill me once he returns to his body!"

"I never said that," the president spluttered.

"You didn't need to say it. You already implied it. POTUS is nobody's fool, and I know exactly how you powerful men operate. I'll get a bullet behind my head one day and that'll be it for me, just like poor Mary-Lou in her yellow bloodied dress."

"I never told you the colour of her dress," the president stared at him with stunned eyes.

"You didn't have to. I already saw her inside that room lying dead on the slab in her yellow dress that was the same colour as her hair!" POTUS shrieked, glaring at the president with terror and hate. "All this time, her corpse was strangling me in my dreams. I didn't know it was you she was after and not me and… "

"God dammit! Don't tell me you had that dream as well?" The president's voice was as stunned as his eyes. "You fucking tomb raider! You literally robbed my body and mind and now my dreams as well? Little deadbeat freak!"

"I'm not a freak! I didn't ask you to enter my body in the first place!" POTUS shouted. He turned back to the Babalawo. "Baba, be my witness, please. You heard what this man said with his own lips. Remember how my mum used to bring me to you so you would cure those December 12th nightmares and the voices. Now we know the true reason for them, and I know this demon will kill me just as he killed that poor girl."

"I told you not to have any fear, good son," the Babalawo's voice was calm, unbothered. He spoke in English, no doubt to ensure the president understood his words. "It will do you no harm. You forget you have a blood bond with it which I have dedicated to the Orishas. It binds two of you together in blood and truth in the spirit realm. Any evil it does to you will be visited back on it threefold, down to his children, their children, and to the tenth generation. That is how the Orishas' justice and retributions work. You yourself are equally chained by the bond and will never reveal the secret shared with you as long as it deals fairly and honestly with you. Your hands must be clean, or the deities will not protect you from its malice." The seer stood up and rearranged his Agbada garb as if ready to leave the shrine. "Now, please let us finish this business without delay so I can go eat. You and your friend have put me through enough torture today," he pulled a martyred face.

POTUS saw the shocked look on President King's face and felt almost giddy with relief—*I'll live after all! Thank you, Ògún!* He trusted the Babalawo's powers and knew that President King was now a believer. With new resolve, POTUS faced the president again. This time, his heart wasn't pounding, and his body stood firm. He knew the possession would work because the president had finally bared his soul. POTUS didn't doubt for a second that the president would return to his comatose body in peace, without delay and without malice. And most importantly, he would honour all his promises, too. Something told him it would be the first time the guy wouldn't cheat or lie because this time he knew that his promise was a promise made to the gods, and the Orishas could be deadly and ruthless in their vengeance.

"I am ready," POTUS said, spreading his arms wide.

19
KARMA & VISAS

Ronke was cremated in a burial ceremony that stunned them by the great crowd of mourners that attended. The entire LGBTQ community from all over the country and several celebrities turned up en masse to pay their respects to her. It was as if a great celebrity had died. Kunle was overwhelmed by the unexpected support and cried nonstop, same as POTUS. Ronke's funeral was the final healing they both craved, the validation of their existence. It told them that they had friends; that despite everything, they were not alone. The shameful, lonely, and furtive burial they had dreaded never materialised, and the triumph of Ronke's final send-off helped heal their grief.

A few weeks later, POTUS paid the medicine man a visit to consult with the oracle about his future. He was met at the door by the little dreadlocked boy that had demanded money from him the last time he visited with Frankie.

"Uncle, I want go America too. Give me visa now," the pint-sized tyrant demanded with his familiar imperious air, as if POTUS carried the entire American embassy inside his Adidas rucksack.

"Visa denied, you little ruffian," POTUS laughed, yanking his filthy dreadlocks with affection. There was an inexplicable something about the little rascal that he liked, a certain brashness that reminded him of himself.

Once seated, he was treated like royalty by every member of the Babalawo's household. From the oldest of his four wives to the youngest of his eighteen children, POTUS witnessed an endless stream of people shaking his hand and bowing effusively to him.

"Oshe! Thank you! God bless you!" They greeted with wide smiles.

"Thank him well," the Babalawo instructed sternly. "Make sure you bow down well to our great son. Without him, Adeleke would not be going to America. Ògún be praised."

Soon, several bottles of beer, Coca-Cola, Maltina, and Guinness were presented to him, together with many skewers of Suya spiced beef.

"Baba, have you heard from the American people about Adeleke's visa?" POTUS asked, eyes wide in surprise and fixed on a couple of packed suitcases in the small living room. Last time he spoke to Frankie, President King had yet to keep to his promise. Furthermore, there had been no announcements about the lifting of visa restrictions for Nigerians either. That last bit had been a tall order and one he knew the president might never fulfil. He had only thrown it in to frustrate President King as he too had been frustrated.

"Not yet," the Babalawo smiled serenely. "But we're ready to hear from them any day now."

POTUS was stunned by the Babalawo's blasé attitude. The seer didn't seem concerned about President King's treachery. From his calm demeanour, one could see that there was not an iota of doubt in the man's mind that President King would honour his pledge.

"But Baba, we both know that the man is a liar," POTUS protested, frowning deeply. "Now he's back in his own body, you can see he no longer has any intentions of honouring his pledge."

The Babalawo patted him gently on the shoulder, his face creased in a smile.

"Fear not, good son," he murmured. "Everything is already in motion in the supernatural realm, trust me. The man made the pledge to the Orishas and will indeed honour *all* our agreements whether or not he likes it. Do not doubt the great Orishas. Just watch and see."

The seer stressed the word, 'all' in a way that sent a sliver of unease down POTUS' spine.

He shook away his disquiet—He trusted the Babalawo and his predictions completely, even as far-fetched as they sounded. If the man said that President King would find his birth mother and give both his son and Frankie the scholarship deal he'd promised, then he had to believe him. After all, he had witnessed the Babalawo's powers and seen what the Orishas could do. POTUS now had his own personal shrine to Ògún in his bedroom and had since renounced Christianity for the traditional religion of his people. Kunle had helped him prepare the devotional shrine, and POTUS now prayed daily to Ògún, offering regular monthly chicken sacrifices to the great Orisha. He also nurtured his spiritual growth with meditations and devoutness at Ògún's shrine, something that pleased both the Babalawo and his dad no end.

A week after his visit to the Babalawo's house, *CNL Anderson Corp* broke the news about the unexpected death of the president's sister, Dr. Delores King. POTUS was scrolling through his mobile phone aimlessly before bedtime, as was his usual habit, when the news came up—***President Jerry King's Sister Commits Suicide!***

POTUS heart plunged— *No! Oh, please God, no!* His hands began shaking as he raced through the report. Despite everything he had later discovered about the president's sister and the terrible Belly-Bury secret, POTUS still harboured a warm feeling in his heart for the steely lady he'd met in his hospital room on that sunny afternoon that now seemed like a distant dream. He had liked Dr. Delores, her posh British accent and her fierce love for her little brother. She had told him he would be welcomed into the King family when he came to America. She was the only one amongst the visitors who made him feel worthy and appreciated. Even with his eyes shut, he could see her piercing green eyes, so similar to President King's, her coiffed waves and the immaculate cut of her grey trouser suit—How can someone like her die like this?

The article claimed Dr. Delores committed suicide following a mysterious mental breakdown that resulted in her experiencing hallucinations and hysteria. POTUS suspected something more sinister— What if the Babalawo's juju was responsible? What if his own hands were tainted with blood? What if the deities equally came after him for whatever reason? One could never tell what might offend the gods. *What if… Oh, great Ògún, have mercy!*

There was no sleep for him for the rest of the night, and early the next morning, he rushed to the Babalawo's house even before Kunle woke up. He was still hyperventilating when he arrived at the whitewashed bungalow.

The Babalawo nodded his head slowly as he listened to POTUS's garbled words. His face was grim, and his steely gaze held POTUS' terrified eyes with unblinking resolve.

"Good son, have no fear. Your hands are clean," the Babalawo finally said, patting POTUS' knee gently. "The woman had a bad debt with the spirits which she could never escape. It would have still caught up with her, even without her brother's dishonesty speeding it up in the supernatural realm. Trust me, the president's time is also coming soon. Just like his sister, he owes a bad debt which he must also pay. He took an oath of blood and truth in this very shrine and then tried to betray it. By his own words, he tied his entire family to his oath, including his sister and right down to the tenth generation. A blood sacrifice is the only outcome when a pledge to the deities is broken. I think, after this, he will honour all his promises. So, have no fears my son. As I said, your hands are clean."

POTUS heaved a loud sigh and thanked the Babalawo profusely— Thank heavens! I don't want to feel like a murderer ever again! God knows I'd never knowingly do anything to harm that kind woman who was nothing like her horrible brother!

That night, he prayed for the soul of the late doctor. He prayed that the seer was right, that the gods wouldn't send evil karma to him as a result of the doctor's untimely death.

It was a prayer he made at an unfortunate hour, while the Orisha's slept with their ears deaf to his desperate voice.

Karma bit POTUS hard with deadly fangs the next time he visited the Babalawo for divination a fortnight later. Even before the seer spoke, POTUS' heart had already squeezed itself into a tight knot of tension on seeing the grave expression on the medicine man's face.

"Good son, it is not good news I bear for you," the Babalawo said, offering him a calabash of warm palm wine, which POTUS drained in one rushed gulp. "It is about your birth mother. I know we had hoped that the American president would find her for you as he promised. But I am sorry to inform you that she now rests with the ancestors. I saw her during my divinations. She dripped water and seaweed from her eyes to her mouth and every orifice and pore in her body," the Babalawo paused as he saw the pallor of POTUS' face.

"Baba, are you sure?" He asked, his voice hoarse, a tight knot squeezing the air from his lungs. "How can you be sure it's my birth mother and not just any other wandering spirit?"

Images of Ronke as he last saw her in his vision on the day she died flashed in his head. She too had dripped seawater just as the Babalawo described—Maybe it was Mama Ronke that he saw in his divinations? His birth mum must be alive... she had to be! She was still a young woman according to everything he'd heard, so why should she be dead? The Babalawo was surely mistaken.

"Good son, I promise you it was your mother I saw in my astral journey. She never made it to America. The smugglers she paid for the passage put her on a boat which capsized before it could get to the white man's land," the Babalawo's voice was hard, devoid of emotion, the voice of pure prophecy. "Her restless spirit told me her sad story. She wants you to know that she's sorry she was not the mother you deserved. Her spirit cannot rest till she has made her peace with you. I was asked to deliver her message and to ask you for forgiveness. She said you must travel to the village of Orugbo in Warri district and ask for Mercy Okosun. She is your blood grandmother."

POTUS was crying silently and hard. He felt a sense of déjà vu, as if he had lost Ronke all over again. Except this time, it was his birth mother he mourned—*It's all been for nothing! All that fighting and bargaining with President King have been for nothing!* He would never get to know his birth mother now. This hole in his heart will never be filled even should he find his maternal grandmother whose name he finally knew.

"I am sorry, good son," the Babalawo's voice was gentle despite the congenital hardness of his gaze. "You can take solace in the fact that she is now at rest, which is more than I can say for the other unfortunate spirits I encounter in my astral travels. The restless dead are forever denied eternal sleep because I cannot deliver their messages for them. It is the curse and blessing of our trade, to be the mouthpiece of the dead," the Babalawo shrugged, taking a bite of the hard, red kola nut before offering one to POTUS.

POTUS shook his head. He didn't think he could stomach anything, not now he knew his long search was finally at an end, a bad end he'd never anticipated. He had always believed that his birth mother was alive, that she was rich and happy in America and would be happy to welcome him with open arms when they eventually reunited. That dream had been his constant companion and comfort from that fateful day of his ninth birthday. Now, the dream was crushed.

As he left the Babalawo's bungalow a while later, his steps heavy and laborious, a strange feeling came over him. It was as if he heard his birth mother's voice inside his ears, whispering comfort and hope into his heart—*You're free, POTUS! Son, you're finally free of Karma's deadly knife!*

POTUS shivered, glancing furtively around as if seeking the invisible ghost speaking inside his head. The feeling of lightness followed him all the way back to his family home—*Whatever bad debt I owe as a result of my involvement in Dr. Delores' death is now paid in full. A life for a life; my birth mother's life for the poor doctor's life. At least, I finally have a blood grandmother, a bloodline I can link to mine. Hopefully, I'll soon find my roots. Thank you, Baba. Thank you, great Ògún!*

The Federal Enquirer
PMD Media, 10 August
(Mike Vine and the news desk)

The White House, CIA Purge!
President King Retakes Control in Dramatic Fashion as Former CIA Boss Chad Rawlings is Fired!

Today, U.S. President Jerry King unleashed a torrent of accusations against the CIA Director, Chad Rawlings, calling him a "worm" and a "snake" before firing him in a move that has stunned the entire nation. The president said there was "unprecedented and mind-blowing corruption among the highest echelons of the CIA" and called former Director Rawlings "a disgrace to his office and the American people."

All of this comes on top of the shocking resignation of the vice president, Franklin Flint, last week, an announcement that sent shock ripples across the world. The former VP gave no details for his resignation but cited pressing family issues. We gather that several top members of staff in the West Wing have also been relieved of their posts. In the meantime, the Speaker of the House, Mary Kay Combes, continues to serve as the second black Vice President of the United States, following Vice President Flint's resignation. She is also the second female Vice President of the United States.

The president's announcement today follows his surprising—and what some quarters have described as "totally incomprehensible"—decision to lift all visa restrictions into the United States to travellers from Nigeria, Africa's most populous nation, with an estimated population of over three hundred and fifty million. Nigeria is currently still battling its homegrown terrorist group, Boko Haram, responsible for the kidnapping of the Nigerian president in 2028 and the bombing destruction of the Nnamdi Azikiwe International Airport, Abuja, in 2030.

. . .

The flurry of decisions and actions taken by President King since his miraculous recovery almost two months ago have led the senate to openly question his state of mind, with some anonymously suggesting to our sources that he might be suffering some unknown side effects of the coma which had him bedridden for 14 days. Other quarters suggest possible post-traumatic stress syndrome resulting from the death of his sister, Dr. Delores King. As readers recall, the president's older sister died after suffering a mental breakdown that left her hallucinating about ghosts and supernatural entities. She committed suicide by hanging, and her body was discovered on her backyard porch. The president was known to be very close to his sister, and those close to him say Dr. King's death has hit him particularly hard, especially at this critical point with the elections looming and his marriage in shambles.

Following the sacking of the CIA director today, the president returned to the campaign trail minus the First Lady, Portia King. FLOTUS' whereabouts remains unknown following her unexplained exit from the White House while President King was still in a coma. The president's daughter, Lisa Hudson, has now moved permanently into the White House to give her father much needed support, a move that would have been impossible had the First Lady been in residence. Portia King, who has no children with the president, is known to be vehemently opposed to the relationship between father and daughter, a daughter conceived while the president was involved in an extra-marital affair with Madison Hudson. As previously reported, Madison Hudson's lover, Tad Hunter, was responsible for the accident that put the president into a coma, and we can report that no charges are to be brought against him for what has now been deemed a genuine accident by the FBI, despite the "Cough-Gate" saga.

. . .

There are also unconfirmed reports that the president has again been visited by his medical team for those strange welts, the three vertical cuts that mysteriously appeared on his arm while he was still in a coma. It would appear that the wounds are finally starting to respond to treatment and have ceased bleeding for the first time since their appearance. It had been reported that the doctors were baffled by the appearance of the injuries, which continued to bleed and fester despite treatment with the strongest antibiotics. All internal and external investigations failed to prove the involvement of any member of the hospital staff or visitors in a malicious and cowardly attack on the then comatose president. To date, the source of the cuts remains a mystery, although Madam Lula, the celebrity psychic, would have the nation believe it was inflicted by the gold greedy goblins she reported during the height of the president's illness. Thankfully, the wounds appear to have had no long-lasting effects on President King, who will today be campaigning in Philadelphia for the last legs of the election countdown.

The latest polls still show the Republican president lagging behind his Democratic opponent, Larry Johnson, by 15 points, according to the Associated Press. Even in the battleground states, the president's numbers continue to plummet in a manner that all but guarantees victory to his opponent come election day in six weeks' time. This is despite his campaign pumping millions of dollars into advertising in a last-ditch attempt to turn things around.

In another development, the Christian coalition, who have claimed victory for President King's miraculous recovery following that amazing world-wide marathon prayer vigil, are once again throwing their divine might behind the president's bid for a third term. They recently held a nationwide prayer-fest billed "The Night of Angels," invoking angels from around the globe to come to the president's aid once again and grant him another miraculous victory, this time at the election polls.

. . .

This is a developing story.

∼

Exactly one week following Dr. Delores's suicide, Frankie received news of his American college scholarship. On the same day, America lifted all visa restrictions for Nigerian citizens. As the news hit the air waves, POTUS didn't know who was more stunned, himself or the befuddled Nigerian populace.

President King's visa waiver for Nigerians ignited fireworks around the country. There was great jubilation in the streets, celebrations in the clubs, and rejoicing in the churches. Numerous local governments organised masquerade festivals and marching parades to commemorate the momentous announcement which took even the Nigerian government unawares. Nigeria had not asked America for that unprecedented favour, nor offered a reciprocal consideration, and both the Nigerian president and his Foreign Minister were scratching their heads trying to figure out what America wanted in return.

They didn't need to wait long.

The Nigerian press, ever so imaginative and vocal in their reporting, soon provided the answers to the citizens. A national paper carried the news about possible secret and lucrative contracts made between Nigeria and the United States, which must have prompted the unheard of visa deal. The paper claimed that the Nigerian government had accepted to host all the dangerous prisoners in Guantánamo Bay detention camp, sacrificing its people's safety for the U.S. visa waiver. The article blasted the deal which would only benefit the rich and powerful who had the money to travel to the States in the first place while sacrificing the safety of the ordinary citizens.

Another national tabloid carried the headline *"Nigeria is Trash,"* reporting that the Nigerian government had accepted to play host to a different type of dangerous entity—namely, a mind-blowing 2000 tonnes of toxic waste and plastic rubbish accumulated by the United States—in exchange for the visa waiver. The paper called on Nigerians to begin violent protests against the filthy deal. A cartoon in the article screamed, *"U.S.A., stick your free visas up your stinky arses. Nigeria will not be your cesspit."* Both Nigeria's search engine, Naggle, as well as Chiggle, the search engine of Nigeria's biggest trade partner, China, also exploded with the news, condemning the USA in endless vitriolic posts about the unwholesome deal.

However, *Naijalanding*, the highest-ranking online social platform, came up with the most-popular explanation for the visa deal which resonated with the Nigerian populace—Nigeria had received the visa waiver deal as bribery for agreeing to host Prince Harry and Princess Megan as permanent residents, to ensure the super popular Princess Megan wouldn't run for the American Presidency and scupper President King's plans for a possible fourth term. It was no secret that the president and his GOP senators had already changed the law to enable him to run beyond the previous two-term mandate. Moreover, Princess Megan was Igbo-Nigerian by ancestry and would welcome a return to her roots.

As the Nigerian president and his cabinet scrambled to find evidence of these conspiracies, POTUS struggled to come to terms with Frankie's imminent departure to the States. Frankie's parents turned up at their house a few days before his departure full of exuberant cheer. His mum brought several Filipino dishes and drinks to celebrate the event, while Frankie's father shook Kunle's hands with uncharacteristic sheepishness.

"Dear friend, how can we thank you and your son for this unbelievable generosity?" He said, pumping Kunle's hand vigorously. Kunle's face remained impassive, neither smiling nor scowling. POTUS knew his father was still yet to forgive Frankie's parents for the way they'd turned on him when the scandal broke and for not attending Ronke's funeral, even though Frankie had been there. But for Frankie's sake, Kunle was doing his best to be polite. Frankie's dad sensed his reticence and rushed over to POTUS, his arms wide open in excessive affection.

"POTUS, wonderful boy!" Frankie's dad gave POTUS a bear hug, tears brimming in his eyes. "Again, we can't thank you enough for your wonderful act of true friendship. Thank you, dear boy."

"No, they're not friends," Frankie's mother trilled, her voice as cheery as someone tripping on Ogogoro wine over-indulgence. "They're brothers; true brothers, forever. I still can't believe that my son's best friend is close friends with the American president!" Frankie's parents stared at POTUS with the same stunned gaze they had worn since Frankie's visa came through.

POTUS knew his blush would have been mortifyingly visible had his skin been the same shade as Frankie's, whose face was already a bright strawberry colour. His best friend still wore the dazed look POTUS had seen the day he received the email to forward his E-passport to the USA embassy for his student visa. Despite everything they'd both experienced, he knew Frankie still doubted the deal they struck with President King and had chucked it all down to some kind of hallucination.

POTUS forced back the tight knots bunched behind his throat— *God! I'm going to miss Einstein more than I'm ready to admit.* The mere thought of not having Frankie in his daily life was a gnawing pain he didn't want to face until he absolutely had to. Several times since Frankie's visa came through, he'd asked himself the same question he'd been repeating for months, *'POTUS, have you made a terrible mistake and allowed your stupid pride to get the better of you, losing out forever on your greatest dream?'* No matter how many times he tormented himself with that question, he could never come up with an answer. Some days he felt he had been a monumental fool, while on other days, he felt he had done right by himself and his self-esteem.

Yet, with each passing day, the demon of discontentment was slowly consuming both his soul and his body, especially after Frankie finally left the country, accompanied by Adeleke, the Babalawo's son. He now found himself struggling to merely exist, eating badly, sleeping badly, dressing badly, and shamefully bereft of his former bling and designer haircuts. Everything was too much of an effort. Only his interest in golf stayed constant, and he applied himself to his game with more discipline and diligence than in the past. He discovered to his joy that the vital tips from President King came in handy, and even his coach had been surprised by his current innovative playing—*Why then aren't I feeling grateful to either the president or even the gods?*

POTUS had never been much into television or politics, but since his strange experience with the American president, he now found himself glued to both *The Great America News Inc.* and *CNL Anderson Corp* on a daily binge, gorging himself on endless hologram images of President King. The booming voice, the piercing green eyes which still winked at random, the hulking presence that radiated immense, menacing power even through the screen. All part and parcel of the mercurial and tumultuous spirit he recalled so vividly.

He wondered if he would ever stop breaking out in goosebumps each time he saw President King's looming image on the telly and his mobile screens—*I wonder what it would be like to actually meet President King in the real human flesh?* He shuddered—*Uh-uh!* He didn't want to find out. Somehow, he doubted he would be as irreverent as he had been when he fought with the shadowy entity that was the president's spectre. He reckoned only the Babalawo and the Orishas could successfully challenge the fearsome force that was President King.

20

JUJU FROM AFRICA

POTUS found his blood grandmother at Orugbo village in Warri district, just as the Babalawo had divined. When he mentioned the village to Kunle, it jogged his memory, and he confirmed that it was indeed the place he'd executed the adoption arrangement with his birth mother.

POTUS arrived on a sunny afternoon as the villagers were about to have their Sunday rice, post-Mass. He was directed to his grandmother's red, mud hut by some curious villagers intrigued by the affluent stranger in the black SUV. On seeing him, Grandma Mercy's eyes widened in incredulity. Before he could introduce himself, she enfolded him in her arms, holding onto him with the strength of ten warriors.

"Omo mi, oh! My good grandson!" The old woman cried, her frail body shaking uncontrollably in his arms. "You have come home to your poor grandmother! What the breeze stole, the wind has returned. The seeds taken by the birds have returned in a bountiful harvest. Ancestors be praised!" Grandma Mercy clung to him with desperate arms as she wept.

Her hug was like none POTUS had ever experienced, not even from his late mother, Ronke. It was an all-encompassing hug from a woman that was even taller than Kunle, despite her advanced age. He felt he was receiving an embrace from his ancestors, a bonding of flesh and souls. It was a hug of blood validation that bunched a tight knot behind his throat.

"Adisa! Adisa!" Grandma Mercy kept stroking his face tenderly with gnarled fingers. "You wear my daughter's eyes even though your father owns your face. I can finally return to my ancestors now I know my name won't be forgotten."

"Ancestors forbid such evil!" POTUS' voice was hoarse as he flung off the curse over his shoulders. "I didn't find my grandmother only for her to leave me too." He hugged her closer, tighter, letting his tears join her own.

He spent the rest of the day with Grandma Mercy, eating the Jollof rice she excitedly prepared for him while chatting with the thrilled villagers gathered outside her home to share the miracle of his existence. Until his arrival, his grandmother had been viewed in the village as an unfortunate old woman, cursed by the ancestors with an empty hut, devoid of loving family. Seeing Grandma Mercy's desperate poverty brought a tightness to his chest—*By the ancestors, if it's the last thing I do, I'll achieve great success and gift her with everything my birth mother would've provided had she survived the journey to America.*

"This is my grandson, Adisa. My grandson, you hear?" Grandma Mercy kept repeating to the crowd in her booming voice, which was strikingly similar to POTUS' own. The pride and joy in her voice made him equally proud. And later, when Grandma Mercy showed him some photos of his birth mother, he was stunned by the unusual pale brown beauty of her eyes—*Now, I finally know where I got mine.*

By the time POTUS finally left the village later that evening, his voice was hoarse from talking, laughing, and crying. He left Grandma Mercy a wad of Naira notes that had her wailing with bliss. He also promised to visit her at least every month. She heaped blessings on his head, calling him by his new name, Adisa, a name he now intended to wear with pride. He carried several photos of his birth mother, together with a plastic bowl filled with his grandmother's Jollof rice back to Lagos. Grandma Mercy also gifted him with another name apart from Adisa—Tunde Adeniran, his birth father's name.

POTUS stored the name away in his mind's freezer, awaiting the right time to thaw and examine it. His birth father's treachery that had led to his mother's doomed journey to America were things he needed to digest before making any decisions—At least, he now knew that he was definitely Yoruba… well, half Yoruba and Half Itsekiri. He finally had roots. Still, Kunle was enough for him at the present time. He didn't need a new father, certainly not one like Tunde Adeniran. He planned to confide everything to Kunle when the time was right and their trust fully restored.

On getting home, POTUS placed his birth mother's photo side by side with Ronke's own on his shrine. He was sure the action would amplify his ancestors' protection going forward. The love and protection of two mothers was a blessing few people received. Ronke may not have been his blood ancestor, but he believed with every vein in his body that they had built a bond of love that was powerful enough to rival that of any blood ancestor's.

POTUS' mobile phone rang as he was about to share supper with Kunle. He glanced at the caller I.D.—*Unknown caller*. He let it ring— Likely another useless idiot. Ever since the scandal regarding his parents, he no longer answered withheld numbers. With luck, people might start getting distracted with their own troubles instead of waddling in the mud of other people's messes.

The phone cut off and started ringing again almost immediately.

"Won't you answer the call, son?" Kunle murmured, chewing a piece of meat in the slow manner with which he now did everything. "Whoever it is seems determined to speak with you."

"It's a withheld number," POTUS pushed the mobile away and resumed eating his prawn fried rice. It was their latest culinary gift from Frankie's mum, who made it a personal crusade to feed them up every Sunday since Frankie's departure to America. When the phone rang for the third time, POTUS cursed under his breath, grabbing his mobile phone as a cat would snatch a mouse.

"Hello?" His voice was taut, his shoulders braced for whatever negativity might spill through.

"Hello, is this POTUS?" It was a woman's voice, a hesitant, soft voice that sounded as if the owner was holding back tears.

"It's Adisa," he said. "Who's this?"

"Oh, sorry. I think I called the wrong number."

"No, no. You have the right number," he quickly cut in before she hung up. "POTUS used to be my name before I changed it to Adisa."

"Oh, thank God!" The woman said, her voice distinctly Nigerian with a slight American twang. POTUS waited for her to speak, but the phone remained silent.

"So, who is this?" He repeated. Likely an old chick he'd chatted up in the old days. *Wonder which one it is. Dupe? Yinka? Lola?* He took a side-glance at Kunle who was now listening into the conversation with both his ears and his entire face. He didn't feel like sweeting up a girl in front of his dad. With a wry smile at Kunle's disappointed face, he pushed back his chair and strolled out of the dining room. He drew the sliding door shut behind him as he wandered into the living room and muted the TV volume.

"So, who's this?" His voice now adopted his sexy, chick-bait drawl.

"I'm calling from the U.S.," the female said before pausing again.

"Hello? Are you still there?" POTUS wondered if the connection had broken—*Rubbish, yeye signal.*

"Yes… yes, I'm here," she murmured. "POTUS, I am… I'm your mother."

POTUS' heart froze. Then it exploded and started racing, pounding, melting. Hot sweat doused his face despite the air-conditioning humming softly in the background. His hand holding the phone went as weak as a baby's grip—*Oluwa! What is this? Is it possible? Could both the Babalawo and Grandma Mercy be mistaken, and my birth mum is alive after all? Oh, great Ògún, save my soul!*

"That'll do. Take her away, and nobody comes in here till I say so. Hello? That you, kiddo?" The raspy male voice cut into the conversation before POTUS could speak, sending sudden icy chills down his spine. His eyes almost popped out of his sockets—*President King! OMG! No freaking way!*

POTUS collapsed into the nearest chair by the grand piano bearing his numerous trophies and news articles.

"I know you can hear me, buddy. So, cut the crap and speak up," the president sounded his usual impatient and condescending self, and in a blink, everything reverted to the old status quo between them.

"Who's this?" Of course, he knew who it was, but he'd rather die than let on.

"That's my boy, alright. I'd recognise that mouthy voice any day. This is your old buddy, the real POTUS, that's the President of the United States to you, pal. Heck! This is some weird shit I can tell you right now. I mean, you're real, and what we shared is real, right? No Disney fairy tale shit. Bet you never expected to hear from me again, right?"

He was right. POTUS was trembling.

"What d'you want, Your Excellency?" He heard the surly quivering of his voice and wished he could muster the old insolence. But he was speaking to the real, living President of the United States, not his fake-ghost. "Who's the woman I just spoke to, sir?"

"She's your mommy of course," President King sounded amused. "Didn't I promise you I'd find her for you? Well, she's here with me now, right in the flesh, no kidding you. But don't go lickin' your chops thinking you've hit the jackpot again, kiddo. You and I still have some unfinished business to sort out. You wanna see your mommy, then you gotta do something big for me. Hugely big, alright?"

Wrong—POTUS wanted to hang up the phone on hearing the president's insults again but curiosity, coupled with the sheer mind-boggling magnitude of the moment, kept him hooked—*OMG! I'm actually speaking with the living President of the United States, the real Jerry King in the flesh!* Clarity returned to his mind—Get a grip of yourself, Adisa Olupitan. The dude is still an arsehole, and he's still lying his head off again! The fact that the president was calling for a favour and demanding a trade-off was proof enough that the woman he just spoke to was an impostor brought in by President King.

"How do I know…" POTUS cut himself short, forcing down his rage—No, I'll find out what the bloody man wants first before revealing I know he is lying. "What do you want from me, Your Excellency?"

"That's more like it. I need you to go to your Barber fella again, right?" President King's voice dropped to almost a whisper. "I mean, I don't know how you Africans do it, but I know what I seen and what you fuckers did to my sister. Friggin' hell! Why for fuckssakes did you bastards have to kill Dels? She never did anything to you, you little punk. You met her as well, you shithead. Goddammit!" President King's voice was a shriek of pain, and POTUS' stomach clenched, squeezing his gut into an agonising knot. "Delores was nice to you in that shitty hospital room of yours, wasn't she? And yet you allowed your witch doctor guy to hex her just because I didn't lift the fucking visa restrictions for you bastards in time. Not to mention all those festering sores from the cuts he gave me inside that disgusting shrine. I did tell you I didn't trust his filthy blade, didn't I? Good thing I got the best physicians in the world or the bloody man woulda killed me for sure."

The president paused while POTUS tried to stifle the waves of guilt drowning him once again in turbulent surges. He had long resigned himself to the fact that Dr. Delores' death was a guilt he would carry to his grave. He knew the blood and truth oath he'd shared with the president had a hand in the doctor's untimely death, just as he knew the president's physicians had nothing to do with the healing of his cuts. By rights, he should blame the president for failing to keep to his end of the bargain. But for his actions, his sister might still be alive. All the same, the guilt held him hostage, and his voice was muted, less abrasive than before when next he spoke.

"What do you want from the Babalawo?" POTUS asked.

"I want him to help me win the election, that's what," President King said with sudden urgency. "Listen, kiddo. I've kept to my end of the deal, right? I've given you fuckers open sesame to America and made your two pals Eddie Murphy clones now they've both come to America on my generosity, right? So, I reckon I've earned some kinda gratitude from the witch doctor fella. I can tell ya right now, since my experience with your Barber fella, I've been channelling all the powerful magic of Africa to myself to get rid of my haters,"

The president started coughing, and POTUS cheered silently for the cough—Good! I hope you choke on your phlegm, you nasty man!

"Get the hell outta here! I told you clowns I don't want anyone in here till I call you," President King roared down the line, still fighting his coughing fit. POTUS heard a door slam in the background before the president grumpily resumed their conversation. "Busybody dumb fucks! Anyways, as I was saying, I don't know if you follow the news, but the numbers ain't looking good for me in the polls, kiddo. They wanna shoot me down. The cheating Dems are trying to steal the election from me with their damned poli-tricks, spreading all kinda lies about me, all hogwash, trust me. But I ain't having none of it, right? I'm gonna kick their asses to hell. They ain't gonna screw me up, hell no! You and I know your Barber fella has some real powerful juju stuff, and I ain't forgotten that weird witch doctor Jesus crucifix I saw in your hospital room. I know there's something strange and powerful going on with you natives, and I want a share of it. So, I need you to go ASAP to your old Barber guy and tell him to do whatever it is he does to secure me victory, right? Tell him I got his son here in the States and if he plays ball, his boy will be just fine, otherwise I—"

"Listen, Your Excellency, you don't want to mess with the Babalawo's son or threaten the man, okay?" POTUS cut him off, his voice hard. He'll be damned before he's responsible for another death in the bloody man's family should the fool piss off the Babalawo. "You'll be burying more than your election bid if you do. You of all people ought to know who you're dealing with by now. Nobody messes with the Babalawo if they value their lives," POTUS shook his head in disbelief.

"Okay, scrap that," President King's voice was a mixture of irritation and impatience, but POTUS heard an underlying fear in the recalcitrant tone. "The witchdoctor's son is fine, alright? Tell him his son's doing just fine, same with your little ch*nk friend. As you said, I'd be a fool to touch them or even you, right? Especially after the blood and truth bond thing we shared. Hell! I've practically got African DNA in me now. I have any more kids and they might even turn out little n*ggers. Shit! I'm royally screwed. No more kids for me. Ain't taking the risk. I mean, my supporters will dump me like a pile of shit if they ever find out about us. You darkies have practically ruined me, you and your damned witch doctor fella. But I don't bear you any grudges. I just want you to do everything in your power to help me win this election and we're even. That ain't too much to ask, right?" The president was now wheedling, just like a child that struggled to understand why he couldn't have all the sweets in the candy shop.

"Listen, kiddo. I know you said you don't want to come over here, but trust me, mighty stuff awaits you here if I win this election. Mighty stuff. And I ain't kidding you, no siree Bob. I'll even chuck in an extra house and a shitload of money for your fairy daddy if you like. Not to mention seeing your birth mother again. I mean, you're still interested in meeting her, right? You just spoke to her right now, so you know I ain't kidding you. It took a lotta hard work for the FBI to trace her, I can tell ya now. So, do me this small service, and you can see your mammy tomorrow, first flight to Africa, suitcase full of crisp American dollars. You told me you like Rihanna and Tom Cruise. They're my great pals, as you know, and I can get you to meet them in the flesh and maybe get to hang out with them. How cool is that?"

POTUS took a deep breath, allowed the myriads of emotions churning inside him to bubble and sizzle till humour finally overcame his rage.

"Dude… I mean, Your Excellency! No way! Freaking awesome! Thanks! I sure want to meet my birth mum and definitely Rihanna and Tom Cruise, too, even if he's an alien. Wow!" He forced his voice to sound impressed, pitched high with awe—*The yeye fool still believes I'm the same old gullible dumb kid from before. Ha!* "I'll definitely speak to the Babalawo tomorrow and let you know what he says'"

"Why don't you call him now and ask him? I can wait. Just link us all on Holo. After all, we're all old friends, right?" The president barked a dry laugh.

"You forget he doesn't have a phone," POTUS said, trying to sound regretful. "Babalawos don't do phones, cameras, computers, or TV. Those gadgets are portals that let in demons and evil spirits. I'm afraid I'll have to call on him in person tomorrow morning and let you know what he says."

"And you can't go there now, being the yellow, little wuss you are, all frightened of the dark and your own shadow, right?" The president sniggered contemptuously. "Woo! Watch out, little scaredy boy! The boogeyman's gonna get you. Friggin' wuss, ha!"

POTUS refused to rise to the president's bait. He was still in shock that the second-most-powerful man in the world was asking for such a crazy favour—*Just goes to show how greed and a shameless desperation to cling onto power can corrupt a man's soul.*

The president heaved a loud sigh. "Guess I'll have to be patient. Alright, I'll call you same time tomorrow. Don't screw it up. In the meantime, I'm afraid mammy dearest remains here with me till our business is done. That's only fair, right?'"

"Right," POTUS was struggling to cling to his GSOH, fighting the rage roaring in his heart—*Stuff the rubbish good sense of humour! The lying demon is already going back on his words!* He knew the woman wasn't his birth mum, but it still didn't make the president's actions any better. *Oh, well. I'll soon show the fool man African magic, alright…*

Kunle was surprised when POTUS got up early to leave the house the next morning. His face wore the anxiety that was now second nature to it.

"Where are you off to this early, son?" Kunle asked.

POTUS sighed softly as Kunle approached him. It was as if his late mum, Ronke, had taken possession of his dad and dosed up his heart with her old fears. He was back once again to being a prisoner of parental love, but somehow, he didn't mind the bars as much as he used to.

"I just need to collect something to post over to Frankie. I won't be long, I promise," the lie rolled easily from his lips. There was no way he was letting his father find out about his dealings with President King—*Poor man will have a heart attack for sure, convinced the FBI and CIA are hunting me for the rest of my life.* He would have felt the same way had he not known the psyche of the president—*Ha! Dude's now a superstition junkie like the next illiterate villager!* He had zero doubt the president was destined to live under the fear of the Babalawo's curse for the rest of his life.

The medicine man listened to POTUS' message from President King before sighing deeply and taking his hand in his calloused palms.

"Do you want to go to America?" The Babalawo asked, his eyes hard, yet compassionate. "I know you sacrificed your place for my son, but now, I can get you there if you wish."

POTUS stared at him in wide-eyed awe. "How, Baba?" He asked, his voice barely above a whisper.

"Leave it to me. Just trust me. Now, when next you speak to the president, give him this message." The Babalawo whispered into his ear. When he was done, a slow smile stretched across POTUS' face, a wicked glint in his eyes—*Oh, yeah babes! That should do it alright!* He could hardly wait to speak to President King.

That evening, President King called as he was, again, having dinner with Kunle. POTUS saw the private number and his face creased in a malevolent grin. He rushed into the living room to answer the phone.

"I spoke to the Babalawo as you asked," he said without preamble. "Your Excellency, I'm afraid the news isn't good," he made his voice sound as solemn as a priest conducting a funeral service.

"What d'you mean the news ain't good?" President King sounded ready to explode.

"Just that, sir. The Babalawo said you're iced out of the White House, basically toasted and done. The oracle revealed your defeat to him, and he said to tell you that the only way to turn things around is to win the election first in the supernatural realm. To do this, you must either come to his shrine for the reversal ritual or he comes to you. He says he can prepare three different charms. It's up to you to decide the one you want and—"

"Give it to me," the president cut him off impatiently. "What are the three charms? I'll decide what to do when I hear them."

"The first charm will work by bringing sudden death to your opponent. He says that's the easiest of the charms, and he can do that without coming to America. All you need to do is send him either a photo of the guy or a personal item belonging to him, and by next week, he'll be a corpse and you will cruise to victory."

The president whistled, long and loud. "Holy shit! This dude's worse than that crazy North Korean bitch leader, Kim Yo-jong. A friggin' one-thousand-carat killing machine. I shoulda known after what he did to Dels. Listen, kiddo, I don't wanna kill anyone. At least, not yet, anyways. Who knows? We'll see. So, what's the second charm?"

"He said he'll prepare a hallucinatory magic cream for you. When you apply it to your face before every campaign, it will bring a fog into the minds of the voters. They'll see you as you looked eight years ago at the height of your glory and the peak of your strength. They'll fall under your spell again and become blind to your opponent's name at the voting booth. Be they Democrats, Republicans, Liberals, or Greens, all they'll see on election day is your name and that's who they'll all vote for until the magic wears off and their eyes open. By then, it'll be too late, and you'll be back in the White House. He says you can only use this charm a week before the election, as it wears off in seven days."

"Holy righteous shit!" The president's voice was almost a whisper, hushed awe layering every word he spoke. "Okay, what's the third charm?"

"He said he can prepare *Satan Tongue Potion* for you and—"

"What the fuck is Satan Tongue Potion?" The president cut him off. "Sounds mighty dodgy to me."

"He said it's a potion you drink to give you a sweet tongue to hypnotise everyone that hears you speak. Whatever you tell people to do, they will obey you, be it voters, politicians, world leaders, or the military. Everybody save the Babalawo and I. He'll give me the juju to resist your voice. But basically, whatever you want people to believe, you just have to say it and they'll believe you once you drink the charmed potion. They will be under your spell as long as you drink it every morning before you speak the first word of the day. Satan Tongue Potion has no expiration date. It's good for as long as you have enough supply and drink it daily."

"That's the one! Hell yeah! I'll go with Satan's Tongue, no contest!" the president's voice was high with excitement. "Holy Mackerel! I knew you guys could do it! That's the Chinese premier quitting his office immediately and that bitch, Portia, giving me a no-contest divorce. Whew!" President King whistled, long and loud. "That Barber fella sure is something. I mean, the guy sent me right back into my body in a blink. The doctors here still can't figure out how I got the three cuts on my arm, but you and I know the truth, right? I tell you, nobody'll believe this shit, not in a zillion light years. Listen kiddo, you and me and the Barber fella are gonna do great things together. Mighty, marvellous, big things that'll change the whole damn world! Screw China and Albania!" President King roared a jubilant laugh. POTUS could almost see him pumping his fists in triumph. An image of the president's giant green hands flashed briefly in his head, the greedy hands of the soul eater, as the Babalawo had called him.

"I think I also want the second charm, the hallucinatory magic cream," the president rushed on with avarice. "Might as well go the whole hog. It'll be fun seeing the voters go blind to Lazy Larry's name. Ha! As you say, I'll be cruising all the way to the White House for as long as I wanna be POTUS, which I can tell ya right now is a very, very long time."

Once again, the malevolent smile creased POTUS' face.

"There's a problem though," he made his voice solemn, just above a whisper, like a person sharing a great secret. "For either the cream or potion to work, they need the one ingredient that will activate them— your blood, Your Excellency. Nothing works without a blood sacrifice when invoking African Juju. That's why the Babalawo said you can either come to him or he comes to you to get your blood."

"It's too close to the election. No way can I leave the country. He can come to me instead. I'll make all the arrangement, no problems and—"

"He won't go anywhere without me," POTUS cut in. "After everything, he doesn't really trust you. Since you and I share a blood bond in the supernatural realm after the ritual in his shrine, I'm his insurance. He can use me against you if you betray him."

"Shit! Tell the guy I don't plan on doing anything to him," the president roared. "Hell! I should be the one worried here. He's the one with all the dangerous juju, and I'd be a fool to mess with him, especially when I need him for my election bid. But if it'll make him happy, tell him he can bring you along. Why not? It'll be interesting to meet you in the flesh, ha!" The president barked a malicious laugh.

POTUS pushed a fist against his lips—*No way! OMG! I'm going to America! I'm actually going to finally see America!*

"I'll get Pansy-Pete to make all the arrangements ASAP. I expect you guys here by next week. You can get your digital passports in twenty-four hours, so that shouldn't be any problem. Tell the Barber to bring loads of the Satan's Tongue juice, alright? I need at least a year's supply."

"Final message, Your Excellency," POTUS said. "The Babalawo says he can't be away for more than three days as there'll be nobody to feed the gods and make sacrifices to them. So, he must be back in Nigeria within three days of his arrival to America."

"Even better. That suits me just fine. I can have you two on the plane back to Nigeria as soon as he's done with his job," the president sounded so pleased that POTUS wanted to spoil his party.

"So, I think I've kept my end of the bargain, and I'd like to speak to my birth mum now and find out when you're sending her home."

"Listen, you little punk. We ain't done till I say so, alright?" The president snarled in another of his mercurial flips. "You'll see mammy dearest when you arrive with the Barber fella and my goodies. Hell! You can even fly back with her when you're done. What do I care? Just don't screw up. I wanna get this shit right."

POTUS held back his rage and bit back his words—No need to antagonise the yeye man. The Babalawo will deal with him well and good.

"One final thing," the president barked. "Do not, under any circumstances, call yourself POTUS when you come here, are we clear? Nobody must know you're the African POTUS, and trust me, when you come to America, you'll realise that there's only one POTUS in the whole damn world and that's me."

President King ended the call.

21
POTUS IN AMERICA

Pansy-Pete was waiting for them inside the plush living room of a secluded two-storey mansion when they arrived with the secret agents in the unmarked car deployed to meet them at the JFK International Airport. As they stepped into the huge house, POTUS pinched his right thigh surreptitiously as he had been doing since he walked into the arrival hall and heard the distinctive twang of the American accent swirling around from a great multitude of ethnicities—*I am in America! I am really in America!*

"We meet again," Pansy-Pete said, extending his hand for a handshake that was as gracious as his smile, taking POTUS' hand into both of his own. POTUS pumped the offered hand enthusiastically, grateful to see that Pansy-Pete's goodwill towards him hadn't dissipated since their first and only meeting in his hospital room. "I hope you had a good journey?" Pansy-Pete was looking quizzically at the Babalawo as he spoke.

"Yes, thank you," POTUS returned his smile. "This is my uncle," he mouthed the lie the president had instructed as he turned to the Babalawo. "Baba, this is the president's main man, Mr. Pete."

The medicine man bowed deeply but ignored Pansy-Pete's outstretched hand. POTUS gave an embarrassed laugh. He knew the

Babalawo never shook hands in case lurking demons jumped into his body through a handshake.

"I'm sorry, but he doesn't shake hands," he apologised, as if he was the one rejecting the courtesy. "It's something to do with his traditional title, you see."

"Aahh! I see," Pansy-Pete didn't see, but he pretended to with a polite smile. "Anyway, Mr. President will meet with you in an hour. He's holding a campaign in New York today but will pop in to see you before then. In the meantime, Lenny here will show you to your rooms before we have a late breakfast around… is 10:30 okay with you? I'm sure you must be hungry after your long trip."

As Pansy-Pete walked away, they were led to their suite by the uniformed white guy with an inscrutable face. He placed their small suitcases next to the centre table and nodded curtly before exiting the suite.

"Good son, is this real, eh?" The Babalawo asked as soon as they were alone, gazing around the luxurious two-bedroom suite with its chandeliered living room and ornate furnishings in awe. "Are we really in America? Will I really see my son, Adeleke, in this America?"

"Baba, it is as our eyes are seeing, oh!" POTUS' laughter was loud and long, like someone drunk on palm wine. "Thanks to you, we are in America! Our feet are standing in this America we see in films, the same America I visit in my virtual world games every day. I swear, once we finish with President King, I'll carry myself out of this place to see better sights."

As he said the president's name, the anxiety he had suppressed since their plane landed resurfaced, igniting his fears—What will the president do to me now that I'm in his country? Can I trust him not to take some kind of revenge on me after everything that's happened between us? I guess all I can do is trust in the Babalawo's powers to keep us safe from the president's malice. If only I could see Frankie right now…

He and Frankie had planned to meet up later that evening. Left up to him, POTUS would have stayed at Frankie's place, but the president had insisted on them staying in the safe house, and anyway, there was no way he could leave the Babalawo on his own. He may be a powerful medicine man, but in the strange world of America, the Babalawo was like a baby without his nanny. Having traversed the virtual hologram world of several states in America in his video games, including New York City itself, POTUS felt almost at home now.

They changed out of their travel clothes into more comfortable garments and joined Pansy-Pete in the opulent dining room. With muted exuberance, they set out to enjoy the sumptuous meal fit for a president amidst lively conversation with their host.

"I'm glad to see you're fully recovered from your accident," Pansy-Pete said with a twinkle in his eyes. "I bet it still feels strange to you that we're meeting like this after everything that happened the last time we met?"

POTUS nodded, overcome by sudden shyness. "Yeah. I mean, I never thought I'd make it to America in a million years. I hope General O'Neill and Chief Jackson are both okay? Sorry about Dr. Delores."

"I see you still remember us well," Pansy-Pete gave a wry smile. "Yes, it was indeed sad about Dr. Delores and very tough for Mr. President. But he's a strong man and nothing holds him down for long. He'll be here any second now. I'm sure you must be excited to see him again."

POTUS wasn't but he smiled and nodded. The Babalawo continued eating in silence, as if he were the only person in the room. But POTUS knew he absorbed every single word he exchanged with Pansy-Pete and much more—*I wonder if he's feeling as intimidated as I am now?*

He didn't have long to wonder.

The president stomped into the imposing living room with a team of menacing security detail, calling out a general greeting with his familiar boom. The sight of the leader in the flesh sent POTUS' heart racing. The living president terrified him. This was a man he dared not give lip or attitude to as he had done in their prior encounters. The raw power oozing from every pore in the president's body reawakened the unease in POTUS' heart—*What if he orders his security guys to arrest me? There isn't really much the Babalawo can do right now to stop him. Oh, God…*

"Kiddo! You little shit! It's great to see you again," the president laughed, seeming genuinely happy to see him. "Well, well! Ain't this something, right?" He turned to smile at Pansy-Pete with a conspirative wink, who returned the president's wink with a reserved smile. "And I see we have your Barber uncle here, too. Good, fantastic."

The Babalawo turned to see the president. A look of horror fell on his face, and he quickly looked away without a word. He remained seated, eating his food once again with the same delicate, silent dedication, seemingly oblivious to the president's presence. POTUS could see the curious looks on the faces of the security guys as he tried to figure out what had brought the strange look on the Babalawo's face on seeing the president—Did he see the secret harm President King plans for us? Oluwa! We're really in big trouble now! I knew we shouldn't have come…

"Guys, you can treat yourselves to some food. Pete will sort you out while I chat with my guests," the president turned to the Babalawo. "I'm mighty pleased to see you again," he smiled, patting the Babalawo's shoulder effusively as if they were long-lost friends. "Let's head upstairs to your suite for some privacy," he winked at them. "By the way, you did well with the Waldorf, Pete. Perfect hotel for our New York visit. Good thing we bought it back from the friggin' Chinese and restored it to its former American glory."

President King briskly led the way to their suite, and as soon as they entered, he shut the door firmly and leaned his back against it. The smile vanished from his face.

"Right, let's get this shit show on the road," his voice was cold and hard. He strode to the centre of the living room and tossed his jacket on the sofa before rolling up his left sleeve. "I got a press briefing and a campaign rally today, plus loads of people to charm and control with our secret weapon. My blood's ready and waiting, and I've got my own sanitised blade. Now, where the fuck is Satan's Tongue?"

It took the Babalawo less than ten minutes to wreak his devastation on President King. A swift blade cut on the president's left arm and the magic was complete. President King almost fainted at the sight of his blood, which was quickly mixed with the *Satan's Tongue Potion* in a small phial. The seer offered the potion to him, and President King drank it without hesitation. The potent sedative knocked him out in seconds, and he slumped unconscious on the leather sofa. POTUS' blood quickly joined the president's blood in a fresh concoction, followed by chants, invocations, and occult rituals. By the time the Babalawo was done, POTUS' prone body joined President King own on the nearby chair.

When next he regained consciousness, POTUS opened his eyes to a horrible new reality. His eyes almost popped from their sockets as he shouted in panicked terror.

"B-Baba... w-what have you done?" POTUS stuttered, staring with horror at his trembling pink hands and pale white arms—*Oh, my ancestors! This can't be happening to me! I can't be trapped inside President King's body! No, no!* "Baba, change me back to myself, you hear? Change me back now. They will kill me if I step out of this room. Oh my God! Oluwa!" He shuddered violently—*Even my voice sounds just like the president's!*

POTUS stared at his own prone body slumped on the chair next to the sofa where the president had first collapsed. The sight sent an icy chill over him. It was like seeing his own corpse. When he caught a reflection of himself in the mirror, the hulking frame of President King in his intimidating poise, his heart almost stopped.

"Relax," the Babalawo smiled. "You will only be the president for a few hours, five hours at the most. Just send them to bring Adeleke and your friend here so we can see them before we return home. Then later, you will attend that conference the fool man mentioned and confess his sins to the American people. This demon wants to continue ruling the ignorant American people, so I will do to him what I did to the former corrupt Nigerian president and get him to destroy himself with his own lips," the Babalawo gave a low grunt, his face grim. "Before I forget, you mentioned that you have the thing that records things in your mind," the Babalawo scratched his head in bafflement.

"Mind Zoome key," POTUS said. He had packed his unique head kit for the trip—Just in case. One never knows with President King.

"Yes, make sure you have the recording of the president and us talking about Satan's Tongue Potion and the elections, you hear? We must show their police proof of what he tried to do. Don't forget to report his confession about the pregnant girl they killed and buried. Her body must be found so that her restless soul can finally sleep. I saw her hovering around the man as soon as he walked into this house. Even now, she's here with us, standing next to your body by the chair. I have promised the poor spirit justice, and I will deliver on it," the Babalawo gave POTUS' unconscious body a vicious look. "Anyway, once you finish the briefing, come straight back here for the body exchange. I will feed the president *Eshu,* the Trick Memory Powder. He will forget everything until we are back home on Nigerian soil tonight. The charm will imprison his mind for several weeks. By the time his memory returns for him to face the wrath of his people, he will be in no position to harm us, nor would he dare touch a single hair on my son or your friend's heads. Now that I have his blood in my possession, he will dance to my tune whether or not he wants it," the Babalawo waved the small phial that contained the president's blood.

POTUS shuddered and glanced down anxiously at the plaster band on his left arm—*Oluwa! Can I really get away with this? Can I really be the President of the United States for even one minute, much less several hours? Sweet Mary and the Apostles! I'm freaking doomed. The Babalawo is going to kill us both...*

Walking down the stairs was the longest walk POTUS had ever taken. His heart pounded so hard he thought his legs would fold under him. When his security detail and Pansy-Pete came rushing out to meet him, he was sure they could see his real face beneath the president's.

"I..." POTUS cleared his throat loudly—*Come on now. Stand straight, you idiot. Talk like the freaking man unless you want to be dog meat. I am the best of the best of the bestest... the best of the best of the bestest.* "I need you to go bring the two Nigerian boys over here right now," POTUS addressed Pansy-Pete directly, forcing himself to hold his gaze—*Can he tell? Did I say it the right way? Fuck! POTUS, just think about how the president talks and walks and mimic it. You've spent enough time with him to be able to fake him. Come on, dude!*

"POTUS-Sir, you mean those two students?" Pansy-Pete pointed upstairs with his forefinger. POTUS nodded and turned to head back to the suite.

"Yeah. As soon as they arrive, bring them upstairs. Hurry now and make arrangements for those two to fly back to their country tonight. My business with them should be done by then."

"Tonight?" Pansy-Pete looked incredulous. "I thought they're here for longer?"

"Changed my mind. I want them outta here by tonight. I have a final meeting with them after my press briefing and that's it; over, kaput. Get them back to their little pig shit country, ASAP." POTUS turned away from Pansy-Pete, clenching his fists to stop the trembling in his hands—*No freaking way! I did it! I pulled it off!*

He re-joined the Babalawo inside their suite, and in what seemed like mere seconds, Frankie and Adeleke were ushered in by Pansy-Pete. The Chief of Staff stared briefly at POTUS' slumped body on the sofa before giving a wry smile.

"I see our young guest has crashed out already. Guess the excitement proved too much for him," he shook his head before walking out and shutting the door gently behind him.

"M-Mr. P-President, sir," both Frankie and Adeleke bowed very low to POTUS, their faces wreathed in terror. They looked ready to pass out. POTUS laughed and hugged Frankie as the Babalawo rushed over to enfold his son in a bear hug.

"M-Mr. P-President, sir!" POTUS mimicked Frankie, who was staring at him gobsmacked, his mouth as wide as a saucer. "Olè! Einstein, you goat! Yes, it's me, Adisa… I mean, POTUS. Baba switched our bodies, so the president is now asleep. Cool, right?" He laughed gleefully, enjoying the stunned look on Frankie's face.

"P-POTUS, is this really you?" Frankie asked, staring up at his face with awe. He was still as short and chubby as POTUS remembered him, and the president's body towered over him. "Are you really POTUS?"

POTUS nodded with another wild laugh.

"Young man, he is your friend, indeed. Do not doubt my powers," the Babalawo said, his face still wreathed in a blissful smile as he clung to his son's arm.

Frankie gave him a hard look, his eyes narrowed in suspicion. "If you're POTUS, then tell me the last thing I gave you before I left Nigeria."

POTUS sobered. "Idiot! You gave me back my gold wristwatch I'd thrown away on my ninth birthday, the one with my parent's initials engraved on it that you retrieved after I chucked it away. I still can't believe you kept it all these years, you crazy bat," POTUS hugged him tightly again, and this time, Frankie returned his hug, hitting him with hard, happy fists.

"Olè! It's really you! POTUS, it's really you! This is crazy shit! I mean, this is just wicked!" Frankie walked round him, poking him, shaking his head, his eyes gleaming with wonder and mischief. "Now, you're really POTUS, you little thief. You are now the President of the United States for real. I can't believe what I'm seeing! Man!"

Adeleke was almost as stunned as Frankie, although his joy at seeing his father quickly overcame his shock. Soon, they were all laughing and chatting as they caught up on home news and American life. POTUS yearned to leave the house with his friends and see New York in all its glory, but knew he had to complete his mission inside the president's body first.

"Motormouth, when you get back into your body, I'll take you on a drive in my car. Boy! You need to see my ride!" Frankie paused briefly before holding POTUS' gaze with pleading eyes. "POTUS, I really wish you'd accept some money from us, honestly," Frankie sounded as guilty as a convicted felon.

"I told you I don't want a cent of what the president paid you, and again, my name is now Adisa, not POTUS," he gave Frankie a fierce look belied by the twinkle in his eyes. "Einstein, you earned that million dollars fair and square, and Adeleke has his family to take care of in Nigeria. I'm cool dude, honest. My dad takes good care of me and your mum makes sure we don't starve." Everybody joined in the laughter.

By the time Pansy-Pete's tentative knock reminded him that he had an important date with the press, POTUS had almost forgotten that he now resided inside the body of the President of the United States. He turned terrified eyes to the Babalawo.

"It's okay, good son," the medicine man gave him a reassuring smile. "Nothing will happen to you. Go and complete your destiny and put things in their right order. In no time, we will be back home safe and well. Trust in Ògún. All is well."

POTUS took a deep breath and exhaled noisily—I am the best of the best of the bestest! He squared his shoulders and rearranged his features into the signature haughty look of the American president. Then he turned and walked out of the suite.

The unmarked fleet of cars that had brought President King to the safehouse mansion navigated the busy New York traffic with efficient speed as POTUS stared out the tinted windows of his car in awe. He saw the familiar sight of the Empire State Building towering over the New York City skyline, and goosebumps broke out on his skin—I'm in America. I'm in New York City! No matter how many times he repeated the words, it still seemed like an impossible dream. An image from one of his favourite films on the Archive Channel, X-Men, flashed in his mind—The Statue of Liberty! Yes!

In an instant, a daring idea filled POTUS' head. He reached into his pocket and withdrew the president's mobile phone. He swiped his thumb to activate the fingerprint security. He was instantly greeted by highly classified numbers of several world leaders and celebrities—No freaking way! He stared at the confidential contact list in stunned disbelief. Many of the names were saved as single letters while others had far-out nicknames typical of the president's usual habit. But he saw other names that needed no introduction, famous names that ruled the world and its affairs together with numerous celebrities—Tom Cruise! Taemin! Sir Lewis Hamilton! The President didn't lie. He really knows Tom Cruise! For one crazy second, he considered stealing the megastar's number for his own use—Perhaps not. POTUS shuddered—*Uh-uh! I think I want to live. No telling what the aliens will do to me.*

Instead, he called Pansy-Pete.

"I wanna go see the Statue of Liberty before we head back to the Waldorf," he said as soon as the Chief of Staff answered.

"B-but POTUS-sir, it's almost an hour's drive, and you have a press briefing in just under an hour's time," Pansy-Pete protested from his car driving behind the unmarked car carrying POTUS.

"Too bad. Shit ass pricks can wait. Holy righteous shit! Am I the fucking president or not? I wanna see the Statue of Liberty now!" POTUS put in as much command in his voice as he'd heard President King do. It was a voice that brooked no argument.

In no time, Pansy-Pete had contacted the Director of the United States Secret Service who approved and transmitted the president's new orders to the security detail, and POTUS found himself headed to Liberty Island—*No freaking way! I'm going to see the Statue of Liberty! God! I can't wait to take photos and show everyone when I get home and…*

Cold sanity hit him—*Nooo! I'm in the president's body! Fuck! Fuck!* He felt like wailing in frustration. As the car whizzed past even more spectacular landscape and famous NYC landmarks, the scale of his loss hit him even more. He cursed the Babalawo silently, wishing once again that he could be free from the dangerous possession. By the time they drove past the newly commissioned super bridge, *The Freedom Bridge*, connecting the famous landmark to land, he was brewing with so much resentment that it took a while for him to absorb the stunning wonder of the famed colossal sculpture from the seclusion of his car. An intimidating fleet of NYPD squad cars already swamped the place before their arrival, and POTUS marvelled at the hyper-efficiency of the president's security detail. It was as near-perfect as the Nigerian president's own, one of the few feats the country had mastered to perfection; keeping their president safe from the terrorists.

As he stepped out of his car, POTUS gasped softly, gawping at the imposing beauty of the lady with the raised torch in all her famous glory. From her lofty height, Lady Liberty surveyed her realm with aloof pride, and POTUS wanted to fall on his knees and worship her like a deity—*I've finally come to America! Thank you, good Ògún! Thank you, great Orishas! I have finally seen the Statue of Liberty with my own two eyes! If I see nothing else in this life, this is more than enough.*

POTUS sat at a massive table facing rows of reporters inside the huge red walled room Pansy-Pete had led him into at the Waldorf. Everything about the room screamed opulence, from the ornate furnishing to the world-famous circular blue and gold seal bearing the distinctive insignia, *The President of the United States.* It took place of pride on the polished desk, while a huge portrait of President King looked stern from the embossed wall. POTUS thought the president looked exactly like what Fat-arse Nurse would have called a bombastic amoeba and a pompositacious ignoramus. He bowed his head, biting his lips, struggling to hold in the bubbling cauldron of gleeful laughter threatening to explode all the way from his belly—*Control yourself, you idiot!* At least the terror that had quaked his limbs from the time he walked into the crowded briefing room had vanished—*The Babalawo wants me to confess everything here and expose President King. Oluwa! Where do I start?*

A reporter raised her screen card with her right hand. Her news outlet glowed brightly on its square surface—*Anna Richards from CNL Anderson Corp.* He screwed his face in disgust, just the way President King did whenever the news outlet was mentioned. Before she could ask him a question he couldn't answer, he dived in with his speech.

"Guys, today's gonna be different from our usual briefing," POTUS said, forcing himself to hold their hard and jaded stares despite the hard pounding in his heart—*Just remember you're President King... that's all they can see; President King, not you. Dude, just act and speak as arrogantly and ruthlessly as him. You can do it. Remember, you're the best of the best of the bestest.* He cleared his throat noisily. "I have an important announcement to make, and I won't be answering any questions when I'm done. So, listen up good."

A hand quickly shot up. The screen card flashed Don Mallory from The Great America News Inc. POTUS smiled benignly at the reporter, just as he knew President King would do. He was a lanky, middle-aged man with the reddest hair ever—Aahh! So, this is what Don looks like.

"Mr. President, can I request an exclusive with you after the briefing, anytime that suits you, sir?" The guy's voice dripped smug confidence, the type that came with knowing you had an ace over your competitors.

"Sure thing, Don," POTUS smiled at him with the president's trademark wink, ignoring other raised screen cards. He drank slowly from his water glass, inhaled deeply, exhaled slowly, squared his shoulders, and started to speak.

"I've come here today to make a confession—" POTUS paused. His words froze behind his throat. Images started to flash inside his head in a dizzying, colourful sequence—his first meeting with President King, their night long chat in his hospital room, the celebrity aliens, the president's warm and kind words to him; his outrage over his shabby treatment by Kunle after his mum's death, the priceless golf tips he'd generously given, Dr. Delores King's warmth and strength, even the crazy experience he'd shared with the president inside the Babalawo's shrine. It was thanks to president King that he had stopped his bad habit of smoking. He owed his reconciliation with his father to the president, while countless children around America owed their safety from paedophiles to the man. Most of all, his Mama had loved the president with a passion that was unshaken, even with his notorious homophobia—*Mama… Mama…*

A tight knot formed behind POTUS' throat—*Why? Why did you have to be such a shithead, Your Excellency? Why couldn't you just remain the awesome dude I'd worshipped?* Rage and bitterness warred in his heart. He wanted to strangle the president, long and hard—*You freaking arsehole, Your Excellency! You freaking liar, yeye devil man!* He was fighting the tears threatening to unman him.

In that instant, POTUS knew that there was no way he could destroy the president in such a brutal fashion before the world. For good or bad, the bond between them was too strong for him to betray and humiliate the man in such a public forum—Mama will never forgive me, either. But justice had to be done. President King had to account for his misdeeds. It was only the right thing to do—*Mama, please understand...*

POTUS began to speak.

"Today, I announce my withdrawal from the presidential race. I will not be seeking a third term in office and will leave it to the party to choose the next Republican candidate that will lead us to victory and become the next President of the United States. Thank you."

As Pansy-Pete gasped behind him and the room exploded in shock, POTUS stood up and walked out into the wide hotel corridor. In a second, he was surrounded by his security detail and Pansy-Pete.

"Get me back to the safe-house ASAP and get Chief Jackson over there immediately. I'll see nobody else till I'm done with Chief Jackson and our African guests, are we clear?" Pansy-Pete nodded, his eyes wide with fear and shock. "And make sure our guests leave on the very first flight outta here as soon as I'm done with them, alright?"

As the dark car cruised back towards the secluded mansion harbouring his real body, the president's mobile phone exploded with calls. POTUS switched it off and heaved a deep sigh, resting his head wearily against the seat—*It's over! I've done it! Mama, I saved your hero, so please be happy where you are now.* All he had to do now was to let the FBI Chief carry out a Mind Zoome on him and extract all the information about the president and poor Mary-Lou Johnson so her ghost could finally be at rest—*If only my poor mother had made it safely to America...*

POTUS sighed again, shutting his eyes. Suddenly, he couldn't wait to leave America and return to the welcoming safety of his African home. The phone vibrated in his pocket. He almost ignored it until he realised it was his own phone and not the president's. He pulled it out. The text message was from Kunle:

Happy 18th Birthday, son! Miss you! See you soon x

∽

The Federal Enquirer
PMD Media, 6 November
(Mike Vine and the news desk)

Republicans Lose the Election!
President King Blames Aliens and African Witchdoctors
for His Party's Woes

Late last night, *CNL Anderson Corp* projected that Larry Johnson has now secured enough electoral college votes to become the next President of the United States of America in what has been described as a landslide victory over his Republican opponent, Paul Giordano. In a statement released by Mr. Johnson, the president-elect said he "was humbled and blessed" and called on the country to come together as Americans after the vitriolic campaign run by both sides.

As world leaders rush to congratulate Mr. Johnson on his victory, the incumbent president, Mr. Jerry King, has claimed large scale voter manipulation by the Democrats in cahoots with their supernatural enablers. Namely, celebrity alien beings from outer space and African witch doctors. Even by the bizarre standards of a president known for making some rather unconventional statements, this latest accusation is pretty stunning and has led to widespread speculation over his mental state, especially following that famous golf ball head injury and subsequent coma he suffered while on the campaign trail.

It is no secret that the president has carried out what some would deem irrational actions since his recovery, including the now infamous withdrawal from the race just weeks before the election, resulting in the sudden nomination of the new Vice President, Mr. Giordano, to bear the Republican flag. Many within the GOP believe that the president's actions played a significant role in the Democratic Party's victory today. Not forgetting the inexplicable waiver of all visa restrictions for Nigerians in a random act that stunned even the Nigerian government who never requested the waiver from the United States. This latest accusation of celebrity aliens and African witch doctors adds more fuel to speculations about his current mental health.

Sending a barrage of *Xitzs* late last night on the popular social media site, *Madxitz*, President King railed against fake news and fake voters. He claimed that he knows the identities of these celebrity aliens and has threatened to reveal their names to the public if the FBI and CIA fail to begin investigations into their nefarious activities. While taking questions from reporters today, the FBI chief, Mr. Daniel Jackson, stated that they have no intelligence on alien celebrities and that they're not investigating any alien interference in the elections at the present time. He refused to confirm whether or not such an investigation would commence in the future. He however confirmed the news of the discovery of the missing college woman, Mary-Lou Johnson, at the house of President King's late sister, Dr. Delores King. There has been speculations about the gruesome discovery and President King's unexpected withdrawal from the presidential race. The FBI has confirmed that the president is not currently under suspicion in the case.

In another development, President King has claimed that both his Secretary of Defence, General Mike O'Neill, and the FBI chief, Daniel Jackson, as well as his Chief of Staff, Pete Daniels, are all aware of the existence of the African witch doctor who hexed the elections. He states that the three men held a secret meeting with the witch doctor's agent in Nigeria. All three officials deny any such meeting and state that their visit to the country was to investigate a case of possible hacking into the national security system after a hoax call to *The Great America News Inc.* by the notorious African teenager that goes by POTUS. Readers will recall the infamous "Remember Belly-Berry" riddle the young Nigerian scammer left with *The Great America News Inc.* after releasing the nuclear codes, which have since been proven to be fake. Chief Jackson stated that in the interest of our national security, the impromptu visit to Nigeria was deemed necessary to question the African POTUS further. However, he refused to answer why the president's Chief of Staff also went on the same trip, especially at a time when President King was still in a coma and Pete Daniels was needed more at the White House than in Africa. Mr. Daniels has also declined to make a statement.

Last night, the conspiracy group, PNUTS, released a series of Xitzs echoing the president's incredible allegations. In a campaign code named, Tornado-OZ, after the classic archive film *The Wizard of Oz*, PNUTS, acronym for "People Not Under Total Slavery," are calling on a mandatory blood test of all American citizens, especially celebrities and billionaires, in order to flush out alien DNA and send the aliens back to their Oz planet. They are also demanding that the FBI initiate robust investigations without delay and for the results of the election to be annulled till all blood results are in and the alien fake voters identified, arrested, and deported back to outer space.

In a recent statement released by the FBI, the director, Daniel Jackson, states they will not be investigating any criminal activities linked to alien election interference or African witch doctors. Both chambers of congress have also confirmed that Americans will not be forced to undertake mandatory blood tests to prove their humanity. The entire country is now fervently following President King's Madxitz feed in anticipation of "The Great Reveal" as the president calls it. This is when he will reveal the identities of the alien celebrities in our midst. It remains to be seen when or if he will finally Xitzs their names. With his fabulous wealth, he will have no difficulties paying them compensation for any defamation litigation they file against him, either in their alien motherland or in the United States of America.

This is a developing story.

Acknowledgments

To my beautiful, gentle and sweet daughter, Carmen Jija Gyoh, whose calm and loving presence never fails to soothe my troubled thoughts. Thank you, my little Mousie. I love you to eternity xxxxxxxx

To my awesome publishers, Jeremy Wagner and Steve Wands of Dead Sky Publishing, who made my dream of African Magical realism a reality. Thank you, guys! My heart to yours! You rock

To my lovely editor, Anna Kubik, for those late-night hours of editing drudgery and her insightful observations. Thank you so much, Anna!

To my amazing book-cover designer, Shane Pierce, who gave me a dream cover beyond anything I ever imagined. You're phenomenal, Shane! THANK YOU!!

To my dear friend, Stuart (Acep) Hale, who read the first raw draft of the story and gave me his candid thoughts which enabled me to craft a stronger story; and for the gift of the awesome word, "politricks". Gorgeous, thanks for your long years of kind friendship and awesome support! xxx

To my soul-brother, Ted (Irish) Dunphy, who has been my shrink, my friend, my brother, my rock and my blessing in countless ways. Irish, you and my Redditch family hold my heart in yours. Thank you for everything xxxx

...AND

To my beloved and loving ancestors, who continue to shower me with endless blessings. Thank you for never sleeping on my watch! I am truly blessed!

ABOUT THE AUTHOR

Nuzo Onoh is an award-winning Nigerian-British writer of Igbo descent. She is a pioneer of the African horror literary genre. Hailed as the "Queen of African Horror", Nuzo's writing showcases both the beautiful and horrific in the African culture within fictitious narratives.

Nuzo's works have featured in numerous magazines and anthologies, as well as in academic studies. She has given talks and lectures about African Horror, including at the prestigious Miskatonic Institute of Horror Studies, London. She is a Bram Stoker Lifetime Achievement Award recipient.

Nuzo holds a Law degree and Masters degree in Writing, both from Warwick University, England. She is a certified Civil Funeral Celebrant, licensed to conduct non-religious burial services. An avid musician with an addiction to JungYup and K-indie, Nuzo plays both the guitar and piano, and holds an NVQ in Digital Music Production. She resides in the West Midlands, United Kingdom.

ALSO BY NUZO ONOH

Fiction

The Reluctant Dead (2014)

Unhallowed Graves (2015)

The Sleepless (2016)

Dead Corpse (2017)

The Unclean (2020)

A Dance For The Dead (2022)

Where The Dead Brides Gather (2024)

Non fiction

Call On Your Ancestors For Success & Happiness (2017)